I0593954

Darque Legends:

Battle of Winter's Edge

Book Four

DERRIEN RELYEA

http://www.thedragonwarrior.com

ISBN 978-0-9905884-6-7 (print)
ISBN 978-0-9905884-7-4 (digital)

Table of Contents

Acknowledgements

Often people ask me how I do this. I ask them, how do I do what? But seriously, I enjoy writing. The words flow off the keyboard onto the page so fast at times, listening to my characters as they tell me the tale of their adventures, and at other times as if I am writing from my own memories long suppressed and suddenly free. However, it still takes time to do this and I work a 'day job' to pay the bills and the publishing. I have dreams of one day being able to retire from that job, giving me the time to devote to writing down all these stories running amok through my memories. And so, I could not do this without help, including my good friend and most talented artist, Lisa Dixon http://lisadixonart.com, who does all the covers and inside sketches for the Darque Legends series, and my awesome publishing friend, Ariel Frailich, http://websiteatelier.com, who does the formatting for me to be able to do the 'Indie Publishing' thing. I also have friends and family who inspire me, and fans who keep me going. And every book that sells, makes me feel like I'm on top of the world. Maybe one day I'll be a writer. In the meantime, I'm grateful to all of you for sharing my stories with me and all your friends and for inspiring me to keep writing them. Please don't stop!

Dedication

This book is dedicated to my very dear friend, Tammy Gallo, who inspired the character of Tammra Dayo, Commander of the Elven Nation. Like Tammra, my friend is beautiful, strong, multi-talented and highly intelligent, and would disagree on all points. But Tammy is more than a Commander. She is a true inspiration. She is what a good friend should be. Compassionate with an innate sense of what everyone needs and wants, and readily jumps in to provide. She has always been there when I've needed her, no matter what. Nothing stops her from doing what she thinks is right, for everyone but herself. Here's hoping that all your dreams come true!

Battle Of Winter's Edge

As a Warrior of the Dragon Clan, she was a defensive swordsman without equal; graceful, deceptively strong, and elegantly frightening. At some point her opponents would come to realize 'twas child's play for the hypnotically beautiful young girl, and they'd begin to sweat and falter knowing when came the first opening she'd send them Past the Veil. When such realization did occur, she'd simply smile and wink and continue her irreverent and constant dialogue. The never-ending babble oft' times provided distraction and gained her advantage even though 'twas not for that purpose, 'twas just her way. Storrm couldn't shut up to save her life.

She also could not remember how she'd gotten here, nor could she recall anything that had happened o'er the past several moons, even though she was quite sure of that timeline. For that matter, just where was here? She pulled the scrimshawed bone picks from her hair, a handmade gift from her elder sister upon gathering her seventeenth winter, releasing the multiple long red braids that swept past the backs of her thighs. Curious. She always let them swing free, except when fighting. Even more curious, the picks simply vanished as she gazed at her hands. Wearing only the width of leather 'cross her breasts, arm bracers, pants, and boots, she stood within a silent whiteness akin to fog, through which even her enhanced vision could not penetrate. She looked around to see where she may have dropped her leather shirt but along with her weapons, 'twas nowhere to be found.

Storrm Aalanna Grifynn, Second in Command to her much shorter and more curvaceous sister Darque, the Battle Commander of the Dragon Clan (and the Resistance, but that could be perceived as bragging), knew she'd gathered o'er nineteen winters, although she looked not a day older than the sixteen she had afore she and Mystynn the Green, Second Prince of the Highland Dragons, took the LifeBond. But what was age anyway? Maturity came with experience and training, 'twas one's level of commitment, one's choices, that carved your path. Although, good genes did help. She and her siblings, Darque, one winter elder, and Fryya, nine winters younger, were unique to Mankind. Redheaded, blue eyed, Dragon-Human hybrids, they came into this world as a side effect told in prophesy centuries after a horrifying experiment perpetrated by the Black, which ultimately led to the Last Holocaust.

Prophesy ran deep in the Dragon Clan and each of the siblings had their role to play. Darque was to bring the Races 'from near extinction, into a new Beginning'. The Battle for the Dragon Clan qualified as their 'near extinction', and they eventually discovered 'twas Kadoor-wide with countless Clans attacked upon the same dawn, the destruction of Mankind and the total enslavement of Highland Dragon, the Black's steadfast maniacal undertaking. This time, as was the last, he'd near succeeded, and now he was determined to continue in his efforts. This time, he'd sworn to finish what he'd started.

The most ancient Magic known, the LifeBond, was recreated to enable them to enter the war with a unique advantage against the Black and his Hoard. Taking the 'Bond fused a Dragon and a Warrior into one fighting force, in which they Shared the MindLink (the telepathy of the Magic bearers, strongest in the Highlands), along with the longevity of the Dragon Race and their Magic (the most vital being the Healing), while their Dragon partners gained the Warrior's fighting spirit, skills, Human tenacity, and their strong will to live. The LifeBond was forever and when one partner Passed the Veil, so, too, did the other.

Shortly after the ceremony, while Darque embraced her destiny and struggled to lead them, Storrm heard her own prophesy. Along with the sense that her span of days was shortly numbered, she would give birth to the first of two generations leading to a girl-child who would carry the blood of the High Races Council: Fay, Dragon, Elf, and Man. This child would end the curse of the future King of Greatest Power. It hadn't taken much figuring to determine who that was: Corbyn the Fay, AKA, the Raven. But of the rest, she and Mystynn were baffled. Warriors rarely got pregnant (she could count on one hand the number of such events in the past few winters, but 'twas certainly not from abstinence), and although she had no desire to seek outside solace from her 'Bond partner, her best friend, and of whom she secretly desired, 'twas not a subject broached by either, even though Darque and her 'Bond, Gunnarr the Mighty Blue, had taken each other as lifemates. That was likely the result of the influence of their ancestor, Darque Abriya D'Rienne, AKA the First Warrior (now a free-roaming spirit of the Keep of St Swiftyn's), the first to take the LifeBond during the ancient War of Chaos, who mated her partner, Solvyngarr, the only other known Dragon/Human lifemates. But they could have no offspring. There were a few Elven/Human half-breeds only recently revealed, previously unknown even to those who carried that bloodline. 'Twas a surprise, but a welcome one. And the Fay and the Sprites had been isolated for so long 'twas believed no mixes from either were in existence. But to have the blood of the Dragon was unheard of and considered impossible. However, that was afore the experiment. Afore the birth of the Aalanna Grifynn siblings. Their Kind was not produced by a pairing. 'Twas in their DNA. Yet, when Storrm heard this prophesy, she and Mystynn knew this not. So, how was she to fulfill such? By the time the siblings learned of their unique Kind, the prophesy had been pushed far back in memory, the intensifying war and the needs of her command taking up their mutual focus, and all their energies.

Sensing her partner was near, without a single weapon Storrm stepped gingerly forward into the nothingness, prepared to fight with using the martial arts techniques of the Clan if necessary, hoping she was not heading o'er a cliff. Hesitantly, she whispered, "Mystynn?" She stretched forth her hands, but although she could clearly see herself, she could see nothing else. 'Twas as if she was in a void. Abruptly, she stopped. She'd heard of THE Void, the place one passed through on the way to the other side of the Veil. Into the Beyond. But 'twas believed this journey was as a heartbeat. Surely this was not... Uncertainty began to engulf her, and she cried out, "Mystynn!"

"I am here." His voice was deep and reassuring, but something was different. Her brows furrowed. Taking a few more steps and reaching into the whiteout as if feeling her way along the darkest corridors in the deepest caverns, her hand touched another's. 'Twas human.

Fingers entwined, her expression clearly one of shock, the most handsome man she'd ever faced pulled her close, staring into her eyes. Dragons did not wear clothing or adornments, and as the man stood there in all his tightly muscled glory, she could utter but one word. "How?" His gaze swept their surroundings with mild amusement, afore returning to her. She swallowed hard, glanced side to side, and bit her bottom lip. "Your voice is different. 'Tis not as deep or resonating."

Undaunted, he replied, "I believe 'tis because Human forms have only one gut. And, my neck isn't as long."

Her volume rising, she squinted, smacked his shoulder, and stepped back half a pace. "One gut? That's all you can say?"

Bewildered, with both hands held upward and his shoulders shrugged he asked, "What? 'Tis the answer to your question."

With heat in her voice, she replied, "'Twasn't a real question. And I expected you to tell me why you're in human form. And if 'tis Magic, why didn't you or Gunnarr ever do this for us afore?

Seems to me, 'twould have made things… a tad easier." As she spoke, she tried not to let her eyes drink in his hard body.

Grinning impishly, he waggled his eyebrows. "Things? You mean, sex?"

"Mystynn!"

Chagrined, he questioned, "Well, what?"

"Can you please get back on topic?"

He took a step further away and cocked his head. "Could you please direct me back to where you wish I was?"

She raised her hands in surrender. "Alright. Mayhap we should begin again. I want to know where we are. And why. And how. And I'd like to know why you're in human form, and how that happened, and when."

His thick arms now crossed o'er his muscled chest, he stated dryly, "Pick the one you want me to answer first, and I shall endeavor to please."

She flicked one hand o'er her shoulder. "Alright, alright. Where are we?"

"You know where we are."

"So, tell me for the sake of confirmation," she insisted.

"We are in the Void."

She tried not to glance down, as he was so good-looking, she could feel the heat rising up her neck and knew she was beginning to blush. "Why are you in human form?"

Dragons could not lie to Humans, but they could redirect. Spreading his hands outward, he shrugged his shoulders and stated simply, "I thought 'twould please you."

He'd pleased her for certain. But there was no time for such. She shook her head to clear her thoughts and continued, "My questions are leading to more questions. Alright. Void. Why?"

"I think you know the answer to that one."

Stamping her foot, her braids swinging, she exclaimed, "But, I don't remember anything! How did we get here?"

"I think you know the answer…"

Cutting him off, she stated, "Fine. I know how." With a sense of unease, she tried to settle her emotions. Pouting, she looked at him with her big blue eyes. "We died, didn't we?"

Humans always confused Mystynn, especially this one. He squinted again and asked, "Is that a real question?"

~~~~~~~~~~

They were in a place where time had little meaning. Passing through the Void happened in the blink of an eye for the living left behind. Nevertheless, even though Storrm could not discern the passage of time, she and Mystynn spoke for what seemed like half a mark as he attempted to explain their circumstances. Throughout, she could not help but feel he was hiding something from her and could only mean 'twas something horrid. Which was most perplexing, as how could anything be worse than accepting the fact that they were dead? Mystynn indicated that she couldn't remember the situation because they were still in the process of dying and it hadn't yet happened. Still, all her memories for about the past winter were Blocked for some reason, and as he made every attempt to steer her not only away from that topic but into continuing their journey, she continued her demands to know why.

Patiently, he tried to explain it again. "'Tis unknown if Humans recall what happened 'til they Pass the Veil. Dragons can sometimes Speak through, and can 'cross the Veil, but usually can't be seen or have any affect upon the other side, and I don't know if you can, except as a spirit, because of your hybrid status and because of our 'Bond. Although other Teams have Passed the Veil, we've Heard nothing from them, hence, we're breaking new ground here."

Storrm was in denial. She wanted to know everything, and not having her memory intact was driving her mad. "How long does this take?"

"As long as you stubbornly refuse to move on, for the 'Bond maintains even Past the Veil, and I cannot go without you."

Raising her hands and looking all around, she asked, "So, this is my fault?"

"Frankly, yes," he huffed impatiently.

She was desperate and tried to negotiate. "But Mystynn, I'm not ready to move on! What if I can't return? What if I didn't get to speak with Darque afore we died? What if we had valuable information that she needs? Surely there's more we can do. Mayhap we can still help in the war effort."

"I would think that knowing you Passed fighting, would be enough."

Crossing her arms o'er her chest, she stated firmly, "No. I want to know not just how, but why we Passed. Just what was the reason for this battle?"

Mystynn hung his head. "I thought you might want to know. I'd rather you not go through it again."

"There's more, isn't there?" Storrm was now convinced he was the reason she could not remember. But why would he Block such from her? She chose to side-step and mayhap she could get to the truth another way. "What if I want to stay and fight for life?"

"We cannot. We must move on," he stated firmly.

Suspicion engulfed her, and she asked with near anger, "Why?" Mystynn would not look up. She took a deep breath as a thought occurred to her. "Was it that bad, that painful?"

Near relieved, his gaze caught hers as he answered quickly, "'Twas."

She sighed, dropping her hands to her sides in defeat. Softly she asked, "Did I die well, Sword in hand?"

Near afore she'd finished, he replied, "Yes. Amazingly you held your Dragon Sword 'til the very end. We lasted far longer than I thought possible, given the circumstances. You were very brave, little one. Our Legend Song will be extraordinary."

Abruptly, she gave voice to that which she'd always felt. "I love you, Mystynn."

His smile was sad as he answered. "And I, you, more so with each passing breath."

"We're not breathing anymore," she countered, trying to make light of the situation. Nonetheless, this truth was amazing, depressing, and funny, at the same time. But, she could no longer pretend. They were in the Void.

They both laughed, and the sound made her happy. She always enjoyed making him laugh. Mystynn was too serious sometimes. But, she had to suppose that this situation was as serious for them as things had ever been, and they'd been through many a battle. Her smile faded. "You knew this would happen, didn't you? Highlands have a sense of their futures. Would you have done anything differently? Are you sorry you took my 'Bond?"

"I would not, and am not," he replied with passion.

Storrm turned about and gazed into the whiteness, her thoughts far distant. After a few moments, determinedly, the Second in Command faced her partner. "Mystynn, I want to go back. Surely there are others fighting with us, or reinforcements are on their way. Could we not hold our position a little longer? We're good fighters, and we've always been strong in the Healing. We should not give up for pain, no matter how bad 'twas. Can we not yet survive?"

He sighed, gazed at the stubborn expression upon his lovely partner's face, and surrendered. "Little one, I knew you'd not Pass easily. Nothing with you has ever been easy. 'Twould appear necessary that I convince you beyond any shadow of a doubt, that we cannot go back. But, if I clear your memories afore we are Beyond, you must be prepared for what we faced."

"I am," she stated with more confidence than she felt.

Mystynn's greatest fear was that with the return of her memories would come disappointment in him, but if he was forced to such, so be it. If she stopped loving him for what had happened, how he'd failed her, 'twas nothing he could do now, and he would keep his promise. "Come, let me hold you close. Though I wish 'twas so, you will not feel me, but know in your heart that I am here and if you need me, simply open your eyes. Place your cheek upon my chest, and I shall take you back in time. 'Twill be o'er the span of but a single heartbeat, but you will experience the events I show you with extreme clarity. 'Twill be as if you are there, living through each and every moment. I will show you not only what happened to us, but what happened to others, and how we were affected."

"You mean, how it all came to this?" She looked around them. "I'm not afraid." Storrm stepped closer, biting her bottom lip gently (a familial habit), with a look of doubt in her eyes. Mystynn hugged her tight as she laid her head upon his chest. She fingered the intricate scar upon his left breast, carved into his scales by the Matriarch herself during the Ranking, when he and his brothers received their leadership ranks after the big battle. It felt so different upon skin. "Don't let go," she whispered, swallowing hard.

Smoothing her hair with his hand, he stated emphatically, "Never."

CHAPTER ONE

Abducted!

FIFTY WINTERS AFORE THE BATTLE FOR THE DRAGON CLAN

PORT O'DINBURRA, ALONG THE COAST OF THE SEA OF DREAMS

~~~~~ IN A DARKENED ALLEY JUST AFORE MIDNIGHT ~~~~~

The ship's new Captain stood in the shadows of the alley, facing yet another hooded man, the second such in the same span of days. Without having earned the title, he flaunted it for all 'twas worth. He'd already been paid for the voyage and would be paid more when he returned after his 'delivery', of what, he knew not, nor did he care. Their cargo was loaded, he just had to sail to the coordinates he'd been given and scuttle in the middle of the sea, ensuring the destruction of the cargo hold. Taking a lifeboat to another ship which would take him home, his reward awaited. He had no issues with betraying the entire crew to their deaths. There'd be no one left to accuse him of such.

His thoughts returned to his new client. He couldn't see the man's face, but then, he'd not seen the face of the last one, either. It made no difference. Solid coin was solid coin. This one didn't seem as evil, though 'twas a toss-up. But having spent his short span of days dealing with evil men, he sneered. "You pointed him out earlier, but he was wearing a hooded cloak. I want a description. How does he appear?"

The man's accent was odd, as if he'd come from some distant region. "Fairly tall, about my height, broad of shoulder, heavily muscled, hazel eyes, and a full head of thick, shaggy, dirty blonde hair. Not only will his mannerisms make him stand out, so too, will his speech. But 'twill be difficult to notice, as he can blend in anywhere with little trouble." Almost as an afterthought, he added, "And he likes to drink."

Too quickly, the Captain replied, "A drinking man is an easy man to take."

The stranger cocked his head as if considering whether to speak. Deciding 'twould not matter in the end, he said, "I give you warning. He is Kreegaren. Very dangerous. If you plan a face-off attack, you will lose. Do not underestimate him."

The name meant nothing but might be useful in the future and he didn't want to appear ignorant, so to divert attention he simply asked, "Why then, do you not take him yourself?"

Many had tried. Many were now Past the Veil. But the man did not say that. Not as young as he used to be, although he'd accepted the contract, he knew better than to try to take Regynn himself and would rather pay another. Mayhap one would get lucky. It could happen. "I must not be associated with such actions."

"Why?" The blurted question was not meant to be spoken aloud. His client stepped back and stared from under his hood, making the Captain shiver. 'Twas frightening, and he felt as if he was as close to the Veil as he'd ever been. He took a breath and fidgeted, suddenly wishing he'd not agreed to this deal. But the coin he'd get from these two transactions would be enough to retire. That thought gave him courage to continue. Opting to move on, he asked, "When do I get paid?"

"Half now, half when you provide proof of his demise," the man said in a smooth tone of voice.

"What proof would you require?" he asked, a sneer curling his lip.

Completely without emotion the man answered, "His right hand."

The Captain considered. Although he had a near full crew, he was still short and if he took the man onboard he'd get work out of him, waiting to take his hand, or anyone's hand, just afore he fled the ship. "This might take a moon or more. How long will you be here? I don't want to end up with a hand I can't sell."

The man knew what the other was planning. After all, 'twas his business to know such matters. Regynn would be taken out to sea and they'd all die, including the Captain. As long as Regynn was aboard that ship when it sailed in the morning, he would consider the deed done and go home, without need to make the final payment. The loss of what he was about to hand o'er was but a pittance of what he'd get upon his triumphant return. His standing was such that if he reported the death 'twould be taken as fact, and if required, he'd already made arrangements to provide a hand that would suffice as proof. Besides, even if he was found out, he was at the end of his span of days and he'd fulfill no more contracts. Assassination for such failure would be quicker and mayhap more merciful than waiting for the Veil to come to him. He gathered his thoughts. He'd been absent from home far too long already. Mayhap this attempt would be the last. "I will know when you succeed." With that, the man handed o'er a velvet bag tied at the top with string. The bag was heavy and when the boy opened it he was ecstatic, but when he looked up again the man was gone, having disappeared into the night. How did he do that, and just how would he know, he wondered? Shaking his head, he peered greedily into the bag once more. He had a plan in mind and the one he was supposed to kill was already inside the tavern.

~~~~~ JUST AFTER MIDNIGHT ~~~~~

Regynn had traveled a very long way o'er the past several moons, but the suffering on her lovely face, the anguish in her voice when she'd guessed that he was leaving despite his attempt to keep such to himself, remained fresh in his mind. Cathay was beautiful, and he was miserable, for their love should never have been. Leaving was the only honorable way out, besides being the only way to keep her safe, but it had not the desired results for him. The young man had not forgotten, he'd not healed, he'd not moved on.

Although he'd arrived just a dawn prior, sitting in the tavern of yet another port district, he couldn't even recall the name of the village with which 'twas associated, which should have caused some concern as he had a very long and near perfect memory. He blinked to clear his blurring vision in the smoky shadows of the room and took another swig of the whiskey. He would've preferred the Vydna of his homeland, but this was interesting. He'd barely finished half the mug and was already feeling the effects. Regynn was a hard drinker when he was bored or not otherwise occupied, and rarely felt any effects from alcohol. This could not be stronger than Vydna. Nothing rivaled Vydna. As he sat, he had a passing notion that mayhap 'twas something to do with their distilling process.

Ever curious, this night he was also distracted and fatigued, seeking solace from the ghosts of his past. Although he'd had some initial trouble, for the past three moons he'd seen no evidence that he was still being followed and he'd let down his guard. As his mind began to drift, so did the chair upon which he sat 'til he suddenly realized he'd been drugged. 'Twas the last thing to occur to him, just afore his face hit the wooden planks of the table.

He'd never learn just how long he was unconscious but when he woke he discovered he'd been divested of his boots and all his personal belongings and his clothes now consisted of rags. Making his way up the ladder out of the bowels of the ship, his head pounding as did his right cheek, the sunlight that greeted him on deck was painful and he groaned aloud. Slapped with a bucket of pitch and a mop, he was set to work along with a handful of others all seemingly feeling as did he, squinting, grimacing, and groaning, with not a blade amongst them. But he wasn't too worried. He'd never needed a blade afore, and the mop handle was solid enough, as was the bucket.

What he did need was to know where they were, for he was an excellent swimmer and if not too far offshore he could simply jump ship and swim back. If such was not an option, he needed to know if he was alone or would have allies he could trust. Quickly learning they were long past even his ability to swim to safety, he began to have hope his abduction was a result of being in the wrong place at the wrong time, as there seemed no advantage or recognition of his status. And as he sized up his comrades o'er the next few dawns he had to conclude that he was on his own, for the others didn't even care they'd been abducted and appreciated what little food they were getting. 'Twould be difficult to sail this ship by himself but it could be done, as could most things in his experience.

As the days passed, Regynn furthered his investigation. First, he clarified that he was on his own. Although the ship wasn't that large, it seemed most of the crew were forced labor as was he, and of criminal background. Second, he had free run, for the few guards were lazy and rarely seen, as they knew that no one would sabotage the ship 'til they got back to shore somewhere. None of them wanted to drown and the ship was old and in need of much and continuous, repair. Besides, they were told on the first day that if anyone was caught not busy at their duties they'd simply be tossed o'er the side as food for the Water Dragons (which held some weight as a threat, even though most considered Water Dragons a myth, for again, no one wanted to drown.). Third, there was one place they could not enter and 'twas the main cargo hold. He'd discerned no sounds coming from within, so at least 'twas not something alive down there, and if 'twas something dead, they'd have smelled it by now. Another point was that if this journey was legitimate there'd be no need to force a crew, which, along with the age and decrepit condition of the ship, meant they were probably all expendable. Fourth, since there were so few guards, they kept the rest of them out of the cargo hold by way of heavy iron locks and the aforementioned threat of being tossed o'er the side. But what his captors didn't know was that due to his ceaseless curiosities, Regynn was highly skilled at near everything. Besides, he loved a good mystery. That cargo hold beckoned him. He must discover its secrets.

Within days his skin was tanned golden brown, his hair sun-bleached back to the white blonde of his childhood, and he'd managed to collect three flat nails o'er half the length of his longest finger, which he kept by creating a fold in the waistband of his pants. His daily routine made him even stronger, his body leaner and more muscled than afore he began his wanderings. The locks on the hold had been there for some time, much longer than had the Captain been in charge, and they'd become caked with rust. Carefully, he'd sneak down to the hold at various times at least once a day to work on those locks, prying the mechanisms loose while leaving the outside unmarked, usually breaking the nails in the process, making it necessary to 'find' another.

Lying awake in his rack that night, he pondered his odds of survival. Finally, he made his choice, got up, and certain his last nail was safe in his waistband, made his way silently through the others, down the halls, and into the bottom of the ship. Positive he was alone, he used the nail to pick the locks, three in all, and entered the hold. Oddly, he felt a warm tingling sensation as he stepped through the door, but it disappeared quickly, and he decided 'twas due to the length of time the hold had been closed.

'Twas so dark he could not see his hand afore his face, and after feeling for it alongside the door, he lit the torch. His eyes fell upon the cargo in the flickering shadows. Barrels. Thirty of them. He squinted. 'Twas no need to run spirits, just what did they contain? He should leave, the crew patrol would be around soon, but curiosity won o'er caution. Reaching for the closest barrel and feeling along the top edge, he carefully pulled the latch to release the lid. Peering inside, he caught the scent of the powder. He recognized that faint odor. And that was when his own lights went out, once again.

A FEW DAWNS LATER

SOMETIME PAST MIDNIGHT ON THE ISLAND OF DREAMS

~~~~~ THE QUARTERS OF THE CAPTAIN
OF THE ELITE GUARD ~~~~~

Caleichante's beauty could stop a man's breath. Tall and lithe, with her pale skin, sharply pointed ears, almond shaped eyes and long, snow white hair pulled back in a single tail with a strip of leather crisscrossed 'round and through it, she had just managed to pull off her boots for the evening and was sitting on her rack trying to unwind when she Heard her Water Dragon. He'd been playing off the eastern coast and the alarm in his voice made her wary.

About the size of the average War Horse, not including their long tails, Water Dragons had short muzzles and wide powerful jaws, giving them a somewhat triangular head. With glittering scales green or browns shot through with flecks of silver or gold and matching slit pupiled eyes, they were quite striking. In fact, some thought their abnormally huge eyes, extremely expressive faces, slit nostrils, along with their enormous saucer paws (even with the razor-sharp claws), made the Water Dragons appear not a threat, and almost endearing. 'Twas near laughable to anyone who knew their true nature. They also had webbed toes and underarms and having to draw their lips back o'er wicked teeth and short fangs, they'd spit and splatter saliva in all directions whenever they tried to speak aloud and sounded less intelligent than they were because of the difficulty thinking in Human tongues. Water Dragons had no rival on all Kadoor for the strength of their bite and could stay underwater for up to a moon using their Magic, as well as able to take another under their Allure just with skin to skin touch, keeping their passengers warm, dry, and breathing at least half that long afore needing to replenish. But passengers took their chances and 'twas advisable to stay near the Dragon's shoulders, as from their hips down their long tails to the very tip, was a serrated and very sharp dorsal ridge which they could lay flat against their bodies or raise up with such speed and force 'twould cut a man in half like a sawblade. Although they were big, they were very flexible, and had thick leathery wings that enabled them to soar for some distances if they came up out of the water with enough power, but they were not true wings and they could not fly as could the other Dragon Races. However, Water Dragons were the fastest creatures in the sea, 'flying' through the waters at incredible speeds. Although intelligent, they were not aggressive and were easily distracted, and if not kept focused, they could be caught and killed. On a side note, Water Dragons were also known as Slyders, for the awkward way they would maneuver on dry land, sliding along on their bellies, pushing with both front legs and then both back legs in a rhythm that made for a straight path along an oil exuded from glands in their sides, which would disappear quickly.

In their typical heavy-lisping, child-like dialog, Schlynn urgently Spoke through the telepathy of the Tie he and Calei shared, his huge round paws gesturing frantically to her as if she could see him, his long tongue slipping 'tween razor sharp teeth and fangs, *"Come, come, Islyth find trouble!"*

Calei could just imagine the splatter of saliva that sentence would have caused and rolled her eyes as she sent her Response. *"Islyth is always finding trouble. What's she done now?"*

His silver flecked brown scales and eyes a'glitter, his short leathery wings and long powerful tail stabilized him in the water as he Replied, *"Islyth follow pirate ship."*

Islyth was a green-gold, meaning she had green scales and eyes with gold flecks and was a good friend of Schlynn's. *"Well, why doesn't she just sink it, like usual?"*

"Islyth say Human aboard. In jail. She like it not."

'Twas interesting, but hardly alarming. Still, Islyth had more sense than most of the Water Dragons, sometimes even her own Tie. She was glad they were friends, as Islyth had survived far longer than any of her hatch mates, and if they wouldn't stay out of trouble, at least Schlynn was safer in Islyth's company, than alone. Thinking about it, she looked at her rack with longing for the day had been hard, but pulled her boots back on, just in case. *"Where?"* she asked.

"Closing."

Really, she wondered? *"Destination a'purpose or by chance?"*

"Islyth say a'purpose."

Now why, she mused, would a pirate ship, with a prisoner, be coming to the island? And, how did it get so close afore 'twas discovered? While these thoughts ran through her mind, Schlynn Answered. *"Deliver cargo."*

Mayhap the Human prisoner was their cargo? If so, Calei was not yet impressed. She cocked her head and furrowed her brow. *"Of what Race is the crew?"*

"Human. Mixed tribe. Smell of Hoard."

Ahhh, now this intel had her as concerned as was Schlynn. Standing up, she firmly Asked him, *"All Hoard, or have had contact?"*

"Contact."

That meant that someone was working for the Hoard, not that the crew were Hoard. And the likelihood of that one being aware of what he'd done, was slim. The Hoard were known to be very devious in their dealings, getting others to do their dirty work for them, usually to their own demise. Besides, although she believed the Hoard was growing, she was constantly chastised and told they had nothing about which to worry. Still... *"Scuttle it, Schlynn. Go help Islyth sink that ship."*

But her Tie Objected. *"Bad cargo. Islyth say need prisoner."*

Perplexed, Calei knew Islyth was prone to spout prophesy occasionally, but 'twas confusing, as how could the Human be both bad and needed at the same time? 'Twould be wise, at least, to go see this prisoner. Her brow still furrowed, she sighed. *"Fine. I need no sleep. We'll ride out there to see this Human. Meet me at the south well of the dungeons. And Schlynn? He better be worth it."*

Her Guard were exhausted after a long day following that skirmish on the northeastern shore. She wondered if the attempted invasion had anything to do with the ship that her Dragon and his friend were now following. Could the ship they'd met earlier have been a ruse to divert their attention? If so, whomever sent that one sacrificed an entire ship and crew to such. What was this 'cargo'?

Choosing to avoid alerting her Guard, she'd pick up some extra help at the docks on their way out to sea. If things got too dangerous she'd Call for more backup, but for now she felt she could afford to let the others sleep as she did a little exploring afore she ordered the Water Dragons to scuttle. Her long slim finger slid 'cross the ivy on her window sill. Drawing her energy to Dance, she disappeared then reappeared in the shadow of the algae covered well in the southern dungeons. Schlynn met her there, and reached out his great paw to touch Calei, taking her under his Allure as she mounted. He turned, and diving into the water, they flew swiftly down and around the underground system, out to the open sea. *"I have a couple of boys in mind, who can help out."*

"The brothers?"

"Yes, the two I spoke with this afternoon, the ones who were so eager to assist last night. Mayhap they would be willing to assist with this mission."

"If get them in Guard, they willing," he stated decisively.

She chuckled. *"I think you're right about that, my friend! Do you remember out of which dock they were working?"*

"Schlynn remember. Schlynn take you."

'Twasn't difficult to gain the brothers' agreement, and as Captain of the Elite Guard, their Master released them to her without question. They both had their own Ties and after waiting briefly for them to respond, they rode out to meet up with Islyth, who led them to the ship. 'Twas still dark when they arrived and looking up from underwater, they waited for the Ship's Watch to move on afore they climbed up the side of the barnacle encrusted hull and vaulted lightly o'er the edge to the deck. Placing a glamour upon themselves to appear as the last Men they viewed from the sea, they walked to the ladder well, and went below. No one was in sight as Calei directed the boys to find the cargo hold while she searched for the brig.

~~~~~ A SHORT TIME LATER ~~~~~

Having dropped her glamour, the Captain curiously observed the Human inside the cell for she'd never seen such white blonde hair on other than a Sprite, but 'twas not like she had a lot of experience with Humans. Her own hair was whiter still, but then her coloring was extreme even for her Race. She stared at the sleeping Man. Something told her he didn't belong with the rest of them. And from the dried blood on his temple, he'd been injured within the past few dawns.

He could sense her presence. Without moving a muscle, Regynn asked, "How did you get on board? You aren't a part of the crew, and we've not docked for new additions since I got tossed in here."

Calei was amused. He was not only astute, he had very good hearing. "I came to see you, actually. My... friends, told me you were aboard and that you were in need of rescue. In fact, they insisted on it. I was just trying to determine why."

"Your friends? There are more of you?" Regynn was up by now and looking for the guard down the narrow and low-ceilinged hallway. "They're in great danger." With her delicate face and pointed ears, the woman was gorgeous. And those eyes! Near mesmerizing. Then she spoke again with a musical chime that he'd originally thought was a residual effect from being knocked unconscious. And it brought back memories.

Mildly curious, she asked, "What do you mean? Why?"

"Well, if you hadn't already taken out the guard at the top of the stairs, you'd be in here with me, but there are more. I know their prowling schedule. I can help, and we can discuss the rest of the details after you get me out of this cell."

Caleichante could sense the Human was telling the truth and that he was not evil. Whether she could trust him, however, was still up in the air. "Yes, that Human will bother no one again."

Evidently, she was older than she appeared, or at least was more skilled. Once again, a memory was triggered, but he filed it away for later. "Ever?"

"Ever."

Since she still hadn't taken a step closer to helping him out of this mess, he continued to negotiate. "Good, that means you're here to scuttle the ship. I'd like to say that I'm a decent swimmer, but 'twould be difficult from inside the hull, and not knowing where land is, might make it even harder. I'd rather not swim for leagues in the Sea of Dreams. There are Dragons in these waters."

She laughed aloud. She truly enjoyed this Human, but she really didn't understand why Islyth thought he needed to be saved. After all, he'd brought up a most interesting quandary. What would she do with him? The Sprites and Man hadn't been allies since long afore the Last Holocaust. Her brow furrowed, she turned about and walked silently down the hallway, starting back up the stairs.

As Regynn grimaced, his rapid-fire mind racing to find some way out of the situation, he decided that even if he was doomed to Pass, he had to tell her. He could not be responsible for what he knew was about to happen. "Wait! Please listen. If you plan to go ahead and scuttle with me inside, so be it, but you need to know what we carry. 'Tis a very powerful poison. Many barrels. The powder is activated by water and they're planning on destroying the barrels along with the ship. If you sink it, 'twould leak into the sea, or mayhap float somewhere and cause much damage to many innocents." Her similarity to those with whom he'd come into contact at home was so compelling, he took a chance. "Do what you will with me, but you have to neutralize the poison afore you scuttle."

Calei stopped and turned her ear toward the Human. Slowly, as he spoke, she made her way back to him, her golden eyes squinting her disbelief. "Why tell me this? If truth, you have mayhap saved many, with no benefit to you at all. And just what makes you think I can neutralize such?"

He'd been right. She could do Magic. He had to capitalize on that. "I know what you are, and of what you are capable. Not only can you discern my truth, you can and must, neutralize that poison."

How the Human knew what she was, could be saved for another time. If he was telling the truth, 'twould be very bad. "Why carry such?"

Regynn stood holding onto the bars, but though Calei remained out of reach, he was a man of honor above all else and would never have attempted to harm her, even to save his own life. Besides, she'd said something about 'friends'. Using information obtained through the past few sennights, along with his own deductions, he replied, "We're heading toward an uncharted island in the middle of the Sea of Dreams. I believe you've been targeted for extinction, for they seek to foul the waters. 'Twould kill many, mayhap even the island itself. 'Twould take decades, if ever, for the island to recover, even if some of your Kind survived to assist. The crew on this ship is expendable, including my captors, though they know not their fate. By your presence, I suspect we're close to your island now. Without neutralizing, you cannot allow your Water Dragons to scuttle the ship anywhere without causing much damage, opening you to an invasion."

'Twas a shock for him to confirm he thought they had Water Dragons at their beck and call, nevertheless, she was very concerned. A whole new batch of eggs were incubating in the Grotto beneath the island even now. Such a poison would destroy them, as well. But the Human's expression gave her pause. Ignoring his remark, she asked suspiciously, "You've seen this kind of thing afore, have you not?"

Regynn hated to admit such and hung his head. "Yes. Another place, another time, but yes."

Calei could sense the Man's conviction. And regrets. Suddenly she remembered what Schlynn had told her. The cargo was to be delivered to the island. Islyth was not referring to the Human. She was referring to the poison. But depending on the size of the load, they'd need something organic from which to draw energy to neutralize such. The Human was needed, just as Islyth said. "How do you know all this?"

Accepting his fate, Regynn stepped away from the bars, sat on the narrow metal rack folded down from the wall, and stated with a sigh, "Trust me, my deductive reasoning has been both a gift and a curse in my span of days."

Calei hesitated but a candle drip and then came forward and with one slim finger touched the iron lock, which fell open immediately. "Your span of days just lengthened. Come with me, I trust my instincts." And my Water Dragon, she thought to herself.

Regynn followed the Sprite out of the brig and up the stairs, scanning for crewmen. There seemed none around. Mayhap his new companion had something to do with that. Trailing her down the narrow hallway toward the cargo hold, he heard soft footsteps coming up behind them at the same time he saw two young boys, both blondes with pale green eyes, walking toward them and looking very much like his rescuer. If these two weren't family, they must be her 'friends', he thought, as the young men's eyes narrowed, and they swiftly took battle stance.

With lightning reflexes, Regynn spun 'round and stuck out his foot, tripping the first attacker, sending him sprawling on the floor in front of Calei, who now faced them, her two companions protecting their flank. There were five of the original brigands, one he recognized as the Captain himself, and along with the three Sprites, Regynn was the only one without a blade. The Sprites were not in the best position, the narrow space making it difficult to swing sword appropriately, and they resorted to their boot blades as the other crewmen advanced. Regynn's tripped man was dead with a broken neck afore he could push back up on his hands and knees, and he tore off the man's sash, wrapping an end around each hand, then turned to face the rest. Calei managed to shove him aside while he was attempting to stand up, placing herself 'tween Regynn and the crewmen, exclaiming, "You are much needed, stay back!"

The two male Sprites suddenly turned around, facing another group of crewmen arriving from the other end of the hallway. Blades flashed, steel sung through the air, blood splattered, while they fought two against one in the confines, preventing anyone from passing them to flank their Captain, for 'twas clear that Caleichante was their ranking officer. He also realized that he was in the middle of this fray, figuratively and literally, as the ship's human Captain spat on the floor and made challenge, yelling, "KREEGAREN!"

The man was trying to disorient Regynn, not that he understood the word, but it made Regynn open wide his eyes and sent him into a fury, for someone knew who, and what, he was. Such provided proof that his addition to this crew had not been by chance. However, they had seriously underestimated him. To himself he swore he'd make them regret their allegiance, and their choice of employers.

Calei swung her falchion wide to block the incoming sword of the nearest crewman. Fighting face to face, 'twas just large enough for the shorter blade to be used to full advantage, and after the block, she twisted and thrust, impaling the man. Falling back into his comrades, they stepped o'er his body and took his place against the female as she backed up for more room.

But Regynn wasn't going to be left out of this fight. He sidestepped them as they passed, and then leaped forward, tucking and rolling into the next two, taking them by surprise. Tripping them both, they fell to their hands and knees onto the wooden flooring and hastily attempted to gather themselves. Regynn quickly wrapped his sash around one's ankle, then twisted and yanked it savagely upwards, slamming the man onto his face once again, afore hitting him hard on the temple with his elbow, rendering him unconscious. Still on one knee, he turned and used the sash to deflect the incoming sword strike, fouling the man's hand and his swing, but not in time to avoid a glancing blow on his shoulder as he scrambled to his feet. Still, the man lost his sword to the maneuver. Regynn stomped the side of the man's knee, dropping him in severe pain, and grabbed the sword as it clattered onto the floor. Thrusting hard past his hip and upwards, he struck true on the ship's Captain just as he attempted to jump on his back. As the sword imbedded into his ribcage, Regynn rolled forward, taking the skewered man with him. Leaving him on the floor, he rose gracefully, withdrawing the blade, all in one smooth motion. Now facing the back of Calei's attacker, her companions, having a hard time with their own fight, had near run into her in their retreat, fouling her swing and opening her to a forceful stab. Using his momentum, Regynn cleaved the man's skull as Calei stepped back, just missing the now downwards and glancing strike, leaving a long, thin, widening red line 'cross her left hip.

'Twas then he noted the boys had successfully finished their fight, the hallway near silent. They had to move quickly, 'twould be more coming, and soon. Stepping back, he took his new blade, and without even looking, impaled the one he'd rendered unconscious earlier. Dead men tell no tales, 'tis told.

Calei nodded her head in approval as they'd not broken eye contact since the Man likely saved her life, and then the four of them turned to the cargo hold. Repeating her earlier Magic to open the locks, they stepped inside, closing and barring the door behind them, and with a quick sweeping motion of their hands, they lit the room so all could see.

As Calei updated her men, they were shocked at the number of barrels. 'Twould destroy the entire Island of Dreams and annihilate the Water Dragons.

Gazing wide-eyed around the hold, Ardryyn, the elder of the brothers, stammered, "But Captain? We've not enough energy to neutralize all this, and there's nothing organic from which to Draw here."

Without even a glance in Regynn's direction, she pointed o'er her shoulder with her thumb and stated decisively, "He's organic. We Draw from him."

Kryllyn wasted no time and reached forth to touch the Human, but Regynn stepped back, and with his hands in the air, his gaze swept from one to the other of his companions. This was too close to his memories. "Whoa. Just wait a moment. Don't I get a reprieve for saving your lives?"

Now Calei looked at him. 'Twas clear he either knew or suspected just how far they could go. "Don't be a whiner. You'll be alright. A tad tired, mayhap."

"What does that mean, exactly?" he asked with suspicion.

"You'll probably miss watching the ship go down."

"I can't swim if I'm unconscious," he protested, as the boys laid hands upon him. Feeling a strange sensation that made him very sleepy, the last thing he heard was Caleichante's voice answering, "You won't need to." Just afore he lost awareness, he had a nagging feeling that something else was wrong. His last view of the cargo hold would cling to the back of his memory for many winters.

CHAPTER TWO

The Norryn

Regynn opened his eyes. Someone was shaking his shoulder and he heard voices asking if he was alright. Even sluggish, his intensive early training made him understand he was in no danger. He frowned as he recalled his first Master when he began his training to join the Kreegare. Her name was Tamm. Those winters he'd spent under her tutelage were tough, but he owed his life to her more times than he cared to admit. He hadn't thought about that woman in a very long time.

"Yes, yes, I'm alright," he managed to respond after a bit, just to get them to stop shaking him. He blinked several times as his vision began to clear, 'til the two brothers standing o'er him with big grins on their faces came into focus. They were on board another ship. Sitting up and gazing around the tiny cabin, he noted that this one was in perfect condition, and by the way she felt, was slicing through the waters at a rather steady clip. "Where am I now, and am I a prisoner?"

One of the boys spoke and he heard that same musical quality he could swear he'd heard afore. "No prisoner. My name is Ardryyn, and this is my younger brother, Kryllyn," he stated while nodding his head toward the other. "You're aboard the Norryn of the Sprite Nation." Smiling, the boys beckoned to Regynn and much to his surprise, showed him around the cabin, which was his to use for the voyage back to the mainland. Not only had he been given prime guest quarters, but also a pair of boots, two sets of clothing (one to wear and one to wash) both of which fit him perfectly, and he even had a small bar of soap, a towel, and a razor, things he'd not enjoyed in many moons.

After he was dressed, the boys, who he quickly learned were far older than they appeared, (apparently much older than was he, but relatively young for a Sprite), led him topside to meet the Ship's Master, and then tour the ship and meet the crew. Evidently, he was considered something of a hero and the Sprites were quite fascinated by him. He was the first Human any of them had met in person and after saving their homeland, they were all quick to show their gratitude. Apart from his heavier build and lack of pointed ears, having about the same average height with his hazel eyes and white blonde hair, he didn't look out of place amongst them. Ardryyn and Kryllyn had been 'assigned' to his wellbeing through the voyage, but he suspected 'twas more of a discovery mission. Although there were places he could not go and things he was not allowed to see, he was given far more freedom than he'd expected.

The story of what happened after he'd lost consciousness was his fame and glory, and he didn't hear the same events told in the same way, twice. His deeds kept growing 'til even he couldn't tell what part he'd played and what part was embellishment. After he'd passed out, the three Sprites used the energy they'd Drawn to Magically neutralize the poison in all the barrels afore several of their Dragons spit forth a forceful and continuous stream of water to cut a hole into the hull, sinking it to the bottom of the sea. Using the opening, Caleichante, Ardryyn, and Kryllyn took hold of Regynn and mounted their Ties who had entered who had entered the ship through the hole. The Water Dragons delivered the two young men and the Human to the Norryn, which sailed out to meet them.

Calei was instrumental in having the brothers promoted to Ship's Hands, which delighted them as 'twas a huge step up from working the docks, and now all they need do was save enough coin for their own weapons so they could apply for the Guard, hoping to get into the Elite. But for the length of this voyage, 'til they delivered the Human to their chosen destination, they were more like glorified babysitters. Calei went back to supervise the cleanup, ensuring there'd be no one left, and watched with smug satisfaction as the crewmen were all dispatched in a Water Dragon feast, afore returning to her duties.

The voyage ended up taking near a full winter from their island back to the mainland, because they had to divert a few days out and go further west than they'd planned. At least, that was the story they told Regynn, but he knew the truth. They were seeking information and they were attempting to guide him to making a certain decision. Knowing he was a rogue, they wanted him to join the Dragon Clan, having no doubt that Battle Commander Grifynn would accept his petition into Training.

While on board, the ship and crew worked several 'contracts' which Regynn was not allowed much knowledge, but he could tell their work was oft' times clandestine, and that each ship worked for itself, the Ship's Master (AKA the Captain) responsible for obtaining and carrying out said work, seeking the most lucrative contracts. However, his own work as an Assassin was similar.

He wasn't expected to do anything during the voyage, but afore the end of the first day he'd pitched in and was soon considered a Ship's Hand, working and living alongside them, learning their methods, their trades, a few words of their native tongue (they all spoke Common, so they could easily understand each other), even joining them in their morning katas on deck where all hands met at dawn to practice their native martial arts and fighting skills, something in which he was very much interested.

The brothers were his constant companions at work and leisure. Regynn's skills were worthy, his strength near equal to the crewmen, therefore he was also paid a Hand's wage in gold and silver as the voyage lengthened, and after he'd paid for all they'd given him that first day he began to collect even more coin during late night gambling, although he drank not, and ate only that which was provided for free. They couldn't be certain but Regynn was surely amassing a small fortune and yet he wove such fantastic tales (to which he received even more coin), made everyone laugh, turned out to be a great teacher of his own style of martial arts (a mix of his Kreegaren training altered and embellished with experience and by need), was an even better student and was truly compassionate, that no one minded losing to him.

It seemed the goal of their fighting style was not only to keep from being skewered, but to selectively touch their opponents while avoiding being touched, and their footwork and hand placements were a graceful dance in which they took advantage of their attacker's momentum, strength, and speed, using such against them to wear them down while expending as little energy as possible, themselves. The techniques required quick thinking, stepping patterns, weight shifting, great speed, strength, coordination and physical control, and he recalled learning similar movements as he was rising in his profession. Thinking about them, he once again recalled his training with Tamm. Although their techniques were not identical, he filed the many moments of déjà vu in the back of his mind, for odd clips of memories continued to surface. Still, he had not enough information to determine their relevance, as fighting techniques could have evolved as similar in different parts of the world, for the end goal was the same.

As the days, sennights, fortnights, and moons passed, he realized the Sprites had given him far more information than he'd given them. And yet, they seemed satisfied with the arrangement. 'Twas clear something else was going on, and one evening he asked Kryllyn, "How do you know so much about me? I've learned much about you but have given little information. I suspect 'tis not needed. Why?"

The boldly asserted truth caught Kryllyn off-guard and he blushed slightly afore responding with equal truth. "We knew your name, where you were from, your status, your affiliation, your honesty, your trustworthiness, all from the trip 'cross the waters via Water Dragon. They are quite Gifted."

Regynn considered this, accepting what he was told as he could not do any research to prove one way or the other. Moving on to his next thoughts, he stated, "We could have been at the mainland many moons ago. Why keep me aboard?"

Without hesitation, Ardryyn replied, "You were given into our care and 'tis our duty to protect you. We couldn't take you back too soon or your enemies would soon learn you were still alive, and you'd be hunted again. And we hoped to influence your decision."

Regynn knew to what decision he was referring. The one about what he was to do now. He'd been kidnapped and the one who'd paid for it now assumed him to be dead. He needed to disappear for a few winters. He nodded wordlessly. Being honest with himself, he needed to not only disappear but become someone else for the rest of his span of days and the Sprites knew this. Remaining a rogue made him a never-ending target. He needed backup.

Ardryyn stated, "We know your word is your life. When you leave us, you will not speak of us or any of the events or things you have seen or experienced. Our existence, the existence of the Water Dragons, will remain a secret 'til such time as we choose otherwise. This is your promise, this is your word."

Touched by their trust, Regynn nodded his acceptance. He'd never broken a promise, save falling in love with Cathay, which wasn't really breaking a promise. He handed her o'er, completed his mission, and then he left. That kept his promise. Keeping this promise should, by Hades, be a lot easier to keep than was that one. Sitting back, he relaxed and asked, "So, what advice do you have for me?"

Ardryyn looked to his brother who responded, "We think you should make petition for Warrior Training at Drekinn and join the Brotherhood. 'Twill be a simple thing for one of your skills and 'twill provide you with a lifelong career, relative safety from your past, and a new beginning."

"Why the Dragon Clan? Why not another?"

Now Ardryyn took o'er again. "Of all the Clans, Dragon is not only a War Clan, 'tis one that keeps the old ways. Your fighting skills will be much appreciated and with your coloring, you should blend in fairly well."

Regynn wasn't satisfied with that answer. There was something the Sprite had not said aloud. "And?"

Kryllyn frowned. "And?"

"Yes. There's more, I can see it in your eyes."

The Sprites knew if the Black returned to the war, so too would the Highlands and Mankind, and 'twould be through the Dragon Clan. Kryllyn looked first to his brother and then spoke. "Um, well, yes. There is more. Prophesy runs deep through the Clan. You have a date with destiny there. Please do not ask me for more. I will give none."

"Will not, or cannot?"

"Both," the brothers chimed in together.

After this revelation, the Norryn struck a straight path to Port O'Drekinn. In the next few dawns Regynn finally opened up with his friends about Cathay. For the first time since departing his homeland, his burden seemed lighter and he began to feel he had a future.

~~~~~ PORT O'DREKINN ~~~~~

Ardryyn was certain Regynn had enough coin to last well o'er a winter and he could manage to hide in the Port District, but the brothers felt strongly that their friend should not wait. "Remember, no one will see you or even know that they have touched you, should you make contact, 'til you are well into the village proper, as the Mist of Forgetfulness that surrounds the ship will envelop you and slowly dissipate as you get further away.

Keep climbing through the Port District, High Gate is unmistakable. Once into the village above, make your way to the Dragon's Den, the castle of the Warrior Brotherhood, and there you can make your petition. Remember what we've taught you, the Battle Commander's name is Grifynn…" Ardryyn winced with the raised eyebrows of his friend. "Forgive me. I'm sure you will remember everything quite clearly." He sighed, and then smiled. "We have a gift for you."

"Seriously?" Regynn watched the brothers exchange glances and then Kryllyn reached into his pocket, pulled out a small pouch, and handed it to him. He sputtered and asked, "What's this?"

"Open it." They laughed at the expression on his face, as 'twas clear the Man had never been given a gift afore. The boys had searched for moons trying to find the rice-like grains on the black market of the many port districts near which they'd traveled and had been forced to Dance there and back to the ship since the Captain avoided docking for fear of losing Regynn too early. They all wanted to keep him safe. 'Twas their sworn duty to Caleichante.

Delighted, Regynn looked inside and then smiling broadly, thanked them both with an arm grasp and hearty slap on the shoulder. "I'd thought never to taste the drink of my homeland again. These few grains are enough for me to grow my own Vydgryn! I know not how you managed to obtain this, but 'tis not in my power to thank you adequately."

The boys were pleased and though it had cost them near all their earnings thus far, it had been worth it to see the look on Regynn's face. Ardryyn broke the ensuing quiet. "I have to admit that you have opened my eyes to the honor of Humans. I will miss you, my friend."

"And I, you." Regynn smiled mischievously, causing the brothers to glance sideways at each other in puzzlement. They had come to know the Man well enough to wonder just what he had up his sleeve. But they decided they must be mistaken as they laid the gangway and watched Regynn shake hands with all the crew afore he simply turned and disappeared into the port crowds in the early dawn light with nothing but the clothes on his back and the pouch in his pocket.

<div align="center">~~~~~ THE VOID ~~~~~</div>

Storrm looked up at Mystynn's face and pounding her fist on his chest triumphantly, announced with satisfaction, "I KNEW he learned those moves from the Magic bearers!"

Mystynn rolled his eyes and hugged her back to his chest with exasperation. "May we please continue?"

"Oh yes. Sorry. I'll be quiet."

NEAR A FORTNIGHT LATER

THE NORRYN

~~~~~ APPROACHING PORT O'DREAMS ~~~~~</div>

The brothers were now fully immersed in their new duties and were exhausted. The Human left them in the pre-dawn marks many days past and they'd sailed without delay into open waters, destination Port O'Dreams for a new contract. They'd chosen double shifts for the next several moons to try to make up for what they'd spent on their friend's gift and were looking forward to making port, as 'twould give them a brief respite. Working hard all day, they still could not stop thinking about Regynn. He had become a close friend o'er the past winter and they'd probably never see him again, but they were pleased they'd found the Vydgryn. Hoping he'd taken their advice and gone straight to the Den, they settled down in their racks and had just closed their eyes to get what sleep they could when the Ship's Master had them awakened and brought to his cabin. Alarmed, they looked one to the other trying to ascertain what they'd done, or not done, to warrant such action.

As they both stood, without a word the Ship's Master reached into his safe on the wall and pulled out two large, extremely heavy bags, handing one to each of the brothers. "This is for you. He made the arrangements within the first sennight he was aboard. 'Twas his wish. He took just enough for one meal and left the rest of the coin he'd earned through the entire voyage. He said he wanted you to join the Guard." He sighed, for he was losing two of his best Hands, despite the short time they'd been under his command. "I contacted Captain Caleichante this morning, advising her that she would most likely have two new recruits as soon as we make port."

CHAPTER THREE
Confirming The Curse

NEAR FIFTY WINTERS LATER

THREE MOONS AFORE THE FIRST LIFEBOND

~~~~~ THE PALACE OF THE GODDESS MORRIGAN ~~~~~

The Sorcerer walked forward, rolling back his hood with both hands, as the beautiful woman reclining upon the elongated, hand-carved, leopard-skin chaise lounge, beckoned. Her palace was breathtaking, and yet, ever-changing as were the moods of the Goddess. Making his way towards the dais, the Sorcerer carefully walked a straight line, keeping his eyes fixed upon his destination so he'd not be lost forever as he stepped first through a jungle with heavy vines hanging from tall tropical-looking trees, large sweet-smelling flowers growing all around, and the sounds of a river gurgling off to his left. With his next few steps he was hit by a blast of hot dry air from the Dragon's Breath, the desert sands shifting ominously under his feet, a venomous snake hissing at eye level upon a huge rock. Eventually, after several such changes, he stood upon the marble floor of an enormous room with carved pillars, the Morrigan still stretched out upon her lounge watching his eyes, his expression.

~~~~~ THE VOID ~~~~~

She'd never seen the Goddess afore and excitedly, Storrm exclaimed, "Ooooh! The Morrigan! She's from whom I took my Battle Name, you know."

Annoyed, Mystynn replied, "How could I not know from whom you took your Battle Name? And you just promised."

"Oh, sorry."

"Shhhhhhhh!"

~~~~~ MEANWHILE ~~~~~

The Sorcerer stood very still, waiting for the Goddess to break the silence. At least she hadn't killed him yet. 'Twas a good sign. Wearing a slinky black dress that molded itself to her upper body and luscious hips, then flowed freely to the floor behind, cut high and off-center in the front with a split even higher, extended sleeves that came to a point at the back of her long fingers, and her stacked bosom held firmly despite a plunging neckline, she was striking. Her dark eyes were shining maliciously, and her smile was cruel as she spoke slowly and with thick contempt. "The Fay exile one of their own, handing him o'er to serve me forever, while he watches every woman for whom he grows to care, forced Past the Veil as his punishment. Nothing he can do, to prevent such. No matter how hard he tries, no matter how strong his Magic, no matter how many tears he cries, the end is always tragic. But they gave me an innocent man, did they not? Filled with guilt for a crime he did not commit?"

Hesitating, his heart raced as fear tried to take a firmer grip. But the Sorcerer thrived on such emotion. Still, he must know, notwithstanding the fact that the Morrigan was much higher in the hierarchy of power than was he, for Bardyn the Bear would not live forever and he had to know if Corbyn's curse was attached to the lifespan of his father. In addition, he'd Seen something that he thought was impossible. Corbyn free of his curse. A curse he'd orchestrated. A curse he would have gladly negotiated. What had he missed? And how? Afore he could respond, she sat upright on the lounge which was now upholstered in red velvet with gold-encrusted ornate ball and claw feet, still staring at him, a wicked smirk upon her gorgeous face. The tip of her tongue slid out to moisten those full red lips and she cocked her head slightly, her heated gaze measuring the man who stood afore her. Then she crossed her long shapely legs and leaned sideways on one elbow as her smile hardened. By the Flame, she knew! She knew why he'd come.

Pleased at his discomfort, she answered his unspoken question. "I was asked to curse the Man. But no one tells the Morrigan how to do that. A curse has a beginning, therefore it must have an end, for 'tis the way of all things. I rather liked the idea of having Corbyn at my beck and call. He has served me well, as I knew he would, without bowing down. The Raven is as my own child. He does not grovel, even to his betters. Me'thinks he is far stronger than the one who sent him here." She pointedly stared at the Sorcerer afore sitting upright again, her creamy smooth shoulders pulled back, the tip of her middle finger sliding sensually down her rather impressive cleavage. "I chose an end most unlikely, o'er which he would have no control, for I desired his company as long as possible."

The Sorcerer seethed. He huffed and chewed on the inside of his cheek as he struggled for control of his rising fury. He must be careful. She was baiting him.

The Morrigan enjoyed the mounting tension. As the Goddess of Fate, War, and Death, she lived for the thrill of the battle, even those she'd not arranged. How could she resist this temptation? The Man came to her, unsolicited, uninvited, to plead for information to confirm the details of the curse of another. 'Twas obvious he greatly feared the Raven. All these winters, she'd wondered. Knowing Corbyn was innocent of his supposed crimes, someone must have framed him. That one would have been the guilty party. But, just identifying that one was not sufficient. The perpetrator must not only be proven, Corbyn must release his guilt-ridden conscience and see 'twas not his fault or he'd remain an easy target. Therefore, the curse was conceived, the exile planned to find the real killer of his lifemate and unborn son, and to prevent Corbyn's murder. There was a spy within the Fay Nation and 'til the truth was uncovered, the Heir Apparent must be protected. Such was the agreement 'tween the Morrigan and Bardyn, the Greatest King.

The Sorcerer began to sweat. Would she ever get to the point? What was the end of the curse?

Her thoughts continued. 'Twould need to last long enough to fulfill the bargain. So, she chose the end to mirror the beginning. 'Twould require a new love. A true love. One who would wrap the Raven and turn him inside out, one he could not resist. But not just any woman would do. No. Corbyn was special. To meet both his needs and to fulfill the longevity requirement, she'd added her own twist. The woman who would end the curse would be one who carried the blood of many Races. Specifically, the blood of the High Races Counsel. Fay, Dragon, Elf, and Man. Forgetting she was still staring at her visitor, she laughed out loud remembering when the curse was set. The implausibility of such happening was so high that she'd thought she just might get to keep Corbyn forever, after all.

The Sorcerer mistook her unexpected behavior. He was so angry his face was turning purple.

With her straight, floor length, pitch black hair and matching black eyes, her perfect pale skin, oval face, high cheekbones, and full ruby-red lips, the Morrigan was not only stunningly beautiful, she was incredibly intelligent, flourishing on all things pertaining to war. She'd always suspected this one as having been the perpetrator of the crime for which Corbyn was accused. But 'twas not her place to supervise the Fay. Still, 'twould be interesting, and having proof would give her an advantage. "You wish to know the end? 'Twill be an exceptional woman who destroys the curse. And I can tell you when. Just two generations from the recreation of the LifeBond, she will be born." She teased him mercilessly, knowing he would not understand.

Assuming she meant that Corbyn would find a Human with whom to have a child, he almost felt safe. Such would never happen after the loss of his 'true love', Hellyn. Or would it? He was the result of a similar situation. Having dredged this painful memory, he glanced up to see the triumphant expression on the

Morrigan's face. In that instant he was positive the bitch knew not only who he was, but what he'd done.

"Why do you fear the release of Corbyn the Raven? 'Twas such a tragedy. As was your childhood. You bear your own curse, do you not?"

Ignoring her latter comment, he spit forth, "I fear nothing."

"Yet you came all this way, just to determine the end of his curse. To try to prevent such, mayhap? I assure you, you have no control here."

The Sorcerer hated being put on the spot, 'twas as standing afore the Black, only with the Dragon, he was the stronger and chose to remain lowly. With the Goddess, he was truly walking a tightwire. "A second generation will not be born if such is prevented by the death of the first," he sneered in defiance.

She'd been amused when the Humans found a way around the Human/Dragon part of the caveat of her curse and if things continued the way they were, the curse could very well end. And soon. Now she was angry but for another reason. This conversation had passed amusing and gone straight to threatening. Just who did he think he was? Did he not know to whom he spoke? He was implying she couldn't hold her curse solid. He was saying he would interfere with what she'd put forth. Ominously, she reiterated, "The birth of the tri-blood girl child begins the end of Corbyn's curse."

With sudden insight, the Sorcerer understood how this could possibly occur. All he had to do was remain vigilant and aware. If Corbyn mated with one of the sisters... killing that one would give him great pleasure indeed. 'Twould be a repeat performance of course, for which he might even take bows this time, how could he not? 'Twas a delicious thought, causing so much pain to the Heir Apparent. Again. He sneered. But he was not known for his tolerance, nor for his patience, or good sense. Letting his emotions get the better of him, he replied impulsively as he locked gazes with the Morrigan. "I vow to kill the babe. This is one child who will not live to see the light of her first dawn."

The Morrigan laughed. She actually laughed. Apparently his audience was o'er, as the Sorcerer watched infuriated, while the Goddess stood up, her arms stretched wide. He ducked, covering his head and face as a thousand screeching ravens flew into the palace near knocking him down, their claws and beaks tearing at his flesh and clothing as they swooped past, flocking together to morph into a billowing iridescent black feather cloak swirling around the gleaming marble as she turned and walked out, leaving him alone in the rapidly dissolving chamber. Gathering himself, he had little time to act afore he dissolved with it, suddenly amazed he yet lived. 'Twas always a gamble when dealing with the Goddess, but the information he'd obtained made this effort worthwhile. Now, he had another appointment.

LESS THAN A SENNIGHT LATER
~~~~~ THE ISLAND OF DREAMS ~~~~~

The Sorcerer sniffed repugnantly and then spit on the ground, clearing his mind. The island stifled his senses, made him feel more agitated by the moment, not to mention how difficult 'twas for him to get here in the first place, for Masking against the Water Dragons was extremely risky and didn't always work. He'd just left one of his contacts, giving her the mirror to pass along to another, implementing a major operation. The feeling of power and control he gained from dealing with that one made him so aroused he'd had to relieve himself, spilling his seed o'er the shoreline sands in disrespectful ecstasy. But now, he had even more important business. Myrrdin. The Elven Prince had been a thorn in his side since afore the Last Holocaust, when he'd managed to slip through his fingers and escape his trap with the help of Corbyn the Raven. Even though Corbyn had at that time just entered his curse with the Morrigan, he was still able to cause him trouble.

Without a bit of modesty, he stood in full view of his skiff's oarsmen, re-tying the leather laces on his pants as he silently reviewed his plans. He needed Myrrdin alive, his Life Source coursing through his veins, but 'twould not happen in any conventional scenario, so a frontal assault or attempted kidnap was no use. And the Krakken was the fastest ship on the seas, so a chase was out of the question. He'd thought long and hard on how to capture the Prince. He felt in his pocket for the blade.

Shuddering, he thought about what had happened so many winters past and called down the curses of the Ancients upon the beautiful Rashei with the long brown hair. He had plans for that one still. However, to avoid allowing another to Cast his Spells again, he'd imbued an ordinary boot blade with one. The bearer of his Spell need only blood himself upon the blade then imbed the blade into the hull of the ship, and 'twould be his. He snorted. 'Twould take proper timing but once imbedded in the Krakken's hull 'twould sail straight for Port O'Kings, and nothing save the death of both the one who'd set the Spell and the Krakken itself would stop it.

Myrrdin would never leave his ship and he had a father-like trust in his crewmen. He'd have no idea what was happening and would be his prisoner within a dawn. He just had to get the blade to his contacts in the Assembly and have them find a disgruntled sailor. This plan would take time to activate, for finding a disgruntled sailor amongst the crew of the Krakken would be most difficult, but the Sorcerer knew with the right encouragement anything could happen. He just had to be patient. And he had to leave. But first, his meeting with Frynbec and Benetyk. Disguising himself with a most powerful glamour so as not to give away his Race, he began the trek towards their rendezvous point.

CHAPTER FOUR

The Winemaker

Kneeling in the thin grass and sandy red dirt, Dyraserrah parted her shoulder length, dark brown, springy curls like a curtain in front of her almond shaped eyes, tucking each side behind pointed ears to clear her view afore she stood up with the help of her boyfriend, brushed the dirt off her hands and knees, and faced Leisalarr with shock. "Where are we?"

Leis, the middle child of the royal Elven brood of seventeen, scanned in every direction as he helped her up. His lean muscle, tall frame, and dark hair were reminiscent of his eldest (and long missing) brother, Myrrdin, whom he'd idolized since he could remember, and at this moment the look on his face and in his dark eyes was just as gritty. The diverse, yet organically sparse landscape, was ominously familiar but not from personal experience. Leis enjoyed his studies and read voraciously as a child. This looked like someplace he'd read about a very long time ago. 'Twas barren, dry, with scrub brush and clumps of reedy grass in all directions. Incredible and colorful rock sculptures with pillars, hills, mounds, arches, and bridges to nowhere, were visible as far as he could see. 'Twas evidently a wind-wasting effect. Gazing up at the blue sky, he noted the bright yellow sun being covered by angry black clouds. Those colors were all correct. And ancient. Both Leis and his girlfriend were born afore the Last Holocaust and had been outside the Wyrdritch as children. Afore there was a true barrier. Afore the morphing of the Protection Spell o'er the ancient forest in which the Elves took refuge from the rest of the world. But since then, the forest moved, colors were ever-changing and nothing like this, and now without the influence of the 'normalization effect' inside, he began to remember how things were, how they should be. "She was right," he muttered without taking his eyes off their surroundings.

"Who was right? Right about what?"

"Anastasia. The Wyrdritch is in real trouble." His little sister's conviction that there was something wrong with the Spell of Protection o'er the ancestral homeland of the Elven Nation sitting in the middle of Darkling Forest led the pair to see for themselves, which also led them to their current situation.

Dyraserrah was getting a tad perturbed and was out of patience. This day had started out badly and appeared to be getting worse by the candle drip. Grabbing his arm to turn him toward her, she stated angrily, "I'm leaning toward US being in real trouble, Your Highness, and I have just three questions. How did we get here, where exactly is 'here', and how do we get home?"

But instead of answering her, he pointed upwards and Dyra's eyes followed. The dark clouds had more than tripled in the few heartbeats of their conversation and she could already see the heavy curtain of rain beginning a league distant. The winds were picking up fast and 'twas a severe storm on the horizon. "You see that? We have to find shelter, NOW."

Searching just a few paces from where they'd so unexpectedly arrived, the wind had become near strong enough to pick up the slight girl and 'twas only the fact that Elves were stronger than Humans, that she was able to keep her footing. But their differences were not that pronounced. Yelling into the rising gale, she drew the attention of Leis and pointed to a rock ledge. She had to yell, to be heard. "I THINK WE CAN FIT UNDER THERE!"

Pelted by straight-line winds carrying all manner of sand, rock, brush, and now piercing rain, Leisalarr grabbed her by the arm and practically threw her under the shelf, diving in after. Rolling on top of her to shield her from the elements, they soon felt the ground under them give way, and after falling a short distance, they landed in a heap on the dirt floor of a small cave. Listening to the fury of the storm outside, they stood clutching each other as their racing hearts pounded at the near miss, backed up as far away from their 'entrance' as they could get, watching the rain waters begin to trickle down the wall from where they'd just fallen. Wide-eyed, Dyraserrah announced the obvious. "If that doesn't stop, we'll drown in here. I'm so sorry I talked you into this."

Leisalarr shook his head and hugged her hard, reassuring her that there was nothing to forgive, then turned all about searching for an escape as the trickle rapidly became a torrential flood. Already ankle-deep in the water, 'twas clearly not an option to exit the way they'd entered. Wading all around the area, they felt o'er the entire wall, and reaching up, they felt the ceiling as well. Nothing. The waters kept rising, now up to their knees with no slackening of the incoming rain. Relentlessly, they continued their search. There had to be another way out. As the water rose to their hips, Leis took Dyra's hand and they prepared to try to cast a Spell to push back the flood, but they knew 'twould be near impossible, as there was nothing organic from which to Draw energy required for such as this, and they'd used much to survive their journey.

Just afore they cast, Leis suddenly stopped and looked at Dyra oddly, prompting her to question, "What is it?"

"Do you not feel that?"

"What?"

Without answering, his expression told her to stop and Cast forth her senses. 'Twas then she felt it; a warm tingling sensation, indicative of Magic, and 'twas not their own. This was a common Spell, and 'twas very near. Leis threw up his hands, seeking information and the location of the Spell, as he trudged desperately through the rising waters toward the far side, close to where they'd first stood. Gesturing wilding, he exclaimed, "Help me! 'Tis here!"

'Twas a Spell Door. Combining what was left of their Magic and Pushing together, they managed to stumble through what appeared to be a solid rock wall, tumbling down a slight decline and rolling into a small room, coming to a stop at the feet of an elder male standing at a table with a look of pure astonishment upon his face. Even though they'd obviously surprised him, his voice was calm, holding no condemnation for their intrusion. "Your Highness? To see you is both a pleasure and not, for it means you are now trapped here, as am I. It has been so long, I am surprised the Wyrdritch yet exists." Taking a sip from the glass he held in his hand, he then put it down on the table and continued, "Please make yourselves comfortable, as I repair the damage to the Spell Door and repel the waters from my home."

~~~~~ LATER ~~~~~

They had no energy to perform unnecessary Spells, so with blankets wrapped 'round them, their clothing drying on a rack at the hearth, they sat at the small handmade table on simple wooden stools while the old Elf spoke of the far distant past, when he'd first arrived. Listening to the fury of the storm outside, he poured them each a glass of wine.

Leis took his glass gratefully and sipped. 'Twas very good. He'd not had wine this good since... dumbfounded, he looked at their benefactor. "I know you! You had a vineyard, made the royal wines!"

With a slight smile, the old Elf tucked his chin graciously and stated with eloquence, "Yes, that was I."

"And now I recall when you disappeared, but 'twas suppressed from my memories o'er the winters, as was much. Why? Why did our memories alter under the Spell? What's wrong with it? Anastasia believes 'tis failing."

"Anastasia?"

"My youngest sister. Oh yes, I should mention there are now seventeen of us. And a new Queen. A long story."

He cocked his head and smiled. The Royal House of the Elven Nation had always been large, and there would be time enough for long stories later. Returning his thoughts to the Prince's questions he had to admit they'd all felt the Spell was failing. "We believed the morphing of the Spell was collapsing the Wyrdritch as well as causing a memory deficit."

Leis looked down as he recognized the consequences of this information. He wanted to return and help, but at this moment it seemed they couldn't even help themselves. "I'm sorry sir, my memories seem to be clearing since we came here but I cannot recall your name."

With a dignified bow of his greying head, he stated simply, "I am Orayalyn."

Now this was welcome news. "Yes! I visited the vineyards often as a child. My younger brother Orasynth, was named in your honor."

A smile came to his lips as he recalled the birth of the Elven Prince. "'Twas a very great honor, indeed," he accepted, afore he began his story. "You were young my Prince, but I remember you as well. In fact, I had just visited Haven and went for a walk by the barrier, something we'd begun to take for granted, though 'twas not natural. If you recall, afore the Last Holocaust there was no barrier, just a simple Spell of Protection, one that basically hid the Wyrdritch from Human eyes. Not that many traveled Darkling Forest mind you, but 'twas a wise precaution. We walked freely through Darkling then. When the barrier was discovered we tried to learn more about it, what had caused it and why. Some of us formed a study group, and I was gathering information. Of course, your father King Jeeryd, wasn't impressed and once Elves began to disappear, he withdrew, decreeing that no Elf could attempt to leave the Wyrdritch and any who did would be severely punished. Most of us didn't believe anyone who was lost had attempted to leave, and in fact we had no clue just how many were disappearing. As the numbers grew, our memories shortened. There was something very wrong. But the King wouldn't listen and forbade further research. 'Twas when your mother Queen

Bryanna, tried to step in and speak for us in support of our efforts, that she angered the King. He declared the rest of Kadoor destroyed and the Wyrdritch was all that remained. 'Twas his belief that the barrier was now the edge of the world. Soon after, the Queen disappeared and then most of our group went into hiding. 'Twas at least another moon later that I made my own fateful trip. I was certain the lost were still alive; by some means they'd penetrated the barrier and I was determined to learn how. As I was approaching that evening I felt a 'pulling' sensation. Reaching out my hand, I saw myself drawn into some kind of portal, rushing me through as a Dance but 'twas not through shadow, nor had I Drawn my energy in preparation." He paused to collect his thoughts. His expression was of one far away, his memories becoming reality once more. "Mayhap I should not have fought the journey so, but as it lengthened I had the passing notion that I'd seen the end of my days. I landed on my hands and knees not far from here. 'Twas most undignified. But after much speculation I determined, one, I was still this side of the Veil, two, the barrier was the result of the morphing of the Spell o'er the Wyrdritch after the Last Holocaust, and three, the lost had all traveled as did I, to some foreign place or other. Mayhap I was not alone in this strange land. But there are few places in all the world that I might have ended up, that could have been worse." His gaze bored into those of the Elven Prince and he asked, "You know where we are, do you not?"

Both younger Elves had remained silent through the elder's story. They each knew in their hearts they'd taken the same journey as did he and were now halfway 'round the world from home. 'Twould be impossible to return the way they'd come and trying to do so a'foot was near as unlikely, for a vast, desolate land, and then the Dragon's Tears lay 'tween where they were now, and the Wyrdritch. Leisalarr took a deep breath, looked at Dyraserrah, and nodding his head in affirmation, answered grimly, "The Rol Dan."

~~~~~ THE FAY NATION ~~~~~

Rhyah hadn't slept in days. The Nation was in turmoil and Bardyn's attitude was not helping, but Corbyn's father wouldn't live forever. Rhyah missed his best friend and lately spent most of his time in wolf form, recalling their youthful pranks. Such was frowned upon by the royal house and mayhap their childhood audacity led to their current circumstances. He could sense the emotional miasma of Kadoor slipping through their carefully constructed barriers, and 'twould not be held at bay much longer. Magic was strengthened by emotion and the Fay were already the most powerful Magic bearers. They must embrace strong emotion once again and they must learn to control it, for the Shunning was a totally unenforceable ban.

Rhyah made his decision. Several others had already abandoned the Nation's borders, and none had returned, nor had they been heard from since, thought to have died due to their inexperience in the outside world. He would not be so foolish. His destination would be the Dragon Clan who one day would lead the Resistance. In the meantime, he would seek out and immerse himself in the strongest of emotions, love and hate, learning how to deal with such foreign senses with minimal repercussion. Corbyn had broken through and he'd still been within the confines of the Nation. Of course, his experience led to his exile.

But there were rumors growing, rumors that Rhyah very much believed. They whispered that the Heir Apparent was framed, that he was innocent of the slayings of which he was accused, and most wanted him to come home. Besides, some believed the royal house was falling apart without Corbyn's steadfast influence. His younger brother Brannyn the Falcon had gone o'er to the Evil One and been exiled shortly after Corbyn was sent away. His mother Alyphia the Fox was being unusually quiet of late, and Bardyn was rarely seen these days outside of his preferred Shift as the Bear.

Glancing around his quarters he noted the pictures of his parents and of his ancestors, treasures most of the Fay did not keep, in accordance with the ban. He'd carefully preserved them, hiding them from Bardyn, and had spent much of the past few winters in the Archives supposedly researching others of his lineage. Such was not discouraged, nevertheless since Corbyn's exile he'd been mindful of his actions for his true research lay in their history afore the Shunning. 'Twas a time when true love was profound, and children remained with their parents, learning how to handle disappointments, anger, loss, as well as happiness, love, and humility. According to what he'd found, there'd been violence but not any more so than now.

He would take nothing with him for he'd be in Shift most of the time. Anything he required, he would obtain. Quietly, he left his home. Shortly after, he was outside the Fay Nation, his point of departure the southeastern region of Wyndsyr Forest in the Razor's Edge. The Wolf padded along on huge paws, his tongue hanging out as he kept up a steady pace northwesterly, toward Drekinn. 'Twas rumored he'd find Corbyn there.

FIRE HEART ISLAND IN THE MIDDLE OF THE DRAGON'S TEARS
~~~~ FLIGHT OF FIRE KEEP, THE CASTLE
OF THE HIGHLANDS ~~~~~

Corbyn had visited Synahmarr several times since her glorious escape from Evanntyr. Rising into the skies like a phoenix, her russet scales sparkling in the fury of the energy storm, she fulfilled that part of the Death of Life prophesy (which would prevent the extinction of the Highlands) while she'd near destroyed a quarter of Evanntyr, where she'd been held captive since shortly after the Last Holocaust. Again, he'd spent several marks trying to convince her to lay her eggs. He knew she was bearing, and he knew the consequences of such, but if he couldn't convince her of the possibilities, he had to convince her that laying was the lesser of two evils. Trying once more, he stated emphatically, "Your return is not sufficient!"

Synahmarr was near her limit. Corbyn did not understand the cruel twist of fate, nor the ramifications. She could tell no one the truth. No one. "All I've accomplished was to prevent the loss of rule for one more generation, taking my place from the Mighty Maahayyel. But even as Matriarch, I cannot avert the Death of Life."

Frustrated and blind to the tortured expression in the Matriarch's eyes, Corbyn replied quickly, "Yes! Yes, you can!"

Her sternness now became a solid rock wall of attitude. "Then I will not! The result would be far worse than our extinction. Leave me, we shall not speak of this again."

As he watched helplessly, Synahmarr walked gracefully out of the conference room in which she'd seen him. Why did everyone think he didn't understand? Of course, he did! He knew exactly what she thought had happened and had tried to tell her otherwise, but she never gave him a chance to explain his theory. He needed it to be reality but 'twould require her cooperation. Mayhap if he presented this argument from a female's perspective? Synahmarr must lay. By so doing, all the Highlands might come out of their sterility. If she did not, the Highlands could very well become extinct. They hadn't had a fertile female except the Matriarch since the War of Chaos. He'd originally believed 'twas due to some kind of Spell, but try as he might, he'd not uncovered such an Allure. He had Kelseacyr, the Elven Skald stationed at the Keep of St Swiftyn's, working on it now. Mayhap time itself would bring back their fertility, and he hoped they'd be encouraged by the new Matriarch's laying.

In the meantime, Highlands would only bear eggs with their lifemate. That meant, if Synahmarr had eggs, which she did, she'd been Claimed, and Highlands mated for life. Corbyn sighed. Knowing the timing of such would help, but he had his suspicions. She'd been kidnapped just afore the Last Holocaust and spent several centuries in stasis waiting for the moment of her release which came as per prophesy and with the help of one beautiful, flaxen haired Warrior by the name of Mynx, who became quite close to the Matriarch. Mayhap she could help him now. He launched himself out the window and made his Shift mid-air. The Raven was on a mission. Mynx was at the Dragon's Den. He had to hurry, he'd been away from Storrm for too long, although she'd not seemed to need his protection. His current Warrior to serve in his curse, mayhap she'd be around for a while. He shook his head. He didn't want to lose this one.

~~~~~~~~~~

Synahmarr placed both her front paws upon the clear encasement in the middle of the open room atop the highest tower of Flight of Fire Keep, and through building tears she stared at the entombed body of her aunt, the Last Dragon Matriarch, forced Past the Veil in the rescue after passing her power and her rule to her niece. 'Twas as if she were merely sleeping.

Syn had the case made specially and 'twould withstand all weather, all manner of destruction, even Flame. When she'd flown back to the castle of the Highlands, her home, after being gone for so very long and never sure if she'd ever return, she'd been so o'erwhelmed by grief that she could not bear to cremate her aunt, sending her ashes into the skies on a funerary flight as was usual. Instead, she'd built this room, this monument to the greatest Matriarch of all time. They hadn't spoken since afore Syn was kidnapped. She needed her now, more than ever. She was miserable. "Oh, Aunt Maahayyel, what do I do? Once again, I've failed my Race. I wish I could talk to you, hear your voice, your wisdom. I need your help to make this decision. If I lay the Black's eggs, he will know, and may yet hold power o'er me through our offspring. At the very least, they may be as evil-hearted as is he. And I could never mate with him again, so these eggs of mine will still be the last. But if I do not take the chance that there may be some good in them, there seems no chance the death of life can be averted. I have ruined everything. What do I do?"

~~~~~ THE DRAGON'S DEN ~~~~~

He'd traveled straight to Drekinn, arranging the meeting with Mynx on the way and now stood in front of her. He'd already attempted to explain his need, and now summarized, "She thinks the Black took her Claim. But I think otherwise. I sense the possibility of another's Claim upon her and believe 'twas a hoax to get her to bow down to him. She has upon her, the residue of Memory Magic." He winced, as 'twas the native Magic of the Fay.

Mynx was quite interested, and since Synahmarr and she were good friends she wanted to help. "But she does have eggs, you are certain? How can we prove 'twas a trick, then?"

"She is so scandalized by her past mistakes that she will not allow me to examine her to prove my theory. I was hoping..."

With a knowing look and a smirk, she cut him off. "You were hoping that she would listen to me, and that I might be able to get her to do what you want."

"That would be the hope, yes."

"And what if 'twas reality? What if she is the lifemate of the Black?"

"Such could very well mean the end of the Highlands."

Mynx sighed. "I know not how to get there. Darque will not allow any to leave the Lairs. 'Twill take a profound event to change her orders, and then I'd have to spend some length of time with Syn to accomplish that which you seek."

Corbyn considered. He felt something was going to happen in the near future that would allow her that freedom, but he knew not if 'twas good or bad. "The time will come; your opportunity will present itself. When it does, you need but remember."

Mynx could not help but think there was something sinister behind the Fay's words, as she warily nodded her affirmation.

THE ROL DAN
~~~~~ OUTSIDE THE HOME OF ORAYALYN ~~~~~

"Hurry, you have to pick as much as possible, as quickly as possible! The Vydgryn rot within a mark after blooming!" The Rol Dan was known for its vicious and unpredictable storms, leaving the old Elf little time to explain to his visitors. The storm continued 'til their clothes were completely dry but as soon as the rains stopped, he hustled them outside through a large enclosed vineyard via a hidden doorway opposite from where they'd made their dramatic entrance such a short time ago (what he referred to as his back door), and handed Leis and Dyra sacks to gather the seed pods of the incredible plant that transformed the parched landscape into a thick carpet of knee to chest high bright yellow flowers growing on every surface as far as the eye could see, atop long spiky stems sprouting from a massive proliferation of the reedy grasses they'd noticed upon arrival. Expecting to wade through mud, 'twas remarkably dry again.

The long edges of the slender leaves were sharply serrated and the hard, spiny seedpods as large as Leisalarr's palm, were firmly attached to the tops of the rigid stems. They proved hazardous to pick so, like the elder Elf, they wrapped their hands with rags. Grabbing as many as they could afore the plants began to slump, they quickly filled their sacks, their pouches, the blankets they'd had wrapped around them earlier, and after some disapproval from their benefactor, even took off their shirts and pants, tying knots in the arms and legs and filled them as well (although this led to some rather painful scratches). The seedpods they'd picked afore the plants began to die back to their prior appearance remained hard and fresh, while the ones they'd not had time to grab, softened to a foul mush afore their eyes. True to the old Elf's warning, the plants had vanished entirely within the mark. Gazing o'er the vast, multi-leveled land, it now appeared as empty as it had afore the flood, the mushy pods dissolving into the ground providing both protection and fertilizer for the seeds within, awaiting the next rains.

'Twas the largest harvest Orayalyn had ever made. Returning to his abode, they shook all the pods onto the floor and then watched in amazement as the elder Elf gathered them and tossed them into the hot coals of the fire. After he'd explained the seeds inside the pods were as valuable as gold in the cities, they cast their wary glances toward each other and then back to him. "I am quite sane, I assure you. Listen."

They listened. Very soon they heard a slight crackling sound coming from the fire that was not the fire itself. 'Twas as popping corn. "Come, come," he said, eagerly gesturing them closer while he stirred the coals with a poker. Apparently satisfied with what he saw, he reached in with a long-handled sifting scoop and gathered the still solid, but now white and spineless pods, placing them in a large cast iron pot which he had hanging o'er the edge of the fire on the other side. When he was done, he repeated the ritual 'til all the pods were thus treated.

Leaving them in the pot for near a mark, he dumped the now thoroughly dried and cooled pods onto the table, carefully preventing them from falling on the floor. Then he gave each of them a bowl and showed them how to crack the pods open and catch all the seeds in the bowl (it reminded them of cracking eggs), making it very clear they must not miss any and that they had to stay dry. The seeds were similar to rice, only a little larger and with a slightly yellow hue. Once all the seeds were gathered, the old Elf threw all the pod pieces back into the fire and they watched in amazement as the fire crackled and flashed while a sparkling green and yellow glow emanated from the flames.

~~~~~~~~~~

O'er the course of the next two days Orayalyn taught the pair everything he knew about the Rol Dan and their situation. By the time Orayalyn arrived others were already there, some for many moons, but they'd not gone far. The winemaker's appearance made them realize they couldn't all live in the small cave, more might still come and there was no chance of rescue if they waited. They had to make the best of this new world. Orayalyn was their elder even then and leaving him in the cave in which they'd all been taking refuge, they struck out to explore, warning him about the storms, promising to return if able, and with the instruction to keep any new arrivals there 'til they did.

As he waited their return, the old man made the best of things, altering his new living quarters to satisfy his sensitivities, making and growing what he required to strengthen his Magic and provide for his needs. But he missed his vineyards. As an agriculturalist, the changing landscape after the first storm fascinated him and by the third such, he'd near perfected the harvest technique, thinking he could use the grains as food. His surplus was a welcome surprise to the returning Elves who had found out much about the land and its people, little of which was good news for the Magic bearers. A group of eleven Elves had left together. Four returned. Orayalyn was quick to note that three of them were once members of the King's Guard and had been trained fighters. Although they were devastated to have lost the others, after hearing of their experiences Orayalyn knew there was nothing they could have done to alter the outcome.

In the meantime, more Elves had arrived, and his tiny cavern home was very crowded. If not for Orayalyn's gardening skills, cultivating a variety of hearty root stock and edible fungi which he'd discovered during foraging, they'd not have survived. When the four returned, they joined with an additional twenty-three Elves. What were they to do?

Arriving alone or in pairs, Orayalyn had interviewed every one of them intensively and 'twas his belief the portals were randomly pulling Elves away from the Wyrdritch at odd times, without warning, and in many different directions. Considering how many Elves were 'lost' prior to his own journey, if there were twenty-eight of them here in less than a full winter, (not counting the seven who'd died on their recognizance mission), there must be multiple such portals and many hundreds of lost Elves. He could only hope that none of the portals led to such places as the lava under Flight of Fire Keep, or directly into one of the many seas and oceans, or even into solid rock. No, he didn't believe any of those were viable destinations, but they could find themselves in the desert sands of the Dragon's Breath, an even more inhospitable place than the Rol Dan, or mayhap the Icelands, where one could freeze to death within a mere few moments.

Their explorations of the land revealed several interesting facts. One, the land was the same out there as 'twas here, as far as they'd been able to travel a'foot, although they could see mountains in the far distance. But 'twas rumored to be extremely cold with constant snows, not unlike the Far Northlands themselves, and 'twas no guarantee forests would greet them if they traveled so far. Sadly, 'twas understood they had little chance of surviving such a journey in the first place. Two, the Vydgryn was as gold for 'twas difficult to harvest, and was the main ingredient in the native spirits, Vydna, the strongest drink any of them had ever tasted. Orayalyn presented them with a full bag of the precious grains. Three, Magic was not tolerated, 'twas punishable by death, and was the reason they'd found themselves ambushed by locals, losing most of their companions rather early in their explorations, after which they learned to hide their true abilities.

The societies in the Rol Dan were made up of Castes, ruled o'er by Warlords. The most feared and respected of the Castes, who had no ruling Warlord, was the Assassins. These worked alone on a contract basis and were oft' times hired by Warlords as private bodyguards or to perform certain tasks that would require their skills, much like the Warriors of the Dragon Clan. And then there was Tamm, an Elf who was hiding in the Assassins Caste, using her skills to excel in her chosen profession, keeping her Elven features hidden under glamour and a full hood. She'd rescued them, helping them to escape their captors. No one knew her history and none of them recognized her from the Wyrdritch, but if not for Tamm, these four would not have survived.

Everything they'd learned about the land, the Vydgryn, and the Assassins Caste, came from Tamm. 'Twas decided the four would return to Orayalyn and bring back any other Elves who might have arrived. Tamm would be waiting. A code was set up through the town of Harsh for any Elves who arrived after this trip, for 'twould be their last. If they tried to return, the elder Elf might be found and killed. Orayalyn was to send all new Elves to them. 'Twas the only way any of them could survive, for they couldn't all stay in the small cave and they couldn't wander about the Rol Dan alone. They'd all become Assassins.

'Twas the momentary reluctance to drain Life Force that lost the other Elves their lives. The survivors quickly saw what needed to be done, crossing the line during their rescue and ensuing fighting. They'd be required to continue such, in the name of self-defense, but the Assassins did not kill indiscriminately. They had contracts to fulfill, protecting by defeating their enemies. As the new arrivals listened, 'twas some comfort. The energy they could Draw from draining Humans would maintain their Magical health as well as keep them hidden. They could not allow the Humans to see how they actually did the deed and if they Drew any energy, 'twould have to be to the death, for if not, their secret would then be known. Therefore, they still had to provide a 'killing strike' for witnesses, if there were any. If they were strong enough, quick enough, and had a good enough grip, their opponent would be promptly incapacitated, and they could finish with cutting their throats or a quick heart thrust. But most of the citizens of the Rol Dan didn't expose much of their skin due to the erratic weather and the intensity of the sun, so they still needed to know how to fight, and Tamm promised that she would teach them.

And there was one more thing. She'd sent a gift. Three grape vines. Small and scraggly, the vines were a sight for sore eyes to

Orayalyn and he would spend many solitary winters nursing them to good health and into a personal vineyard of which to be proud.

~~~~~~~~~~~

On the night afore Leis and Dyra departed, the elder Elf brought out three hand carved and sand rubbed cups, offering up a toast. The man was not only a fine winemaker, he was a gifted craftsman. "I had begun to think the Wyrdritch destroyed. Your appearance has given me hope that mayhap one day, I shall return." The sparkling moisture in his eyes made the pair understand what he carefully didn't verbalize. He was requesting their promise to take him home, dead or alive. Acceptance of the promise in their eyes, he relaxed and stated, "To your success, and our homecoming." Leis and Dyra met his cup with theirs but had a hard time swallowing past the tightness in their throats. Silently, they agreed. They would take him home, one way or the other.

~~~~~ WYNDSYR FOREST ~~~~~

Rhyah sat panting under a tall pine tree, its bushy, short-needled branches providing some cover from the rain. As he was even now, he'd spent much of his time traveling in Shift, for 'twas the most efficient method under the circumstances. He'd made several attempts to approach the local wolves of the region, but it hadn't taken long to realize things were a tad different in the real world, and a lone wolf was viewed with distrust. Since he was not a member of their pack, he was considered an outcast and intruder. Even though he was bigger than most of them, fights ensued. He'd had to move on. Still, he considered every encounter a learning experience. Staying in his chosen Shift longer than ever afore, he'd allowed himself to fully open his senses, truly feeling the frenzied emotion of the hunt, the metallic taste of blood, relishing in the exhilaration of his kills. He'd studied the pack order hierarchy mentality, and their fights led him to discover his talents in such. He was quick, agile, stout, daring, and ferocious, and although he could easily have taken down his opponents, being in Shift for lengthy periods made him begin to think more like a wolf, and 'twas the desire to be part of the pack that he felt the strongest, the disappointment of rejection near suffocating.

Still, he knew that learning to accept and deal with the emotions with which he was now being bombarded, was safer in Shift than in his true form. Unless he was o'erwhelmed, that is. He licked his shoulder where the once gaping slash was closing. Another reason not to change. Wounds tended to heal much faster this way, as Shifting was Magic and Magic was healing. A circle of life. And death.

His wolf form fought for supremacy o'er his rational thought patterns. His reasoning could suffer. Large yellow eyes scanned for dangers as he felt the pull to remain as a wolf. Mayhap 'twas why the others never came back. Stuck in their preferred Shifts. The longer he waited, the more likely was his own fate. He licked his shoulder once more, bowing his head to keep the rain out of his eyes, allowing it to roll down his muzzle and drip off the tip of his black nose as he stared at the wet ground in silence.

CHAPTER FIVE

Last Sentinel Of Harsh

Fully hooded, Leisalarr and Dyraserrah walked into the tavern at the edge of the city, in search of the shadowed table in the farthest corner. 'Twas near an exit into the back alley. From what little they'd seen thus far, Harsh lived up to its name. The floors of the shabby buildings were made of raw planks covered in mostly threadbare braided rugs, there were no paved roads, only boardwalks along the buildings, and unlike what the Elves were used to, there was no landscaping, either. The few trees appeared stunted and wind sculpted. Back home in the Wyrdritch they'd be considered scrubs and were apparently lucky to be alive, as were many of the residents. For a Race so attuned to nature, 'twas a very dismal environment. There was no doubt 'twould be next to impossible to fuel their Magics in such a land.

There seemed to be only one waitress, a young girl of mayhap thirteen winters who wore a pair of leather strap sandals and a flowing, pale blue, unadorned, ankle length, soft cotton tunic. 'Twas clearly not made for her and being too big, she'd belted it with a sash wrapped at least three times around her tiny waist to avoid stepping on the hem. But the wide scoop neck kept sliding off her shoulders and the long sleeves kept unrolling, covering her hands past her fingers. Her long blonde hair was braided in a circlet around her head and then joined to a single tail wrapped with a strip of leather. In contrast, the customers were covered head to toe, dressed as were they, although most had their sleeves rolled up and hoods pulled back revealing a multitude of skin and hair colors, mostly worn in shorter styles. The young girl was working hard to deliver everyone's orders, and walking deliberately toward the corner table, Leis made certain he showed no deference to his girlfriend as they passed. Once seated with their backs to the wall, they quietly observed the other patrons.

Since there weren't enough living organics for them to Dance (besides the fact they knew not where they were), the journey had been a'foot and they'd left the elder Elf near a fortnight past. The massive storm they'd experienced the day of their arrival did not repeat itself but Orayalyn had said 'twas the norm and that they were few and far 'tween, which was why the Vydgryn was so special. The seed pods had not contained many grains but collectively they each had a small bag and just afore they left, the old man handed them two bottles of his best wine and another three bags each of the Vydgryn that he'd been collecting, with the warning not to let them get damp. "It doesn't do me any good out here and I can always collect more. Besides, I have a feeling I've seen the last of my visitors. And mayhap soon, the last of my days here." Leis shook his hand and the Elder's grasp was still as strong as he'd remembered from his childhood. Dyra hugged him and kissed his cheek, making him blush and sputter. Without another word, he'd gone back to tend to his vineyard, muttering to himself as they'd turned and walked toward the eastern horizon, fearing they might never see him, or home, again.

Although the place was packed, no one looked their way and by observation the one young girl was doing all the work, waiting and clearing tables. Soon however, she came by to ask if there was anything they wanted. Clearly but softly, Leisalarr recited the words Orayalyn had made him memorize. "Vydna. And you shall leave the jug, for me'thinks 'tis better than in a glass, and a cup simply smothers the aroma," while Dyra knocked once on the table with her knuckles, indicating the same for her. The girl appeared somewhat skeptical but said nothing as she waited. Orayalyn had told them where to sit and how to order, warning them not to reveal the fact that Dyra was female nor to show too much of their Vydgryn. However, they pulled their bags out and each offered up a pinch of the small grains, dropping a few in the middle of the table where the flickering light of the candle made them appear more yellow than they were. They brushed them off their fingers to the stunned incredulity of the girl. Wide-eyed she backed up without touching the precious grains and stammered under her breath, "I'll bring your order as soon as possible m'lord, but it might take a while. Forgive me. Please forgive me."

Leis was afraid of this. He looked to the exit and then caught Dyra's eyes, noting her understanding of their situation. They'd discussed it at length during the long and sleepless nights on their rough trek to Harsh, while the Prince helped Dyra enhance her skills with a blade. They'd come up with every possible scenario, both good and bad. Orayalyn hadn't had contact with his brethren for many winters and things might have changed. Still, the old Elf insisted 'twas the only way he knew to contact the others. If this went a'foul they could soon be in a fight for their very lives. Dyra's hands snaked into her large bell-shaped sleeves as she took a firm grasp upon her blades, while Leis placed his hand upon the grip of the blade at his belt. If they could not make skin-to-skin contact with their opponents they'd have to rely on the blades, and they'd probably be fighting against swords. Tensely, they watched as the girl crossed the tavern, slid behind the long counter, and disappeared into the back through a heavy curtain, their eyes shifting to the exit once more. Should they wait, or make good their escape now?

As the moments slipped past, Leis surreptitiously placed his hand upon Dyra's arm to convey his decision. They had nowhere to go. They had to try to locate Tamm. 'Twas their only chance to survive in this unforgiving place. But Humans lived such a short span of days. Were any of these still aware of the old codes? Did any of them still align themselves with the Assassins? According to Orayalyn, no new 'lost ones' had come through the portal in many decades and therefore those now living in Harsh might not be on their side, or were at the very least, totally ignorant about them. And how did they even know Tamm was still alive? In fact, 'twas no real assurance the Elf ever existed. After all, Orayalyn stated he'd not seen her himself. Mayhap those who returned had already aligned with the Warlords, or even the Black, to enslave the rest. Were they making a deadly mistake?

<center>~~~~~ THE TAVERN KITCHEN ~~~~~</center>

The elderly woman grabbed the young girl by her shoulders and turned her forcefully 'round afore she could sneak out the back way. Frantically, she implored her, "You mustn't! The Warlord is no fool, 'twill bring down great tragedy upon our heads!"

Defiantly, the girl shrugged out of her grasp. The woman was not her mother, nor was she any blood to her, although as an employee of her parents, the former owners of this tavern, she had cared for her and her little brother for the past few moons since they'd died as a result of poisoning. As long as they worked, that is. And work, they did. Day in, day out, without a break, 'til she and her little brother fell into her blankets in the corner of the kitchen, oft' times without supper if the woman decided they'd not worked hard enough that day to pay for their own keep.

Grabbing her cloak and speaking in a rasping whisper, she slipped into the gathering dusk. "I have done everything you've told me to do, but I see you now. I betray not the Assassins. But since you will not even try, despite your promise to me, then I will save my brother myself. The price upon the heads of those two will buy his slave contract and matters not from whom we get paid. The Vydgryn they carry is enough to do the job if this goes a'foul. Whomever gets here first can have the strangers, and I get my brother back!"

"No!" she cried, but the girl was gone. Defiant little shit. Apparently, she could control her no longer. The child's parents were kind, but that only made them easier to poison to obtain ownership of the tavern and keep the children as her slaves. However, she'd continued her greedy habits and having 'forgotten' to pay taxes just a few sennights prior, the Warlord's troops came to collect. She'd managed to scrape up enough to pay the back taxes and the interest 'requested', then thinking the boy was her own son, they took him in retaliation and to prevent her from forgetting again.

This night had been long in the coming. She went back to the doorway. Pulling the curtain just enough to peer out at the customers in the front, she scanned to the corner where sat the newcomers and prayed to the Fates they'd not all be hit when the Assassins came for them. But 'twas an empty prayer from her lips. The girl would send the message, alerting both the Assassins and the Warlord, and 'twould be the end of her. The Assassins were not to be trifled with, but neither was the Warlord of Harsh, and his forces would get here much faster than could the Assassins. The tavern would not survive this time, and nor would she. She shook her head. There was no option. Closing the curtain and going back inside, she emptied the safe and pocketed the night's coin, donned her cloak, and stepped out into the darkness. The customers, and the tavern itself, were on their own.

~~~~~~~~~~

As a small child, Brecca's parents taught her the secret code to notify the Assassins if ever strangers appeared in Harsh. She'd never even seen an Assassin, although she knew they were at the palace. Nonetheless, she'd never thought to hear those words and the surprising occurrence gave her a chance to save her brother. She knew she'd not return to the tavern and left nothing behind, for she had nothing to take. Her first stop was to the home of the Blindman. She trembled with the rush of energy she felt when he'd gazed upon her as if he could see her deceit while she'd recited the stranger's words. For several long moments, afraid he knew of her plans, she stood under the unnerving scrutiny, her heart pounding, afore he'd simply flicked his fingers toward the entrance, dismissing her without a word.

Now she was running as fast as she could toward the palace. She didn't believe the Assassins would come, yet she'd kept her word to her parents, making the necessary connection afore putting her real plan into effect. She had no faith in the old codes, or the myths of the travelers from another world. Such had not happened since afore her grandparents' spans of days, a familial task handed down through the generations without proof of having ever been reality. That task ended with her and her little brother, for they were the last. Yet, she wondered. The strangers had come, they'd said the words. No, she kept telling herself, she could waver not, she believed not in the code. However, she did believe that she could save her brother.

~~~~~ THE PALACE OF THE WARLORD OF HARSH ~~~~~

Gliding along, the Assassin easily kept pace just behind the Warlord's son as he rambled through the palace searching for tonight's pleasure. A depraved little bastard was this one. Preferring the young to the mature, with no regard to gender, he'd take his pick of the slaves and at times use them 'til he'd forced them Past the Veil. The only good thing about his greedy desires was that if the slave survived the night 'twas unlikely they'd end up in his bed a second time, for he enjoyed terrorizing the virgins and rarely wanted 'used goods' again. 'Twas most distasteful but the Assassin said nothing. Slaves had no rights and the man was within his. Nonetheless, she'd recently relieved her brethren in this contract simply because they'd not trusted themselves to fulfill it without prejudice and had pleaded for another assignment.

Although they could refuse any contract, once accepted 'twas difficult to break. Such would lower respect for their Caste, and having that respect was paramount to their safety. Promising her brethren 'twould be done, she'd promised herself the pleasure of the kill once it could be achieved without associated risk to them, an opportunity for which she'd searched daily o'er the past sennight and 'twas becoming tedious. Still, the Assassins had a reputation to uphold, and none of the slaves were of their Race. Slaves died on a daily basis in the Rol Dan. And, if the real identities of the Assassins were known, they'd be hunted and killed without question. 'Twould be all-out war and due to sheer numbers they'd be o'erwhelmed despite their skills. She was the best of the best, the rest of the troops near as good as was she, but they could not stop a war in the open. They needed help, and their own fortress.

'Twas something happening afar, and her senses told her another war approached. Every fiber of her being cried out in warning that the Black had returned. 'Twas also time to renegotiate the Harsh Warlord's contract and they wanted no more of this anyway. So, she would wait 'til dawn for that opportunity to present itself. If it did not, she'd conclude their business arrangements afore making her own opportunity, and then simply disappear. They'd maintained a presence in Harsh since shortly after the Last Holocaust, when the Kreegare had been created. But o'er these past many decades they'd become convinced there'd be no more arrivals. Mayhap the Wyrdritch itself, was no more. At least the Warlords of Harsh had always paid well.

Playing bodyguard to this one's son had been one of their more lucrative assignments (and active, as everyone wanted to kill the man). Still, to survive what they knew was coming, she wanted more. Much more. They'd already begun building an impregnable fortress in the lands to the east, with rich vegetation and some of the most ancient trees left in the world, separated from the mainland of the Rol Dan by a continuously frozen wasteland giving rise to the notion that nothing but more of the thick layers of ice and snow lay beyond. Most of the Kreegare had migrated there even now, as their disappearance was being orchestrated so that 'twould be many moons afore 'twas noticed. Her thoughts returned to their preparations. The fortress had been and continued to be, siege-stocked o'er the past several winters for what was on the horizon, but they'd need to lay in more supplies to bring in all their forces and survive in isolation for any length of time. Imperceptibly she shook her head. That kind of funding would not come from this Warlord alone, but every contract helped.

The young man's wanderings ceased as he grabbed a little boy from under the kitchen braziers where he'd been hiding, and dragging him along, the Assassin followed. She ground her teeth as she tried to find a way to free the boy, but 'twas not an option. His quarters were luxurious and spacious, but she was not allowed to follow him inside for 'twas her duty to stand guard at the closed doorway, allowing no one to enter. Her heartbeat quickened, for she knew he'd take this one Beyond with his accursed cravings. She'd had enough of this, she thought to herself, and decided 'twas time to Drain the bastard. Damn the Fates, she'd forfeit their payment afore she'd put up with this any longer.

That's when she heard the commotion at the front gates and within a heartbeat, troops were running through the hallways. Her attention shifted from the bedchambers to the coming troops and afore she could move, the troops collided with her and dragged her away on their hasty journey. Her nostrils flared in anger as she tried to push her way back, but 'twas against the current of o'er two dozen armed men. Instead of fighting, she backed up tightly against the wall and watched as chaos erupted. A mere few heartbeats had passed when she abruptly saw the Blindman trying to enter the same hallway, getting jostled this way and that by the gruff troops, his long scarf tied in a specific pattern of knots she'd not seen in many decades. Then within a few moments from having been forced down the hallway, she cursed her Elven hearing as the little boy screamed in torturous pain resulting from the cold-hearted abuse. The debauchery had proceeded much quicker this evening than usual. When the troops had all disappeared around the corner, she listened carefully, blocking out the noise fading into the distance. But the little boy made no more sound through the heavy door and she knew she was too late to save him. Her jaw twitched in loathing.

Focusing her hearing toward the commotion at the gates, she learned a young girl was being taken directly to the Warlord. By her description, 'twas the daughter of the last Sentinel of the tavern at the edge of the city. Had she betrayed them? Why notify the Blindman and then come here? But those same troops that just ran past to collect the girl would soon be dispatched to the tavern and there was no time to waste. She shook her head as thoughts of the girl's future came unbidden to her mind. She would be taken to a painful death or enslaved for the rest of her span of days. Once, she would have done something. Such held meaning. Honor. The Code. But now, she had many others depending on her. The girl was not one of them.

She looked back at the door with uncertainty. Her personal code was being torn asunder and she knew not what to do. Her senses confirmed the boy's death, and mentally crossing off the Warlord's payment for services rendered as a loss, she swore his son would die this night, regardless. But first she had an extraction to perform.

As she ran through the city to the tavern she could only shake her head at the unlikely cascade of events unfolding. When she'd relieved her brethren in this contract, the Second, Cassiopeia, had chided her for going solo. She'd responded with the obvious. Harsh had become little more than a tomb as far as any noteworthy activity was concerned. She should have listened to her. Now everyone was too far away to provide her any backup, leaving her completely alone. Shivering, long buried memories burned in her mind with the similarities 'tween the past and present. Grinding her teeth once again, her eyes narrowed as she continued.

THE TAVERN

~~~~~ WITHIN THE HALF MARK ~~~~~

Leis was getting edgy. The girl had not returned, and the other customers were taking notice. No one came through the curtained doorway leading from the kitchens and just as they were beginning to shout in aggravation for their drinks and supper to arrive, Dyra grabbed his arm and yanked him under the table. He'd been watching the other customers and like them, had his eyes upon the curtain while Dyra had been watching the entry through which stormed uniformed troops. Turning o'er benches and chairs as they bullied their way toward the counter looking for the strangers, the men made enough racket to disguise their movement under the tables. Dyra indicated with a nod that they should try the exit. For some reason it seemed clear to her senses. There was danger, yet there was also something else. Leis was dubious about that 'something else' but they couldn't stay hidden under the table in the thickening shadows for long. They stopped crawling when the tavern became quiet as the frightened customers revealed their presence.

~~~~~ THE BACK ALLEY ~~~~~

The Assassin stood close enough to touch the uniformed men huddled near both sides of the door, their hip length hoodless capes pulled back o'er their shoulders, their swords in hand as they waited for the strangers in the tavern to try to exit. So silent was she that they'd not noticed her arrival, and now the darkness assisted her actions. Not that she needed assist. She hadn't even pulled her sword yet. Stepping up behind the one in the rear, she slipped her right hand to his bare neck and Drew while at the same time her left arm wrapped around his waist to hold his body in front of her like a shield. She was so fast, the man's reactions so minimal, the others didn't even look back at them. Placing her right hand o'er his, she took control of the man's short curved sword. She frowned. Unwelcome memories threatened to distract her. 'Twas as her own falchion from days past. The one she'd lost after the ambush. The ambush that destroyed her people and sealed her fate. They'd been betrayed. But by whom? She thought she knew, but 'twas too horrific to confirm, even to herself.

She dragged her thoughts back to the present. Facing the backsides of the other six men, she stood perfectly still, her disguise ridiculously simple, ever amazed that Humans had such inferior vision as well as inferior hearing, strength, and speed. Unless they took a close look her way, they'd not notice her presence. Taking this man was not much risk for one of her experience, but she didn't want to alert the other troops too soon. 'Twould not be long now. She prepared to Dance as she listened for them to enter the front door of the tavern. 'Twould be her signal to strike. Any noise resulting from the deaths of these would not be noted during the ensuing chaos. She just hoped the strangers had remained close to the exit, for she didn't want to lose them.

~~~~~ INSIDE THE TAVERN ~~~~~

The sounds of multiple sets of booted feet came closer and Leis and Dyra scrambled under yet another table. Further from the exit with each move, 'twould be their only advantage. Having been directed to the strangers in the corner, the men were not expecting attack from behind. Leis leaped out at the shoulder of one of the men, pushing his sword arm into the air and then twisting, tripping him, and forcefully rolling him o'er his hip to the floor. Gaining control of his weapon in the process, the man was gutted afore he could regain his feet. Leis turned quickly to face the next threat. The sword was of much poorer quality than the blade he had at his belt, but it significantly extended his reach. Smiling in triumph as he caught Dyra's eyes after she'd killed her first attacker, 'twas clear she was using every trick he'd taught her on their journey to Harsh. With so many left he could not help her and satisfied in her ability to hold her own defensively, he returned his attention to the fight.

~~~~~ THE BACK ALLEY ~~~~~

As the commotion began inside the tavern the troops outside stood perfectly still, apparently waiting for the strangers to exit and not about to join in the fight. The Assassin was disgusted at the spineless ambush tactics. Her dark eyes flashed. Dropping the dead man, with lightning like speed she Danced from man to man, ripping their cloaks away from their necks, dispatching them with ease afore any even comprehended their danger.

'Twas a Dance technique she'd essentially created, a fighting style using the enemy's own shadows, boosting her own energy with each kill. 'Twas very dangerous, requiring extreme precision, for if one missed their timing both the host and the Dancer would Pass the Veil in horrendous agony. She'd taught the same technique to the Kreegare and each was expert in using not only their enemy's shadows but their partner's. There was one setback with the technique, if you considered it such. Without entirely completing one Dance afore moving into the next, one might appear to the naked eye as wispy tendrils of smoke, not fully materializing 'tween locations and giving the impression of being near everywhere at once. Throwing each other forward, sideways and back in such a manner, a pair with this knowledge and skill could 'leapfrog' themselves into position as if through teleportation, a mythical Magic derived from faulty memory and vision, that none of the Magic bearers had ever been able to accomplish. Still, her techniques had created the myth itself and helped them to win the war, but as far as she knew, had vanished to time afore the Last Holocaust.

Seven down, at least fifteen inside. She could hear the screams of the customers as the troops invaded the tavern. And something she hadn't expected. She heard the screams of the dying.

~~~~~ MOMENTS LATER ~~~~~

After slicing a path through three of the troops, spattering their Life Source o'er the entire tavern, Leis and Dyra stood back to back in the middle of the room facing off the last dozen when suddenly one of the men appeared to be enshrouded by a black wraith of swirling mist, immediately dropping to the blood-soaked floorboards with an astonished expression. For a fraction of a heartbeat the opaque mist coalesced into the image of an Elf, but then the mystery female disappeared, the wispy blackened tendrils snaking behind another. She was Dancing and moving so fast, her image was but a blur. Dumbfounded, they'd never seen such speed or daring. To Dance in such a fluid environment was considered impossible, still, her tactics jarred a memory in the back of Leisalarr's mind. This had been done afore. But there was no time to analyze the familiarity, and hoping the mystery woman was on their side, they gathered their wits and returned their focus to the fight.

~~~~~ INSIDE THE TAVERN ~~~~~

An eerie silence descended upon the tavern broken only by the heavy breathing of Leis and Dyra as their eyes scanned the carnage. Neither of them had ever been in such a fight afore. Neither of them had forced another Past the Veil. There was blood everywhere, but although their mouths were open, they spoke not aloud, somehow understanding the scene spread out around them was more for show than to produce the end result. Only the three men they'd forced Past the Veil with their blades, had been killed by blade. The rest were Beyond afore they were cut. 'Twas as if the cutting was but an afterthought. Vampyre. They'd seen it happening with their own eyes.

Leis jerked abruptly as he felt a strong hand grab his shoulder and push him toward the exit. "Move!" a female voice hissed, and grabbing Dyraserrah's hand, they gratefully stumbled through the butchery into the cool night air. He'd not realized the smell of blood could be so potently nauseating. But rest was not forthcoming. With Elven vision, even in the darkness they could now clearly see the tall hooded Elf as she stood beside them scanning the area afore she simply pointed to another building 'cross the alley. Using hand signals that reminded him of something from the past, she told them to follow quickly. Dyra had the say in her trustworthiness but when Leis looked to her, the expression she wore was uncertain. Still, she nodded to go with the Elf, so afore they lost sight of her in the shadows, they pulled on their hoods and ran to catch up.

After racing from one hiding place to another for near a league without seeing anyone in pursuit, they were thankful when they saw her enter one of the smaller buildings that sat alone. Most of those they'd passed o'er the last mark had been attached one to another to create several small units in each block afore an alley would appear, forcing them to run along a wooden walkway and find shelter in the shadows of the next block of such structures. Businesses intermingled with hovels of living quarters as they continued their journey through the back alleys of the outskirts of Harsh.

Slipping inside after the Elf, they near ran into her, stopping cold in their tracks to stare straight ahead at the atrocity that now confronted them. The place had been trashed, near everything moveable had been strewn about and broken. But worse, in the flickering shadows of the firelight coming from the hearth behind him, an elderly Human male hung by his ankles from the ceiling rafters, his arms tied behind him, his throat slit. Blood covered everything and was puddling on the floor. Dyra dropped to her knees, puking. This hadn't happened that long ago. A mark at most. Leis stood stalwartly, his hand upon her shoulder for support, swallowing hard trying to avoid puking himself, his eyes riveted to the horrific scene. 'Twas clear he'd been tortured and if not blind afore, he was by the time he Passed the Veil.

"Help me," the Elven female quietly stated as she stepped forward and reached up to cut the ties that bound the Man to the rafter. The action made them realize how tall she was, even for an Elf, and she was strong, but her manner was gentle and reverent. Obviously, this male had meant something to her. Leis reached out and with equal reverence cradled the Human as he was released, gently laying him out on the floorboards. Dyra stood up and assisted him in the effort after wiping her pale face with her sleeve.

Unexpectedly, the Elf righted a tall stool from under a round table in the confined space and sat down with a sigh. Leis and Dyra nervously looked to the doorway, watching carefully. They waited for her to speak, wondering if they had time for this. Surely, they were being tracked or would be soon. She began to speak in a low voice, "Harsh has come full circle. 'Tis time. He was the last. As is the girl child." She paused and looked around. Grabbing an intact bottle of whiskey on a shelf behind her, she opened it and offered Leis and Dyra a drink. When they declined, she shrugged and continued with her thoughts. "The Warlord's elder son had this Human blinded when he was but a child, as punishment for helping the Assassins. 'Twas rich! He'd never helped us, there'd been no new arrivals for decades. But his father handed down the responsibility to him and such became known to the son. There are spies everywhere in the Rol Dan." She shrugged her shoulders and pushed her long feathered black hair behind her pointed ears. Lifting the glass in salute to the corpse on the floor, she took a few sips, wiped her mouth on the back of her hand, then continued. "We disposed of him in a most gruesome manner of course, with no one the wiser. These people are a superstitious lot. That in and of itself, helps us. The Blindman, as he became known, was well taken care of from then on. We met his every need. He became a trusted friend. He'd inherited his father's scarf to signal new arrivals, but I never thought he'd use it 'til tonight. He did well when he was called. He faltered not. But his actions led to his demise." Once again, she paused as if considering if 'twas brave or stupid of the Man. Gazing from the Blindman to the new arrivals, she gulped down the last of what was in her glass, grabbed another partially full bottle from behind her then stood up, emptied the first bottle o'er the Man, the floor, and the furniture, then set it down on the table. "I regret I was not here to prevent this. He was a friend in a land of few friends."

Leis and Dyra glanced at each other. They knew why she wasn't here to prevent this. She'd been saving their butts at the tavern. And the Blindman was dead because he'd fulfilled his family obligation to signal the Assassin, for Assassin she surely was, that they were there. And the 'girl child' was surely the young girl from the tavern who disappeared. Her job would have been to tell the Blindman and from there they surmised he managed to tell the Assassin and she came to rescue them. But what had happened to the girl child?

"Come," the Elf said afore she threw the bottle she held into the hearth, causing a flare that lit the whiskey on the dry floorboards and would soon reach the table, cutting them off from her. Hurrying 'cross the hut, they followed as she pushed past the curtained doorway into the back room just as the whiskey exploded into flames. The Human and all he had would soon be ablaze.

She exited through a small hatch behind the cot in the corner of the dark room and squeezing through they raced after her as she ran down the back alley. Stumbling to catch up, Leisalarr hissed loudly, "Wait!" But the Elf slowed not. They'd not even had a good look at her. All they'd seen thus far, were her hands and her head. "At least tell us your name!" Becoming angry, Leis stayed Dyra and they stood panting in the dirt.

Now the Elf stopped too, her voice low and somewhat odd, her hesitant response draped in antiquity. Without glancing o'er her shoulder, she said, "They call me Tamm." And then she started running again.

Tamm? So, they'd found her. And yet, Leis had a feeling there was more to their rescuer than that to which they'd been made privy thus far. If only he could remember. Once more, Leis looked first to his girlfriend and when Dyraserrah nodded, together they turned and gave chase, still not knowing who she was, where she was going, or what she planned to do with them. All they knew for certain was that death surrounded her and the blaze behind them was reaching toward the skies.

~~~~~ THE PALACE OF THE WARLORD ~~~~~

'Twas a mere candle mark prior when Brecca found herself in chains standing afore the Warlord in disbelief. She'd come here to bargain for the life of her brother but now she was desperately trying to find a way to bargain for her own. 'Twas late and the Warlord had been awakened, his troops hustling her into the audience chambers to allow him to hear the story from the child's own lips. She'd trembled despite her bravado, clenched her teeth and set her jaw in defiance.

But nothing went the way she'd envisioned and now she was shivering in the cold air of the bedchambers of the Warlord's son, where she'd been sent immediately after being threatened into submission spilling her story about the strangers. She'd not mentioned the Blindman but somehow, they'd known anyway. Still, she was proud that they'd not learned such from her. The information about the strangers was what she'd come to tell, therefore, she didn't consider herself as having been broken. However, once she'd been handed o'er to the son, things took a definite turn for the worse.

The evil young man standing naked o'er her as she knelt with her head bowed, knew not 'twas her brother lying on the floor, dead, tossed aside like garbage. She tried not to cry as she sensed 'twas what her oppressor craved. Stone faced, her heart closed as she squeezed shut her eyes. When she opened them, the light of rage burned for anyone to see, but the man was blind to such. He was used to getting his way, intimidating others, bullying them into doing whatever he wanted. Brecca sneered at him, openly making eye contact, knowing 'twould make him angry enough to kill her. She needed him angry. So angry that he'd do something stupid. So angry he'd provide her the opportunity to fight back.

He slapped her so hard, spit flew out of her mouth and her head jerked aside. Her tongue slipped out and she tasted the blood from her cheek and split lip. She could take a bit more of this and then she'd feign being as tame as a kitten. With nothing to use as a weapon but her teeth and the chains securing her hands behind her back, she glared at him again. His face a mask of fury and desire, he grabbed her by her hair and threw her against the wall 'cross the room. Rolling to her side, she tried to get up, but he pushed her back down, forcing her face to the wooden floor, and then he kicked her right side, surely cracking a few ribs in his eagerness. He was actually becoming stimulated.

Gasping, she didn't try to get up this time. She lay on her side trying to take a breath, but the effort brought tears to her eyes. His leer penetrating, his tongue licking his lips in high arousal, he asked, "Had enough yet? Oh girl, I want you. I may have to be careful though, so I can keep you for a few nights." He cupped his rising cock and stated, "Yes. I'll be careful." Thinking he'd finally broken her spirit, she allowed him to believe that, and gingerly spit out the blood from her cheek while elevating her shoulders to steady her ribs. Her head was pounding. Likely a concussion. She needed to keep her wits but didn't care what happened to her after she'd done the deed. She just had to convince him she had no fight left.

Her head jerked up and back as he grabbed her by her shoulder and arm. Lifting her slight frame easily, he threw her on the tall mattress of his huge canopy bed, laughing all the while. She bit her lip to prevent crying out, but the pain was excruciating, and she was unsuccessful. Panting, she felt the mattress give with the added weight of another person crawling in beside her and with horrifying clarity, reality set in. She was about to be raped.

~~~~~ MEANWHILE ~~~~~

Leis and Dyra were not used to running non-stop for such long distances and they began to fall further and further behind. They didn't want to lose her, they knew not how to get out of the city or where to go, so they doubled down on their efforts and used Magic to increase their stamina and pick up their flagging speed. Immediately, they felt as if they'd hit a brick wall and came to a sudden halt. Catching their breath, Tamm stood in front of them, frustration upon her face. "Never use Magic for purpose other than fighting! And never where can be seen!" Lowering her voice, she sighed. "I apologize. You made it clear you could not keep up earlier. I should have slowed down."

Leis and Dyra panted as the Prince replied. "No need. We'll do our best to keep up. We didn't think, and such a mistake could have been devastating. I have not been in combat situations afore, and Dyra has only my training under her belt."

Tamm nodded. She liked his honesty and responsibility. "I will train you, should you be accepted and decide to remain."

As they rested, her words made them realize the race was not won at the end of this night. They still apparently had to pass some kind of acceptance to get into the Kreegare. He could understand. They'd not had new additions to their ranks for many decades, how could they be certain Leis and Dyra were trustworthy? Just afore they took off again Leis looked around and gathering his senses he began to wonder about their direction. They'd arrived at the edge of this city and they were certainly heading deeper into it now. He could see the darkened outline of the Palace just ahead as they prepared to continue. Why were they going there?

"We go to fulfill a promise I made to a little boy," Tamm stated, answering the question he hadn't asked aloud. Her voice hardened, her brown eyes narrowed. "Leave now or come with me. There is no turning back. If you come with me now, you come to stay. If you are not accepted into the Kreegare, you will be forced Past the Veil. And, if you want to make it through this night alive, you will do everything I say, exactly when and how I say it."

By the Ancients, just what was this promise? Making their choice and accepting her terms, they followed, running in silence. Both knew 'twould be their rights passage. As of this moment, they were in training to become Assassins, and if they failed, they died.

~~~~~ THE CHAMBERS OF THE WARLORD'S SON ~~~~~

Brecca knelt upon the bed, hands still chained behind her back and head shoved 'tween the man's bare legs, leaving her off balance and pressing her cheek against his inner thigh so her face wouldn't be shoved into his genitals or into the bedding, suffocating her. His laughter filled her ears, the smell of death, her brother's death, filled her nostrils as she squirmed to get her balance, to get away. But she was still dizzy, she couldn't take a breath without severe pain, and her head was pounding. Her mouth began to water. She was going to throw up, she could feel it.

She was a slave now and he could do this every night if he so desired. This was not how she'd planned things to turn out. She'd not live this way, and she'd not allow this man to live after killing her little brother.

Twisting her head, he drew her closer to his throbbing, elongating cock. She squirmed against the soft skinned thing, her lips closed tightly. But she was losing the battle. She'd soon pass out and there was no telling what he'd do to her then. She chose her fate. Using her only weapon, she opened her mouth and let him thrust deep. Pushing against his intrusion with her tongue, she avoided gagging just long enough to clamp down hard. She'd not get another chance. With a mighty grunt, her teeth tore through the man's flesh, the bitter taste of blood filling her mouth as was the air filled with his agonized screams. Kicking and pushing swiftly up and back with her shoulder, she rolled o'er and off the mattress, bringing her still chained arms in front of her body, looking for an escape route she knew was not there.

Panic stricken, she could move no faster for the pain. The doors opened, and the guardsmen entered. Accepting her soon-to-be demise, the heavy rush of adrenaline had her falling to her hands and knees as she defiantly spat out the evidence of her guilt on their boots in a rush of blood along with the severed member. Puking in revulsion, she scrambled to her feet, for she would not be cut down on all fours like an animal. But instead of the expected sensation of cold steel on her neck she watched them drop to their knees afore they fell on their faces leaving her with an expression of pure astonishment. Looking up, she had to squint to see into the shadowy doorway where stood what could only be, three fully cloaked Assassins.

~~~~~ THE WILDS OF BYNDYNN FOREST ~~~~~

Rhyah sat in Fay form, a shimmering golden glow of Allure emanating from within as was with all the Fay, his thick back-swept pointed ears as wings against his head. He was a handsome man. Naked, leaning back against the trunk of the old oak, he rested one arm upon his bent knee, the other leg stretched out straight as he surveyed the area. He'd not seen another Fay in any form since leaving the Nation, and 'twas concerning.

Although he'd made some progress with moderate level emotion, controlling the added energy effectively in fueling his Magic, he'd made the decision to continue to work on developing the strongest emotion, to break through as had Corbyn. 'Twas love he need command. But how best to do so? His roving gaze focused on nothing as his mind drifted, attempting to formulate a plan of action that included locating the Heir Apparent.

Love. Thinking about his best friend, he knew Corbyn had been successful in finding that emotion. Living it. Breathing it. Believing it. Aching for intimacy, to have and to hold someone like a priceless treasure and to be treasured in return, to live out his span of days with a partner who sparked his desire, whom he could drive to the brink of ecstasy with his touch, was becoming an all-consuming determination.

And what of this growing urgency to travel further northward that could not be shaken? He woke from his dreams of late, shivering in an icy grasp that would release him not and yet 'twas warmth and deep passion that enveloped him like a blanket, calling for him to come. However, the dreams would fade as soon as he became aware and comprehend them he could not. Was it a prophesy? A Vision? He sighed. If and when he could remember the details of the dreams, mayhap he could follow, but 'twas nothing he could do about them now. Only time would tell.

Shaking his head, he stood up, and putting off the sensation his destiny lay in the distant north, he chose his next task. To conquer the strongest emotion, he must try once more to form a mate relationship, and since he didn't trust himself to do so with a Human, he would tackle the issue in his wolf form. From his study of the family units of wolves it should be similar, he thought to himself. Making his Shift he padded off on his massive paws, tongue lolling out of his muzzle, wicked teeth glistening, and eyes a'glow.

<center>~~~~~ THE PALACE ~~~~~</center>

Leis barred the door behind them as Tamm surveyed the damage to the young man's crotch with an admiring eye. He deserved so much more, but she couldn't have delivered it and was pleased. The girl had her respect, she'd done what was necessary. But she was not Elven and therefore would be left to the will of the Fates. After Draining the thrashing man, she wiped the blood from her hands on the expensive silk sheets and returned her gaze to her 'recruits'. "He keeps his Vydgryn in the chest," she stated dryly, nodding her head toward the lockbox in the corner of the room. Understanding her intent, Dyra walked quickly o'er, the locked chest no challenge for her Magic, and began filling a scarf she pulled from the dresser. Tying the makeshift bag, she tucked it into her sash at the same time Leis was approaching the girl.

Although 'twas Dyra who had the most reliable ability to 'see' into the hearts of others, Leis stared at Tamm, something ancient and perplexing just out of reach of his senses. The Assassin stared back as if daring him to recall that which was in his memories, afore her quiet voice broke through the hushed room. She knew what he was thinking. Nodding toward the girl beside whom he now stood, she stated with some remorse, "Leave her, she's not one of us. She could turn." 'Twas clear the Elf didn't trust easily and Leis was still unsure if she trusted them. And yet, her words dredged memories that muddled his mind even further. Squinting, he continued to stare at her, the past rising to the edge of recollection. Knowing his response might enflame the situation even more, he could not leave the child. "So too, could one of 'us'," he stated boldly.

The brief flicker of pain and regret in her eyes made him vow to himself that he'd unlock her secrets, and soon. Standing stock-still, she said naught while Leis looked to the little girl. "Come," he told her, and she took his hand, her gaze flickering 'tween the two Assassins warily, understanding something had passed there, something about her, but not knowing quite what.

While Leis picked up the girl and removed her chains, Tamm went to help Dyra and together they hastily filled several more bags that the Elf pulled from her cloak, afore they heard troops coming down the hallway outside the chambers. Nodding toward the tapestry behind the headboard of the massive bed, they ducked inside a trap door leading into the passages 'tween the walls of the palace. Leis and near chuckled. Some things never changed. As they disappeared, the Warlord himself broke down the heavy door and entered, leading his troops to find a vacant room full of blood and death.

Tamm knew the Warlord would be well versed in all the passage entries and she ran through, the others racing to keep up. Leis and Dyra could hear no one following them and were concerned they'd be met at the exit, but just a few moments later, Tamm rounded a sharp corner and stopped at a small widening in the passageway. From a crack in the outside wall came a sliver of sunlight showing the dawn was upon them and so too, upon a large growth of algae growing up the inner wall. "No!" Leis cried, for he thought Tamm meant to Dance, abandoning the girl to the Warlord.

"Shut up! Give her to me and do exactly as I," Tamm stated in hushed tones that harbored no room for insubordination, as Leis did as he was told. With a touch Tamm used her Magic to stop the bleeding and speed along the process of healing Brecca's worst wounds, afore tucking the child gently against her chest, frail arms and legs wrapping painfully around the Elf.

Leis and Dyra watched her Draw her energy from the organics on the wall. Tamm Drew deeply, above and beyond what was considered necessary, and they did the same. Fearing the unknown, remembering no living thing outside to where they might be heading, they were confused but said not a word. Then Tamm reached forth and grabbed each of them, literally throwing them through the wall. Not as in breaking through, but as in Dancing through, and afore they realized it, she was with them, ahead of them, behind them, pushing and dragging and throwing them along her signature like fish on a line. They soon discovered they hadn't needed to have a known destination as they were not avoiding solid structures, they were moving through them, and if they didn't succeed, they'd all perish. They began to assist her in the effort and following her Allure through the Dance, they found themselves at the far edge of the city once again. But this time, they were on the northeastern edge. They'd come clear 'cross the entire city, and not only was that amazing, Tamm was still holding the little girl tightly to her chest, her thin arms and legs wrapped around her under her cloak.

Allowing but a brief respite, Tamm used even more Magic to finish Healing the child afore setting her on her feet. 'Twas done quickly, without flourish, and with barely an acknowledgement from the Elf as she cast her gaze upon her brethren. "I can see from your faces, neither of you have ever traveled that way afore."

She paused as she considered. She had to accept the fact that the technique she'd pioneered, taught to her brethren, used so effectively through the war, appeared to be all but forgotten. Taking a slow breath, she continued, "'Tis but one of many new experiences you will encounter, for you have much to learn to become an effective Assassin."

Both the younger Elves were still trying to regain their energies, sitting on the sparse grass and Drawing freely from everything within reach. "I thought we'd passed that test already," Leis panted, referring to their recent kills.

Without a hint of irritation, she responded, "You have killed. That means only that you CAN kill, it does not mean you know HOW to kill well enough to not BE killed. Survival is utmost in any warrior's training. To survive, you must be better, quicker, smarter, than your enemies. You must combine speed, surprise, and skill. You must have an advantage of which your enemies are not aware. And, you must leave no trail." Her glittering eyes flashed to the little girl. "What is your name, child?"

"Brecca," she answered with her chin up, no longer surprised by the happenings. Her eyes locked onto the Elf's, knowing the strange one considered her a hindrance. She was that 'trail' just mentioned.

Despite all she'd been through and what she'd seen, Tamm could sense no shock from the girl and nodded with cautious approval. She was a brave little one. Even with dried blood upon her face, the child knew to keep her wits, and words, to herself. The corners of her mouth uplifted slightly and gathering Brecca to her once more, she caught the eyes of Leis and Dyra, where her faint smile dramatically disappeared. "Come. We have a long journey ahead of us."

'Twas at that moment Leis glanced at Dyra. Carefully maintaining a neutral expression, his eyes told his girlfriend that he'd remembered. He knew who Tamm was. He knew the past that haunted her.

CHAPTER SIX

All Things Puzzling

MIDSUMMER

O'ER THREE MOONS AFTER THE DRAW OF THE DOMES

O'ER A WINTER AND A HALF AFTER THE FIRST LIFEBOND

~~~~~ ICE MIST FALLS ~~~~~

While searching for the squad of Dragons whose mission o'er six moons past was to complete the destruction of Drekinn and secure both the True King and the child, Fryya, the Hoardsmen sent word that they'd found evidence of an old battle in the Ice Mist Falls region. Now standing amidst the vast glorious spread of falls and waterways, he felt not the breathtaking splendor. In its place was a burning hatred, for here his Dragons met their fate, ambushed and slaughtered by a mere few LifeBond Teams who should not have survived the Battle for the Dragon Clan. Had they survived their attack upon the Lairs? He couldn't help but wonder. Even though there'd been many witnesses to the destruction of all three suspected Lair sites near four moons past, 'twas not like Darque to do such a thing. Still, they had no evidence of survival. Thus far. Disdainfully, his loathing shifted from the Clan to his own forces and the obvious destruction to which they'd succumbed here. They deserved such a fate for their stupidity.

Several marks did he spend walking the area, open senses gathering information, piecing together the story of their demise. He breathed in their shock at the ambush, their dismay at the interference with their Healing by some outside force, Saw the Thumper fall to the grounds below. But standing where the Clan shield covered with Dragon scale had landed, 'twas not to be seen. Mayhap an animal had dragged it away? 'Twas not buried in the mud or the lush growth at the edges of the wide river. He placed his hand upon the bare ground and closed his eyes.

Suddenly, he leaped back as if burned. 'Twas with such shocking speed that he collided with one of his men and together they tumbled o'er the edge into the frigid waters. He was livid. Standing knee deep, soaked to the skin, he Reached forth his hand and the hapless Hoardsman who'd just come sputtering out of the water himself, clutched at his neck as the Sorcerer clenched his fist. Without even touching the man, his life was taken from him as his throat was crushed, his body floating down the river to spill o'er the next falls. The Sorcerer was still angry, and gasping, he was assisted out of the water, where he dried himself instantly with a wave of his hand. Still shaking with emotion, those who'd assisted him were frightened but wise enough not to indicate such. As soon as he was deposited upon the shore on his feet, they distanced themselves so as not to catch his notice, or his ceaseless ire.

The 7th Prince. The Sorcerer had felt Bryynn's presence when he'd tried to divine what happened to the Thumper. Having lay in the open o'er six moons, 'twas finally picked up by the Prince. Could their slowed Healing phenomenon during the battle have had something to do with him as well? Mayhap with such information he could deduce the Magic of the 7th Prince. But 'twould have to wait. Bryynn was here. He'd hatched and was close to half a winter of age. That would make him near a quarter grown. Gathering his senses and taking o'er a mark to calm himself, he decided he would reconnoiter this area closer. There might just be more to discover here, than the whereabouts of a shield. He ordered his men to make camp.

~~~~~~~~~

With the elegance and grace of her Kind, Empress Bronwyn of the Ice Dragons sat unobserved, close to the tree line of the river away from the spray of the falls. Her usual coloring was as the frozen waters of her home, the Icelands, where her delicate beauty glistened in the sunlight during the short summers. Her Magic now camouflaged her like a chameleon to appear as the trees and rocks with which she was surrounded. Near invisible, she watched openly as the Hoardsmen searched for evidence of the battle.

Although all Dragons could access the Memories of the Ancients, it did not mean they had perfect memories. Ice Dragons, on the other hand, had eidetic memories. Anything they saw or detected was emblazoned upon their minds forevermore. They could also 'taste' scents for leagues, which helped them locate the treasures they so craved. Motionless as if frozen for days at a time, they could sit or stand anywhere unseen by most eyes, but it mattered not, for their forte Magic was Mesmerizing. Not the Memory Magic of the Fay, 'twas more closely related to an ancient Human practice known as hypnotism (which they most likely developed from dream-state memories of encounters with Ice Dragons). With such, they could make anyone believe near anything, and so they'd managed to remain a myth to Mankind throughout history, Mesmerizing those who happened to catch sight of their long slender necks and muzzles, delicate gossamer wings, shimmering white water-color scales that matched their enormous eyes and rather impressive fangs, into ignoring said experience. No one who had ever actually seen an Ice Dragon realized such, thinking 'twas a trick of the light or their own imagination. Mayhap 'twas a dream. 'Twas a powerful defensive Allure, as Ice Dragons were the most fragile and even though quite strong in flight, they could be easily o'ercome in a fight. They had the ability to spit a net-like spray of ice that would capture and hold near anything, and if focused that spray would become a stream which would carve rock in half (not unlike the Water Dragons). But as their cousins required access to water for such, the Ice Dragons required cold to accomplish this Magic, which wasn't readily available outside of their home environment, leaving them fairly defenseless. Therefore, they'd developed a clandestine and solitary way of life. Despite their vulnerabilities, Ice Dragons were extremely intelligent and courageous (although some would think them simply foolhardy), and would go to great lengths to travel, investigate, and satisfy their curiosities while in search of treasures of all kinds which they would stash back home in their elaborate crystal caverns carved into the glacial land. Yet they cared little about the rest of the world, thinking their woes did not and would not affect the kingdom of the Icelands.

'Twas not a shield which tempted Bronwyn away from her home at this time, making the long and dangerous journey to Ice Mist, drawing her as a moth to the flame. The tip of her delicate pink tongue slipped forth 'tween her long fangs and she tasted the air once more. Following the scent, her crystalline eyes squinting in the sunlight, she sharpened her focus 'cross the rivers and lakes toward the farthest western edge of the region. One of the Fangs of Solvyngarr. Of all places to be lost, she thought to herself. But her treasure was there. And she had to get it afore did the Humans, for she knew they were evil and would try to use it for great harm. Bryanna would be pleased. 'Twould be her crowning jewel, even though 'twas not hers to keep. This required protection. Still she wondered. 'Twas no ordinary blade, so how had it come to be here? And for that matter, where were the other three? She wrinkled her slender nostrils. And just how would they get it back to Abriya?

Waiting in perfect stillness 'til long after dark, Bronwyn began to move slowly back into the tree line, afore she took wing 'cross the vast waterways to the far western edge. No one saw the Ice Dragon as she secured the precious blade within moments after landing, and then quickly flew off to the north, toward home.

HAVEN

THE WYRDRITCH

NEAR TWO WINTERS AFTER THE FIRST LIFEBOND

~~~~~ O'ER SEVEN MOONS AFTER THE
DRAW OF THE SPELL DOMES ~~~~~

Tall, pale skinned and lithe with delicately pointed ears as were all Elves, Queen Alyssa had not every attribute of her people. She touched the corners of her eyes and shook her head. Hurrying to her dressing room, her face shielded by her hands as if trying to make a difficult decision, she wondered what she would do if someone had noticed the failing glamour. She'd been so busy, she'd not checked afore presiding o'er the Assembly this afternoon and now she was worried. Examining her appearance in the mirror, she ran her fingers through her Spell-darkened hair and had a sudden thought. Alarmed, she realized she'd never revealed to Anastasia that she had to continue to upgrade the Allure she'd set upon her at birth or her eyes would revert to their normal appearance. Elves and Sprites had an upward tilted, almond shape to their eyes, and not having that characteristic would surely disclose their mixed breed ancestry.

Alyssa's mother had carefully kept her glamour throughout her span of days and when her noble daughter was born with the same features and blonde hair, she'd set the glamour for her child, one that would last 'til puberty. Once Alyssa reached age, she was taught to maintain it herself, to the point that she thought nothing of it, for 'twas part of her normal routine. Still, she'd also been taught that if anyone found out, 'twould have dire consequences. Raised in a time of war, with Jeeryd stealing the throne afore they were all thrust into the Last Holocaust, anyone with Human or Sprite blood would have faced censorship, exile, even death. Not to mention that the Elven Nation, led by the insane and evil King, were told frequently and without shame that Humans were at fault for the devastation, and they would never have accepted her as their Queen. Her Magic was strong and Jeeryd never discovered her secret, for which she was most grateful. He was a horrible father and was not present at the birthings, therefore 'twas no issue with placing the glamour for not only Anastasia, but Coltyn as well. Her midwife was very trustworthy, as she'd been the one who'd assisted with Alyssa's birth and knew all her family secrets.

Fortunately, unlike her mother, Ana had been born with brown hair, and 'twas just her eyes that needed to be hidden. Still, she wondered if Anastasia's glamour had begun to falter and as she thought back, she couldn't be certain it had been in place consistently during the last several moons afore she left. 'Twould have begun to flicker, not just drop off all at once, but should she send word? Then again, with whom could she trust such knowledge? No. She'd have to rely on the changing times and Ana's strength of character to weather the coming storm, for the truth would come out, and soon. She thought about the Sprites and half-breed Elves who had stayed with them just a few moons past. Caleichante, Prince Kevon, and the Warriors Bastyen and Graasyn had been accepted by the Nation once Alyssa accepted them. Diadranei was the only pure breed Elf among them. She chuckled at the irony.

The Assembly meeting o'er which Alyssa had just presided, discussed the Healing of the Spell o'er the Wyrdritch and the fact that the Healing itself had altered the morphed Spell o'er the forests that was causing the Highlands so much trouble. The Aversion Spell, as it had become known, was not actually a Spell but a result of the morphing of the Protection Spell, which occurred during the Last Holocaust. Since that time, the Aversion spread like a fungus o'er all the forests, affecting all Magic bearers, but particularly the Dragons, and made it near impossible for them to enter or cause damage to the trees. This had proven harmful and beneficial in that the forests were protected from the destruction of the evil Dragons of the Hoard and was used to help hide and protect the Bog Lair of the Resistance. Now that Persephone had managed to Heal the Spell, the Elven Princess reported the Aversion would continue to erode as if it had never been. Although unsure of how long this might take, Darque would need this information as soon as possible.

The Assembly meeting had also brought up much new intel. It had been near two full winters since the LifeBond 'tween the Highlands and the Dragon Clan, bringing Humans back into the war. And less than a full winter past, the Spell Domes were set, with Princess Anastasia playing a crucial role in their completion. 'Twas very dangerous indeed, but brave. She also learned of the Lady Tialani's suicide to prevent her own arrest as a spy and Anastasia's role in her capture was now legendary. She was proud of her daughter. However, rumor had it that Tialani was not the only spy amongst the Sprite Nation and she could not but be concerned about her daughter's continued safety. She would have to trust the Elite Guard, now led by Captain Naftaleah, to ferret them out and keep Ana safe.

Since the Elven Nation was in recovery and preparing to send out the Call to Return, she had chosen just five representatives to send to the Resistance, organizing them under the command of the Sprite team already at the Keep. Captain Natanamia would lead the entire team. Although her stepchildren were elder, 'twould avoid any issues with who held the higher rank. Her chosen were good fighters but had not been tried in real battle yet, therefore they would be learning as they worked alongside the Sprite Elite team who'd already seen fighting and who themselves were under the Battle Commander.

Of the Queen's stepchildren, the eldest, Myrrdin, was already living and working amongst the Sprite Nation. Persephone would stay and continue her work on the Healing of the Wyrdritch and any still affected by the old Spell of Protection, as well as provide assistance with the Call to Return. Thyrazin, Fyrdien, Irylane, Beralarr, Enlyrod, Dyrachin, and Englyrim, would remain in the Queen's Guard, while Orasynth, Malyrist, Laratyn, Gylrann, and Gylragg would go to the Keep. The middle son, Leisalarr, was still missing and as soon as they had someone to spare, a search party would be sent forth. That left her own. Anastasia was promised to Kevon, living with the Sprites on the Island of Dreams, and Coltyn was too young to leave Haven.

Yet the most interesting intel of this day, was something of which the Battle Commander might be surprised. Still staring in the mirror, her imagination transformed her own face to the face of the Fay, Rhyah the Wolf, who'd recently been reported by her recognizance teams to be roaming Kadoor. She was concerned for his wellbeing as most of the Fay had been totally isolated since afore the Last Holocaust, and their youth would require practice to handle the miasma of emotion in the real world. Emotion powered Magic, and the Fay were already the most powerful. If one weren't strong enough or skilled enough to handle the influx, terrible things happened. 'Twas time for the Fay to drop the ban on emotion, 'twas a ridiculous ruling in the first place, set up as a politically correct response to fear, after the War of Chaos.

Alyssa knew that Rhyah had a date with destiny. He was to travel to the Icelands and bring the Ice Dragons to the Resistance via their Empress Bronwyn, who was now Tied somehow to a woman she could not envision. She speculated the dream was sparked by Rhyah's initial appearance outside the Fay Nation. Rhyah must be found, brought into the safety of the Resistance, and taught how to handle his new-found emotions afore he was sent to fulfill his destiny. This information, along with the rest, must be taken to the Battle Commander immediately.

After deciding now was not the time to announce her Human ancestry, she set her glamour once again and called for her step-children, briefing them on their new roles, including the information the young men were to report upon their arrival. Darque was said to be stationed mostly at Drekinn Lair in the Dragon's Den as of times of old when her father, Grifynn, was Battle Commander of the Dragon Clan. They were expected. She sent the young men to pack and then watched them as they left Haven, Dancing away. Once again, she touched the corners of her eyes but this time 'twas to wipe away the tears. Even though they were her stepsons and close to her own age, she loved them and prayed for their protection and success afore returning to her duties. They would be missed.

DREKINN LAIR

~~~~~ THE QUARTERS OF STORRM AND MYSTYNN ~~~~~

</div>

Storrm stood staring at the tapestry, the morning light beginning to stream in behind her from the cliff face as it reflected off the Sea of Dreams. She and Mystynn had their pick of quarters, but they preferred their original cave, the one they'd chosen just afore Darque was promoted to Second, the rank she and Mystynn now held.

So much had happened since then. During that first winter after the LifeBond they'd been snowed in at Drekinn and Darque encouraged them all to pursue creative outlets. Darque was a gifted artist, her specialty in scrimshaw, and she'd set her talents upon the baskets of Dragon teeth she'd collected as salvage. Now that the teeth were being used as spear and arrowheads, Warriors considered finding her works amongst their supply, to be a good omen.

Storrm's talents lay in sewing and design. She'd made flowing curtains, pillows and privacy screens, wall hangings, and native dance costumes for the others. Her creations even now graced the entire Lair and lifted their spirits, making them feel at home, transforming the endless hard stone of the extensive caverns that riddled the land under Drekinn Village and the Dragon's Den, into even more colorful and comfortable living spaces. But 'twas her tapestries that had everyone in awe. She'd traded them away o'er the following few moons but kept this one. 'Twas an intriguing scene, depicting a stunning forested region with waterfalls and mountains peaking through the canopy, but there was one mountain which had a massive, triangular shaped ledge fronting a vertical crevasse through which only one Dragon could fly, or three could walk shoulder to shoulder, and if one stood upon the ledge, the entire region was in view. When she'd made the design, she was convinced there'd been a battle there. 'Twas as a dream, for she didn't recognize the place.

As she'd done every day since they'd returned to Drekinn, she stared at the tapestry trying to recall why it appeared so familiar. Suddenly a deep voice rumbled through the caverns. "Storrm!"

"I'm coming!" she yelled back, but Storrm moved not, her gaze riveted upon the tapestry. She needed to get to the Cave of Voices where the Spell Door was located, which would take them into the dungeons of the Dragon's Den above. But she couldn't stop staring at the scene in front of her.

~~~~~~~~~~

Mystynn sat down in the cavern, staring at the Spell Door, trying to make himself fairly comfortable because his partner just said she was coming. He knew enough to realize how long that might take but he Blocked his thoughts from her. Lately, he'd been Blocking many of his thoughts from her. He was afraid he was not much of a priority to Storrm. Mystynn was something of a charmer of the females of his Kind and he'd never been rejected. But he'd never cared as much afore. But then again, she was Human. Well, not entirely Human. Just the same, he felt lost as to how to proceed and decided mayhap he should talk to his elder brother, Gunnarr. He snorted. That would be a first. Afore the LifeBond, Gunnarr was the one who always came to HIM for advice on females. Nonetheless he must have done something right because it hadn't taken the High Prince long to Claim Darque as his lifemate. He looked o'er his shoulder. No Storrm. He closed his eyes, dropped his head, and sighed.

~~~~~~~~~~

Storrm knew they were waiting for her in the Pits. For the next moon she'd be in command of Drekinn and 'twas her duty to lead the katas. Still puzzled, just afore departing she glanced back o'er her shoulder for one more look. Then shaking her head, she turned and walked out. Mystynn would be impatiently waiting for her at the Door. She said she was coming! Men. Mattered not their Race. She just didn't understand them.

~~~~~~~~~~

Since 'twould be a while, Mystynn Cast forth his senses to locate his brother and after hemming and hawing about how life might be with one of another Race, he finally came out and Asked him, *"Do you miss the Mating Flight?"*

Gunnarr could sense the feelings 'tween Mystynn and Storrm, and wisely did not joke with his obviously distraught brother. Taking a more serious tact, he Replied honestly, *"What I have, far surpasses what I have not. Are you thinking of doing the same?"*

Mystynn Replied with misery in his usually carefree voice, Sputtering, *"Me? Oh no. I mean, she deserves far better than I."*

Knowingly, Gunnarr Responded, *"Ahhh. But what does she WANT?"*

Afore Mystynn could absorb the question and formulate an answer, he heard Storrm walking up behind him.

~~~~~ THE VOID ~~~~~

Storrm completely missed the fact that she was the female being discussed by Mystynn with his big brother, wondering if Mystynn knew her thoughts back then. Still confused about their status, she pushed away, keeping her hand on his chest. She chose to ignore the conversation to which she was just made aware. She loved him but apparently she was correct in that he'd wanted another. Nevertheless, she was so perplexed by the tapestry that she failed to notice the tension emanating from her partner. "I know that region, I sense a great battle was fought there and yet, I cannot recall the specifics. I was never very good at memorizing the prophesies, but this place intrigues me. 'Tis both stunning and threatening."

Mystynn dropped his chin and gazed into her striking blue eyes. There was an urgency in his voice as he redirected her. "My dear, your incessant chatter is part of your unique and charming nature, but you simply must stop interrupting. You have no idea how difficult 'tis to relocate my place on the streamline of Memory."

"Sorry. I'll keep quiet 'til we return to the beginning."

"That would be a miracle," he chuckled. "If you were capable of doing that, you'd not be you. And strictly speaking 'twill be the end, not the beginning."

Storrm frowned, bit her bottom lip to prevent a retort, and Shared his vision once more.

LATER THAT MORNING

~~~~~ THE OFFICE OF THE BATTLE COMMANDER ~~~~~

</div>

Storrm sank into the Dragon chair with a sigh, the soft, generously stuffed leather cushion a luxurious sensation compared to the stone upon which her butt had been spending most of its time of late. Even cuddling up with Mystynn was not very comfortable, as he was thick leathery scale o'er rock hard muscle. However, thinking of his good looks, along with his ferocious fighting skills, unique sense of humor, compassion, and intellect, made her tingle.

In the past there were times when Storrm felt sorry for herself. She was always second. Second born, second in all their classes and training, second for anyone's attention, Second in Command, second to everyone who needed to talk to the Commander, second place to Darque in everything they'd ever done throughout her entire span of days. But seeing what Darque was going through, all the decisions she had to make, the responsibilities that came with being first born and the 'answer to the prophesy', she knew she would not want that position. Second was fine with her. Besides, once she took the 'Bond with Mystynn, she became first in someone's life.

She and Darque were inseparable prior to the 'Bond but Darque had raised her, becoming more like a mother or a mentor than a sister or a friend. Mystynn was her best friend. Even so, he seemed aloof when she tried to flirt with him, not that she had all that much experience with flirting, and his quiet hesitance convinced her that he didn't want her in that way. He hadn't actually said such aloud but when he sensed her arousal she felt as if he were pushing her to look for satisfaction with her Warrior brothers and would probably be pleased if she fell in love with another man. Any man. As long as he was HU-MAN. She sighed in disappointment and then glanced about the office afore returning her attention to her sister.

"Storrm? What are you thinking? You're not with me here."

Her mind wandered back a candle mark, to the short-lived bliss of lovemaking in the big Warrior's private quarters in the Lair below. She wasn't certain she'd recognize the man again, unless of course, he were naked. That image she'd never forget. Nonetheless, 'twas just a diversion. As had been the others recently. She'd needed to release tension. Sex was commonplace, with partners easily found within the Brotherhood, and her Warrior brethren encouraged her to partake of the willing males, or even to choose a willing female to partner with if she so desired, to provide said release. So, she'd tried. Her love for her LifeBond partner unrequited, she realized now that she was attempting to find love elsewhere, but thus far, she'd had no luck. Although there was no disrespect, she'd felt no such emotion for her chosen partners, nor from them. Release tension? In her mind, though she did have excellent results, as achieving orgasm had never been difficult, all such events had created more tension and it became a vicious cycle of regrets. 'Twas just not fulfilling. After this latest 'release' she'd vowed to avoid such again and had just managed to lace up her pants as she'd barged late into Darque's office, noting an amused, though pained, expression upon the Battle Commander's face.

Realizing she'd rather Darque not know of her issues, as her sister's seemingly perfect union with Gunnarr made her jealous, she sat upright. "Well you know I've got your back," she winked. Then, apologetically, she continued, "'Tis nothing. What were you saying?"

Darque sighed and knew 'twas truth that regardless of the situation Storrm would always have her back, so she could forgive her distraction. They'd been swamped and had slept little since the Spell Domes were Drawn down to protect the Lairs. The Sprites and Elves had assisted with that endeavor, including Diadranei, Caleichante, Captain Natanamia, Prince Kevon, and Princess Anastasia. Shortly after, the young Prince and Princess were escorted to the Island of Dreams by the Captain while Dia and Calei stayed with their lifemates, Bastyen and Graasyn, doubling the Stealth Ops most respected Team to fight for the Resistance.

Darque was very happy with the relaying system her Communication Teams were working, using their Link to send and receive messages from anyone who needed such. Rolf and Nalwynn were stationed at Drekinn Lair and Axyl and Haniyyah maintained the communication Link from the Keep and the Bog. 'Twas much more efficient and quicker than using the old system of Runners, although they still used Runners to take messages to and from those who had no direct access to the Link, such as the Elves and Sprites. Although they could use telepathy with their Water Dragon Ties, they did not have the ability to Send or Receive as did the Highlands.

Within a moon, after letting things settle a tad, she'd sent Warrior Teams out to the ports and to some of the other Clans to gather intelligence. So far, what information they'd received suggested that the other Clans had been hit as had they, skirmishes had increased upon the Outlands, and 'twas rumored that survivors were being taken as slaves. But 'twas still early and such was difficult to confirm. She'd also sent a Team to reconnoiter Tupry, the outlaw village in the Razor's Edge where anything could be bought for a price and was considering sending more to King's Gate to try to infiltrate the village and eventually the castle. 'Twas an extremely 'hot' location but someone needed to find out what the Black was doing. He'd been very quiet since the big battle, letting King Shytin and the Sorcerer, living and working out of Evanntyr Castle, handle everything. She had a plan to hold more LifeBond ceremonies to build up her Fleet as their ground forces of Free Warriors were now quite limited, less than 300 since the completion of the Domes. The new Dragon Matriarch, Synahmarr, was preparing for her role in that endeavor. And they'd begun a census, not even sure who'd survived the Battle for the Dragon Clan, and 'til the Domes were secure they'd had no time to do other than survive themselves.

Darque set up a command to seek missing Warriors as well. There was no record of who'd been deployed and who'd been stationed or were on leave at the Den, who would've fought in the big battle. Apparently, her father kept track of all that by memory. Everyone was ordered to make their own lists of family, friends, anyone they knew or could remember, even for the Warriors to seek their past sponsors. As there were no Warriors to spare for such a task, the lists were given to Master Tyrza who had incorporated them into the children's education curriculum. They were being checked and cross-checked and any known dead were recorded and re-checked against records from the battle, although Flame, the Magical brew spit forth in the Highlands' fiery breath, generally left little to recognize.

To honor those who'd been forced Past the Veil, Darque had asked for a wall upon which all their names could be engraved. She'd nailed a paper list outside her office at the Den in the days after the battle and she wanted to enlarge it, creating a memorial. This could be accomplished with the help of the Water Dragons who could literally carve the names into the rock by spitting, using a finely focused stream of water, with the guidance of the Master Masons and Craftsmen. The Wall of Valor was in the works and Darque was in favor of using the walls surrounding the Training Pits as 'twas not only an enormous space, 'twas where every Warrior had taken the Oath since the Last Holocaust. 'Twould be as bringing them home.

Those they could positively say were Past the Veil, shortened the list of potential deployed and missing elsewhere. If those Warriors had attempted to return after the battle, they'd have been greeted with the Illusory Spell o'er Drekinn, making it appear that all had been destroyed and there were no survivors. Now the Spell Dome, more powerful still, would make it impossible to even locate Drekinn. The Domes made the Lairs undetectable, and the Gatekeepers could send anyone who got too close, through a portal to the other side or anywhere they chose. Since going through a portal was something they would not recall doing, 'twould seem as if the Lairs no longer existed or could not be found. Most Warriors were deployed or worked in pairs as a Team. Darque's earliest estimates were near two hundred, but with the newest estimates, 'twas conceivable that o'er a thousand Warriors were out there somewhere. Mayhap more. 'Twould be necessary to seek them out and bring them back.

Shortly after the Domes were completed 'twas discovered that the Water Dragons could still use the wells. Since the Water Dragons had created them, most built long afore the Last Holocaust, allowing them travel inland by way of the vast underground river systems that spider-webbed their way throughout the mainland, they knew that both the Keep and the Den had wells. However, her Warriors had excavated much of the Bog Lair themselves and were certain there was no well at that location. Darque didn't like it but 'twas nothing that could be done to alter the Spell now. Besides, the wells were easily defendable, could only be navigated by the Water Dragons, and having a 'back door' seemed a good strategy. Which was why she was intent on moving King Gabriel from the Bog to the Keep.

Thus far, only Islyth and Schlynn, lifelong friends and partners in mischief, were allowed to come and go as they pleased, so they could visit Caleichante and bring information about what was happening on the Island of Dreams. But the other Sprites had Ties as well and she had to make a decision on their status soon. And after making this discovery, they found that the native animals, birds, and insects of the Talons could come and go without difficulty, however when Corbyn attempted to penetrate the barrier in his preferred Shift as the Raven (or in any other Shift) he was unable, and they deduced that no Shifter would be able to sneak in under another form. Nevertheless, they could conceivably enter through a portal, disguised as someone else. Although they could post guards at the wells, monitoring the incoming was another issue.

Darque looked again at her sister. "We have to expect refugees. Intel says the Outlands are under hit and run attacks. Nothing focused yet but 'tis only a matter of time. Their goal, if they have one, seems to be simple enough: to prevent the survivors from getting organized as an opposing force. And Abriya has mentioned Shahanalaa requires a key which we have to find, along with the fact that we have yet to find the actual door from the Keep into this region."

Storrm thought a moment. "Hunting has been good, but 'tis mostly outside the protection of the Dome, and we need more farmland." She paused as she thought about how they were to accomplish that. The Dome o'er Drekinn Lair included enough farmland to provide for those few currently stationed there, but not enough hunting area and opening Shahanalaa was their only safe option for all three Lairs. "I'd expect the door to be in the bowels of the Keep. Such a huge separate environment would require an entrance at ground level, don't you think?"

"Not necessarily," Darque countered. "It could enter upon a cliff for all we know. But we have several Teams searching on all levels now. I don't understand why we can't find the entry, as from description 'tis massive."

Storrm nodded and chewed on her bottom lip as she thought. "Do not forget 'tis protected by a Spell from the Ancients. We could walk right by and not see. Have you asked Ama? Surely our mother who was born here, would recall the location of the entrance."

Their mother, Aalanna Myriam Treygyn, was full Rashei, born and raised in the Keep. Just prior to the event that forced their entire population into the Otherworld, Aalanna was secreted out and moved to Drekinn. Corbyn had assisted in this rescue effort, using his native Memory Magic for her own safety, with Aalanna believing 'til recently, that she was a born and bred Clansman. "She recalls nothing of the region. Either she was too young, or not being able to see the entrance itself continues to block her memory. Corbyn merely untethered her altered memories, leaving us at the mercy of her recall."

Storrm squinted. "Tell me again why the Dragons can't see all this from the air?"

"I know. 'Tis odd and 'twas my question as well. Abriya explained 'twas created by some kind of 'burp' in the Beginning as all the Magic settled. The same phenomenon that protects it from above, protects it from extreme weather. I have a theory that the entire region is within a monstrous cavern or 'tis under an ancient and extremely powerful Spell. Mayhap both. And mayhap the same Magic that created it protects it still. 'Twould include its own lighting, climate, animal life. We already know, or have been told, that Shahanalaa has all these things as well as abundant water and vegetation. All I know for certain is that 'twas how the Rashei fed their society in the generations they inhabited the Keep and we must re-open it to feed our growing population."

"And there might still be some of them in Shahanalaa, unaffected by the Spell that made the rest of them disappear?"

Speculatively, she replied, "Yes, 'tis possible. From all evidence, the event that took the Rashei occurred in the early morning and they might have had a working detail there who may have been unaffected. They may still be alive and unable to leave, although this occurred o'er half a century past. Once we open Shahanalaa again, they might or might not be affected by the original Spell, forced to join the other 'spirits' wandering about the Keep." Darque paused. Thoughtfully, she added, "Also, 'tis possibly where Myriam hid Abriya's Dragon Sword."

Raising her hands in animated surrender, Storrm summed up their frustrations. "All this is possible. Mayhap this and mayhap that. We know not much for certain."

"No. We know not near enough for my satisfaction. About anything." She still didn't know how they were to find and 'rescue' Rhyah the Fay. Wolves were common in the mountains and when the Fay Shifted to their preferred form 'twould be most difficult to tell the difference. She'd put her Teams on watch for Rhyah, and Storrm would mention such to Corbyn the next time he deigned to make an appearance. She had to think he was their best chance since Rhyah reportedly was his friend in childhood.

Changing the subject, Darque continued, "I think everyone is learning to handle the new arrivals. Have there been any incidents?" Strictly speaking, the Dragons themselves, both Water and Highland, were relatively new arrivals, creating a whole new society and environment to which most were no longer affected. Making use of one of their lesser Magics allowing them to enlarge spaces, the Highlands could walk freely about the Lairs, but doing so in such a manner used up their Magic unnecessarily and created an odd optical illusion that could be disconcerting to others, therefore they preferred to perch upon the walls of the Den and the Keep, roaming through the smaller areas of the Lairs only when necessary. The Bog was already large enough for them, as 'twas built as a training facility for the Fleet.

"I've heard of none, thus far." Storrm thought about the other new arrivals. The discovery that some of their own people were half-breeds of Elven and Human descent, including the Warriors Graasyn and Bastyen, was not as much of a shock as might have been expected, and they, along with the Elven and Sprite forces under Captain Natanamia, were blending in well with hardly a side glance of note.

Then there were the Daggogh and the Gordatch, contingents of the People of the Razor's Edge and the Raptor's Talons (the two major mountain ranges in Kadoor) who were now residents of the Lairs. Their appearance was by far more remarkable than pointed ears. With tattoos and painted symbols covering most of their bodies, their hair cut erratically, partially plastered in colorful spikes, the rest braided with feathers, shells or precious gems, and wearing even less than a Warrior on leave, heads turned when they walked past. And they brought their Night Beasts (also known as the Kahyah) and Night Wings. These were bred by, and partnered with, the Hunters of the People. Both creatures were fierce fighters and had played an integral part in the success of the last battle. The Wings, fox-faced, bat-like flying animals who fought with long fangs and talons, mostly subsisting on the blood of their victims, stood waist high on the average male and were quite at home in the cavernous Drekinn Lair. The Beasts, on the other hand, standing shoulder to shoulder with their Handlers, preferred the outside areas and the openness of St Swiftyn's Keep, and although the children were enamored of them as they were big enough to ride, they preferred to be asked first, for they were sentient as well. They had no access to the Link and being the result of the cross breeding of the available big cats and wolves at the time of the Last Holocaust they had no better dexterity, nor could they speak Common or any other tongue but their own, however they could and did communicate with Gheryh the Word Sayer, co-leader of the People along with her mate, Kyrag.

The Danah and Danoh of the People were currently staying in the Keep and when Darque had attempted to formally introduce them to the Warriors as was her duty as Commander, after having gone through multiple such introductions of people and names with which she was unfamiliar, she'd faltered, citing, "… the Danoh, um, 'ah', Danah, and the Danoh of the People, the um, uh, Gordogh.. no, Daggogh and uh Gordatch…" Frustrated, she blushed as she finished, "Gheryh and Kyrag…" while concurrently Speaking with Storrm, *"How by the Ancients do you talk so much, without ever getting tongue tangled?"* Storrm laughed and Replied, *"You did stumble o'er that a bit, didn't you?"* Darque was embarrassed as she'd continued to show the ruling partners around the Keep, reluctant to admit her sister was correct, *"yeah, well, yeah."* Storrm Replied again, acknowledging the fact that everyone thought she talked ceaselessly, *"'Tis an art, you know."* Darque dismissed her with one hand o'er her shoulder, Teasing, *"One in which you've had much practice!"* As Storrm left the area for her own duties, with a sparkling grin she Reminded her, *"You know I'll always have your back."* Darque smiled appreciatively as she passed by, and Stated, *"One of few truths to which I cling, my sister."*

Storrm chuckled once more as her thoughts returned to the Night Beasts and their ongoing 'troubles' with the children. When the Kahyah grew tired of all the petting and hair pulling, they would simply stand up and wander off with exaggerated intolerance, sometimes dragging the children along as they wrapped themselves around one leg or another, keeping their eyes tightly closed to avoid being swished in the face by a long tail, laughing hysterically 'til the Beast located his or her Handler to remove the offending being. King Gabriel himself had a big female Kahyah partner known as Traddya. Since Gabriel took the 'Bond with Daynahmyn, Traddya spent most of her time with her mate, Ryygg, who was partnered with Gheryh, but would visit her old Handler as frequently as possible as she considered him one of her pups.

Another new arrival was Crytcha, the sole representative of the Borkahn (commonly known as Trolls afore the Last Holocaust). The most differing in their appearance from the other Races (even the People), thick-skinned, boxy, and hairless, able to crouch and blend into the very landscape disguised as a boulder, part of a rock formation, or even 'disappear' into part of the rock wall, Gorch's daughter, having less than thirteen winters, was an unexpected arrival and officially a refugee, as she was sought after by an opposing Borkahn faction led by Roack who had already abducted her once, handing her o'er to the evil Pitch Elves of the Talons afore being rescued by Diadranei and Bastyen. Although Crytcha had entrenched herself into the Clan by helping to defend the Spell bearers during the struggle to Draw the Dome o'er the Bog, she was still somewhat of a loner.

Darque appreciated the fact that she was gaining skilled fighters, but fighters didn't spend all their time fighting and she didn't need any non-productive mouths to feed. Everyone in the Clan worked, even the children, and therefore she'd set a sideline task for the newcomers. "I want Natan's team to vet the refugees. They can detect a spy much easier and with more surety, than any human." She thought about her briefing with the Elves upon their arrival when she'd asked them for this service. Orasynth, the eldest of the five brothers, had been the first to respond. Carefully choosing his words, he stated, "Humans effortlessly deceive even themselves and therefore Human deceit can be muted to our senses. Also, the attempt to discern deceit in another Magic bearer can become quite muddled if such scrutiny is resisted." He shook his head and finished, "We cannot be certain we can detect a spy."

Darque understood his doubts. "Do your best, for your best is above and beyond ours in this endeavor and 'tis all we have for now. Many new refugees will soon arrive, and we have little space to keep them apart from everyone else while we try to vet them, aside from the fact that 'twill be near impossible any other way, as records, references, Clan leaders, even entire villages, are being destroyed. 'Twill be a hurried process, stressful but most important. I trust your best judgments o'er the instincts of others."

Orasynth had heard that Humans were quite unrealistic about the abilities of Magic bearers and after hearing this he was relieved. The Battle Commander was someone who seemed to have a solid grip on reality and was not only strong physically, she was emotionally sound, and her battle strategies were equally so. He bowed his head and replied, "So be it, Commander." Taking their leave, they went to work out a plan in preparation for their task. The Elves were a proud people and would certainly do their best for the Commander, for 'twould not only affect their safety and the safety of the Resistance but 'twould reflect on their Nation. Queen Alyssa had freed them from their own father, the evil King Jeeryd. They would do anything to please their stepmother.

Storrm considered the plan. "Agreed. I've spoken with the Elves and they're highly intuitive, as are the Sprites. Initially, they seemed surprised at the dry humor and harsh language of most of the Warriors but they're beginning to hold their own." She grinned and wrinkled her nose. "I suspect they have their own such humor, in their own language, of which we are missing much!"

"No doubt. But 'tis not insolent and for that, I'm grateful. We seem to be attaining an integrative fighting force." She paused to reflect but suddenly Heard the voice of Rolf's Nalwynn Reporting they had guests. Smiling, she continued, "And on that note, I have an appointment. Natanamia and her team are just arriving and I'm giving them the tour of the Den and the Lair, after which I'll return to the Keep. The Sprites and Elves are going to stay in the Den for a few days. When Gunnarr and I leave, you and Mystynn command Drekinn while Kydra holds the Bog with Ragnyrr."

CHAPTER SEVEN

The Kreegare

THE DRAGON'S DEN
~~~~~ LESS THAN A MARK LATER ~~~~~

Elder Warrior Regynn was the one Warrior in 'Bond who, unlike any other, was unaffected by the absence of his partner. 'Twas not that he didn't care or that he wasn't aware of her absence, he just didn't seem to experience the same anxiety the others had to endure. But then again, he was unlike the other Warriors in many ways. 'Twas most likely due to how his mind worked, becoming totally engrossed in whatever project in which he'd taken an interest. His big green Sydrayyah was currently hunting, leaving Regynn in the library absorbed in a project he'd begun moons past. He'd discovered a formula in the Archives of the Ancients which described an extremely powerful explosive stick of which he could not decipher the name.

Common Tongue was the result of many different languages meshing as survivors banded together from all backgrounds after the Last Holocaust and therefore Ancient Tongue had altered significantly. The Elder Warrior also had to deal with the fact that the Ancients themselves had their own version of Common and they all spoke their own regional tongues as well. All in all, Regynn, doubtless the most intelligent of them, was the one most likely to understand and combined with his incessant need to discover and tinker and learn, he had taken the post of Clan Historian after the Passing of the last to hold the position.

He'd been successful in creating an explosive stick of similar effectiveness in hopes that 'twould become a powerful addition to their arsenal against the Hoard but had been unable to test it prior to the Battle of Ice Mist Falls. When Fryya 'borrowed' one of his altered 'hot candles' which he'd modeled after their fireworks, she'd successfully managed to do his testing for him and put down her first Hoard Dragon by herself. All it required was entrance past the near impenetrable scales and Healing of the Highlands (which she'd accomplished using one of Darque's matching blades which sadly, she lost) to implant near the heart, and the blast killed instantly. In point of fact it not only killed the beast, it destroyed his carcass, dropping it in a blob on the ground in which Right to Second, AKA Third Fighter Kydra, near died from aspiration. But that was another story. Now he was preparing to finalize the formula and mass produce it for the rest of the fighters.

The new stick he named Flamite, as 'twas descriptive of how it worked and closely resembled the name he'd been unable to completely decipher. The size of the stick that Fryya used was too difficult to deliver other than by hand as 'twas too heavy, however, a smaller version could be easily delivered via their new arrows tipped with Dragon teeth which could penetrate the scales, and as long as it didn't get lodged in their heavy ribcage 'twould destroy the heart, which along with decapitation was the quickest way to kill a Highland. Larger sticks of Flamite could be attached to spikes launched off the ramparts by huge crossbows and some of the Warriors, especially those in 'Bond with enhanced strength, could use a medium sized one on regular arrows. 'Twould stop the foot soldiers of the Hoard as well. Even though the Highlands were the hardest to kill, if their Healing Magic was severely compromised, they would Pass without the destruction of head or heart but that took much and caused too many lives to be lost in the effort. So, destroying the heart or decapitation was still considered the primary goal.

The possibilities for his re-invention intrigued Regynn and as he entered the hallway to make report to Darque, he looked up just as the group of Sprites and Elves approached him in the corridor of the Dragon's Den. As was typical, he'd completely forgotten his appointment. The Magic bearers were being briefed at, and touring, all three Lairs, and Regynn was supposed to meet with them, giving them the tour of the library. Behind Captain Natanamia there stood the five Elven Princes and the Sprites, including Lyrianei and Kalisadei, who'd been members of the chase team following the abduction of the 7th Egg from the Island of Dreams, and sisters Datyniah and Dalakiah. Then he squinted and looked past the female members to the brothers standing in the very back. Stepping out eagerly, he burst forth, "Ardryyn! Kryllyn! What are you doing here?"

Grasping arms, the pale green eyes of the blonde-haired brothers lit up in unison, wide smiles of anticipation upon their ever-youthful faces, as they hugged each other in greeting. "Regynn! We could ask the same of you, me thinks," declared Kryllyn with enthusiasm. "How long's it been? We thought you'd be Past by now, or close to it. You're looking rather well for an elder Human. 'Tis the LifeBond?"

"I haven't seen that many winters! But yes, 'tis indeed. I've had many benefits from taking the 'Bond."

Curiously, Ardryyn asked, "And your woman? Did you ever hear what became of her?"

"Cathay followed me! She's here now…"

As Regynn caught the eyes of his Commander mid-sentence, Darque tilted her head and crossed her leather-braced arms o'er her chest while her gaze shot from the Sprite brothers to her Warrior and back. "'Twas my understanding that you two had never been to the mainland." Her enquiring gaze shifted to her Warrior. "Regynn, I know you were an Outlander afore you joined the Clan and took the Oath. Am I to believe you are that well-traveled?"

Regynn coughed and Natan cupped her hand o'er her mouth to keep from bursting out laughing at the expression on his face, while wide-eyed, the Elves and the rest of the Sprites stared in amazement at their two male counterparts, who were now casting their gazes everywhere but upon the feisty Battle Commander, leaving Regynn to explain.

Pointing first to the Sprites and then to Regynn, Darque motioned o'er her shoulder and demanded, "You three. My office. Now."

'Twas not exactly the tour Natanamia thought they'd have, but she knew well the Human's fiery temper and with great interest to discover what was going on for herself, she stepped aside and waved her team past, to follow Darque down the corridor. All she could hope was that Lord Rohar would not be told to recall his representatives and that they hadn't just lowered Darque's respect for the Sprite and Elven Nations.

~~~~~ DARQUE'S OFFICE ~~~~~

Captain Natanamia had the blonde hair and light eyes that were the opposite of their cousin Race, the Elves. They did, however, share a build that was generally tall and lean, pale and ever youthful. Her green eyes now focused upon those of the brothers, she was amazed. 'Twas odd enough that any living Sprite had a connection with any Human prior to this deployment and to her own experiences o'er the past winter, but, "Mariners? You worked the ships afore you joined ranks?"

Although they briefly discussed having accompanied the Human to Port O'Drekinn, the specifics of how they'd met Regynn would have to come from former Captain Caleichante. "Yes, Captain. We had no home, no family. My brother and I worked our way up from the docks to the ships. Once we had enough coin, we purchased our weapons to join the Guard and begin training." The boys' appreciative gazes flickered to the Warrior afore continuing, "Our lifelong goal was to be one of the Elite."

Natanamia stiffened as she recalled that exact sentiment spoken by another Sprite so many winters past. Her little sister, Niamia. She licked her lips, swallowed hard, and returned her gaze to Darque who now sat back in her chair watching the Sprite Captain handle her team. Regaining her composure, she returned her focus to the men and declared quietly, "Go wait outside."

Darque motioned to Regynn to follow the Sprites, and once she and Natan were alone in the office, she stood up. Although both women planned on getting more of those 'specific details' on that past mission from Calei, 'twas not a priority. But afore Darque could dismiss the affair, Natanamia spoke. "I must apologize for this breach in confidence. I knew not that they had been off-island. I did not lie a'purpose."

Darque felt the conversation had taken a wrong turn, for she was not particularly concerned. Trying to steer it back on track, she replied, "Pfffft! Ignorance of fact is no lie. I should apologize to you as well, my friend. Regynn came to the Dragon Clan as an adult and with nothing but the clothes on his back, he pounded his great fists upon the front gate of the Den, ready to make application to Warrior Training afore he'd been in Drekinn a full day. Although he'd drop a few hints through the winters, and some of his fighting skills I now recognize are Sprite inspired, no one ever really knew his past. Nor did we care. He's been a good Warrior and a member of the Brotherhood for more of his span of days than he was not."

Natanamia listened quietly but was still troubled. She was representing the Sprite Nation as well as commanding the Elven entourage; her team should be exemplary in all ways, not to mention that the Battle Commander held rank o'er them all. "I am open to your suggestions. I can replace them or have them punished, as you will."

Darque shook her head. "Me'thinks they're good men, but then I don't know them as well as do you." She watched her friend's eyes and the indecision she saw there reminded her of her own, not that long ago. "Natan, I sense a need to succeed, that is unnecessary. A little friendly advice…? When I took o'er from my father, I thought I was well prepared. I'd been groomed for command my entire span of days, and I felt like I'd worked for it and earned it. I quickly discovered I knew little, about even less. But I do know what is important and that what I should know, will rise to meet me. In brief, you can't know everything, you can't be prepared for everything. You just do the best you can, day to day."

Natanamia plopped down in the huge wingback chair and smiled. "You're right. I'm trying too hard, as usual. This assignment means the world to me, I just don't want to fail."

"Fail? Hades no!" Darque thought about the loss of her friend's sister and the terrible trials through which she'd fought. "Much has been asked of you o'er the past winter, and much has been expected. I think you're doing fine, if what I think holds any weight for you."

"By the Ancients, you're the 'one of prophesy', the one who will bring us all back from near extinction. I'd have to say that yes, your opinion holds much weight."

Darque shook her head. "I'd rather think that outside of all this, we are friends, and not just because of those words. In fact, that notion is sort of creepy. I didn't ask to be 'the one of prophesy', 'twas a matter of birth order." With a wink, she teased her friend, "Besides, I do respect my elders and you are far older than I!" Laughing, she reached into the cabinet and produced a bottle of mead and two glasses. Half filling them, she handed one to Natanamia while they discussed the next leg of the tour, forcing her team and Regynn to wonder what was happening as they waited in the hall.

LATER

<div align="center">~~~~~ REGYNN AND CATHAY'S QUARTERS ~~~~~</div>

Full wakefulness struck with a fury as Regynn relived his near-death experience during one of his early deployments as an Assassin in the Rol Dan with his partner, Cassiopeia. 'Twas a rare occurrence for the Warrior to have such nightmares, but he understood with clarity the reason behind this one. Sitting upright, he eased off the mattress to avoid waking his lifemate, Cathay. He'd not meant to fall asleep, but they'd both been up working all night and he was out early this morning, so when he'd returned to their quarters, he couldn't help but stretch out beside his still sleeping woman just to be near her for a time.

The next thing he knew, he was that young man again, just out of training, partnered with a much more experienced Assassin for his own protection. 'Twould be so 'til she felt confident in his skills, and that he'd not run off and get himself killed alone. They'd been on a mission to deliver an orphaned child to his grandparents in a distant and warring city. Betrayed and ambushed, the details didn't mean much now, he'd found himself in a precarious position while protecting the child and fighting off a frontal attacker when another came from behind. Cass yelled, which made him turn his attention to the new threat.

Everything had happened so fast. For many winters following, he'd told himself he'd been mistaken. He must have been mistaken. He had but a heartbeat to avoid being stabbed in the back by this new attacker and could not have managed while still holding safe the child. He faced the reality that he was about to Pass the Veil and could do nothing to prevent such. Cassiopeia had just gutted one of the ambushers as the new attacker rushed past her to kill Regynn and take the child. Her sword swinging around from her previous maneuver, she'd not be able to reverse her momentum fast enough to deliver a killing blow to save Regynn. So, with her other hand she'd reached out, her fingers just sweeping his bare arm as he passed by, managing to divert his attention. But his reactions seemed slowed. With his momentum and the position of his sword, he should have been able to kill her and still would have been able to deliver the strike on Regynn. But at the same time, she'd struck him what he'd thought was but a glancing blow with her sword, and he'd dropped to the ground, dead. In the meantime, Regynn had turned within a heartbeat and killed his frontal attacker.

The entire incident occurred o'er the drip of a candle. Regynn had tucked the incident away in the back of his memories for they'd no time to think more then. Changing directions, they'd mounted the ambushers' horses and ridden off into the night to successfully complete their mission. The events of that fight were not confirmed nor related even once they'd returned. Cass merely glanced at Regynn when they'd made report to Tamm, leaving out the details of the ambush, and he'd been promoted to full Assassin, sending him off on his own or with a partner depending on the level of need. Cassiopeia was his usual partner, but 'tween them, that night was never mentioned.

Now that he had proof of how the Sprites killed by Draining, 'twas a short leap to the deduction that was so long in the coming. He was now convinced she'd used the blade after the man's death, pretending to give the killing strike. Confirmation in his mind, he knew what he must do. He left their private quarters and headed toward the office of the Battle Commander for the second time that morning.

~~~~~~~~~

Regynn stood at Battle Ease in front of the desk. 'Twas half the day since he'd left Darque after debriefing about the events in which he'd met the Sprite brothers. She'd not called him back, but after finally connecting all the dots, he'd returned on his own, looking uncomfortable while he tried to gather his ideas into some sort of logical order. For lack of a reason, she'd just asked him if he was there because he was having regrets about his earlier statement. "No Sir, I didn't believe the existence of the Sprites or their Water Dragons meant anything to the Clan then. Nevertheless, you wouldn't have me break a promise, would you? I knew they'd all join us eventually. Besides, I didn't really see the Dragons. I was unconscious at the time. I honestly didn't remember them at all."

Darque was staring off into space while listening. She had to agree with him and his words jogged her memories. Grifynn had made oblique references as she was growing up that didn't make sense at the time, but now she knew were related to his own knowledge of the Magic bearers. If the former Battle Commander didn't care about such information, why should she? Besides, both the Sprites and the Elves were now a part of the Resistance and any point taken now, would be moot. She shrugged her shoulders. "Of course, you're right." She glanced at him. "If you think of anything else that might help, I expect you to make report." She dropped her gaze to the ever-growing mountain of paperwork stacking up on her desk, afore returning her attention to Regynn. "Is there something else?"

"Uh, yes. I've been working on my latest weapon, the modified hot candle. 'Tis a success, and I've figured a method of delivery other than the one Fryya chose." He paused and scratched his chin. "I'm calling it Flamite."

"Wonderful! Get that information to Alric, and his team of Weapons Apprentices can begin. Mayhap Silas with his Blacksmiths could be useful, as well," she added, more to herself than to the Warrior.

Regynn was pensive. "Yessir." He shuffled his feet but did not leave. He cleared his throat and took a deep breath. "Commander?"

"Yes?"

"Things have been coming together." He hesitated again, memories of working with Cassiopeia flooding his thoughts.

"What things?" Darque quietly waited for the Warrior to continue, but he simply stood there, looking at her. "Your horse is at the gate," she said, puzzled by his behavior and the look in his eyes, as she tried to encourage him to speak his mind, and for the second time in the past two winters, asked, "Where are you taking me?" So much had happened, of this he was correct. What more could he reveal?

His gaze upon the front of her desk, he stated, "You know about me and the Sprites."

When he stopped yet again, she tried to nudge him along. "Yes. We discussed that earlier." She leaned forward, a quizzical expression now plastered upon her face as Regynn seemed somewhat reluctant to continue, which was seriously bizarre, for whenever anyone gave him an open gate to speak his mind, even though 'twas interesting information he conveyed, he usually spoke 'til one had to make him stop.

Sighing deeply, he appeared to come to a difficult decision. Squirming a tad, he then repeated, "You know about me and the Sprites." His eyes caught hers afore he continued, "But you know not about me and the Elves."

<center>~~~~~ O'ER A MARK LATER ~~~~~</center>

Once Regynn loosed his tongue, information spewed forth to the utter astonishment of the Battle Commander. Everyone knew Regynn was an Outlander, but as he was extremely close-mouthed and kept secrets like no other, from whence he'd come had always been a question. Now Darque understood much. Suspicions, past events, fighting styles, even his favorite drink, Vydna, came together to complete the puzzle. Regynn was born and raised in the far eastern region known as the Rol Dan, beyond even the Dragon's Tears, of the Caste of Assassins. He'd worked his way up to the smallest and most elite of that Caste, known as the Kreegare.

Castes in the Rol Dan were like Clans in Kadoor, in which you were born, raised, lived and worked your entire span of days, but not everyone in the Assassins Caste became Kreegare, like not everyone in a War Clan became a Warrior. However, not everyone in the Kreegare were from the Caste originally. Although there were a few Outlanders in the Warrior Brotherhood, the vast majority were of the Dragon Clan, like most of the Eagle Warriors were from the Eagle Clan, and so forth. However, there were far more 'Outlanders' who had risen to the level of the Kreegare than Caste members, per ratio. This had always puzzled Regynn, even though he knew not much about the happenings in Kadoor prior to his travels, but once he'd joined the Dragon Clan, the odd ratios puzzled him even more. The Kreegare of the Assassins Caste had actually formed not long after the Last Holocaust, per their history, but from whence had those 'Outlanders' come? They were highly effective in their chosen professions, and much feared. 'Twas said (and some believed strongly) that the Kreegare could kill with a look and a touch and that most of their victims died afore the killing strike was even swung, however there were no witnesses to such. The fear of mysticism raised their effectiveness and they made no effort to quell the rumors.

But through his winters of service, Regynn began to believe the rumors were true. Saying naught, but observing much, he filed the odd bits of information away for some future connection. During his training, he could swear that he'd seen the pointed ears, the slanted eyes that occasionally showed through some kind of mental suggestion to see otherwise, and of course there was that incident with Cassiopeia. 'Twas all a trick of the light or too much Vydna 'til Calei and the boys rescued him from that ship. Thinking his fellow Assassins may have been associated with the Sprites as had he, he'd kept his mouth shut. And then the events of the past winters convinced him that his fellow Assassins were not merely humans who'd had associations with Magic bearers, they were actually Magic bearers using glamour to alter their appearance. With the arrival of Princess Anastasia and her entourage, along with the gift of the Spell Domes, even more of the pieces came together and the final addition of their current situation made him believe the Kreegare were mostly lost Elves from the Wyrdritch who used their Magic to remain unseen and to protect each other, as Magic was forbidden in the Rol Dan and any caught using it in any form were handed a death sentence. 'Twas one of the Kreegare's most common assignments. Paid to kill those who were thought to practice Magic. Regynn had always found such to be highly hypocritical, considering the average man and woman of the Rol Dan thought the Kreegare used Magic, although they'd never say such aloud.

One of the issues he'd struggled with after meeting the Elves, was their length of days. If his fellow Assassins were Elven, they'd been there for centuries, so how did they hide the fact that they'd live far beyond their human counterparts? That question, along with many others, was answered when he, along with the rest of the Clan, learned that both Shayla and Grifynn had successfully managed to live through many life spans with no one the wiser. And, he'd never been sent on an assignment to fulfill the sentence of someone who was accused of Magic. Now he knew why. How dense could he have been? "I don't believe they ever killed them. I believe most of the lost Elves who ended up in the Rol Dan, are still alive."

Darque stared at him. She always thought there was much more to the man than what was known. She could sense it. But now, she was stunned at how much more there was. Assassins were known even in Kadoor, and much feared. With each new revelation, she wondered if her father had known these things. 'Twould have been nice of him to share with his successor, but then, his death was not exactly a planned event. Nevertheless, the importance of this information was immense. As she spoke, Regynn interjected 'til their comments ran o'er each other. "We need to inform those Elves that the Wyrdritch survived and the Elven Nation has sworn allegiance to the Resistance."

"No."

"We need the Kreegare on our side."

"No."

"The Evil One may be there even now, recruiting, spreading his hate and brutality throughout the Rol Dan. There could be many in need of rescue. Many refugees to bring to the Resistance."

"No."

"If the Kreegare swear fealty to the Black…"

"No."

"I need you, Regynn! The Clan needs you!"

"NO!"

Darque held her breath. No Warrior had ever left the Brotherhood. Not alive, anyway. Though there was a formal declaration of leaving, that Regynn himself had dredged up in the Archives, no one had ever taken it, for the Oath was 'til death, and given the sensitive information they obtained through membership in the Brotherhood, leaving meant death, either by one's own hand, or by that of the Battle Commander. She watched his eyes and his sword arm, though he carried not a sword. If he left his blade upon the desk in front of her, she knew 'twould mean the same thing.

Regynn's eyes reflected much turmoil as he slowly reached for the blade upon his belt. Wisely, Darque said nothing as his hand rested momentarily upon the leather sheath, afore, much to her relief, he broke eye contact, turned brusquely, and walked out.

~~~~~ THE QUARTERS OF REGYNN AND CATHAY ~~~~~

Her soft, high pitched voice broke through Regynn's explanation of what had just happened. "You're blessed she didn't fire you on the spot!" Cathay was also an Outlander, and now that the cat was out of the bag, everyone knew she and Regynn were from the Rol Dan.

"One is not fired from the Brotherhood," he stated, wisely excluding the fact that 'twould have meant his death. Not that it had ever happened afore. At least, not to his knowledge. He wondered. Mayhap he'd just struck upon a new research project.

"Only because no one has ever threatened to quit afore!"

His mind elsewhere, her tone brought him back to the moment. "I didn't threaten to quit, I merely…"

"…refused an order."

"'Twasn't an order. Exactly. It hadn't gone that far. And I made a vow when I left, that I'd never return, as well as my vow to you. I will not leave you again."

"Seems to me, you made a vow when you took the Oath to serve the Battle Commander and the Brotherhood. Your allegiance is to the Clan now. Not the Kreegare. That was a life span past, and much has changed."

He sighed. He could never have quit the Brotherhood, would never have fought against the Battle Commander, let alone commit suicide. 'Twould be totally out of character and the very notion was ludicrous, besides the fact that he was in the 'Bond now and his death would mean Sydrayyah's.

He considered, as he felt he was going to be leaving soon on this mission of which he'd instigated, despite how he felt. "'Twill be very dangerous. The Kreegaren Elves know not who I am now, only that I abandoned my position and my Caste. As far as I know, they think I am dead. Not to mention that I have not set foot in the Rol Dan for o'er fifty winters. If I am recognized, they will not give me enough time to explain, they will simply kill me."

"They haven't managed that yet. Even as a human, you earned your way into their ranks, and now that you are in the 'Bond, you have the strength and reflexes of your youth, more so. You will be fine. Besides, Sydrayyah was recruited from there, and lived there since the Last Holocaust. You, I, Sydrayyah? There are none in all Kadoor who know the Rol Dan better than we."

Opening his mouth to reply, the words were abruptly forgotten as he stared at her, unsure of what he'd just heard. He furrowed his brows and cocked his head. "Surely you aren't suggesting that you go with us?"

"I am not just suggesting. I also made a vow. I will never stay behind again. I will not let you go without me, and Sydrayyah won't allow it, either."

His expression now one of true confusion, an emotion with which he was not all that familiar, he questioned, "What do you mean by that?"

"Oh? We've Spoken occasionally, has she not mentioned?"

He was simply stunned. *"Sydrayyah? How long have you been Speaking to my woman?"*

Sweet innocence in her Voice, the big Green Replied, *"Since afore she left the Rol Dan in search of you. I've known her for some time."*

Regynn wasn't sure what to think. *"You knew her afore you took my 'Bond?"*

Syd narrowed her eyes. *"Don't even begin to chastise me. When she left, 'twas to discover the fate of a man missing o'er thirty winters and thought by most, to be Past the Veil. We share a bond of our own. Forget you not that if it weren't for my help, the two of you would never have found each other again!"*

WITHIN A FEW DAWNS

<div align="center">~~~~~ THE TRAINING PITS OF THE DRAGON'S DEN ~~~~~</div>

Regynn stood beside Sydrayyah, a scowl of worry upon his face as he boosted Cathay aboard and helped her strap onto the saddle. She was so small compared to the big Green. Frowning, he shook his head and unstrapped her, hushing her protests while he positioned her to the front of the saddle so that he'd sit behind her, fearing she'd fall off. He wanted some control o'er a situation in which he'd lost all such. He scowled again as he glanced at Sydrayyah's eyes and then half smiled. He could forgive her eventually, although they'd not Spoken since that day in Cathay's quarters. He patted himself down, ensuring all his small arms were secured, and even carried a sword for this trip. It had been so long he'd had to dust it and clean off the tarnish when he'd taken it out of his weapon's hold at the foot of his rack. Regynn was like all Warriors, with much appreciation for the steel, and none would carry a tarnished weapon. Even though his best fighting techniques were in hand-to-hand, using martial arts styles learned through much training and practice and refinement, he was an amazing swordsman and taking no more chances with the life of his woman than were being forced upon him.

Darque had insisted upon an 'escort' of sorts, forcing the Warrior who usually worked alone, to take a Team with him. 'Twas actually a welcome notion and he'd immediately requested Ardryyn and Kryllyn, but 'twas the older twin Elven Princes, Gylrann and Gylragg, who'd been the ones chosen. It made sense. Being Elven, they would surely be more welcome than Sprites to those who probably had no idea they were all now allies, and being royal, if the Kreegaren truly were Elven, they'd be more easily recognized, although Regynn was unsure if this was a good thing. Could go either way. He sighed and mounted, taking a firm hold on Cathay. Their supplies were tied up behind the saddle and he was as confident as he could be, that they were ready for their mission. Nevertheless, he was not a diplomat, but all his arguments o'er the past few dawns had met reality in that, he was Kreegaren. If anyone could seek an audience with their leader, 'twould be Regynn.

For the past few days he'd worked out with the brothers to learn their styles and they, his, so if they were forced to battle, they'd have the best odds, able to work together as a united team. He'd found little differences in those of the Elves and those of his Sprite friends and knowing the two Races had split up generations past brought up so many questions he had to force himself to keep his focus on the task at hand. Glancing 'cross the sands, he noted the Elves standing in the doorway beside a rather large plant that had been one of the additions made when the Sprite/Elven entourage arrived. Small trees, bushes, and ivies now dotted the entire Den and the Keep, and were even being grown at the Bog, providing them the necessary organics to Dance and to fuel their Magics.

He took a deep breath. *"I apologize for my behavior, Sydrayyah. Mayhap I was jealous."*

Sydrayyah sighed and Responded with sincere depth of emotion, for she wanted only the best for her 'Bond and his lovely lifemate. *"I am not angry. Forgive me for not Telling you sooner. I just could not find an opportune moment to do so."*

"I understand."

Knowingly, Syd wrinkled her brow ridges. *"Cathay is tougher than you think, my friend. You were apart for a very long time. She survived much."*

He considered the meaning behind her words, knowing that Cathay must have learned to fight to protect herself. *"I should have been there."*

"You did what you could to protect her. And, you are here now."

He nodded his head, fully understanding that Cathay was not a part of this Conversation, as well as that 'twas himself he needed to forgive. *"I love her. She is my life."*

"I will not fail either of you."

Regynn caught the gaze of Gylrann, or was that Gylragg? Shaking his head, he noted the smug expression upon the boy's face, the laughter in his eyes at his unspoken question. Apparently, they were easily mistaken one for the other and thought 'twas humorous. Mayhap 'twould be helpful. He mused upon that notion for a heartbeat, then through Sydrayyah, conveyed the coordinates of their trip to the brothers. Through a series of stops, they would make their way to the Rol Dan. Although Syd could fly them all, 'twould be exhausting. So, the Elves would Dance as far as they could, while Syd would use the timefold in flight, providing coordinates to organics along the way, and arriving at each of their destinations within a few candle drips of each other. The Highlands' ability to Push aside the physical and enlarge space for themselves led them to discover this advantage, creating a fold in time that allowed them to fly at speeds to rival a Dancer's Dance. The entire journey would normally take less than a fortnight, but they had to beware the Hoard and they all had to eat. Using Magic made one ravenous and fatigued, therefore they hoped 'twould not take more than a moon or two.

Regardless, 'twould be much faster than travel a'foot, which could take well o'er a winter.

The first legs of the journey would be made with little effort, and Regynn squeezed Sydrayyah's sides with his knees to signal his readiness. Launching from a dead stop in the sands, her muscled wings beat as they took flight. Once outside the Dome, she Pushed, and they vanished from the skies. The boys Drew their energy and disappeared, following quickly behind the big Green.

CHAPTER EIGHT
Medusa

Travel had been a tad difficult at times, but the company eventually worked out the issues of accommodating their different practices and now they were camped upon the far shores of the Dragon's Tears. Cathay spoke softly to her traveling companions as she turned the spit ever so slightly. Sydrayyah had offered to assist by cooking the rabbits with one fiery breath, but they'd been moving from one location to another at a breakneck pace 'til now, and Cathay needed the time 'twould take, along with the process of actually cooking, to help her focus her thoughts. Slowly, she stated, "I think 'twould be safest to try the cities of Dominion or Abhorrence first. Either one is large enough in which to hide, and we could obtain information at the taverns along the outskirts. Assassins were known to be everywhere in the larger cities and I doubt 'twould have changed. If necessary, we could try Tyranny, although I have no desire to ever return. I would probably foul the mission there anyway, as even though I've been gone for many winters, someone might yet recognize me."

Gylrann and Gylragg, oft' times simply referred to as 'Rann and 'Ragg, helped Cathay clean up after all had eaten their fill, while Regynn prepared to continue their mission, saddling Sydrayyah. The Warrior had not said much during their meal, listening to everyone's input. He didn't want to return to Tyranny, either. Warlord Takes of Tyranny had been his childhood friend. They'd grown up together, training together. When they'd been separated at just nine winters, Regynn staying with the Assassins and Takes returning to Tyranny when his father was forced Past the Veil, they'd lost touch. Nevertheless, long after Regynn became Kreegare, Takes sent for him, giving him a most important assignment. All the Warlords of the Rol Dan were constantly fighting but Takes had secured an alliance with the Warlord of Odium, a small city in a distant quarter of the land, and he required a bodyguard to pick up and safely deliver the daughter of the Warlord, to Tyranny, to mate with him and bring their cities together. Such would create a 'cage' around the cities 'tween them and Takes was certain 'twould increase his power and control. Of course, during the journey Regynn fell in love with Cathay, but 'twas nothing to be done. And when he discovered Takes' real plan to conquer the Warlord of Odium using his daughter as hostage, he'd weighed his options. Finally, he realized he had none. Odium was too small to attack Tyranny to rescue their Princess and could not have protected her from Takes if they'd been successful in doing so. And if he took Cathay back home, she'd be killed, and her city leveled. Leaving her with Takes suddenly became her safest position in all the Rol Dan. And if 'twas discovered their love for each other, she was doomed. So, he fled, making it appear he was a traitor and sealing Cathay's safety with Takes. But even though Takes' life had ended horribly, and Cathay had escaped with the assistance of Sydrayyah (he still knew not the details of that daring venture and Cathay had long been silent in her protection of her benefactors), he felt guilty that he'd not been there for her.

Regynn considered their plan, though 'twas dicey. As they had no other known contact person, and the Sentinel of Harsh might or might not still be there, he decided 'twould still be the safest and most obvious starting point. If they could locate the Sentinel, they could contact Tamm. Going first to the other cities would increase their chances of exposure. He wanted out of the Rol Dan as soon as possible. The very air he breathed here, was irksome.

Regynn helped Cathay mount up and watched the twins Draw their energy as he Told Syd to take them to Harsh.

MEANWHILE
THE KEEP OF ST SWIFTYN'S

~~~~~ O'ER EIGHT MOONS AFTER THE
DRAW OF THE DOMES ~~~~~

The dark-skinned man with the pale little girl returned, only now they were riding on a black horse. 'Twas clear they were looking for the Keep. The Battle Commander hadn't seen them the first time they'd come 'round, but this time she'd been called forth to determine their fate. O'er two moons earlier, the man and child were sent away through a portal to avoid confrontation. But after hearing report on the pair, Darque wondered. Were they the Eagle Warrior and Natan's niece? If so, she had to hope that eventually they'd find their way back. Although Natanamia had originally come to St Swiftyn's to meet the Warrior who was trying to rescue her niece, she'd left for the Island of Dreams to escort Kevon and Anastasia shortly afore the pair's first appearance and she couldn't fault the Gatekeepers their choice at the time. After all, she couldn't always be there to help make every decision.

Standing upon the wall, her eyes lit up as she viewed them. Her vision was sharper than most, her hybrid status combining with her LifeBond to enhance all her senses. She nodded to the Gatekeeper on duty and watched with satisfaction as the two, along with their horse, disappeared outside the Dome to reappear within a cell block of the Keep along the wall of the Ward. Once their identities were confirmed, they'd be allowed their freedom. She was pleased. Natan would be thrilled, as Darque suspected there was something going on 'tween the Sprite and the Warrior, and so would Caleichante, as the horse was surely Demonseed, lost on her journey to the Wyrdritch. Myrrdin would also be pleased, as 'twas his horse originally 'til Calei confiscated him when she'd disembarked the Krakken.

THE ROL DAN

~~~~~ THE CITY OF HARSH ~~~~~

Brecca listened carefully to the whispered words as she eavesdropped. 'Twas time to leave. Unseen, as soon as the adults left, she rolled out from under the brazier, fully dressed in simple pauper's tunic and boots, and felt for her weapons. All there. All well disguised. Her cloak was hidden in the outskirts of the city, along with her leathers and a stash of supplies she might need if she had to flee. She half smiled to herself. The young girl who'd been the last Sentinel of Harsh, was the first human since Regynn to join the Kreegare and had been assigned her first solo mission: infiltrate her old tavern and keep tabs on the activities in Harsh. Her partner and trainer, Cassiopeia, was pleased with her progress o'er the past winter, and was maintaining an equally incognito presence closer to the palace.

No one had recognized Brecca from afore. A winter's healthy growth, hard training, and a short shaggy cut of her long blonde hair along with a width of leather 'cross the evidence of blossoming puberty, she'd easily passed as a young boy to join the kitchen staff at the tavern. After last winter's blood bath, the tavern was cleaned and reopened, and those who might have seen a familiar face avoided the area as rumors of the slaughter included Magical influence, while those brave enough to give the new owners a chance, found good food and drink and a welcome atmosphere. It had become one of the major gathering centers for the lower classes.

Her position had given her unique intel, as the people of Harsh whispered freely in her presence, ignoring her as if she were another table or chair. Sifting through all the rumors of late, she'd pieced together the truth and 'twas now urgent to return to her brethren with the news of the recent arrival of strangers, for 'twas certain there was more to these than met the eye. And along with that was the information she'd just obtained about the Warlord's plans to attack the Kreegare. But first, she had to get to Cass and then out of the city. 'Twould take them less than a sennight to return to Tamm and make her report.

THE KEEP OF ST SWIFTYN'S
~~~~~ THE OFFICE OF THE BATTLE COMMANDER ~~~~~

Darque smiled at the Eagle Clan Warrior standing in front of her, the odd-looking child in tow. Having expected them, she understood Flyrra's half-breed status and had heard of her coloring, but actually seeing her was undeniably remarkable. After a short de-briefing session in which Flyrra never let go his hand nor moved a muscle ('twas as if the child barely breathed), making her easy to forget (which she suspected was the point, and mayhap encouraged by a touch of Magic), she steered them towards the mess hall for something to eat, as well as to meet up with Natanamia. The Sprite Captain was eagerly awaiting Kayarr and Flyrra but hadn't been available for the de-briefing and sent Darque a message that she'd meet them as soon as possible.

~~~~~ MOMENTS LATER ~~~~~

As they approached the mess hall, Kayarr could see the Sprite of his desire 'cross the crowded space. His hand on Flyrra's shoulder, he steered her a little faster toward the entrance. His attention upon their destination, Kayarr flashed a huge smile and raised his hand to wave at Natan, trying to catch her eye. Inside, the steady stream of children, Warriors, and other adults was irritating to the sensitive ears of the half-breed. Kayarr failed to notice Flyrra's escalating tension as they entered the large area. Everyone was either socializing or eating at long tables, sitting upon equally long benches.

~~~~~~~~~~

Flyrra was confused. Surely Kayarr wouldn't put her in such a position. She knew not what to do. She had no idea how this worked. What were the rules? Who did she have to attack so that she could eat? Mayhap 'twas similar to the feeding pits of the Black's Lair, where she'd have to make a snatch and then protect what she'd managed to grab. Her eyes darted from the full plates to the tables, then to search for exits and guards, then person to person, as Kayarr's were fixed on the Sprite now making her way toward them. Everyone here had a weapon. She prepared herself.

~~~~~~~~~~

Just as Natanamia was close enough to catch the look on Flyrra's face and sense her rising emotions, the little girl went full feral. With lightning speed, she reached up and grabbed a piece of meat from a young boy's plate, knocking him off the bench in the process and hissing as she backed away, stuffing her mouth with the juicy tender meat the likes of which she'd never tasted. Several boys and a few girls began to tease her as she crouched and continued to hiss while trying to eat as fast as she could, to avoid having it stolen away.

At first, Kayarr wasn't sure what was happening as his attention darted from Natanamia back to the child. Time seemed to stand still and as the Warrior understood he had but a heartbeat to prevent a catastrophe, Crytcha stepped 'tween the little girl and the others, grabbing the child, lifting her to her face and staring at her huge black eyes. Flyrra struggled to look at the taunting children just o'er the Troll's shoulder, but could not get out of Crytcha's grasp, and furious, she locked gazes. In the span of a few breaths, Flyrra calmed down and buried her tiny face into Crytcha's stony chest. "No hurting," Crytcha emphasized as she held up one hand, presenting her wide back to the boys who had begun to hurl food and cups. Although the children took her statement one way, Kayarr knew 'twas the other way 'round, for Flyrra could have done much damage if not for the strange looking being who was but a child herself. Amazed, 'twas clear that the Troll seemed to understand the situation as well.

'Twas not exactly the way Kayarr had envisioned their first day. Crytcha refused to release Flyrra and they all walked out after calming down the other children. "I apologize for my daughter. 'Twas a misunderstanding," stated Kayarr to them, with a dumbfounded Natanamia at his side. A total of seven children had participated in the 'assault', which they understandably thought was a defensive action on their parts, and they all marched to the Commander's office following Kayarr, Natanamia, and Crytcha, still holding tightly to the silver haired girl who'd wrapped her scrawny arms and legs around the giant as best she could. In this position, Flyrra looked like a rag doll that Crytcha was embracing.

~~~~~ THE OFFICE OF THE BATTLE COMMANDER ~~~~~

"'Tis no way for future Warriors to behave. Those who will wield much power, must show restraint and integrity."

One of the boys blurted forth, "We were defending each other. We knew not about her upbringing. Besides, we saw no weapon, no evidence of Magic, only her ill manners." When the boy noted Darque's stern expression, he dropped his gaze. "My apologies, Battle Commander."

Darque bit back her retort, speaking slowly, "I understand. Still, you are lucky to be alive. Magic bearers are themselves weapons, and they are everywhere. Many are now allies but many are not. 'Twould be wise to distinguish such afore you jump to conclusions, for although all of you are doing well in your training, fighting a Magic bearer takes special prowess and true knowledge of what you face."

Another boy stepped forward from the others and boldly asked, "But how can we fight that which we do not understand or see? 'Twould be good to have a demonstration of such power, to prove 'tis so."

Darque was a skilled Warrior, not a particularly patient woman, but Ragnyrr was teaching her effective communication that did not include swinging sword, the gritty Commander's preferred method of solving an argument. The Third Prince, in 'Bond with her Third Fighter, Kydra, was becoming quite the diplomatic negotiator, and was the epitome of patience. She held her tongue and said that which she felt should be said, rather than what she wanted to say, which she'd save for the next time, if there was a next time. "Your curiosity shall be provoked more and more in the winters to come, with exposure to many more Races. But these are allies and guests, and such 'proving' could be seen as provocation. Things could turn ugly. Surely 'twas not your intent to cause harm or to insult?" When the boy dropped his gaze sheepishly while offering up an apology, she continued, "But you may be correct in that it may benefit us all to learn first-hand of what others are capable and not rely on rumor and myth to improve our tactics, as fear is poor fuel for Battle Lust. Mayhap we shall have a special class. I will speak to Master Tyrza. In the meantime, I believe Flyrra deserves an apology for your behavior, and Flyrra should reciprocate."

Crytcha still had a grip on the thin child and dipped her head to whisper something to her. After apparently not getting the answer she was seeking, she firmly repeated. Shortly, she relaxed her grip and after facing the group of children directly for the first time, Flyrra turned to look for Kayarr. They hadn't really gotten a good look at the child afore. Some of them backed up a pace, all of them startled, which none would admit in the presence of the Battle Commander. After all, 'twas just a little girl who hardly had any meat on her bones, who wouldn't even look them in the eye. Mayhap 'twas why she'd stolen the food. But there was something about her which made them all uncomfortable.

Trying to be brave, the eldest boy stepped closer and held out his hand. Flyrra stared at it, not knowing what to do. Kayarr leaned o'er to whisper in her ear and holding her shoulder she gripped the boy's forearm with a surprisingly strong hold for such a scrawny child. Keeping her head down, she stated mechanically, "I'm sorry. 'Twas wrong of me to take your food. I knew not your customs. 'Twill not happen again."

Her apology was oddly unemotional, but the boy was sincere in his reply. "Well, 'twas not my food, but thank you. I am sorry we had such a bad beginning. Please return and allow us to start o'er."

Kayarr recognized she'd reached her limit and if he didn't help her get out of this situation soon, someone would get hurt. He squeezed Flyrra's shoulder in support, but the others saw it as a command, for Flyrra immediately turned and flew into his grasp. He picked her up and held her tight as she buried her face in his shoulder.

All she had to do… but no. She would not cause trouble for Kayarr. These were his people. Trying to regain her control, she kept her eyes closed, the others viewing her behavior as a display of fear and timidity.

Darque dismissed the children, sending them back to the mess hall with cleanup duty their penalty, but asked Kayarr, Natanamia, Crytcha, and Flyrra, to stay a moment. Once they were alone, without mincing words she asked, "What is her forte Magic?"

Kayarr winced and replied, "Her stare. She can discern deceit. Make people uncomfortable, force them to tell the truth."

Darque could also discern deceit, not the same way in which did Flyrra, but she knew the Warrior was not telling the whole truth. Her eyes unreadable, she asked, "And?"

Kayarr winced again. He'd hoped not to go there so quickly. He wasn't certain how 'twould be taken, and since Flyrra had been raised the way she was 'twould take time for her to learn restraint. If she ever did. Her Magic had helped her to survive. Would it now cause them to be ostracized? He'd returned to the woman of his dreams, but Flyrra knew not her own blood and trusted only him. He made his decision. He'd leave with Flyrra if she was not welcome. 'Twas clear to him now that the child needed him and he could not fail her again, nor could he leave her here with just anyone. Even Natanamia, who now stood beside Crytcha, did not fully understand her niece's Magic, for she'd never laid eyes upon her afore this morning.

The Battle Commander cleared her throat, reminding him that she was waiting for a full disclosure of the child's abilities.

She was thought to be a half-breed Sprite and Elf, so she carried their Magics. She considered what she already knew, and about what had just happened. Apparently, she could force someone to speak truth when she stared at them, but what else? Suddenly, she understood and was appalled. Angrily, she addressed the child, her face still buried in Kayarr's shoulder. "What did the Black call you? By what name were you known in the Hoard?"

After a few heartbeats, a soft, miserable, muffled voice answered, "Medusa."

Darque stood up fast, slamming her fists upon the desk, her eyes fixed upon the Warrior as if he held their very destruction in his arms. Although not much taller than most of the older children at the Keep, the Battle Commander had a presence that made everyone aware of her power. 'Twas as if he'd been pushed, yet stepping back a pace, he did not look away. Kayarr felt horrible for Flyrra. She'd revealed this name to him even afore he'd helped her escape the cage in the caves of the Pitch. He felt guilty that he'd not been paying more attention when they entered the mess hall, for he was distracted. He should have done more to prevent the confrontation, he should have expected her reaction and been prepared. "She is just a child," he began with a frown.

Her eyes a'Flame, Darque spit forth, "She is a child with unspeakable power and no social skills!" Kayarr broke contact and dropped his gaze to the floor, knowing the Commander was correct in her assessment, and as Darque reined in her anger, she furrowed her brows and continued. But even afore she asked, she knew. "Of what exactly, is she capable?"

Kayarr chose full disclosure o'er attempting to cover for the child, hoping for a solution that did not include them leaving the Keep. He'd be hard pressed to keep Flyrra safe outside of the Resistance and if Darque rejected her, he knew of no others who would accept the threat of her presence amongst them, even if any others still existed. Catching the Battle Commander's gaze once more, he replied, "She is as strong or stronger, than I, but cannot sustain such once fatigued, and therefore is not big enough to defend herself for long. And... she can force others to do things they would not otherwise do." He saw the look upon Darque's face and cleared his throat afore he continued. "She can make her enemies commit suicide or kill each other. 'Tis how she survived in the Hoard. She discovered this Gift early in her life. Although she must maintain eye contact, 'tis not a weapon to be taken lightly, nor used only against humans. She's defended herself against animal and Dragon attacks, as well."

Darque considered his explanation. Without control, Flyrra could cause much injury and even death. But she'd been much injured and was only defending herself. Would she use her Gift to 'defend' Kayarr? Would she use it on impulse, in anger, misunderstandings, arguments, just to get what she wanted? She sighed. "I cannot allow her to hurt others," she began. But Kayarr and Natanamia chimed in together in protest, coming shoulder to shoulder in defense of the little girl who still hadn't looked up, keeping her face pressed firmly against the Warrior's leather chest pad. "I will leave with her, if she's not allowed to stay." Turning their gazes to each other, their mirrored sentiments surprised them.

Darque sat down and held up her hand for silence afore continuing her thoughts. "By the Flame, you two, don't be ridiculous. That was not my intention. But we must have a plan to teach her restraint!" She could sense that the child had spent much time hooded for the protection of those around her, but 'twas a totally impractical solution here. She chewed her bottom lip for a moment, thinking. "I understand that most Magic bearers have a mentor early in their lives, to teach them how to use their Magic appropriately. Since this is apparently a Magic that isn't commonplace, I am asking for your suggestions."

Natanamia looked at the child then back to Darque with a frown. There was more to her niece than they thought. Elven and Sprite surely, but was there something else? Choosing to keep such thoughts to herself, she began, "Strictly speaking, 'tis not unheard of, but history mentions such a talent being rare amongst the Magic bearers, even in Ancient times." Seeking to lessen the impact of her abilities, she continued, "Mayhap she has just used a common Magic taken to the extreme in her extreme situation. She may have altered our ability to discern deception and combined it with our natural affinity for nature. But no Magic bearer has attempted to force his will upon another to such a degree..." She faltered as she realized that 'twas exactly what the Sorcerer and the Black were doing. Forcing their will upon others to kill. She grimaced and had to admit, "I know not. She is young, her Magic may alter as she grows, but usually such just becomes stronger."

Darque nodded her head for 'twas so. Magic had limits, but no one was certain where they were. And every Magic bearer was different. Just as every human was different, their talents and limits depending on the decisions they made and what they valued, as much as their genes. What it all came down to was, "Can she be taught to appreciate life other than her own and yours? Can she be trusted to live amongst those here?"

Finally, Flyrra turned her head and stared directly at Darque for a moment, afore dropping her gaze. 'Twas something she rarely did and thus far only with Kayarr, who'd proven he could tolerate such. It seemed to help her make a decision. Her musical voice very soft, she stated, "Please don't send me away. Kayarr has taught me there is a difference 'tween good and bad. I want to be a Warrior too. I can fight the Evil One. I know him well. I hate him."

Darque's heart broke with the anguish she felt coming from everyone in the room. But she also felt the truth. The little girl had been through so much and just wanted a chance. The Resistance was all about chances to survive, to fight evil. What she needed was a way to teach the child while keeping those around her safe. As an idea took shape, she addressed Crytcha. "Just what happened in the mess hall?"

Crytcha stepped forward from where she'd been standing against the far wall. Her huge blocky hands held fingertip to fingertip in front of her chest, she stated, "Little one felt attacked. She wanted to sting them, like angry bee. Misunderstanding. Needing calm."

"So, you just stepped into the stream of Flame?"

As if 'twas nothing, she shrugged her shoulders and with her hands now palms upward, replied. "Me, she cannot sting."

Kayarr set Flyrra on her feet again while Darque sat back in her chair, one finger o'er her lush lips as she beamed in excitement. Catching Natan's attention, she nodded her head and with Kayarr looking bewildered, the Elf began to understand what was on Darque's mind. 'Twas brilliant. Crytcha had been with them since the Domes were completed, remaining a loner for she was so different from the others. No matter how hard some of them tried, Crytcha simply felt left out because of her size and appearance. The only member of the Borkahn to inhabit the Keep, she could not go home 'til her father sent for her and that would probably be many winters to come, if ever. Now came Flyrra, who, after this incident, would likely have a difficult time with acceptance despite Darque's hopes. However, of all those around her, including her own aunt and the Warrior whom she'd clearly claimed as her father, Crytcha was the only one to whom she could cause no harm for although they were not a Magic bearing Race, Magic had little to no effect upon the Borkahn. If they would both agree, 'twould be the perfect plan.

"Crytcha, Flyrra, I am assigning you to each other's care and company. This is a battle exercise. Flyrra, when you are not with Crytcha, you are to remain in your quarters. You must always have Crytcha with you wherever you go, even when you're with Kayarr and/or Natanamia." She looked to the Warrior and the Sprite who both nodded in affirmation. They understood how important this was. If Flyrra failed, there was nothing else to be done. They were on board with anything that would keep her safe with the Resistance. Turning her attention back to the children, she continued, "You will learn how to plan your life around a partner, how to trust a partner, how to cover your partner, and how to be patient when you want something for which you have to wait upon your partner." Both girls were still quite young, even though Crytcha towered o'er everyone in the room, and they both were excited at the 'assignment'. Darque was reminded that her assignment was pretty much how life became for the 'Bonded. "I'll discuss this with Master Tyrza so that she can include it in your studies. And Flyrra?"

"Yessum?" Kayarr whispered in her ear again, telling her the proper salute for the Commander, and she immediately rephrased, making both the Warrior and the Commander smile. "Yes Sir?"

Darque leaned forward and laced her fingers together. "I want to emphasize that this is an assignment, not real war. You must promise not to harm anyone here, no matter how upset you are. If you become angry or fearful, let Crytcha help you as she did today. Remember where you are now. Remember you no longer live in constant danger, needing to defend yourself. We are different, and we have different ways of doing things, different expectations. If something happens, we all need to learn from the experience. But if you cause harm, it cannot be reversed. That one will never trust you again. That is not how a Warrior behaves. Do you promise?"

Her mother had been unaffected and Flyrra had long ago decided 'twas in their familial blood, so she had no doubt her aunt could hold her own against her gaze. But Kayarr had been the first Human she could look at with any control and not cause inadvertent harm. Now came Crytcha, whom she'd tried to harm and could not. 'Twas a wonderful freedom she'd experienced. Flyrra's eyes seemed to shine a bit more than they had but with her, 'twas difficult to tell. She nodded her acceptance of the terms. 'Twas not a difficult decision, she didn't mean any harm to these people, 'twas the unintentional slip that she feared. And she hadn't shown Kayarr her full power. She need not have eye contact nor one-on-one attention. She merely required her vision. If she could see them, she had complete control of them. Not even the Black was aware of the full extent of her Magic. Learn restraint? She'd learned timing, appropriate location, secrecy, and endurance, to restrain herself surrounded by the worst of the worst. What she needed to learn was trust.

As they turned to leave, she peeked o'er her shoulder and smiled shyly at the Commander afore she hurried to catch onto Crytcha's huge hand, engulfing hers near to her elbow. The little girl had to turn her head straight up to see her new friend's face, but everyone could feel the happiness emanating from the pair. As they left the area, Darque's acute hearing picked up Flyrra's whispered comments to her companions, "'Twas amazing. When I looked at her, she flinched not." 'Twas sad in a bizarre way. What the child was forced to do to survive, made Darque very angry. She hoped her little social experiment worked, for she could think of no other option.

As she returned her attention to her paperwork, she had a stray thought. With all the events crowding the morning, she'd near forgotten one very important bit of intel. Flyrra grew up in the Lair of the Black. A Lair they'd not been able to locate since joining the Highlands in this war.

CHAPTER NINE

The Intel Spell

After barely escaping the tavern avoiding certain capture by the strangers, Brecca and Cassiopeia traveled non-stop back to the Fortress. The strangers intrigued both her superiors and she'd chewed her lip wishing she'd confirmed their identities afore she'd left. Feeling dejected and that her first mission was a failure, the slight smile of approval on Tamm's face relieved her fears. "You did well, Brecca. And the information about the upcoming revolt against the Kreegare is confirmed by intel from the other cities. We have begun full withdrawal even now. The strangers you met in Harsh will reveal their true intentions soon enough. Our first duty is to retrieve our own." She glanced to her Second. "My meeting with the winemaker is long o'erdue."

Cass called for Leis and Dyra, the pair having risen to the top of their brethren. Most of the Kreegare had no prior fighting training, being lost Elves of all backgrounds from the Wyrdritch. The Prince and his girlfriend, having joined just o'er a winter past, discovered they had great talent in their new lives, and trained hard. Attaining the ranks of Third Fighters, they worked as the Second's right hands and bodyguards to both their immediate superiors. Usually working in pairs due to their unusual Dance technique, the newest Kreegaren had proven to be swift, vicious, and skilled, provided with much experience o'er the past few moons as their world became more and more dangerous.

~~~~~ MEANWHILE ~~~~~

Even though Regynn was not only a Warrior of the Dragon Clan but an accomplished Assassin knowledgeable in the art of making himself near an illusion to others, they'd had to obtain information quickly. And although they'd made every attempt to keep to themselves and not raise any alarms, 'twas a small city with a superstitious people. Sydrayyah had remained outside the city limits, hiding in the caves and rocky formations of the sparse land, and when they'd heard the rumors spark, Regynn knew 'twould not be long afore they'd be taken into custody. 'Twas only the little boy's subtle warning provided at breakfast, that gave them sufficient time to escape. Regynn shook his head. The 'little boy', whom Cathay had determined early on was really a little girl in disguise, had been most attentive to their needs, and the warning was not offered consciously. If he'd not already been aware of the girl's subterfuge, watching her without her knowledge, he might have missed the fact that although very young, her signature techniques identified her as Kreegaren. He had to admire her skills to attain such a position and wondered how she'd come by such, as she was most surely not born of the Assassin's Caste and was not Elven.

Nonetheless, the girl's story mattered not at this time. 'Twas Regynn's responsibility to keep everyone safe, and after fleeing Harsh just o'er a sennight past, he'd been reluctant to carry on the mission with his entourage, seriously considering doing so alone from here on out. Cathay and the twins reminded him that if they didn't continue their journey soon, 'twould matter not to which city they went, the dangers would only increase with time, as rumors in the Rol Dan traveled faster than the fastest horse. His thoughts strayed back to the girl, whom he'd attempted to contact, but she'd disappeared just after the 'warning' and prior to his chance to question her privately. 'Twas the wisest move to leave rather than make the effort to locate her.

He made his decision. Speaking to Sydrayyah, he laid out his plan. *"I can think of no better strategy than to begin in the nearest city and move from there. We have a good chance of finding an Assassin at any one of them. All we need is one good contact."* He could feel her disappointment weighed as heavy as did his, in their loss of the opportunity to find such a contact with the little girl at the tavern. But 'twas all water under the bridge now.

"I have coordinates in my mind," she'd Replied with confidence when Regynn Shared his memories of the other cities, and the most likely places to start.

Sydrayyah then made her decision. Altering their course from the location Regynn had given her, she chose another. Regynn didn't know everything about the Rol Dan, and neither did Cathay. But there was one who was certain to help them find the Kreegare quickly and with the least amount of danger. She chose to go as directly to the source as possible. Speaking to the Elven brothers, she Asked, *"Do you recall the winemaker?"*

Syd understood them as they immediately thought of Orayalyn, one of the lost Elves from their childhood. Astonished, the boys accepted the coordinates, Drew their energy, and disappeared a fraction of a candle drip after Syd took wing.

~~~~~ SOMEWHERE IN THE DARDEN REGION
OF SOUTH BYNDYNN FOREST ~~~~~

The Sorcerer held mixed emotions since hearing that the Destroyer was being sent to retrieve the child. Flyrra had proven difficult to kill but without the assistance of the Eagle Warrior she'd be out of his hair and not causing him all this trouble, for the Pitch Elves should have finished her. They failed. Although, 'twas not his ass in the sling this time, 'twas the Destroyer's, and since he himself had no desire to fetch Flyrra out of the midst of the Resistance where she'd apparently found refuge, the Elf could do his best. With any luck, he too would fail and 'twould make his own position more secure.

The Destroyer had always been presumptuous in his abilities. Who cared that he'd created the Pitch, his evil permeating through their beings, perverting their Magic to the point they were now considered a different Race? How did that rank above his own services to the Black, gaining the Destroyer the position of Second in Command instead of he, himself? But the Destroyer was just a self-hating Elf who'd mangled his own vocal cords to hide the unique and musical quality. He shared not the blood of the Fay, and although all Magic bearers could perform the same Magics, some were more adept at certain styles and types as the Races had their differing strengths and talents, therefore when the Destroyer pulled a Shift 'twas rather disjointed. The Sorcerer sneered. Thinking back to when he'd openly prowled the halls of Drekinn as a spy, he took great pride in his own ability to pull a decent Shift, even though his Magic was oft' times boosted by the Evil One himself to ensure success. But the Black was so angry with his Second in Command, there'd be no assistance forthcoming for him during this mission. If mission, there was.

They'd suspected Flyrra survived after the Pitch lost her, and then when the big Warrior escaped as well, they deduced the two had joined forces. The Human couldn't possibly know what he was handling, or he'd run in terror. Yet no matter how much they'd paid, no matter how many they'd tortured, there'd been no trace of either of them since their escape.

The Sorcerer still believed the Lairs had not been destroyed and 'twas some unknown Magic making them invisible, but he'd been unable to prove his theory. So, they'd waited these past many moons for the child to send her signal. Once she did, they would know exactly where she was and could retrieve her with ease. The Lairs survived. She was there. Her return was inevitable.

~~~~~ NATANAMIA'S QUARTERS ~~~~~

Kayarr stood at the entry and glanced longingly inside, just o'er Natanamia's shoulder. Holding onto Flyrra's hand, he knelt beside her. "The Warrior's Barracks is no place for you, little one."

She pouted. "As if I haven't seen it all?"

Kayarr dropped his gaze to the floor and tried not to laugh. Or cry. Either emotion would be an appropriate response to her precocious statement. She hadn't seen HIS all, and along with that not being an option in his or Natan's mind, there would be little time to spare for the child in the next few sennights and 'twas decided he would live in the Barracks with the other single Warriors while he was learning his way around. "You'll stay here with your Aunt Natanamia. We both have new worlds to explore and lessons to learn, and I expect you to honor your commitment to the Battle Commander. I'll visit as often as I can. You have but to call for me and I will come." Handing her o'er to the beautiful Sprite Captain, he couldn't believe 'twas so difficult. He'd been in many a battle but walking away from those two was the hardest thing he'd ever done. Natan and Flyrra stood forlornly silent and motionless, watching his back 'til he disappeared down the passage.

~~~~~ A DESERTED CORRIDOR OF THE KEEP ~~~~~

Fryya was holding Walkyr tightly to keep him from banging his head against the stone floor. His Visions were getting worse and since they were nearly the same size, she struggled to protect him from harm. Just afore this one hit, they'd been discussing her plan to get the adults to allow them to join the Brotherhood. This Vision only made her more desperate to fulfill that quest and take the Oath. As soon as 'twas o'er she'd drag him to the clinic.

But then he panted, "Warrior Regynn and Cathay!"

Startled, she asked, "Are they safe? Did they make it to the Rol Dan? What do you See?"

"The Commander of the Ancients. Many lost ones. Regynn knows not what they face. 'Twill be o'er afore 'tis begun."

"What Commander? What lost ones? Just what are they facing?" she asked, nose wrinkled in befuddlement.

In his delirium he mumbled, "A fight the Warrior should not win." Perplexed he continued, but, "Escape by pruning shears," was all he managed to say afore he slipped past consciousness. 'Twould be a while afore she could wake him. At least 'twas good news. Or it seemed to be good news. As she pondered the meaning of this Vision, for 'twas mystifying, she sat with his head in her lap and finger combed his shoulder length straight brown hair while she leaned back against the wall, closed her eyes, and quickly fell asleep. 'Twould be a very long day.

<center>~~~~~ DARQUE'S OFFICE ~~~~~</center>

Kayarr stood behind Flyrra as she sat in the middle of the desk in front of the Battle Commander. For near a mark, Darque sat with her forearms crossed and resting on the desk, facing the cross-legged little girl. Both had furrowed brows, both chewed the inside of their cheeks as the lengthening silence filled the office.

Flyrra broke that silence with her melodic voice as she repeated her earlier answers to Darque's questions. "I am sorry. I cannot think of a single moment outside the Lair. We traveled frequently but I was always hooded." She stared at her hands in her lap and with intense sadness mixed with anger, continued, "I once saw the sunlight reflecting off the trees outside the Lair, but 'twas for just an instant afore I was knocked unconscious. I was caught off-guard. I never let that happen again."

The child was so upset that she could not help more, that Darque tried to comfort her. "I am sure if you had any recollection of the area, 'twould not be of much benefit, for from what you do recall, 'tis obvious the Lair is in caverns in a forested region. As we suspected. And that could be anywhere. Do not fret, and do not feel persecuted, for you must understand that we had to ask."

"I understand. 'Tis what a Warrior does." Flyrra looked up and meeting Darque's gaze, she forgave her the increased harshness of the interview as both the Battle Commander and Kayarr shared their increasing frustrations. They'd had high hopes, and those hopes were now dashed.

Darque sat back, a smile upon her face. The tension in the room slowly dissipated, as did the headache. Flyrra had thought 'twas the result of the intensity of the emotions in the room for the past mark and that seemed likely, as the pain was near gone now. Hitting her like a flash of lightning when first she was questioned about the Black's Lair, with her unique facial features she was able to hide the discomfort so as not to appear to be avoiding the questions. She'd honestly tried to help and was extremely disappointed in herself, her expression reflecting the mix of physical and emotional discomfort.

Kayarr gathered the little girl to his arms and turned about, ready to leave. Darque squinted as she caught the look on Flyrra's face. Something wasn't quite right. Thinking she understood, she nodded to the little girl hanging o'er the Warrior's shoulder and said, "Flyrra, do not concern yourself with this any further, for you have done all I could ask. I consider this matter closed. You are a member of the Resistance now. I want no nightmares from bad memories dredged this day. You are not only safe here, you are much loved."

Flyrra had to swallow hard as she nodded her acceptance of the Battle Commander's words. 'Twas no love in her early winters, save the handful of times she'd seen her real mother. Now she was surrounded by the emotion. She'd do anything to show her love in return. How she'd wished she could help them find the Black's Lair. The thought made her cringe as Kayarr carried her out the doorway, but the sudden flash of pain was gone as quickly as it came.

~~~~~ THE LAIR OF THE BLACK ~~~~~

'Twas triggered, the Spell broken. Flyrra had sent out her Call. After all these many moons they had a Link to locate the child. The Black swaggered through the caverns toward the torture chambers, where he knew he'd find his Second in Command. The Elf could locate her now by using the Link 'tween them. Sneering, he knew his necromancer believed the Lairs of the Resistance still existed, but even this was not proof. All this proved was that the girl was still alive and had been questioned about this very location.

He furrowed his brow ridges and stopped mid-stride. Wrinkling up one nostril, he wished he'd thought of this Spell. 'Twas the work of the Sorcerer and Linked the Black and the Destroyer to the girl child. The necromancer had wanted to include himself, but he was not to be so trusted. The Sorcerer had failed him too many times. Nevertheless, he thought as he continued to his destination, two things were very clear at this moment. One, the Spell was brilliant, and two, why had not the Destroyer come to him already with the knowledge it had been triggered? 'Twas fear and weakness he sensed during their discussion of this mission to retrieve the mixed-blood. Could he trust no one? Did he have to do everything himself? Curling his upper lip in disgust, he hurried onward.

CHAPTER TEN

Commander Of The Ancients

"HOLD!" Orayalyn roared, turning his head swiftly to catch the eyes of all who had so abruptly invaded his peaceful existence. His back was bent from long marks gardening throughout a lengthy lifespan, but he stood courageously as tall as was possible in the middle of five Assassins on one side of him and two Elves, two Humans, and one very large green Dragon on the other, risking his own life to prevent the clash. His long, thin, elderly arms reaching out to either side with one palm held outward and still grasping his pruning shears in the other, he glared at the entire entourage of all those recently arrived and the authority which emanated forth was such that everyone suddenly stopped in utter shock. 'Twas not the only shock of the past few moments, but 'twas the most productive.

This entire cast of characters had all unexpectedly appeared at his home to fetch him to safety within a heartbeat of each other, and drawing weapons all 'round, he could tell 'twould be much blood shed for no reason. He'd already registered Leis, Dyra, and Cassiopeia as familiar faces and 'twas clear he was the one everyone was trying to protect. Brandishing his pruning shears, he stated firmly and eloquently, "I may be old, but as yet I am not blind, as are you, apparently. Look about! I am in no danger excepting that which could occur from you fighting each other! Stop. Now." He nodded toward Leis and Dyra who slowly rolled back their hoods. Although no one put down their weapons, neither did they move, all cautiously eyeing those 'round them.

With hearts still racing at the startling confrontation, Leis and Dyra grinned in sheer delight at the twin Elven Princes and signing the all-clear to the rest of the Assassins, 'Rann and

'Ragg near leaped into the arms of their elder brother. Hugging and crying tears of joy, for they'd thought never to see each other again, Tamm abruptly widened her eyes as she recognized Cathay and Sydrayyah. As they all chattered excitedly, Regynn stood alone and bewildered. It seemed everyone knew someone, but thinking him dead ages past, they'd not yet come to the realization of just who he was. Thus far. Still, they'd need to know soon and with that in mind, he asked, "Is there any real purpose to my presence here?" He gazed curiously at his mate as she greeted Tamm like a sister, afore he continued dryly but without any animosity, "'Twould seem you could have accomplished this entire mission on your own."

~~~~~ LATER ~~~~~

Tamm was pensive as everyone crowded inside Orayalyn's living area. She now recognized her former Human comrade but held conflicting emotions about the fact that he was still alive. O'er fifty winters past she'd sent the remaining Human associated with the Kreegare after him. That one had returned home triumphant, although he'd Passed to natural causes less than a winter later. Apparently, he'd failed and now thinking back, she had known the truth. She understood that she'd purposely ignored the obvious simply because she'd liked Regynn and hadn't really wanted him to die. So, she'd declared the mission successful, fulfilling her duty, subconsciously hoping Regynn was alive and well all these many winters.

Brecca had come along to learn (as well as the fact that Tamm had taken the child under her wing) and recognizing Regynn and Cathay, without interrupting, she'd mentally added her information to the narrative.

Tamm knew Cathay from Tyranny, having helped her escape from the evil Warlord Takes. "How did you think he'd died?" she questioned sarcastically while shrugging her shoulders as if 'twas nothing to take out a Warlord in the Rol Dan. 'Twas o'er twenty winters past, and she allowed her mind to drift back. She'd personally negotiated the bodyguard contract for Cathay, befriending the tiny woman with the heart melting smile and honest opinions and learned why Regynn had betrayed his Caste. The story of her love for Regynn along with her faith that he yet lived, gave Tamm reason to help her escape the abusive relationship. Recruiting their mutual Dragon friend, Sydrayyah, they'd hustled Cathay out of Tyranny after Takes somehow fell off the ramparts and drowned in his own moat (although he was a fine swimmer like his childhood friend, Regynn). The disproportionate damage to his body had been officially recorded as due to the fall. Sydrayyah flew Cathay safely 'cross the Rol Dan and the Dragon's Tears after which she'd retreated back to her den in the cold region past the wastelands, known as the Sakyn Forest, the region in which the Kreegaren Fortress was even now being completed, leaving Cathay to her own wiles. 'Twas an extremely dangerous mission but if Regynn was still alive, Cathay would find him. She'd hoped they were happy. Now she saw that they were. Tamm found herself wishing she had time to learn of the pair's adventures through those winters. She had few Human friends. Even now, Regynn and Cathay were at the top of the list.

Tamm returned her attention to the others. She recognized not, the twin Elves, for they'd obviously been birthed after she'd left the Wyrdritch. But Cassiopeia did, and confirmed they were the Royal Princes Gylrann and Gylragg, pointing to each in turn while naming them. The twins laughed as they pointed to each other, indicating she had them mixed up, and their mirth lightened the mood. Working her way around the small space, she now stood shoulder to shoulder with Regynn. "You vouch for these Elves?" she questioned quietly.

"That I do, Tamm," he replied without hesitation, appreciative of her acceptance and trust in him after all this time, even though he could sense a wariness.

She simply nodded her head, keeping her eyes upon his, searching his soul for any hidden untruths or betrayal. Apparently she found none, as she broke the contact and faced the groups, her voice soft but commanding, gaining instant silence and attention. "We came here to fetch Orayalyn. You came here, to find me. I deem your mission a success, however, ours has just begun. With the revelation of the upcoming revolt against the Kreegare, we need all vacate this area afore any other decisions are made. We leave for the Fortress without delay."

Given less than a quarter mark to prepare himself, Orayalyn looked about his home and with a leather bag, carefully picked out a few of his most treasured items, all of his own creation. And then as an afterthought he ran into the vineyard, quickly returning with dirty hands, a full bag, and a smile upon his face. After all, who knew what was available where they were going?

Regynn, Cathay, and Orayalyn then mounted Sydrayyah, while Brecca stepped aside with the Elven Assassins. Sydrayyah took the coordinates provided by Tamm afore the Kreegaren entourage disappeared.

~~~~~~~~~~

Following as swiftly as she could through the timefold nonstop, it still took the three of them near a sennight to get to the Fortress, several marks behind the Elves. 'Twas an imposing sight that met their gaze against the backdrop of ice capped peaks and monstrous evergreen trees, some larger than the Dragon's Den itself, and spread out o'er many leagues. They'd traveled far beyond a frozen wasteland of dry, cavernous mountains with minimal organics, to discover the vast old growth region in the most distant boundaries of the Rol Dan known as the Sakyn Forest. The Fortress was built into the solid rock of one of the mountains, o'er a running waterfall with a river that split beneath the main Ward. One of the massive trees grew up in the middle slightly off to one side 'tween the split rivers, with two more at the twin towers, a part of the tower living space themselves. 'Twas quite impressive and equally impenetrable. No one could reach the Fortress given normal means, and even for a Dragon to perch upon the walls was dangerous by its design, leaving only safe landing and perch space for one of the mighty beings. There was no road, no climbing path, no way to navigate the rivers up the falls and no way to repel to or from the Fortress walls, let alone the fact that 'twas distant to the wastelands providing little hope of anything sustaining life beyond. Tamm was rightfully proud of what they'd accomplished. The others were impressed by the ready organics she'd found in this land.

THE FOLLOWING DAWN
~~~~~ THE GUEST QUARTERS IN THE TOWER
OF THE KREEGAREN FORTRESS ~~~~~

</div>

The Magic bearers had to sleep several marks straight and then stuff themselves to regain the energies lost to their traveling. Once satiated, Gylrann spoke with speculation. "I swear I'm correct. Leis must know this too, yet it appears he's said not a word. Mayhap he felt he had to hide this knowledge for his and Dyra's safety."

Facing the Elven Prince while Sharing the conversation in Link with his 'Bond, Regynn listened quietly as 'Ragg continued their thoughts. "Agreed. Leisalarr was always a history buff. He would've recognized her. I am clueless as to why he would keep such knowledge to himself, unless 'twas for their own safety, or he was infiltrating for more intel."

In response to Regynn's question, Sydrayyah Answered, *"I have known her for many winters, and she is honorable to this day. We are in no danger from her past, although I know not what 'tis, for we shared an agreement that such would not be revealed or discussed."*

"Was such an agreement entered into as a pact?" Regynn asked.

Hesitantly came her Reply. *"No."*

"Then I believe 'tis time to have that long deferred discussion."

~~~~~ LATER ~~~~~

Racing through the stone hallways toward Tamm's office, Brecca was amazed at what had been completed since she'd arrived just o'er a winter past. And so many of the Kreegare were now based here, she was just as amazed that she'd rated her own room in the upper levels of one of the massive trees. Not only was she the youngest here, prior to the return of Regynn and Cathay, she was the only human.

After Regynn's disappearance, Tamm refused to accept another Human, though a few could have made it by their level of fighting skill. She'd thought long and hard whether to send another to take out Regynn, and shortly after she made the decision, she'd made the long journey to Tyranny where the Warlord Takes ruled, to do damage control, ending up negotiating a new contract. 'Twas a herald to Tamm's skills that she'd worked out the bodyguarding detail on his new mate after Regynn had disappeared. She and Sydrayyah befriended Cathay, and through the many winters following, she'd kept tabs on the female. Sydrayyah had taken up long term residence in the far distant mountains where their fortress was even now being completed, and Tamm requested the big Green help in her daring plan to assist Cathay, as Takes was a selfish, spoiled, hateful, vile, and odious Human and made everyone miserable. Even after nearly thirty winters, Cathay never gave up hope that Regynn lived, and although he'd know not her situation, he would still be in love with her. She could feel that truth even now. Their love remained strong throughout their many winters apart.

Brecca hated to be late to her training, but she could not wait to make report on what she'd heard less than a mark earlier. Eavesdropping on the newcomers, she'd not recognized the name by which they'd called Tamm but knew 'twas important by the emotions surrounding them all as 'twas spoken aloud. Sneaking away from her first class, she knocked on the massive door that stood floor to ceiling and heard Tamm's voice bid her enter. Pushing hard, she stepped inside near out of breath, her eyes widening at what she beheld. All eyes upon her now, there stood Tamm's personal Guard, Regynn, Cathay, Orayalyn, Gylrann, Gylragg, and the big green Dragon she'd come to know as Sydrayyah off to one side in her bubble of Allure, all facing the leader of the Kreegare and her Second in Command, with Leis and Dyra standing at their shoulders one step behind. Quietly, she slipped through the crowd and took her own place at Cassiopeia's left. As was everyone else, her hand rested upon her short sword as her eyes swept 'cross the room.

~~~~~~~~~~

Regynn stepped forth, stating without preamble, "We have no proof of this claim however, any doubts 'tween us would weaken our new-found alliance and should be cleared afore we go any further."

With Regynn's nod, Gylrann also stepped forth and without hesitation stated, "You are Tammra Dayo." At the name, every Elf in the room, apart from the Princes, stifled a gasp of disbelief. Leis and Dyra stood warily but said not a word. Brecca squinted as the name was repeated from earlier but kept her silence. Cassiopeia's eyes flicked warily from one to the other. Tamm's expression was clearly forced calm, her eyes burning... fear? Repugnance?

'Rann continued. "Mayhap the Draining of Humans has kept you alive and youthful all these centuries, yet 'tis clear you have avoided falling to the same fate as the Pitch. Such an ability would be helpful to the Resistance and I believe 'twas how the Elves fought in the War of Chaos. Such knowledge has been buried and forgotten by most, but as a Prince of the realm I've had access to this and much more, and have long studied our history, as have we all." 'Rann and 'Ragg pointedly cast a quick glance to their elder brother, yet the expression on Leis's face revealed not his thoughts. Returning their attentions to the Kreegaren leader, 'Ragg stated, "There is no doubt of your identity in our minds. We see no reason for you to deny such."

Tamm's lip curled and her nostrils flared. Distastefully, and clearly avoiding casting her own gaze to Leisalarr, she plastered a smile to her lips and replied slowly and clearly, enunciating each word as if saying them left a nasty taste in her mouth. "You are mistaken. Tammra Dayo was a traitor to the Nation. She died imprisoned long afore the Last Holocaust. Long afore you were even born. She is dead."

Now Leisalarr shook off Dyraserrah's hand and stepped around to face his commander. "Tammra Dayo was no traitor. She did not die in the dungeons of Haven. She escaped and lived. And now I understand how 'twas done."

Tamm glared at her bodyguard. "What do you mean?"

Dyra now joined her boyfriend in support at his side as he continued. "The Dance techniques Tammra pioneered for the War of Chaos, allowed her to disappear from the holding cells, and from Haven itself." He shook his head. "Everyone knows Tammra Dayo was framed, yet she shouldered the burden of the ambush of King Lucien and his death, along with his sons, the Princes Typeth and Grygoth. 'Tis surmised 'twas because she felt she'd failed them and deserved such a fate." After a brief hesitation Leis spoke up again, with 'Rann, 'Ragg and even Cassiopeia in agreement. "Tammra Dayo was a heroine of our Nation, blindsided, used, and ultimately betrayed, but to us, she has not been forgotten." Tamm could not speak. She could not formulate her thoughts. She simply stared as Leis continued. "Jeeryd was the traitor. King Lucien's nephew. My own father. He was in league with the Black to steal the crown and Bryanna. Everyone knows this." Now catching her eyes and not letting go, he repeated, "My brothers have confirmed that Jeeryd is dead. You escaped. You lived. And 'tis time you return in glory to help the Nation once again."

She could no longer deny the truth. She nodded her acceptance of the facts. Licking her full lips, she asked, "You knew who I was all along?"

With a slight nod and a guilty grin, he answered, "I figured out the truth shortly after we met, afore we even left Harsh."

"Why then did you not say something?"

Leis's smile widened. "I was a tad more concerned about surviving and protecting Dyra at the time, than with admitting I knew who you were. We knew not how long we would be here, and we needed to blend in, not cause waves."

"'Twould have been a tsunami." Tamm relaxed as she admitted to the truth and to the many changes they'd endured o'er the past winter. Then she sat up straighter and questioned, "To whom do you owe your allegiance, Prince Leisalarr? Do you stay with the Kreegaren, or do you return to the Elven Nation?"

Leis and Dyra hesitated not in their combined response. "We stay." Then Leis stated, "Our place and our brethren are here. There's naught to which to return. Dyra is an orphan and I might as well be. My father meant nothing to me, my mother is one of the lost ones. I am not needed in the Royal lineage, I gave up my accession when Dyra and I made our vows as Assassins, and we will fight at your side wherever you lead. Our allegiance is to you and the Kreegare."

"'Tis good." Tamm's serious countenance returned quickly as she leaned forward on her desk. Waving at Cass, Leis, Dyra, and Brecca, as well as her Guard, she looked to the newcomers. "Yes. I am Tammra Dayo. I was the Commander of the forces of the Elven Nation during the War of Chaos. You need fear me not, nor the techniques I need teach you, for one does not become Pitch simply through Vampyrism. 'Twas a carefully orchestrated hoax along with much propaganda to turn us away from our own Magic, to weaken us after the war, making us easy fodder for the

Black. The entire Kreegare is proof of this, as is the Elven Nation itself, for we all descended from those who participated in that long-ago war, using my techniques and natural Elven Magic."

~~~~~~~~~~

O'er the next mark, Tammra (who now accepted them calling her by her given name) explained her history and laid out her plan. After her harrowing escape, knowing she'd be hunted as a traitor to the crown without the ability to prove her innocence, she'd managed to journey to the Rol Dan where she'd successfully infiltrated the Assassins Caste. Becoming much respected and sought after for her skills, she was able to hide in her adopted homeland. However, when shortly after the Last Holocaust she discovered a stranger accused of performing Magic, she suspected 'twas her brethren. Rescuing Cassiopeia and killing all the witnesses, they created an even higher level, the Kreegare, the most skilled of the Assassins Caste, into which they brought all the other 'lost' Elves arriving in this unforgiving land. Of course, when one can feed from the Life Force of another, near instantly forcing that one Past the Veil simply by touching skin to skin, one had to hide such an ability. 'Twas a walk in the meadow, given their chosen profession.

Tammra still had her doubts about allowing the outside world into their realm, but she did see the logic of training the newcomers. Therefore, o'er the next few moons, Regynn, Cathay, 'Rann, and 'Ragg would live with the Assassins and enter intensive training to incorporate the Kreegaren Dance techniques and fighting skills into their own abilities. Tammra Dayo's forces had learned to Dance with extreme precision to advance safely and to protect each other by using this partnering technique and long-distance Dance. Although Regynn had a head start on the fighting skills, strictly speaking Humans could not Dance. Wherein two Elves or Sprites could throw each other forward, passing and sharing energy and then throwing the other (a maneuver that caused Cathay to envision a fly fisherman in action), a Human partner could participate, traveling with and prolonging the distance and time achieved within their Elven partner's Dance by allowing the Dancer to Draw energy, equalizing that of the effort of the Dance itself. Creating the Allure of the Dance and beginning with skin to skin contact, the Elf would throw the Human forward, then follow, Draw energy, then throw the Human forward again, the Human creating the end organics needed for the Dance. The Magic bearer need only refrain from completely Draining their partners, pacing themselves, and the Dance could reach blurring speed. As long as the Human remained within the Allure trail (the 'fishing line') to return back to their partner for the Draw of energy, they were safe. 'Twas akin to racing down an elongated slide or through a portal. In this manner the partners would be able to travel great distances, with or without known organics at the end, as well as traveling into place for quick and efficient kills during a fight. A skilled Human partner (such as Brecca had become) would make the team almost as fast as two Elves or Sprites. And the twins should have no difficulty learning the techniques as they would use their twin sense to help guide them, picking up the maneuvers very quickly.

Although 'twas argued (with Regynn doing the majority of the arguing) that attempting to teach Cathay such methods would be too dangerous for her, she'd insisted she be allowed to try, and after much practice she was able to learn to travel with an Elven partner, point A to point B. 'Twould not be as fast or as efficient, but 'twas better than the alternative and provided her with some protection, as she need not be abandoned if rapidly vacating the area became the necessary option.

During this time Regynn never stopped trying to get Tammra to reenter the war, choosing sides, bringing the Kreegare aboard with the Resistance, a subject upon which she steadfastly refused to comment. 'Twould mean much change for the Elves and they were all trying to deal with much change already. The morphing of the old Protection Spell o'er the Wyrdritch (which failure sent them all to the Rol Dan) along with the Healing of said Spell, the death of King Jeeryd, the alliance of the Elves and the Sprites, as well as their alliances with the Resistance, swearing fealty to the newly crowned King Gabriel who was still considered a usurper throughout the rest of Kadoor, was all suddenly thrust into their laps. Cathay encouraged his efforts, for she knew the Elven Commander was listening, and the Warrior did not back down.

Regynn was no diplomat, but his opinions were intelligent, educated, and just plain common sense, and o'er the next several moons Tammra's stance of isolation for the Kreegare began to soften. Once a mighty warrior, always a mighty warrior. And she had her bodyguards putting in their opinions at every opportunity. But there was yet something in her past that she refused to discuss. Something that had caused her to accept the blame for the ambush. Something so horrible that she would be angered when anyone tried to get her to talk about it, and therefore, they stopped trying. 'Twas much to digest and giving Tammra some space seemed the best plan. Yet, Regynn knew they would have to return to the Keep soon. He dared not make any attempt to get word to Darque, as if caught, their tenuous alliance would crumble. Tammra would not be betrayed again, and she and her Kreegare would not return to the Elven Nation. They were a distinct force and they stood alone, and they'd not be commanded by other than Tammra. They'd made that perfectly clear. But his own mission could not be abandoned forever. Surely she knew this. Regynn felt she was testing his honesty.

MEANWHILE

EARLY WINTER

~~~~~ THE KEEP OF ST SWIFTYN'S ~~~~~

Kayarr visited Flyrra and Natanamia at the end of the day as often as he could, and Flyrra hugged Kayarr afore going to bed. But when she didn't let go as quickly as usual this night, the Warrior held on, gazing into her eyes in question. He was always interested in her progress, and she was making much. "What happened today, sunshine? Are you and Crytcha doing well?"

She giggled, and then her face got serious. "Yes, Crytcha helps me when I feel pressured." She stopped and changed subjects abruptly. "Most of the other children lost their parents in the Battle for the Dragon Clan."

Her socialization skills were improving as he hadn't thought she'd know anything about any of the others this soon. He waited a moment for her to continue and then prodded, "Yes, 'tis true."

"Most of us are orphans."

He liked that 'us' part. "And?"

"But they know who their parents were."

"Oh. I see. Well, you knew your mother."

"Yes, but she's dead."

"True."

Flyrra dropped her gaze for a heartbeat. "The others call their mothers, Ama. I called mine by her given name, 'twas all I knew. And now I have a new Ama. My aunt Natanamia is more mother to me than was Niamia."

He nodded his head in agreement with her statement, choosing not to say anything yet, for he knew not where this was going, nor what response she was seeking.

After a moment of intense thought, she continued. "They call their fathers, Aba. I didn't know my father. He might still be alive. But even so, he'd be of the Hoard. Niamia, I mean, my mother, told me I was the product of a rape."

The Warrior was not often caught off-guard by the girl's frank statements and made every effort to not display such sentiment when he was. She was bluntly honest in all things. "But she also told you how much she loved you, and she tried to protect you."

Flyrra looked down again and nodded silently, afore she went on with her thoughts. "First names seem cold. Show a lack of commitment."

Kayarr was almost amused and would have been had he not known Flyrra so well. She was trying to say something profound and he marveled at how much she'd learned in just a few sennights here. "I know what you mean. I called my own father, Aba. Many in Kadoor do the same. 'Tis a colloquialism of Common Tongue."

"It showed how much you loved him."

"Yes, I suppose."

She didn't say anything for a few more moments. Kayarr just held her on his lap as she stared off into space. Bedtime could wait. 'His little girl' had something on her mind. Natanamia glanced around the corner holding a glass of wine, and he held up one finger as a signal to give him a little longer. She ducked back out of sight.

Abruptly Flyrra faced him and asked, "May I call you, Aba?"

'Twas one of those times he was caught off-guard. Natanamia gasped around the corner. He blinked. Then he tried to swallow and found he had great difficulty doing so. Finally, he looked her straight in the inky depths of her eyes, and said quietly and with great emotion, "'Twould mean much to have you call me, Aba."

Immediately, Flyrra jumped down from Kayarr's lap, and holding onto his hand, she stated as though she'd just won a huge victory, "Then you can't leave! My Ama and my Aba must live together. That's how 'tis done."

They both heard the wine glass hit the floor and Natanamia came stepping out, her eyes gleaming with moisture, holding her hand o'er her mouth trying not to cry. She gathered herself, and lowering her hand, she stated, "I swear I didn't put her up to that, Kayarr, I'm sorry."

Kayarr had a wicked grin on his face, and with mock seriousness he stated, "But we must comply, the child is correct. Her Aba and her Ama, must live together. You've become her Ama, and seems she's chosen her Aba. Therefore, I believe we must do as she says. After all, we can't have her expectations dashed, can we?"

Licking his bottom lip, he gazed hungrily at the beautiful woman in front of him, the woman he'd wanted to pledge vows to and with, since that day they'd met in the tavern near two winters past.

Natan could scarcely get the words out of her mouth. "I thought you were leaving again."

No longer teasing, he replied, "Although I will likely need to retrieve the other Eagle Warriors soon, Darque is Battle Commander, so I've officially completed my original mission, and this morning she asked me to stay. Seems the Music Master position is open, and along with joining the Resistance, she wants me to help rekindle that profession. I was thinking about accepting her offer. I said I had to discuss it with you first."

Flyrra smiled triumphantly as she knew there would be a mating ceremony in the near future. Mayhap her new friend, Ardyth, would help her make something she could give them as a gift. Natan was always looking for baskets to use.

CHAPTER ELEVEN

The Daring Duo

"Ahhh Shayla, that son of ours. I know not what to do! How can I keep the boy safe, if he is forever 'losing' me?"

Lying naked upon the enormous feather mattress, a cotton sheet spread haphazardly 'cross their heated bodies, Shayla rolled o'er and swept the hair off Cayell's handsome face with her fingers. Snugging her knee tight 'tween his long legs, the course auburn hair rubbed against the smooth skin of her thigh warming her deep inside as she smiled at the reference to their Claim son and his favorite pastime, 'losing' his personal bodyguard and the man who'd Claimed him after Kallyr's death.

'Twas most unusual for a child's Claim parents not to be mated to each other but the war brought on many changes, and given Shayla's busy schedule as Clan Healer, the situation had been working fairly well. Except for the increasing frustration o'er the past few moons. Such was two-fold. Cayell and Walkyr were more often at the Keep now than at the Den, which meant he and Shayla saw less of each other, and 'twas Cayell's duty and privilege to keep the boy Seer safe at all times, meaning he was ever at Walkyr's side. But now that the Lairs were protected by the Spell Domes his duty had become slightly less intense. If the boy stayed inside the Dome, that is. Earlier this evening he was discovered outside upon the plateau with his best friend, constant companion, and main troublemaking instigator, Fryya. The gutsy girl with the long thick mop of curly copper hair had excused their excursion to 'Walkyr needing to clear his head from having so many Visions lately'.

They'd arrived at Drekinn Lair just the previous evening to move their belongings. The Keep would become their permanent residence per orders of the Battle Commander as 'twas her feeling that both Fryya and Walkyr needed to spend more time 'round the other children. Cayell wasn't too happy about this as he'd become rather attached to Shayla and although she was much older than he, having lived multiple lifespans with the help of the Blood Crystal, she didn't look, act, or feel so, and neither seemed to notice when they were together. Having been thrust into each other's lives since the beginning of the war they'd discovered much common ground, and not just their unique parentage of the Seer. Although as a Warrior, Cayell could not take on a formal Apprenticeship, he'd learned he had quite an interest and innate sense for concocting healing potions and diagnosing all manner of problems, and Shayla had been informally teaching him in their spare time. She'd appreciated his input, clear vision and deduction and he'd rapidly become her sounding board on the many complexities of her duties. Then to their surprise and delight, they'd become lovers amidst the many stresses.

Shayla and Cayell recognized that with their responsibilities they'd have little time together, but their hearts would not listen and as the moons passed, they each held tightly to the memories of their brief trysts, trying not to talk about their hopes and dreams for 'twas likely what they had now was all they would ever have, and 'twas cherished. Her duty was to remain at the Den as the resident Healer and his duty, both as a Warrior and as a father, was to remain with Walkyr. "I think Fryya is a bad influence. Mayhap 'twould be better to leave us here and to move Fryya to the Keep, alone."

Shayla laughed aloud for she felt the same but 'twas rooted in more selfish reasoning. She kissed his neck and sighed. "Although Walkyr has gathered near nine winters, he is wise and has seen much more than he should. I recall Darque and Storrm were as precocious as their little sister and even though they were not raised together, blood is telling in their deeds for Fryya is just as bold and brash." Shayla had raised Walkyr. 'Twas interesting to note, since Shayla and her brother, Grifynn, the former Battle Commander of the Dragon Clan, who, due to the Blood Elixir and the Blood Crystal of Shayla's creation, had lived since afore the Last Holocaust, she was not only generations older than her handsome young lover, she was aunt to Darque, Storrm, and Fryya. She had to think about that a moment. If Fryya and Walkyr ended up as more than just best friends, she'd be her aunt and her mother-by-vows. Since there was no blood relation 'tween her and her Claim son such was not an issue but 'twas somewhat amusing.

Cayell was gazing at her with a strange look in his eyes. Speculative. Deep. She furrowed her brows. "What?"

"The boy should take the Oath and join the Brotherhood," he announced unexpectedly.

"WHAT?" His statement came completely out of the blue and her response was a tad louder than she would have liked.

He gripped both her shoulders. "Seriously, Shayla, think about it. He is much sought after by the Hoard; his Gift is too powerful. His Sight too accurate. He needs more protection than I can give, especially now. If he were in the Brotherhood, I'd have help, he'd be surrounded."

"But he's just a little boy!"

Cayell hugged her to his tightly muscled chest. "He's a battle-hardened little boy. In the first winter of the war alone, he forced more men Past the Veil in battle than did I 'tween the time I took my Oath and the Black's return. And he did so with much skill, despite not having many winters of formal Training."

Hesitantly, she replied, "But that doesn't make him eligible."

"Yes. It does. We're in a declared war." Afore she could voice the protest in her heart, he continued, countering her thoughts. "Grifynn never declared but Darque did, and since she is now Battle Commander, that changes all the rules."

Raising up on one elbow, she asked, "What do you mean?"

"Going through formal Training is no longer a requirement. Going through a real battle and surviving, is."

"But he's the Clan Seer since Kallyr died. What of his position?"

"A good Seer can always See. As a Warrior, he can be permanently stationed with Darque, and if he was ever to take the 'Bond, he'd have the Link to relay his Sight from wherever they were. The Commander and the Clan would still have their Seer."

She was quiet for a few moments as she absorbed all he'd said. 'If he was ever to take the 'Bond' was an ominous statement which her lover seemed to be trying to hide in all the other information he'd given. Suspiciously, she asked, "What else does he require?"

Without hesitation, Cayell responded. "Parental permission, and a Warrior to sponsor him."

Now Shayla was becoming irritated. "And you are the Warrior going to be his sponsor, I suppose? You're his Claim father, you can do it all by yourself. What do you need from me?"

"I can be one or the other, not both."

"Oh. I see. This wasn't about you thinking he'd be safer. You want me to agree to provide parental permission."

Patiently, he replied, "Yes, 'tis my thinking that he'd have additional safety. But he wants to be a Warrior, Shayla. The way this war is going, none of us know if we will live or die afore the next dawn. 'Twould be a shame to disallow his dream, never to make his mark. And the Brotherhood was hard hit. We're in need. Besides, 'twould break up the 'daring duo' for a time, for although Fryya is just as skilled and has also met the battle requirement, she'd be hard-pressed to find both a sponsor and parental permission. Grifynn is but a spirit without say, and Aalanna would never agree." He frowned. He really wouldn't mind if both the children were inducted. But Fryya was not his concern. Walkyr was. And the boy had near begged him to get Shayla to agree so he could take the Oath. He loved that boy. He'd do anything for him. 'Twould be the answer to his own dream, having his son join and stand beside him. And being in the Brotherhood would not get him into more fights, as he'd already proven that nothing could keep him OUT of a fight. If he should Pass the Veil fighting, better he do so as a Warrior.

And then, there was the bonus of mayhap being able to spend more time with Walkyr's mother. He grinned wickedly and locked his legs around Shayla's knee, lacing his fingers with hers, dragging her closer so they were chest to chest, and kissed her deeply, passionately. Opening his eyes, he saw the desire in hers and felt his manhood rise again, pulsating in an ever-increasing pounding rhythm with the thought of what was to come. She grinned and licked her lips and his breath stuttered as he released her, urgently pushing her head down his strong body, her tongue cooling his heated skin as she wound her way ever closer, past his navel, tantalizingly swirling through the line of hair that ran down the middle of his muscular belly, lower and lower. And then with his gasp in her ears, she engulfed his rock-hard shaft and began once more, to pleasure her lover.

MEANWHILE

<div align="center">~~~~~ OFFICE OF THE BATTLE COMMANDER ~~~~~</div>

Storrm sat in the monstrous, hand-carved, wingback chair 'cross from Darque's huge oak work desk in the Commander's office in the Den. "Darque, you know she qualifies. She's more than qualified. She's as good a swordsman and fighter as were we at her age, mayhap better, for she's already fought in defense of her life and the lives of others." 'Twas always a feeling of lingering resolve here, of times past, memories both good and bad. So much had happened in this office throughout their relatively short spans of days. She sighed. She wasn't here to dredge up the past, she was here to discuss very important business. A new inductee to the Brotherhood. Their little sister, Fryya. "Yes, she's younger than were we, but she'll soon enough see ten winters, and we were pioneers as well. The youngest ever to take the Oath. This is war and 'tis time to break such records." She tried not to second guess what her older sister was thinking, as she noted the growing scowl upon her face. At least Darque hadn't said anything negative yet, and mayhap she'd not have to pull her ace card. Darque could bypass the rules, after all, she was Battle Commander and what she ordered took precedence o'er everything else.

Darque had only arrived from the Keep less than a mark prior and Storrm was waiting for her, about to pounce with the need to discuss their little sister's future. "I know all about the rules of the Brotherhood, I tutored you, if you recall, and I know war changes things radically. I am certain you wouldn't be here with this petition if you weren't providing her sponsorship. But war does not change the fact that she has a living parent, and since she is underage, that parent must agree." She watched Storrm's face and the way she bit her bottom lip. Darque didn't really want to have this discussion, she was swamped with work, had missed katas, and was not a fan of this idea. Having her little sister take the Oath and join the Brotherhood at such a young age was not what she'd want for her. Being a Warrior wasn't just a job, 'twas a lifestyle, and 'twas for one's entire span of days. There was no quitting, no changing your mind. Like taking the 'Bond, joining the Brotherhood was a commitment that would end with one's Passing, and that Passing would likely not be as an Elder. She smiled slightly as she felt that Storrm had no answer to her point. Darque didn't want to try to convince her mother to let her induct Fryya, although 'twould be good to rebuild the Brotherhood with such talent, and as her sister, she'd be very proud. She did not want to pull rank, either. The Brotherhood was still reeling from events o'er the past two winters, and 'twould be too much for her to ask of them at this time. She felt she was up against a wall, but she also felt safe. She had Storrm against that same wall. "So? What does Ama say?"

Darque had sheltered her younger sister, standing at her side through thick and thin, but although Storrm had often teased Darque, she'd never bested her too-serious sibling. Darque's humor leaned toward dry and sarcastic and often as children, Storrm was left to wonder. Darque was the tutor, the trainer, the mother figure for the many winters Aalanna was held captive at Evanntyr Castle. Now, Storrm was about to 'spring one' on her sister that just might blow up in her face. She'd not given that notion much thought, and it caused a frown as she stated, "Ama refuses to sign the release."

Darque misunderstood her sister's expression and stated with finality, "So be it."

Storrm stood up dramatically and rested her hands on the edge of the desk, leaning forward with a slight smile upon her face, as she stated, "But you can."

Now Darque was flustered. She didn't like the feeling. "You mean as Battle Commander? I think not."

Storrm twisted and leaned her hip against the desk, peered o'er her shoulder at Darque, and grinned broadly with pure satisfaction. "There would be no opposition to such from the rest of the Brotherhood, for you'd not sign as Commander." She stopped, and staring at her sister pointedly, she continued, "You would sign as her mother. Her Claim Mother. If you recall, you Claimed her after you rescued her from the Battle of Kaddart, afore we knew she was our own blood, and that Ama yet lived. Furthermore, those documents were never dissolved after Ama returned. Strictly speaking, you are still her mother and can give your consent without pulling rank."

Darque simply stared. And although her mouth opened and closed, no sound emerged, as she could come up with no retort. Storrm was correct. She raised her eyebrows as that truth washed o'er her. 'Twas unfathomable.

NEAR A MOON LATER

Flyrra waved to Storrm, who stood beside Mystynn watching the dawning skies while the little girl and her best friend gathered mushrooms. Flyrra loved these outings and was happy that the Battle Commander was now allowing such. She turned toward Crytcha when she heard the Troll's gentle voice beckon her come to another area, where she'd apparently found the motherlode of all mushroom sites. 'Twould be good, because these were to be added to the feast tonight, to celebrate the new Warriors. But she frowned as she realized 'twould shorten her time out with the Second in Command.

Once they'd finished, they'd have to hurry to get ready and get to Drekinn in time for the ceremony. Crytcha was being ferried by the one Dragon who would have no difficulty with her: Gunnarr himself, but Flyrra would be riding with Storrm and Mystynn, something she'd dreamed of doing. As of this day, due to their assignment forcing them to always be together, they'd neither of them ridden the huge beasts, but for this night, Darque had given them a special reprieve. She sighed. 'Twas both good and bad to have such restraints. Then she grasped her basket and hiked o'er to where Crytcha waited.

DUSK

'Twas fitting to hold the ceremony in the massive Training Pits of the Dragon's Den, the first since they'd entered the war, where new Warriors had taken the Oath since 'twas built after the Last Holocaust. But the Oath itself was older still. Nevertheless, only Grifynn through his many 'lifespans' along the tenure of his elongated span of days, had ever presided o'er the Acceptance and although Darque was much honored, she was also much saddened, for the two new Warriors standing afore her would not only be the first she would receive and the first to accept during a time of war in their modern history, they'd be the youngest. She and Storrm once held that record, taking the Oath at the ages of twelve and thirteen, just four winters afore the first LifeBond. She reflected upon the circumstances of those times and upon how much the times, and they, had changed. Her father was forced Past the Veil in the Battle of Evanntyr where she took her field promotion, and promoting Storrm to Second Fighter, they'd entered the Battle for the Dragon Clan as their first test of leadership. Destiny Called. Her prophesy began.

'Twas cold in the Pits and wearing full leathers and knee-high fur-lined boots, her attention returned to the two youngsters both on one knee afore her with barely disguised eagerness, their breath but frosty puffs as they tried not to make a sound. Scanning the decks surrounding the Pits, she found them flowing o'er with spectators, every available Warrior and Clansman attending. Even King Gabriel with his ever-present bodyguard, double, and half-brother Rakkah, sat watching with expectation. Their Dragon partners sat behind them, and the Free Dragons who'd joined the Resistance in anticipation of the Blood Call of their partners in the upcoming Third LifeBond ceremony, also sat, reverently waiting for Darque to proceed. The lengthening silence was becoming awkward.

Yet she was not ready to continue, her heart aching for what these two would lose. Warriors fought hard, played hard, and loved hard, for they knew they'd likely Pass the Veil hard. It could be a lonely existence, fraught with constant pain both physical and emotional, even though there'd never been a Warrior who'd regretted their Oath. 'Twas a certain satisfaction in being one of the best, a protector, and now the leading last line of defense against the Hoard.

Her mind drifted again. Remembering her protests, her misgivings for this very event, her every objection had been countered. Still, 'twas a most difficult decision but 'twas hers alone to make. The war itself was the final factor that shoved her o'er that edge of indecision. The Resistance needed fighters. No, these two had not gone through traditional Trials on the path to this moment. Instead, they'd both been through actual battle, shedding blood in defense of others as well as themselves, and with the way of life to which they'd all been forced, and to which they were all resigned, 'twould not be long afore 'twould happen again. Their ranks were seriously depleted in the Battle for the Dragon Clan and 'twould be tragic for such as these to go Beyond without making their mark, for both desired to be Warriors. They'd declared their intent, giving their lives to the Brotherhood, and would fight their entire span of days, however long the Fates gave them, for the Resistance. 'Twas that for which Fryya would have been raised had she been birthed at Drekinn, but for the past two winters she'd been rapidly catching up, aggressively determined she'd not miss out on her true destiny. She'd already killed her first Hoard Dragon.

For Walkyr, however, 'twas not his original destiny. Extremely gifted, he was promoted to Clan Seer after Kallyr was killed. Afore the war his life would have been protected, kept close to the Battle Commander, a position Darque had wanted to maintain, not in spite of, but because of, the many battles to come. But times change, situations alter expectations, and plans were modified to meet the need.

The expectant hush upon the crowd and amongst the near three hundred Warriors who stood flanking the two new arrivals in the Pits, finally broke through Darque's contemplation. In somber reverence she licked her full red lips, took a deep breath, and stepped closer to the candidates. 'Twas time. Drawing her Dragon Sword from the ornate scabbard upon her back, specially made from Spell-altered Dragon scale, the scraping sound produced was as metal on metal, singing through the quiet of the spectators. She addressed them collectively, Pushing her voice throughout the area so that all could hear her words. As she spoke, she took a two-fisted grip and raised her Sword high, then slowly and gently laid the flat side upon each of their shoulders while saying, "I, Darque Aalanna Grifynn, Battle Commander of the Dragon Clan, the Resistance Forces, and the LifeBond Teams, do hereby accept your Oath and grant you full rights as members of the Warrior Brotherhood." She flipped her grip and stabbed the Sword into the sands at her feet. "May you live well, fight well, and die well, with righteousness above all else. Arise, fellow Warriors, and greet your brothers and sisters-in-arms." As the two children, for children they yet were, stood up, Darque held their gaze with her own and added for their ears only, "Oath accepted with regrets for your lost youth. I love you both, I would wish you a long span of days without war to be faced, but such is not ours to be. Nevertheless, I shall not forget your personal oaths to me, to stay clear of the dangers and remain where I put you! And you'd best not, either."

In response, Walkyr winked and Fryya stuck out her tongue, grinning mischievously. Darque sighed. If they weren't such talented fighters... Shaking her head, she raised her Sword once again and circling high in the air, she cut downward in a sweeping motion to the side, breaking the silence and officially ending the ceremony with everyone raising their voices in cheers and regards afore hurrying off to join in the revelry of the now open celebration. The official swearing of the Oath was done in her office at dawn with only their sponsors and witnesses present, then repeated in the Pits for all to hear just afore she accepted them.

Only another Warrior could sponsor a new Warrior and therefore Cayell stood for Walkyr while Storrm stood for Fryya. To share this honor, Darque noted her aunt Shayla stood arm-in-arm with Cayell, with whom she'd been spending a great deal of time o'er the past winter. She smiled to herself. Shayla had practically raised her and was like a second mother. The Clan Healer had been lost without Kallyr and Darque heartily approved her budding relationship with the handsome, and very capable, Warrior. Aalanna stood with Storrm behind her youngest, belatedly though still reluctantly in support of the induction. There would be mead, ale, wine and whiskey free-flowing, and a huge party in the Great Hall this evening, with dinner and dancing. Even the Shyffah had sounded for the first time since the big battle.

As the two new Warriors ran toward their brethren, memories of her own induction came abruptly to her mind and blushing, Darque shook her head, exclaiming, "Be careful tonight!"

Fryya stopped just long enough to smile o'er her shoulder at her big sister, and quipped, "As were you?"

Sternly, Darque responded, "If you weren't a Warrior, I'd turn you o'er my knee and tan your butt!" But the two were mingling, disappearing amidst the boots and pants and weapons.

Once out of sight, Fryya faced Walkyr, and shrugging with her hands in the air, exclaimed excitedly, "See? Another bonus!"

~~~~~ THAT EVENING ~~~~~

The Great Hall of the Dragon's Den was enormous but even so, all the Dragons present had to use their Magic to give them room to stand and walk about freely, which gave the odd impression they were occupying the same space as those they passed by or stood near. Nevertheless, being within separate transparent sparkling bubbles went along well with the elaborate and colorful decorations for the celebration ball honoring the new Warriors.

Standing next to one of the many buffet tables lining the walls, Walkyr missed his mouth. Not as in, he didn't have one, but as in, he was trying to eat and was distracted enough that he planted the food he held in his hand, upon his chin. Shaking back to his senses, he looked around to see if anyone had noticed and of course, everyone had. Warriors and guests were breaking into grins and soon the entire hall broke out in snickers which near o'erwhelmed the musical presentation being led by Warrior Kayarr and his friends. He could feel his face light up bright red as he tried to find a napkin, and when that effort failed to produce, he sighed and wiped his chin on the edge of the tablecloth. Reaching around him for another glass of mead, Daxx, with his

'Bond Linayyah standing by, slapped him heartily on the back and he near fell on his face, while Cayell mysteriously appeared out of the crowd to help him find his feet again afore everyone went their separate ways and Walkyr found himself alone at the table once more. From under long mahogany lashes, his eyes sought out his best friend. Where did she go now?

Walkyr had never worn such clothing. In black knee-high boots, a pair of supple, snug fitting, black leather pants, and long-tailed black silk jacket with a white silk blouse that laced up the front, he'd been boggled trying to find a place to secure his weapons. Finally, Cayell helped him dress and arm himself appropriately for which he'd been grateful, and just afore they'd been presented to the entire Clan and the Brotherhood in attendance, he'd seen Fryya for the first time as she stepped up beside him. Wearing a floor-length, diaphanous gown of glittering black with a matching sash cinching it at her tiny waist, her voluminous, curly, bright copper hair pulled back and braided atop her head, he was speechless. She was so beautiful. He'd been distracted by that image all night. 'Twas becoming obvious to even the ones who didn't know him well.

Shayla smacked Cayell on the arm and glowered at him. All he could do in response was shrug his shoulders with a pained expression. The daring duo were together again. And now that they were both Warriors, there was nothing to keep them from getting into even more trouble together. Except orders. Cayell looked at Shayla who looked back, each knowing what the other was thinking. 'Twas a plan. They'd speak to Darque this very night. That is, if they could get to her through the festivities.

'Twas at that moment Warrior Daylyn screamed for the Healer, her voice echoing through the Hall. "One Warrior down! Walkyr's down!"

Followed closely by Shayla, Cayell raced 'cross the Great Hall, pushing past Daylyn's 'Bond, Makyyan, protectively leaning o'er the Seer. As he got his first glance at the boy, Fryya sat on the marble floor holding her best friend's head in her lap as Walkyr gasped in his recovery from a most violent Vision.

~~~~~ SHAYLA'S QUARTERS ~~~~~

It had taken some time to get everyone to settle down and allow Cayell to carry Walkyr out of the Great Hall, but instead of taking the boy to the clinic, Shayla steered them to her private quarters.

Cayell was confused. "I don't understand. His Visions have never been violent, a tad crazed, mayhap, excited, but not seizure-like. What's caused this, Shayla?"

Fryya listened to the adults and bit her bottom lip to keep from revealing the secret she'd sworn with Walkyr. His Visions had become increasingly violent of late, moons afore they'd taken the Oath. As his Sight ramped up in both frequency and physical impact, the two friends concluded that Walkyr was doomed. Simply stated, if they could find no cure, the Visions would kill him. Thus far, they'd successfully managed to prevent Cayell and Shayla from discovering the problem by 'losing' the big Warrior and avoiding the Healer, but as things worsened his Visions gave him little warning if any, and they'd been hard-pressed to sneak away in time to avoid discovery. Sticking to her best friend like glue, Fryya had been sworn to silence, for Walkyr took his position as Clan Seer seriously and did not want to be cured, feeling the cure would subdue his much-needed Gift, and even if it eventually took his life, the Battle Commander required what he Saw to the very end. But Fryya could not sit idly by and allow such to happen. So, she'd schemed to get the adults to permit them to take the Oath in hopes they'd then be able to Cast their Blood Call and take the 'Bond in the coming ceremony, fully expecting a Dragon partner could help Walkyr control his Visions. They'd hoped their secret wouldn't be openly revealed afore they'd accomplished their goal, but mayhap such was not to be. Should she break her promise to her best friend?

~~~~~ LATER ~~~~~

Fryya never left Walkyr's room, falling asleep on the cushion beside his bed. He raised his head slightly and tried to regain his focus as he looked around, finally recognizing Shayla's quarters at the Den. So soft was the cushion, that Walkyr was not sure if he saw Fryya tucked into its depths or if 'twas another Vision, 'til she opened one eye and glared at him. "You ruined a perfect evening," she stated with feigned malice, but then relented, her expression clearly showing her relief that 'twas apparently not his time to Pass. She wasn't certain what she would do without him. They'd been best friends since she was rescued and since then, had rarely spent a day apart.

He sighed and questioned softly, "How long have I been out?"

"Longest ever," she whispered in reply, while glancing nervously o'er her shoulder as she stood up and gave him a hand to help him off the mattress. "'Tis dawn and you had the Vision after midnight, so near five marks. They'll be coming in here to ask of the Vision. What do I say?"

"You promised. As far as you know, 'tis the first such…" he began, but in walked Cayell and Shayla, quickly donning their robes. 'Twas obvious they'd not been sleeping, having been otherwise occupied, prompting smirks of awareness and raised eyebrows from both children. The amusing circumstances helped cover their prior conversation and glancing one to the other, they sat down while Walkyr prepared to relate what he'd Seen.

LESS THAN A MARK LATER
~~~~~ OFFICE OF THE BATTLE COMMANDER ~~~~~

Warrior Walkyr had just been dismissed, literally running into Warrior Fryya waiting outside in the hallway (having been dismissed first), and grabbing her by the hand, they raced to the Pits for katas (they were late) to be followed by Training (against Shayla's wishes). Despite their resolve to keep their pact, Darque and Storrm saw through the inconsistencies in their stories, and with timing provided by Cayell and Shayla for all their most recent 'outings', the subterfuge of the newest Warriors was uncovered. Now Darque, her sculpted, leather braced arms crossed o'er her chest, stood facing the Healer, Cayell, Storrm, and Kydra, while she chewed on her bottom lip. No one said a word, 'twas quiet as a tomb.

Suddenly the room resounded with everyone speaking at once. Darque's ears were inundated with, "They didn't...", and, "Surely 'twas not...", along with, "I'm certain they meant...", and finally, "But we can't...", afore she put her hand in the air to shut them all down. Silence reigned again while Darque took a deep breath, then began, "First, they have taken the Oath and they are Warriors. They shall be treated as such." She noted the wincing expression on every face afore continuing. "Second, their indiscretion does not deserve discipline. They were keeping a pact. One which was entered into prior to their Oath. They should be commended for such an action." She was reminded of Regynn and his vow to the Sprites. Continuing, she said, "And they did offer up the truth when asked directly for such. And if you recall their exact words, they never actually lied, they merely... misdirected." At which time she cast her gaze pointedly to Storrm, who was quite adept at misdirection. The Second in Command had the grace to appear pained.

Cayell stepped forth. "So, no discipline required?"

"Not this time. But if they do anything like this again, I shall have them in front of the entire Brotherhood," she promised.

There ensued a collective sigh of relief, for none wanted to see the children in trouble. But now the conversation, and their concern, took another path. A much more serious one. The Vision itself.

CHAPTER TWELVE

The Third Lifebond

'Twas mid-winter and the solstice would soon be upon them. Darque consulted with Synahmarr through Gunnarr's Link and 'twas agreed they must take the risk, for they needed every Team they could make. Thus far, everyone who had stood for the 'Bond had volunteered, and Walkyr's Vision simply reinforced the fact that Magic was dangerous, and no one knew if they would take the 'Bond. However, not only would she not force the current list to participate, she recognized that new relationships had been forged since they originally volunteered. There was Tyrrsyn and Tyrza, Torstynn and Raynah, just to mention two. After Speaking with the Matriarch, she'd set aside the old list of candidates.

Katas were ending but Training had been delayed per the Battle Commander's order, as she wanted to speak to everyone present. For the first time in ages the Den held most of the Warriors in the Brotherhood, including First and Second Flight. Those who were usually stationed elsewhere would be returning to the Keep and the Bog later this day, and the crowd stood restlessly waiting. Even King Gabriel and Rakkah were present, and though the King did not interfere with the decisions of his Battle Commander, he did wholeheartedly agree with this one. 'Twas perfect timing for such an announcement.

Standing on top of the wall of the spectator's decks so everyone could see, she was reminded of having done so once afore, a very long time ago. 'Twas in her seventh winter, and she'd become convinced by a Vision that she and Storrm could fly. Taking her little sister by the hand, they'd boldly leaped off the wall into the sands below, amazingly causing only some minor scratches, but near pushing Grifynn into apoplexy. They'd promised never to try to fly again. She had to conquer the strange mix of amusement and sorrow such a memory evoked. 'Twas a promise the sisters had kept 'til they'd entered the war.

Now her attention returned to the present and the upcoming Third LifeBond. Synahmarr and the Ancients were near ready to Brew the Magic and she and the Warriors had to be prepared. She'd decided, despite Walkyr's Vision, to go ahead with the ceremony, but 'twas undeniably one of the most difficult decisions she'd had forced upon her since taking Command. These were Warriors and they all knew the odds of taking the LifeBond had never been one hundred percent, but no one had failed thus far. This time however, 'twas a different story. The odds just lowered significantly. For each Warrior sending their Blood Call, 'twould be even at best. She cracked her knuckles. Walkyr's Visions were just as powerful as afore, but they were causing the Seer so much trouble he was losing the details. She ground her teeth wishing she had some of the finer details of this one.

Raising her Sword, the shuffling and clanking stopped as they stood at ease. Now addressing the rapt audience, she Pushed her voice, so all could hear. "I have rescinded the list of participants in the Third LifeBond." Afore she could continue she had to quiet the confused, and quite vocal, Warriors. "No, do not think we stop the ceremony. But although we need to make as many 'Bonds as possible 'tis also true we need to keep every Warrior we have, and more. I do not want to lose any of you." As she surveyed them, all crowding in closer, she continued, "Everyone knows the power of the Clan Seer, and what Walkyr has Seen changes everything. It has been confirmed that the LifeBond will produce at least one failure." The uproar muffled her voice and finally getting them to quiet down, she began again, "'Tis no doubt, and cannot be altered. However, we know not for certain if 'twas the third ceremony he Saw, nor whom, nor if 'twill be more than one to Pass in the attempts. I could stop it but like I said afore, we need the LifeBond. I considered long and hard, and this is my decision. We will continue to recreate the Magic of the Ancients, hoping at the very least that what Walkyr has Seen is not in the upcoming ceremony, as well as 'twill be only one loss. But since we have no such details, I have cancelled the current list of volunteers and will await new ones in my office o'er the next three dawns. There is no shame in not coming forward. The prior volunteers will be given first chance, but consider well, this offer. As I said, we need standing Free Warriors as much as we need those in 'Bond." With that, the Battle Commander stood down and left. The hush o'er the crowd lasted but a moment as they collected their thoughts and wrapped their minds around what was just said, afore it changed to a mad rush to exit the Pits, with near everyone heading straight for the Commander's office.

THE WINTER SOLSTICE
NEAR A FORTNIGHT LATER
<center>~~~~~ TRAINING PITS OF THE DRAGON'S DEN ~~~~~</center>

Darque had no lack of volunteers to stand for the Third LifeBond. Walkyr's Vision could have been from any future ceremony but in her heart she believed 'twould happen tonight. She'd attempted to avoid all chances, even waiting for the Winter Solstice in a desperate attempt to tip the scales in their favor. With every Cut she made with the ceremonial knife, releasing their Blood Call and sending each of her Warriors into the Magic flames dancing toward the starry skies, with every Dragon reaching into those flames and yanking their new partners through to the other side, she barely breathed as she mouthed her prayer to the One, "Not tonight M'Liege, please, not tonight," wordlessly hoping they'd misinterpreted the Vision.

In the biting cold, Synahmarr was glorious. The Ancients surrounding her, she was so imposing she hardly had need of the others. Thus far, everything had gone without a hitch. Darque could feel the energy bathe her body inside and out, tingling, warming, invigorating. 'Twas like neither of the prior ceremonies, more powerful than anything she could imagine. Surely such power could prevent the tragedy, she thought to herself, knowing such thoughts were in every Warrior's mind as she stepped forth to make another Cut, sending Aspynn, Astraa's sister, to the fire to be pulled through by none other than Maakayyel, youngest sibling of the Last Dragon Matriarch and Gunnarr's uncle. Soryn was already learning how to partner with Pelayyah, sister of Petrayyah and Sydrayyah, both having taken the 'Bond prior, and Drysalyn partnered with Danniagg, Korriagg's brother. Then Prysym went through with Rasparyn, a simply huge Dragon, followed by a pretty female Dragon named Zymaalynn and the Warrior Valkyn.

Five successful LifeBonds thus far. The stars were sparkling above the Pits, but all eyes were upon the candidates still standing naked on the sands, waiting their turn. With hardly a sound, murmured prayers were offered up to the One True Liege as the Magical fire burned fiercely, a veritable red and yellow inferno licking toward the skies and lighting the entire area as if 'twas full day.

Darque stepped toward Alyyse, raised the sacred knife and then quickly brought it down to make the Cut upon her thigh. Alyyse's eyes widened but not with pain as she was drawn without conscious thought toward the fire. A long forepaw reached through and Alyyse was yanked into the blistering heat. Darque took a breath in relief as the pair burst forth from the other side, but 'twas not the expected pairing. Alyyse had been taken in 'Bond by the stunning female Kyralayah. Darque nodded her head to acknowledge Gunnarr's Words, *"The LifeBond is about pairing fighting partners. 'Tis not about mating, my dear. You are the exception, not the rule."* Such thoughts brought heat to his loins and his Voice was husky with desire, despite the situation.

Following this unusual pairing was the female Warrior Paydynn, taken by the male Dragon Korriagg, then the female

Warrior Kytahna and the male Dragon Dylordynn. The male Warrior Hadyn went next and his 'Bond with the female Dragon Delfyyan went without a snag. Darque was becoming more confident as each new Team was created. Making the Cut for Maddyx, one of her male Warriors, the male Dragon Varrdayyn pulled him through the fire, but her brows raised not this time. Like Gunnarr said, this was not about mating. However, she couldn't help but wonder if the same sex Warriors and Dragons partnerships created tonight might have an interesting time with their own mating. After all, most Warriors of the Clan had little to no qualms about sex, whenever, however, and with whomever, as they might not live to see the next dawn. Such was not frowned upon as was considered normal, and even though most such relationships were not same sex, there were a few. Still, if the female Warrior had sex with a male, while Sharing such with their female 'Bond, and vice versa…

Distracted momentarily by these fleeting thoughts, Darque made the Cut for Mace, twin of the Warrior Mynx. As he stepped toward the fire, time abruptly slowed. Even her senses were muted. Sounds seemed distant and unintelligible as if she were hearing them from another world. An increasing pressure began to surround her, and an eerie mist filled the Pits. Out of the corner of her eye, she noted Synahmarr had risen to her feet, and with her head down, she appeared as one pushing to keep the gates closed against an opposing force. But what was she really fighting so hard to keep closed? As the sun dawned upon her, Darque's eyes darted back toward the fire, and she watched in horror as a ghostly foreleg grasped Mace's arm. His Blood Call had reached through the Veil. His partner was Beyond. The contact brought a groan of near pain from the Matriarch as she sat back hard on her haunches, having lost her balance against the drop of pressure she'd attempted to use to prevent the joining. Mace remained perfectly still as his expressions shifted from confusion to discomfort to disbelief as he and the ghostly Dragon maintained their grips. Within a heartbeat, his expression became one of determination followed by acceptance. 'Twould seem they were Communicating through the Link already established by the impending 'Bond.

The petite female Dragon Spoke with Mace, her voice full of regret. *"I am Maddokyn. Forgive me, this has never happened afore. I had no idea I could still be Called from the other side. But the Spell was not Brewed to allow one to return as in life, and Humans cannot survive the journey 'cross the Veil."*

Mace was confused. His partner was Beyond? How could this have happened? But he knew they had little time and his Warrior training kicked in as he asked, *"What do we do?"*

"You can resist. Let go and you may yet survive."

"May? And what of the others? What of the success of the ceremony?"

Apologetically, Maddokyn Replied, *"All those touched this night will die as the Magic fails behind us. 'Twill create a whirlpool of destruction encompassing and extinguishing all around you."*

Decisively, Mace Responded, his hand firmly grasping the Dragon's forearm, not allowing her to pull back. He was yet amazed that he could feel her as solid, when he knew she was Beyond. *"That is not acceptable. I will not, cannot, cause such to happen just to try to save myself. There must be another option!"*

Sadness filled her Voice. *"There is but one. Sacrifice yourself. You must allow me to pull you through."*

Barely hesitating, he asked, *"Will such an action allow the others to continue safely?"*

"Yes."

With firm conviction, he Answered, *"Then take me."*

"You fear not the Veil?" Maddokyn asked in wonder.

Mace's Voice was full of acceptance, no anger, no fear. *"I am a Warrior. I only fear failing my brothers and sisters-in-arms. The LifeBond must succeed for them to carry on the fight, and if my sacrifice will allow that, then so be it. I am ready."*

And suddenly, Mace was gone. The Dragon yanked him into the fire and they did not reappear on the other side. Darque was stunned as if paralyzed as the moments dripped past. Her heart raced and her breath stuttered as with physical pain, a stabbing sensation in her gut at the realization of the fulfillment of Walkyr's Vision. Mace. 'Twas Mace he'd Seen. Her ears picked up the soft weeping from the spectators above the Pits, and she identified the strangled moan of Mynx, his flaxen haired sister, as their twin link was severed with his Passing.

And then she Heard another Voice. Synahmarr. *"MOVE Battle Commander! Make the next Cut! The Magic begins to fail. We must reach a leveling or I will lose containment of the energies invoked this night. The Warrior's sacrifice will have been in vain and 'twill end in disaster!"*

The other Warriors still stood upon the sands, waiting their turn to take the Cut. They'd flinched not, but they were all still caught up in the Magic and likely unaware of what had occurred. Forcing herself to move, the eerie mist that had filled the Pits dissolved as Darque stepped toward Darrtan. As he slowly reached into the fire, Darque's eyes riveted to the flashing lights of the blaze, and she let out her breath in relief when he successfully passed through with the female Dragon Illsyyah. Quickly she sent Warrior Baylis into the fire and she made it through with a male Dragon known as Maklarynn. 'Twas as if nothing had happened prior to their Cuts. No change was noted in the appearance of the fire, there was no hesitation in their journey through. She wondered if they knew of Mace's demise or would have to be told later. Surely their Dragons would inform them.

Spinning back toward the lineup of Warriors to continue the ceremony, the fire abruptly crackled and popped loudly, changed from the fiery red and yellow furnace to a cold blue light, afore simply disappearing, leaving the seemingly untouched body of Mace in its wake, lying face up in the sands. Her hand still holding the knife, she looked for Synahmarr, the Ancients surrounding her as if she needed assistance to stand. The Warriors who were still waiting their turn looked around as if they'd just awakened from a nightmare, the story of what they'd missed circulating rapidly as the rest of the Clansmen came to assist them with their leathers. The pressure of the surrounding Magic lingered, while exhaustion, excitement and grief permeated the Den.

<center>~~~~~ THE FOLLOWING EVENING ~~~~~</center>

The twelve new Teams of 3rd Stable stood solemnly at their 'Bonds sides around the edges of the Pits, while the rest of the Warriors and those living in the Den gathered in the spectators' stands once more. What should have been a celebration had become a time of mourning. A funeral pyre was set up in the middle of the Pits and she hoped 'twould give Mynx some closure. She would never see her brother alive again and she was not taking this well. However, she, like her twin, was a Warrior and she wanted to make him proud. She stood just behind the Battle Commander, the torch at her side, ready to be lit.

Darque's grave voice was heard throughout the area, no Push required, for all was still. "We come together to pay tribute to, and honor, one of our own. Mace was a true Warrior, a faithful Brother of the Clan. With full knowledge that he could be the one of Walkyr's Vision, he stepped forth proudly and without hesitation, took the Cut," she stated with a nod toward the new Teams afore continuing, "as did you all." Darque swallowed hard. She thought of all the Warriors in the past who had fought and died and for whom they'd had this very ceremony. Their names were now carved into the walls surrounding the Pits, a display of courage and spirit that descended through the ages. She was grateful to all who had gone afore her, leading and following, fighting to the Veil. But Mace didn't get to fight. He didn't even have his sword in hand as he left this side of the Veil. His willingness to do what had to be done regardless, humbled her. "Mace knew he was leaving us, and yet he willingly sacrificed his life for the lives of

those left behind so that we may carry on the battle in his stead."
Pausing, she glanced downward and finished. "May his journey
through the Void be brief and painless, and may he find solace
Beyond."

Looking up at the surrounding Warriors, she began the Chant
of Mourning. Her own voice steady, her chin high, as Battle
Commander she recited: "One Warrior down, a brother has
Passed." Her statement was followed by all the witnesses present
chanting in unison, "He kept his Oath unto the last." 'Twas near
deafening there were so many. Darque took a deep breath and
continued, "And how do we honor him, our brethren?" The final
line in the Warrior's Mourning Chant, reverberated enthusias-
tically throughout the Pits, "In Legend Song he will live again!"
In hushed reverence, the spectators' stands fell silent once more,
and Darque swallowed hard. A single tear spilled o'er her cheek
and she brushed it away.

Turning to Mynx, she used her own torch to light the girl's,
and watched wordlessly as the tall blonde walked toward the
pyre. Hesitating for but a moment, a prayer upon her lips, Mynx
then bent down and lit the fire, stepping back a few paces as it
roared toward the heavens. Mesmerized, the Warrior moved not.

Darque finished without her. "And continue this war, we will.
Mace's sacrifice was not, and will not be, in vain. 3rd Stable will
begin training this night," she ordered, dismissing the event.
Everyone shuffled out of the Pits, a rising anticipation already
o'ercoming the sadness. Darque stared at Mynx's back. She could
only imagine the pain the other felt in the loss of her sibling, and
her heart ached. She prayed she'd never have to endure such.

DARQUE'S OFFICE
~~~~~ A FORTNIGHT LATER ~~~~~

The lovely Warrior with the flaxen hair stood nervously afore
her desk. Goldenrod, her Battle Name, had been instrumental in finding Synahmarr and keeping her alive afore she broke

free of her prison in Evanntyr to answer the Death of Life prophesy. They'd become friends, and Darque knew that she and the Dragon Matriarch shared an unusual Link from their experiences together. Darque also knew that Mynx was at her limit and needed respite. The Warrior was working hard, giving her all, training every day for marks, but she was distracted by her brother's loss and such was taking a devastating toll on her reflexes, slowing her actions. She was not only a detriment to herself at this point, she was a detriment to her partners. Darque needed Mynx back at her sharpest, her most skilled level. Such was the life of a Warrior. Yet, Mynx had refused to take a break. She'd refused to miss training and had been pushing herself o'er the past fortnight, to little avail. 'Twould appear as if the harder the Warrior tried, the worse her timing suffered, and such would soon result in serious injury if something didn't change.

She eyed the Warrior as Mynx surreptitiously rubbed her left side where Darque had seen her slip up just this morning. She'd missed the block and allowed her opponent to land a solid strike that could have been fatal if they'd not been using practice swords. Darque knew she was in a lot of pain, but 'twas not the expression showing on Mynx's face. Lately she was always a step behind her opponents. The Trainers had been working with her to bring her back up to level. The expression showing clearly on her face was one of self-disgust.

Worried about why she'd been called to this meeting, Mynx blurted, "I apologize for my mistakes, I'll try harder, I can do this. I'm a good swordsman. Mace taught me…" Mentioning her brother had her choking up and unable to continue.

Darque felt badly for the girl, but she had to get back in line. Nonetheless, Mynx was near her breaking point. 'Twas just this morning, after watching the girl's most horrible performance yet in the Pits, that she and Gunnarr came up with a brilliant idea. At least she hoped 'twas brilliant. The situation had been nagging at her and she'd had no answer 'til she and her mate were inspired by Mynx. Firmly she began, "I understand. But I am sure you understand that you must o'ercome this distraction. Mace would not want you like this. He would be disappointed."

Mynx could not meet Darque's gaze and desperately attempted to keep the tears from spilling o'er her cheeks as she looked down and blinked several times. Finally, she managed to squeak forth, "Yes Sir."

Darque nodded, recognizing the girl's valiant efforts and then continued with a sly smile upon her lips, "To that end, I have a deployment situation for which I think, even now, you are perfectly suited. 'Tis an isolated and dangerous assignment that could last many winters. 'Twill mean leaving immediately. I want you ready within the mark."

Bewildered, Mynx looked up but could only ask, "Sir?" Gone were the tears and in their place, a sense of growing wonder. Leave the Den? Leave Drekinn? The home in which she'd been born and bred, side by side from birth with her twin, along with all its memories? She'd refused to leave on a 'break' afore, she was a Warrior and proud, she'd somehow muddle through this and come out stronger, but a deployment wasn't a failure nor was it a refusal. This was an assignment, something that would keep her occupied and useful without the constant reminders. With great expectancy, she waited for Darque to provide more information.

"I find our world changing. I have few Warriors to spare for such diplomatic positions, but there is one that I must fill. I need someone to become liaison and personal bodyguard to the Dragon Matriarch, Synahmarr. I need someone there to keep up our position and alliance and to keep me informed of all happenings as well as to protect her, as she is now at the top of the Hoard's most wanted list and refuses to acknowledge her own danger. She has only the Ancients and as yet, they are not fully convinced, either. 'Twill take someone who can get close to her and stay there, gaining her full cooperation without anyone suspecting the real mission is not diplomacy for if there is a spy at Fire Heart, or one is able to infiltrate, I need to know. 'Twill be perilous and take a delicate touch. I see no one more qualified than you, Mynx."

Mynx was stunned. Such a position was considered very high ranking and she'd only been employed once afore; as bodyguard to Darque's little sister, Fryya. 'Twas a very long time ago and as she recalled, she'd not truly shined in that position.

Her thoughts clear in her expression, Darque stated, "You were young and inexperienced, but you still did well. And you did very well on your own with Synahmarr in the Witch's Dungeons. The cunning and skills you displayed to keep her alive, clearly show your training is that of a Warrior, and your heart tells me you will lay down your life to protect the Matriarch, without thinking twice. No other can create the kind of relationship with Synahmarr that I want, and you already have."

Suddenly Mynx remembered another conversation that would require her and the Matriarch to work together. Briefly, she wondered if Darque knew. Then, acknowledging both her relationship with the Dragon and her Commander's knowledge of her personal needs, she stated, "Thank you. I will not fail you, or my brethren."

"Just don't fail Syn," Darque whispered to herself, as she watched Mynx turn and leave, hurrying excitedly to pack and make ready to be flown to Flight of Fire Keep. Although Mynx no longer had any family to keep her in Drekinn, 'twould be an interesting existence for her as 'twas a castle built for flying giants and she would be the only human who'd ever lived there. Nonetheless, Mynx had a smile on her face as she near ran down the Great Hallway. Gunnarr's rumbling approval mixed with Darque's own satisfaction at what she hoped was the perfect solution meeting all their needs. Synahmarr was proving to be a most stubborn Matriarch and she'd been in stasis through most of the ages since the Last Holocaust. Darque hoped that with Mynx's influence, the Dragon would gain a bit more respect and patience for the needs of her human counterparts as well as an understanding that she had to protect herself.

She thought about what Corbyn had revealed to Storrm and agreed that 'twas necessary for the Matriarch to lay her eggs. If anyone could convince her, 'twould be Goldenrod. Mynx would make report as requested on that venture, directly to the Raven, as they'd worked out an agreement of sorts this very morning. She would give the Warrior her final orders to include this, along with all the other details of her mission, afore she was flown away. Yet of more immediate importance, she hoped that with Mynx's influence, her upcoming meeting with Synahmarr might have the positive outcome she so desperately required.

CHAPTER THIRTEEN

Child Of The Borkahn

O'ER A MOON LATER

FLIGHT OF FIRE KEEP

~~~~~ LATE WINTER/EARLY SPRING ~~~~~

Synahmarr looked so different. They'd communicated through the Link o'er the past few moons, but the last time Darque had seen her was when she'd escaped her prison, having been held captive in the dungeons of Evanntyr Castle since just afore the Last Holocaust. Her russet scales once filthy, dull, and ragged, now shimmered in good health. Her speech was eloquent, slow and commanding as befitted her position and reminded Darque of her predecessor, the Mighty Maahayyel. As expected, and hoped, Warrior Mynx stood just to the Matriarch's right shoulder, her hand ever upon the broadsword at her hip, even for such visitors as the Battle Commander. She'd apparently become well accepted.

Syn began with an explanation. "Maddokyn died in the Battle for the Eagle Clan and although she wanted to, she could not cross the Veil even for the LifeBond. The Magic was not meant to bring a partner from Beyond and the binding would have taken the Warrior regardless. She did the appropriate thing. If she'd not taken the boy through, all those around him would have died as the Magic collapsed. There was far too much energy circulating. I am more powerful than I knew."

Darque understood and appreciated the Matriarch's strength, for 'twould be needed in the war. Nevertheless, they'd lost a Warrior and a LifeBond Team, for which she was not very appreciative. Coming straight to the point, she asked, "Can you alter the Magic to allow them through?"

Synahmarr's eyes darted around the table afore she softly responded. "I can."

Darque squinted. There was something going on here, that seriously concerned her. "Will you?"

The Matriarch sat on her haunches, her front paws together talon to talon, at the head of a massive half-round table open in the middle. The Dragons sat not on chairs or benches, but the Ancients encircled her, sitting as did she, to both sides along the outer rim of the table, while the Battle Commander stood inside and just in front of Syn, who was quiet for a moment. The Matriarch turned not her massive head but 'twas clear she was in Communication with the Ancients afore she replied. "You must understand this is not a simple task. There are many issues to be considered. We honor the dead by allowing their rest and freedom once they are Past the Veil. As you know, the original Magic was such that all Highlands were forced to answer the Blood Call of their partner." She glanced again to the others afore continuing, "Some believe, theoretically, 'twould take away freedom of choice from those Beyond. I do not believe that is so, since Beyond has its own laws of reality and time." The Ancients sat stone-faced but Darque could sense some animosity as well as encouragement within the mingling emotions with which she was surrounded. "I believe I can alter the Magic to allow them to answer. However," her glance flickered around the table once more afore she continued, "they will still have a choice in whether they do so. I know not if this will help create more Teams, nonetheless, 'twill avert more tragedies such as just occurred." Synahmarr nodded toward Mynx near imperceptibly, and the Warrior's eyes glossed o'er slightly in an expression of appreciation. 'Twas the only outward sign that anything had passed 'tween the pair afore she finished. "But as you know, those whose Blood Call is sent and not answered, even though they may touch spirits with their LifeBond partners, will face heartbreak and devastating loneliness for the rest of their span of days, 'til they are joined Beyond."

Darque thought about Regynn, who had gone through many miserable moons of just such an unanswered Call, awaiting Sydrayyah's arrival from the Rol Dan and the next ceremony to bind them. But Regynn was different and such would not be the same with another Warrior. She nodded. 'Twould mean a great sacrifice, mayhap losing them to depression, their desire to be with their partners, dealing with the rejection. 'Twould mean issues on the battlefields to come. But what else could she do? They could not lose more the way they lost Mace. Then she recalled the Matriarch's words. "You're saying those Dragons who are Past the Veil, would need choose to participate?"

"Precisely."

"And how exactly, do we get them to do that?"

Dipping her chin, the Matriarch replied softly, "I know not."

Her response was surprising, and totally unacceptable. There was always another option. Mayhap with encouragement, someone to teach them that 'twas now possible, and how to accomplish the deed. But 'twould mean someone already Past. What would Grifynn do? Her father might even be the one who could help. But if he went back to the Beyond, the Sorcerer would be able to enslave his spirit. Surely there was a way out of this dilemma. Still, the Ancients were waiting. She must take her leave as she was expected at the Keep soon. She made her decision. "We have no choice. Alter the Spell."

NEAR A SENNIGHT LATER
<center>~~~~~ THE CLINIC OF THE KEEP OF ST SWIFTYN'S ~~~~~</center>

Chynnar faced Cayell and smirked. 'Twas not her usual case and strictly speaking, should not be amusing, but seeing the tall Warrior holding the youngest Warrior in the Brotherhood o'er his shoulder like a sleeping baby was a sight. As they'd arrived from Drekinn Lair just a mark earlier, the boy had thrashed in yet another powerful Vision, the worst they'd witnessed thus far, and it had taken her, Kelsey, Fryya, and Cayell to prevent him from harm. "He will likely sleep for several marks now. I gave him something to help ease his restlessness." She was very concerned. Walkyr's Visions were increasing, becoming more violent and seizure-like in their impact upon the boy. She'd already discussed his situation with Kelsey and they'd devised the concoction together. But in her heart, Chynnar knew 'twas getting worse and if they could not gain control, the boy would eventually succumb to the stress.

As Fryya anxiously stood beside him, Cayell said, "I'll take him back to our quarters, and then go make report." Fryya immediately nodded and silently followed them down the corridor to stay with her friend as he slept.

~~~~~ THE OFFICE OF THE BATTLE COMMANDER ~~~~~

Cayell was more than concerned and as he made report, he struggled with his emotions. Walkyr was his Warrior Brother, but also his son. "This one was bad, Darque. He Saw a vicious battle. The Black and his Hoard were chasing someone, and at the same time being chased, with nothing but death surrounding all. 'Twas in a forested region unknown to him, and he cannot identify the location though he felt a familiarity he cannot explain. The odds were absurd and confusing. There were many others fighting with us, whom he did not recognize. The evil, the hatred, the brutality, unprecedented in his mind. Not only did having the Vision cause shock to his system, but so too, the content was shocking as well. He admitted to me that this Vision has been repeating and keeps strengthening in detail as if 'tis morphing, ever changing, but he is certain 'twill happen soon."

"The Black led his Hoard? He was present at the battle?"

"Yes. Every time he has this Vision."

Giving voice to that which they both hoped, she questioned, "Do you, or he, suspect this battle was at his Lair?"

A satisfied smile crossed the Warrior's lips and his eyes flashed. "We do. He has Seen many of the Hoard inside and outside of the caverns, both man and Dragon." Then his smile left him, and he cracked his knuckles in agitation. "And yet, he seems to describe two separate settings for this battle. 'Tis possible that he Sees the fighting both inside and outside of the Lair, but this I cannot tell for certain. All I know is that the battle is huge with many fighters, many unknown to Walkyr. And the prize is a girl-child."

EARLY SPRING

~~~~~ THE KEEP OF ST SWIFTYN'S ~~~~~

</div>

Crytcha had been living alone and as was one of the main-stays of her Race, had managed to get a hive of bees to take up residence within a vast fissure along the outer wall of the Keep that extended into one of the cavern chambers, tending them in her spare time, harvesting the honey for everyone to enjoy. But Flyrra could sense her loneliness. The only child of the greatest leader the Borkahn had ever seen, she would never let her father down by openly admitting such. Still, Flyrra knew.

Flyrra was small and skinny for her age, but now that she was in a healthy environment she was growing fast, and with her shoulder-length, straight sparkling silver hair, and triangular face with huge black upswept eyes making her appear something like one of the giant wasps of Abysmal Gorge, she was rapidly becoming popular for being uniquely pretty. Most of the Clansmen had long hair, thick, luxurious, oft' times curly and usually red or blonde, but the few who were different were not unlike the dark-haired Elves, so her coloring drew everyone's eye. Initially she enjoyed the attention but 'twas not fulfilling, as she observed her best friend looking forlornly about, wherever they went. Crytcha, four winters her elder as near as anyone could tell, had confided in her that she felt left out and ugly. Towering o'er every-one, her Kind had no body hair and she could literally make her-self appear to be a part of the rock walls without anyone the wiser, which she was doing more and more of late.

Flyrra had been making good progress with no mishaps requiring Crytcha's assist in the past few moons, gaining total control of her Magic. She'd decided not to look anyone in the eye, especially when she was frustrated, even though she needed not such focus. Her decision was based upon the fact that her direct gaze was a bit creepy for most others and she was trying to fit into her new environment.

One evening while she lay in bed staring at the ceiling, she thought of a gift she could give her friend to make her feel better. But it had to be a secret. Getting up and stealing through their small quarters, she worked her way quietly to the big bed upon which lay her parents in the side room off the main living area. Flyrra knew Kayarr and Natanamia were instantly alert from the moment she'd left her own bed, and she reached up and gently shook his shoulder, softly pleading with him, "Please Aba, please ask the Battle Commander for an audience. I need to talk to her alone. I need a favor. Please?" Kayarr turned his head towards Natan but she only looked puzzled and shrugged her shoulders while shaking her head. Since Flyrra could not go anywhere without Crytcha, they wondered if the two had a falling out. They attempted to question her but Flyrra wouldn't say another word. Finally, Kayarr agreed to ask and the child smiled broadly as she went back to bed.

~~~~~~~~~~

The morning after Kayarr met with Darque to convey his daughter's request, he took Flyrra by the hand, and for the first time since their arrival mishap, they walked through the Keep alone together to the Battle Commander's office. Once there, after Darque gave her approval, Flyrra surprised Kayarr and made him wait outside.

"I have a request, Sir," she began, and then proceeded to describe what she wanted to do. Darque had been keeping tabs on the child and was well pleased. She nodded her head and shared in Flyrra's excitement, encouraging her as she attempted to organize her thoughts. The little girl's imagination was blooming since her arrival, but she'd never attempted anything like this afore.

When Flyrra was done talking and had agreed to Darque's terms, which included staying with at least one parent at all times outside of her quarters, or with the Second or Third Fighters (a step up, giving her more freedom of movement within the Keep), she sent the child to Ardyth, as she and Cathay had spent much time together, sharing their sewing talents and becoming good friends. Ardyth was entranced with the project the little girl envisioned and had Flyrra come by her quarters after classwork and training every day for a full moon, teaching her to sew and helping her to finish her creation.

On the first night, Ardyth spread a large selection of strips of leather, ribbons, sparkling gems, feathers, and shells from which to select, upon the long low table in the living area, and Flyrra was delighted, not knowing which to pick or what to use first. The tip of her tongue sticking out slightly, she meticulously chose her colors and the extras, and then taking needle in hand, she worked. Ardyth was just as careful not to complete the project for Flyrra, as 'twas clear she wanted this to be a special gift just from her to her best friend. Even Axyl could see how much effort the little girl made trying to do something she'd never attempted afore and using not a hint of Magic. Bryynn and Haniyyah would lie on the enormous woven grass mattress on the floor off to the side of their cavernous quarters and watch the little girl's hands shake, her tongue sticking out, occasionally furrowing her brows and looking up at Ardyth to see if she was doing a good job.

Night after night she returned with either Kayarr, Natan, Storrm, or Kydra (when they were available), unbeknownst to Crytcha. Finally, Flyrra was satisfied. Ardyth gave her hearty approval of the child's handiwork and helped her wrap the gift afore she left. Flyrra could hardly wait for the next afternoon. She would give it to her when Crytcha dropped her off at her quarters to return to her own.

~~~~~ THE FOLLOWING NIGHT ~~~~~

Flyrra's heart was in her throat as she walked home along-side Crytcha. The closer they came, the more she feared. Would Crytcha like it, or would she be hurt by such? 'Twas suddenly a possibility that her friend would think it looked stupid or that Flyrra thought she was ugly. Near deciding not to give her the gift after all, Natan met them at the door as they arrived, the box in her hand. Flyrra shook her head. She was broadcasting her emotions so loud-ly, even her mother Felt them, but Natan didn't back down, holding forth the gift. Flyrra sighed, took the prettily wrapped little box, and with her head lowered, handed it to Crytcha. "I hope you like it. I made it myself." Speaking aloud brought tears to her eyes. She bit her tongue, trying to prevent them from spilling o'er.

As 'twas for Flyrra, this was a completely new experience for Crytcha. She was at first confused but had been studying other cultures since her arrival and understood the meaning behind such a gift. She tentatively opened the box, careful even with her huge blocky fingers not to tear the pink and purple ribbons. Peeking inside, she instantly knew what she saw. 'Twas a beauti-fully braided and decorated leather headband with several large crystals and very narrow glistening blue and silver ribbons intri-cately braided and sewn all around, creating a short fringe in the front, lengthening slightly around the back.

Crytcha choked, her tongue sticking to the roof of her mouth. Suddenly her throat was so dry, she couldn't speak or swallow. She could sense how much time and effort was put into the cre-ation of this gift and grinning, she put the headband on, adjust-ing the buckle and clearing her throat afore declaring, "Now we look like sisters. I am beautiful like you!" Touching Flyrra's long shining silver hair and then her 'hair' of ribbons, her narrow eyes gleamed with moisture, her appreciation clear to anyone. Kayarr and Natan were standing in support of their daughter at the open doorway, watching behind Flyrra's back. They too were quite pleased, for both children.

Even though the Troll could physically crush near anyone, 'twas not what defined her. Somehow Flyrra found her voice. "'Tis not the headband that makes you beautiful, Crytcha. 'Tis your spirit, your heart, your gentle ways, your loving acceptance and honesty." She hung her head, unable to look her friend in the face. "'Tis your forgiveness of me and the way I left you to rot in the caves of the Pitch."

Crytcha remembered well those dark and frightening days of captivity, but things had changed. She shrugged. "I was rescued. As were you. Makes no difference by whom, or when. You did what you had to do, helping many. Leaving me was the only way you could do that. I could not have been helped by any other than by those who did the deed."

Flyrra hugged her hard. "I don't deserve such a good friend."

"We shall be friends, always." Then she leaned o'er and gave the little girl a gentle hug afore she turned away. Waving, Flyrra bid Crytcha goodnight, and watched her disappear down the long corridor, her headband sparkling with each step she took.

~~~~~~~~~~

As Flyrra did her chores that evening, she thought about Crytcha. While Flyrra had a home and parents, Crytcha lived by herself in the rough crevasse where she made her own food and tended her bees. But her friend was lonely and enjoyed their time together, even though much of it was in classes and training. A lot of the other children lived in what closely resembled the Warriors' barracks. She wished she could share her good fortune. In a reversal of their past situation, she decided she may not be able to do much for the others, but she could do something for Crytcha.

Walking back to the main living area, she sat cross-legged on the floor staring up at Kayarr and Natanamia. Both were home near every night lately. Crytcha hadn't seen her family in winters and might never again. As was her way, she blurted forth, "Darque and Storrm and Fryya are sisters. Many of the others have siblings. I want a sister."

Kayarr near choked on his wine, spewing it forth o'er the couch, and Natan helped him clean up while trying not to laugh too hard. Even though his skin was dark, 'twas clear he was blushing. His black brows furrowed as he caught Natan's gaze. "I had no idea what parenthood entailed. I wonder if others have such issues?"

Natan smiled sweetly, knowing for what he thought the child was asking. Pushing her long blonde hair behind her pointed ears, her green eyes sparkling, she exclaimed, "'Tis certainly entertaining!"

~~~~~ A SENNIGHT LATER ~~~~~

'Twas early Spring and Crytcha's formal Claim documents had been signed o'er to Natan and Kayarr without hesitation. Although 'twas quick and easy, 'twas also ominous of just what Darque knew of the child's future. Meanwhile, Flyrra had learned to speak to others by maintaining her focus slightly o'er their shoulders or at their ears, something that she occasionally found amusing, but few understood her mirth. She no longer required Crytcha's constant companionship, although in spirit, they were near inseparable. Nevertheless, now that the girls lived together they seemed to spend much more time apart. Flyrra enjoyed Survival Training and was becoming quite adept with throwing weapons. She was excelling in both classes. In fact, she was doing so well that Darque dropped the partnering requirement and Flyrra was now allowed to go outside the Dome on forays without Crytcha, although she still required supervision for her own protection. She loved going out with Storrm and Mystynn and she loved to fly, now that she could see her surroundings.

Since Crytcha had little need of a weapon (although Alric had created an extra-large War Hammer for her that only the strongest Warriors could even lift), once she mastered their identities and how they were used so that she could defeat them, she was assigned a new project. Darque began a Mastery program of Beekeeping through the Master Chef and Master Gardener sections. 'Twas no one better suited to help establish this new Master's program, than one of the Borkahn.

With both children doing well and their previous tight supervision requirements cancelled, Natan was kept quite busy with her command duties and more often than not, was away for days, while Kayarr (along with a slight nudge from Darque) had decided 'twas time for him to seek out his brethren, the eleven remaining Warriors of the Order of the Eagle and bring them back to the Resistance. With some reluctance, he left on his mission. But once outside the Dome, his true Warrior stride kicked in and he felt energized. Still, he'd be happy to return, knowing 'twould be several moons in the making of such a return, so, balancing stealth with speed, he disappeared into the depths of Byndynn forest.

CHAPTER FOURTEEN

Rhyah The Wolf

The sun was setting and 'twould soon be time to return, but Flyrra loved sunsets. The semidarkness of dusk, the shift in the temperatures, the sharpening of the scents, all combined to increase her fascination and focus. She'd not been allowed outside the Black's Lair without a hood, forcing her other senses to their peak even afore she'd been rescued. Now she could add her vision to the multitude of sensations and 'twas glorious.

Glancing up, she couldn't see Storrm but knew the Second was there. Her breath frosty in the early Spring air and her bag full of the last winter mushrooms, she leaned against the trunk of the enormous pine waiting for Storrm to call her, hoping that would not happen too soon but of course 'twould. The Second in Command had allowed her to get further away than usual and taking a deep breath of the crisp air, she savored her freedom.

Suddenly, from just north came the howls of a wolf pack. On the move, 'twould seem they were also on a direct line toward her. Mystynn had gone south to hunt just after dropping them off and had not yet returned. As the approaching sounds became menacing growls from two distinct directions, Flyrra sensed 'twas a large pack chasing down a single challenger. In a few heartbeats they clashed into each other, snarling and grunting. She heard screams of pain and fierce defiance with branches breaking as heavy bodies crashed through the underbrush, closing in on her location. 'Twas happening so fast she could do nothing as the chaos, with much blood-letting in the making, roared closer and closer and she was cut off from the Second. Her eyes darting this way and that, she had just about decided 'twould be the better part of valor to run in the opposite direction, when she heard Storrm scream.

"Flyrra! Where are you?" the Second yelled through the increasing noise. But afore she could respond, a huge ball of fur rolled toward her, claws slashing and fangs biting as the two opponents exploded out of the forest into the clearing several Dragon lengths away. Instinctively aware she would be caught up in the fray if she tried to run, she dropped to a crouched position, one hand on the ground in front of her and the other out to one side for balance and support, casting her gaze around the area as she sized up the skirmish. She had to make sure she could see all her opponents. Multiple sets of glowing eyes shone from the forest, encircling the fighting pair. The blood and saliva splattered her face, the sound of Storrm's footsteps was muted, her voice seemingly leagues distant, as Flyrra set her Magic.

The two gray wolves were locked together in a fight to the death, feeling and hearing nothing outside their private war. But one was different. More than three times her size and much heavier, Flyrra immediately noted the near healed laceration upon that wolf's shoulder, now re-opened and spurting blood. After a moment's confusion, her senses told her that one was not really a wolf. 'Twould seem they'd found Rhyah. The problem was how to get him out of the fight without further injury to any of the pack, or herself. Darque had taught her she must be more discerning with her Magic, and during her brief hesitation the Fay was injured again. Causing much damage to his enemy, he was still unable to land a killing blow. The pack leader had greatly injured Rhyah early in the fight, and the loss of Life Source was causing much fatigue, slowing his reflexes. He could not Shift, or he'd be torn limb from limb afore he could set his Magic. If he stayed in Shift, he would soon become too fatigued to continue the battle and Flyrra doubted she could talk the wolf pack and their leader into just leaving the area. She prepared herself to kill them all to rescue the Fay.

A few heartbeats after the two fighters came snarling into view, they were closely followed by Storrm as she slashed through the underbrush. Sword held high, she ran toward the wolves fearing they were there to attack Flyrra, ignorant of the true situation. With the entrance of the human, the rest of the pack charged out of the forest to join the fight.

Now the little girl was truly alarmed. Fully aware that she would have to do something for which she would probably be punished, mayhap even banned from the Resistance, she wasted no more time. Tilting her head slightly, 'twas the only outward sign that she was doing anything, but 'twas suddenly followed by muffled silence while every creature, including the Second, came to a screeching halt. Storrm's eyes widened as she found herself unable to control her own body, forced to drop her Sword to her side while watching the power of the half-breed's Magic unfold.

Flyrra knew she'd have to answer for the use of Magic against the Second in Command, but she couldn't think on that now, for stopping her was imperative afore she further injured Rhyah. It had been a long time since she'd powered up against more than a handful, and never against a mix of Races. As she struggled to gain control, she counted a dozen in the wolf pack coming out of the forest and could only hope she had them all in sight. Thankfully, they were smaller than their leader who was currently pitted against the Fay. 'Twas the largest Magical Hold she'd every thrown. Now for the action.

Sweating and grinding her teeth with the effort, she Pushed her will upon the wolf pack, and separated the fighters. Howling their anger, all the wolves were dragged back through the leaf litter and the mud created by melted snow, their unwilling paws trying to keep their position, making ruts in the ground as they stepped back while at the same time, biting at the others. With snarls rising, they were forced to face each other at the tree line while Flyrra concentrated her focus upon Rhyah and the leader of the pack. Infuriated by her Magic, the wolves of the pack turned against their own, while both the original combatants desperately tried to fight the Hold, reaching out to each other, angry with their inability to finish the kill. Slowly, the distance 'tween them grew as they were forced to move away, still biting at the air, slashing with their claws. Never taking their eyes off each other, the leader was forced into his pack, all tearing each other apart, massive injuries evident to the Second in Command as she stood paralyzed, wondering what Flyrra would, or could, do next.

Involuntarily, Rhyah laid down on the ground as blood and fur flew everywhere, covering the small clearing. Still snarling, he was deep in animal mentality and seemed not to know what was happening, just that he was being prevented from finishing off the one who'd attacked him, keeping him from the female he'd tried to claim as his own, stealing her away from the pack. When the female rejected him, his anger took his reason, clear thought eluded him, and the fight was on.

The pack leader had become prey, and he, along with the rest of them, ripped and tore at each other 'til all were lying on the ground, either dead or soon to be so, with wounds so horrific 'twas difficult to view. Watching them bleed out upon the forest floor, 'twas one of the most gruesome scenes Storrm could ever remember. Oh, she'd seen death afore, rivers of battle blood, but never caused by unwilling participants against themselves and their own. The battle had been a macabre and cruel joke, the barks, shrieks, growls, and snarls echoing in her ears long after 'twas quiet once again.

Breathing hard, Flyrra waited for several moments as the forest sounds slowly returned. Rhyah continued to fight her Hold on his mobility and she feared he'd cause more damage to himself, along with possibly his own death if he attacked the Second. She couldn't let that happen. She also had to brace herself for the Release as she was not even certain Storrm would give her time to explain, and she pondered just running away and leaving the two of them. But not understanding that 'twas a rescue effort, they'd become prey to each other, and she could not allow that to happen. She carefully avoided eye contact with the Second, whose rage bored through her soul and made her shiver.

Timing was everything and when she felt Rhyah, still in wolf form, was so depleted by loss of his Life Source that he'd not be able to continue to fight, she Released them. Although she'd seen the entire ordeal, Storrm's muscles and reflexes took o'er and she swiftly raised her Sword and near stumbled forward afore she caught her balance. Her head turned rapidly from Flyrra to the wolf as her understanding that 'twas the Fay, registered in her expression. Not sure how to handle the situation, she ignored Flyrra while she quickly scooped up the near comatose wolf lying and panting on the blood-soaked ground.

Mystynn returned at that moment. His opinion they should kill the half-breed then and there was clearly difficult to keep to himself. Without even bothering to Speak, he stated angrily, "She could have forced you Beyond as did she the wolves! How can we trust her?"

With a head nod toward the little girl, standing where she'd earlier crouched but having not moved since the Release, Storrm responded, "We'll discuss this later. With Darque." Mounting Mystynn with the severely injured wolf in her arms, she was amazed at his size and weight. If not enhanced, she'd never have been able to pick him up, let alone carry him. She adjusted the near lifeless body 'cross her lap in front of the saddle, and then after a moment's reflection, reached out her hand toward the little girl.

Flyrra had been holding her breath wondering if she'd be abandoned out here, not sure what to do if she were. When she saw Storrm reach out, she ran gratefully toward the Dragon, but her newfound hope was dashed by the coldness of the Second's emotions sensed through the skin on skin contact. Hanging her head, she did not let go, and allowed herself to be pulled up to sit behind Storrm. Holding on tightly, she squeezed her eyes shut against the rush of wind as Mystynn took wing to return them to the Keep. She'd loved living with the Resistance. She'd loved her new family. And she knew not where Kayarr even was, let alone how to find him.

Leaving a giant wet stain on the back of Storrm's leathers, the tears she shed came not from the cold of flight.

~~~~~ THE CLINIC OF THE KEEP ~~~~~

Upon arrival, Storrm restricted Flyrra to her quarters with a posted guard outside her entry, as she raced to the clinic with the wolf in her arms. Mystynn followed, as he did not trust either the girl or the wolf.

Now she looked upon the Fay in his true form. Afraid he'd lose himself to the Shift with his failing Life Force, he'd changed, making it even harder for him to Heal. Black eyes closed, forehead glistening with moisture, his shaggy brown hair streaked with strands of silver and black was matted down with sweat and blood. Perfect skin glowing as from within with Allure, he would stand at least four hands taller than herself, she mused. Her fingers pushed a strand of his soft hair behind one fan shaped ear, pointed backwards like miniature wings aside his head. The Fay lay lifelessly on the rack covered with a blanket, as Storrm glanced o'er her shoulder to note Kelseacyr concocting a potion. Quietly, she asked the Skald, "Will he live?"

The longing heard in that low voice made Kelsey look up curiously. With little concern, she stated, "Rhyah is strong, but I am Elven and know not much about Fay anatomy. Therefore, I've sent forth a Call to Corbyn. Once the Raven arrives, he can help me figure out what I might be missing, and if he lives 'til then, he should improve."

Storrm knew the Skald was much better than for which she gave herself credit so if Kelsey had little worry, Rhyah had a good chance. She picked up the edge of the blanket 'cross the Fay's bare waist and peeked. What she saw there, made her blush. She'd seen plenty of Warriors completely bare and they'd never made her look twice, so she couldn't understand why there was a difference in her reactions now. The quickening in her gut and the moisture that came unbidden 'tween her thighs was surprising. But then again, what was she thinking? He was Fay. The Fay had some weird attraction that she suspected was in their blood. Still…

The flustering moment was broken by the abrupt appearance of Kelsey at the head of the rack and Storrm dropped the blanket with a guilty expression. A knowing smile upon her lips and her brown brows raised, Kelsey stated, "Help me hold him upright and get him alert enough to drink this." Without a word Storrm did as she was told, cradling the Fay in her arms as she sat behind him, providing support for Rhyah to sit up for the tiny Skald, who stood even shorter than Darque. With great effort the Fay opened his eyes and once again, Storrm felt that strange emotion in her gut. If Mystynn refused her, mayhap this one… she had to admit he was all hard muscle and quite handsome, and the Fay were the strongest of the Magic bearers. She could do worse.

~~~~~~~~~~

Outside the clinic, Mystynn stood near shaking with his own unexpected emotions. He'd seen Storrm's reaction to Rhyah, watched with jealousy as she'd admired his form, and Felt the arousal such had produced. Although he wanted her for himself, she deserved better, yet she'd not found a Human to mate, seemingly uninterested in her own Kind other than the occasional release of sexual energy. Most of the other Warriors found such release much more frequently and he'd been somewhat concerned she'd never find a match. Mayhap Rhyah was the one to stir Storrm's heart. Such a pairing would be good for her. In fact, what better match could he have envisioned? The Fay would never take a 'Bond, therefore, he would not be as burdened by having to Share their mating habits. Mystynn had decided long ago that he'd not take his own mate and therefore he could more easily Block such if necessary. 'Twas with a heavy heart that he determined to encourage their relationship. At least he would always be her 'Bond, keeping her safe. No one could take that away, he thought, as he continued to Block his muddled emotions from Storrm.

NEAR A FORTNIGHT LATER

~~~~~ THE KREEGAREN FORTRESS ~~~~~

</div>

'Twould be near the end of the Spring Melts back in Kadoor. Standing in the middle of the open Ward, surrounded by the entire Kreegaren force of near two thousand Elves all dressed in full Assassin's cloaks would make the average person, even a Warrior, feel a tad intimidated. But Regynn was not average and through the long winter, these Elves had all become friends. He faced Tammra, his fellow travelers stepping up behind him as they grasped arms.

She stood eye to eye with the Warrior and locked gazes. "Everything good has the potential to be bad, if forced upon you. 'Tis freedom for which we fight. The right to life, the right to choose." Tammra reflected on her words repeated from long ago and did not try to hide her emotions, but she was not quite ready to commit to yet another move. "I will give your proposal an honest hearing, my friend. But know that we are safe here, the Fortress is impenetrable, and we can live out our lives in security if we stay. Swearing fealty to your King Gabriel and bringing my forces under Battle Commander Darque, is not seen by most of my brethren as a step up. Nor have they all been convinced of the danger the Black and his Hoard bring to us. Although none wish to return to the Elven Nation, few of these Elves have military training in their past and none fought in the last war. They care little about the rest of the world."

She paused, noting Regynn's expression of disappointment afore she continued. "But I do. As the former Commander of the Elven Nation during a war of major impact, I see the danger all too clearly." Regynn's disappointment changed to hope afore she concluded her thoughts. "Nonetheless, I will not force my troops to join your Resistance. They will follow me anywhere I lead, but I must have their full agreement. Times have changed. I have changed." She loosed Regynn's arm and they stepped back a pace from each other. Nodding her head, she then stated, "Worry not. I have a feeling we shall be coming to visit, very soon. After all, we must deliver our most honored guest back home." And with a sly smile, she turned with them, her ever-present bodyguards Leis and Dyra beside her, and walked them toward the outer wall where Sydrayyah stood waiting. Cathay mounted, then Regynn. They were sad to leave behind Orayalyn, who'd chosen to remain with the Kreegare and Leis and Dyra for a time. Then hopping to the top of the wall and once again bidding Tammra goodbye, they took their leave. The Elven brothers Danced together and disappeared into the chill early morning air, following the Dragon.

Tammra watched the cloudless skies for a time after they'd gone. Winter was near o'er and Spring was just around the corner. The Spring Melts in the Sakyn Forest region had proven to be similar to Kadoor's, but with the light snowfalls through this past winter, they should not be as heavy or last as long, and mayhap by that time she could convince her troops that they must at least make a cursory visit to the Resistance. As most of them had expressed a desire to reunite with family, but not to stay there, they were planning a trip soon anyway. They could mayhap, stop there on the way to the Wyrdritch with the winemaker. 'Twas as good an excuse as any. Figuring in her mind, she would have at least a full moon or more to convince her people to take heed of their visitors' warnings. Wishing her new friends fare travel, she turned abruptly, left the Ward, and walked back to her office. 'Twas duty as usual.

MEANWHILE

LATE SPRING

~~~~~ THE CLINIC OF THE KEEP ~~~~~

</div>

Storrm arrived early in the afternoon to check on Rhyah's progress. A quick visual scan of the clinic revealed no Fay. Kelsey wandered into the room to see who was there, her arms filled with bottles and bags and dried herbs. With her long brown curls bouncing, her lovely voice answered Storrm's unasked question. "I couldn't stop him. He just got up and asked to leave. Darque came and escorted him away about a mark past."

Turning without a word, she breezed out of the clinic on her way to Communications. Axyl and Haniyyah supervised messaging from the Keep. They could relay any information to and from all three Lairs, with Rolf and Nalwynn stationed at Drekinn Lair in the same capacity. They'd never failed her afore. Her temper flaring, her steps hard and swift down the hallway, she came to an abrupt halt. Furrowing her brows, she wondered. Had Darque given her orders for Watch and allowing Flyrra out of detention, other than what they'd previously discussed? And what about her orders regarding the Fay? That, they'd not discussed.

Mystynn's Voice boomed mid-sentence in her mind as if he'd been trying to Speak to her and she'd been Blocking. Throwing her hands down to her sides, she realized in frustration that she had been doing that very thing, and her distraction had eroded the Block. She'd not wanted Mystynn to know of her feelings, or hopes, regarding Rhyah. *"Can you Hear me now?"* he Asked her in an amused voice. 'Twas a phrase he'd heard Humans use often 'tween the War of Chaos and the Last Holocaust. His witticism fell on deaf ears, however, as Storrm did not share those Memories.

"Yes. I can Hear you now." She sighed. *"I'm sorry. I must have been Blocking for some reason,"* she added, afore trailing off in her apology. Why did she have to say so much? Why couldn't she have left it at, 'I'm sorry'?

His bruised emotions went unnoted, and Mystynn was glad. He'd not wanted to hurt her. He knew she'd been Blocking, and he knew why. But Darque had taken her leave, given o'er the Keep to their Command, released Flyrra from detention back to her training and classes, and provided orders to deal with the Fay. Now he repeated those orders to Storrm.

"Was she upset?"

"I did not note such emotion, but her orders were relayed through Haniyyah," he reminded her. Letting her off the hook, he continued, *"I doubt it. You and she had your face-to-face earlier, so taking her leave was merely protocol. She wanted you to be aware the Fay had left the clinic and has been given private quarters and free roam of the upper levels of the Keep. She also wants you to keep an eye on his progress as he is still healing and should report daily to Kelseacyr for wound care."*

Mystynn then Told her he was leaving to hunt the high peaks outside the Dome and would be out late. Storrm bid him fare hunting, while wondering if the Fay were looking for her. She blushed at her own thoughts. For Flame's sake, she was an adult, why did she have to act like such an adolescent when it came to Rhyah? Taking her own leave of the clinic, she decided to get something to eat. She bit her bottom lip in reflection. 'Twould be nice if Rhyah were in the Mess Hall.

~~~~~ LATER ~~~~~

As it turned out, Rhyah was in the Mess Hall when Storrm arrived, and walking up beside her in the line, he'd offered a friendly smile and easy-going manner, despite the physical pain with which he was dealing. Through the afternoon, her fluttering gut settled under his charming good nature, causing her to laugh openly, or lean closer, enthralled as he told her tales of his childhood. But 'twas not just his life of which they spoke. The Fay was a very good listener as well, but she was needed in the Ward and her Command duties called.

As she stood up, so too did the Fay and the fluttering in her gut returned with a vengeance to his deep masculine voice, while his firm yet gentle touch upon her arm, brought a tingling 'tween her thighs. "May I accompany you on your rounds?" he asked, his black eyes flashing their lighting streaks as was the 'tell' of the Fay.

She was honored that Rhyah had chosen to show his real form. 'Twas a form that elicited many admiring and envious glances from the other Warriors in the area. "'Twill be easier to keep my eye upon you, if you are with me," Storrm said, her usual demeanor returning, her confidence building. 'Twas clear by the Fay's roaming gaze, that he appreciated what he saw when he looked at her. "Come. I go to the Ward to supervise training. Are you a swordsman?"

With a wicked grin, Rhyah responded, putting forth his elbow for Storrm to grip as they walked toward the exit, "I look forward to displaying my meager skills in handling my sword, though I am quite certain you can teach me much." The double entendre did not go unnoted.

~~~~~~~~~~

As they walked into the training area of the Ward, Storrm questioned, "Where are you sleeping tonight?" Her face turned instantly crimson. Taking a step back, she stammered, "I mean, I just understood that you were given private quarters and that's convenient." Her eyes caught those of the Fay, his expression heated, hers mortified. "I mean, 'tis less likely you would have interference with your healing process. You'll get more rest in private quarters, 'tis quieter than in the Barracks." Still attempting to recover, she finished, "I just wanted to ensure your comfort, and that you knew your way around."

Sliding one hand down to her low back he pulled her near, closing the gap that Storrm had attempted to widen during her babbling, without remorse. "I'd say 'tis more convenient for getting to know you better, and that would increase my comfort greatly. And are you offering to show me around?" he questioned, his eyes slowing drinking in Storrm's strong, lean, youthful body.

Storrm didn't bother to protest. His actions were not threatening, and she was quite flattered by his attentions. After all, she'd never thought herself the prettiest or most desirable Warrior in the Brotherhood, but she seemed to have entranced the Fay. With more control, she stated, "I have to wonder how you rated such privacy."

Appearing somewhat confused, Rhyah replied honestly, "'Tis my understanding that your Mystynn discussed the arrangements with the Battle Commander afore she left for Drekinn."

Surprised, Storrm's deep blue eyes widened and she opened her mouth to speak but could find no words. Her famous, or rather, infamous temper flared yet again. If this was what her sister and her partner wanted for her, this was what they would get. Besides, there was always the chance that the Fay was someone with whom she could spend her life. With Mystynn regularly Blocking her from his attentions, she was lonely. Standing closer to his broad chest, she could feel the heat coming through the borrowed leathers, the seams straining to contain what was abruptly rising 'tween his legs. After a slow sultry glance downward, she caught his eyes again and stated teasingly, "Have you a sword?"

"I believe I have just proven that," the Fay replied with an awkward grin. He had not intended for this meeting to go quite this direction, this quickly. But there was something about the Second in Command that drew him and made him yearn to take her then and there, despite the fact that they were in an open Ward. Was this true love? His hand unconsciously rubbed 'cross the left side of his ribcage, just o'er his breast. He'd received a vicious bite wound there and the dressing o'er both his chest and his left shoulder seemed bulkier than 'twas when he'd left the clinic.

Her smirk was contagious as she replied, "I meant a sword for fighting. We're in the training area. We should practice."

"I don't mind practicing whatever you want to practice," he laughed, and Storrm just shook her head and stepped away, walking o'er to the racks along the wall. Following her beautiful backside, multiple long thick red braids swishing past her calves, Rhyah adjusted his pants for ease of movement with a self-chastising grimace and then just managed to catch the sword Storrm tossed his way, afore it hit him in the face. He was definitely going to have to step it up or this luscious creature would think him an idiot.

~~~~~ HIGH ABOVE THE WARD OF THE KEEP ~~~~~

His long black wings iridescent in the skies, Corbyn had flown in earlier from Fire Heart, where Mynx reported Synahmarr had finally agreed to lay her eggs. He mused o'er his last 'conversation' with the Matriarch. His own voice rang through his mind, "If viable, they must hatch, if not viable you must lay them so you can fly again!" She'd been enraged in her response, "You would have me fly with the Black?" Calmly, he'd replied, "No. I would have you fly with your lifemate." The Matriarch had squinted in suspicion, her voice a low growl from deep in her throat. "What do you know that I do not?" Corbyn had then vowed, "I know that your memory has been altered. And I know that I will find the one who did Claim you. This I swear."

Thus far, he'd had no luck in fulfilling that vow, but now that she had agreed to lay her eggs 'twas one less worry, and he could relax for a time. 'Twas then he was delighted to discover his childhood friend had been located and brought into the Keep. 'Twas exciting, and yet, seeing Storrm and Rhyah together brought forth conflicting emotions.

He hadn't seen Rhyah since he'd been exiled. 'Twas the end of one life and the beginning of another. Yet lately he'd begun to question the parameters of his curse. Why was he sent to prevent the death of so many Warriors? The Morrigan knew when they would die, death could not be prevented, 'twas the way of life for a Warrior. So why was he required to suffer so, by watching, waiting, attempting to prevent the inevitable, his emotions worn ragged as he grew to love them all in his own way? Reflecting further, he wondered about the parallel to his past life, losing Hellyn and their unborn son to such butchery, a death he could not prevent because he was not there. The death of every Warrior he served had come by the sword, and his duties had prevented his presence every time. Just like with Hellyn. Coincidence?

His latest Warrior to serve was Storrm, and he'd protested greatly. Never afore had he been angry with the Morrigan, the potent emotion flooding his senses. Always he'd taken his assignments and followed her directions, sadly knowing to what end 'twould lead, and enduring as best he could. But this time was different. With every fiber of his being, he wanted to prevent this one's death.

Corbyn knew his best friend well. Rhyah was not one to wander from female to female. He wanted Storrm and once he'd chosen, he would remain loyal to the end. Rhyah would be as devastated as had he been upon his own beloved's loss, when Storrm succumbed. Serving Storrm meant she didn't have long. But how long? Moons? Winters? He never knew. Should he prevent their growing relationship? Save Rhyah the pain? No. Storrm deserved some happiness, as did Rhyah. Loss was ever present in the lives of all, 'twas not he to blame, and one simply learned to deal with such emotion. His beady black eyes glittered as he pondered those thoughts.

~~~~~~~~~~

Rhyah proved to be a decent swordsman, and Storrm enjoyed their duel. For more than a mark they practiced. With his direction she improved her weight shifting and stepping while she taught him the turn and swing techniques of the Clan. But 'twas when she noted the darkening stain creeping 'cross his left breast that she dropped her sword and stepped up, her hand reaching for him, her eyes concerned. "We've done too much for today. Let me take you back to the clinic. That dressing needs changing. I fear we've opened the wound again. Did you feel nothing?"

"I felt it long ago." Holding his chest with his right hand, he passed the borrowed sword to her with his left as they walked out of the Ward together, heading back to the clinic.

Storrm noted his pain and weakness, and chastised him, "You were hurting, and you kept fighting. Why did you not tell me?"

Flashing a brilliant smile, he stated, "I did not want to stop. You are a most fascinating woman, Storrm. But now, although I hate to admit such, I do need rest." Then with genuine eagerness he asked, "May I see you later?"

Standing at the entry to the clinic, Kelsey came o'er and practically dragged him back inside, fussing at them both about doing too much and making her job more difficult. Then Corbyn appeared from behind the tiny Skald, and Rhyah's eyes lit up. The good friends embracing, Rhyah suddenly broke the grasp and looked o'er his shoulder for Storrm. She was gone, and he knew not her answer to his query. Reluctantly, he turned away and followed the Skald and Corbyn into the clinic.

THREE DAWNS LATER

~~~~~ GUEST QUARTERS OF RHYAH ~~~~~

</div>

Kelsey had released the Fay after gaining his promise he'd not participate in anymore fighting practice 'til the wounds had a chance to heal sufficiently so as not to reopen. She'd attempted to have him Shift back to wolf form to aide such healing, but he'd refused, saying he wanted to experience all this new life had to offer. Everything was so different outside the Nation of the Fay.

Due to a very potent concoction suggested by Corbyn and provided by Kelsey, he'd slept from dusk to dawn for the past two nights and 'twas now dawn again. His sensitive ears could hear the generalized ruckus with which he was surrounded as those in the Keep woke, and everyone went about their morning routines. Now that the Domes were in place, the morning katas of the Warriors were held in the open Ward once again, the Battle Drums and Pipes providing rhythm as they moved in coordinated synchronicity. Each age and skill level had their own katas, each coordinated and incorporated into the next level so that 'twas a huge dance of awe-inspiring grace and force. He'd not wanted to miss such but he'd promised and so he aimlessly wandered about his quarters, waiting for Kelsey to bring his breakfast. That was also a part of his promise. Not to leave his quarters for the next few dawns. That part was the most difficult to accomplish, as his body began to warm with the rush of blood from thinking about the Second in Command. 'Twas all he could think about, it seemed. The Skald had been providing his meals and performed daily dressing changes. His normal curiosity was straining for release, tension was building. But he had to admit, his wounds were better already. Still, the company of his kinsman was expected this morning as well as the Skald, and much awaited, even more so than breakfast.

Throughout the long nights Rhyah had dreamed of the woman in the Icelands. He didn't understand how she could be there in reality, but he knew not what she might represent otherwise. Only the Ice Dragons could live in the Icelands. 'Twas far too cold. But o'er the past few moons the dream had become near constant in his sleeping marks, making him yearn for the freezing temperatures, the ever-present ice and snow, the raw beauty of the stark landscape drawing him like a moth to the flame. He'd long past determined that the beautiful woman was Elven, and although 'twas somewhat ludicrous, he was beginning to think 'twas Queen Bryanna herself. And she rode upon the Empress of the Ice Dragons, Bronwyn. With each dream, he felt she was trying to tell him something, and that she had something to give him. He could not ignore the call. He knew his destiny lay to the far north. And yet, 'twould be suicide, he thought, as he squinted trying to make sense of such. Even in wolf form, he'd not live long. Was he to accept this dream as literal? What did the Fates have in store?

Kelsey came early but brought not his meal, stating as she cleaned and re-dressed his wounds that Corbyn had taken that duty out of her hands this morning and should arrive soon enough. This proved to be truth, for as soon as Kelsey walked out, Corbyn strode in past her, holding onto a plate laden with food. His mouth watered as he took the offering and then the two friends sat down while Rhyah ate and Corbyn talked. So much time had passed since they'd last seen each other. They had some catching up to do. Without giving much detail, Corbyn told his friend what he could and once Rhyah had his fill, the Raven sat back with great interest, listening to all that had happened during their separation.

Rhyah finally quieted for a moment and then he broached the subject they both had tried to avoid. "You and I know the Shunning was a direct result of disagreements 'tween your grandfather and your father." He noted the grimace upon Corbyn's face as he recalled Corlyn the Lion, who fought in the War of Chaos and was an original member of the High Races Council, and his son, Bardyn the Bear, who had grown up feeling demeaned and o'er-shadowed by his famous, or mayhap infamous, father.

After a brief pause with no comment from Corbyn, Rhyah continued. "The younger Fay all realize the truth, that we must embrace strong emotion as we did during the War of Chaos. More of us want to leave the confines of the Nation, to seek a way to fight against the Evil One, standing shoulder to shoulder with our allies in the High Races Counsel once again." Still no comment from his friend. In growing frustration, he summarized, "The Fay want you back, Corbyn. They want you to return and take your place as the Greatest King, and Bardyn will not be able to prevent it for much longer. His health wanes as does his span of days. The Bear has spent more of his time in fur these past few decades, than in skin."

Now this disclosure had Corbyn's full attention. He'd always wondered how fared his family. Knowing Bardyn was near his end of days, hit him hard. Despite their differences, despite being exiled and cursed, Bardyn was a good man, had tried to be a good father and ruler, and they'd always loved each other. Corbyn had felt like a failure not only to Hellyn, but to Bardyn and the Nation as well. He needed to be there for him. But how? Could the curse be ended? He sighed. "I can't say that such news is welcome, my friend. But 'tis good to know."

Moving on to another topic, Rhyah asked about the parameters of Corbyn's curse. 'Twould be horrible to be the bringer of death time and time again. He could not understand how Corbyn managed to survive. The Raven reflected momentarily and then as he finally understood himself, revealed, "I am not the bringer of death. I merely delay it for as long as possible. The hopelessness and defeat of knowing the result of my efforts is for naught, are the true constraints of my curse."

Noting Rhyah's flagging endurance, Corbyn stood up. Just afore he took his leave he stared at his good friend. Should he say anything? Feeling oddly hypocritical, he made his decision and stated softly, "Remember always, that you are in control of your emotions. No one can take your control, you can only give it away. Do not allow such in your journey through life. Do not allow others to control you through your emotions." Rhyah appeared fully engaged in his words, and Corbyn hoped he'd conveyed enough information to help his friend through the upcoming events in his life. Sensing they both had much to learn still, he turned and walked down the corridor pondering his own sentiments.

CHAPTER FIFTEEN

Prophetic Misunderstandings

In the Raptor's Talons, late Spring was arguably the most unpredictable of the seasons. Mid-day could be near hot and sunny while dusk might bring the sense that 'twould snow again at any moment, forcing the need to rekindle the evening fires. 'Twas such an evening as this, that Storrm found herself in Rhyah's quarters standing naked on the fur rug that lay in front of the fireplace, a fresh stack of split wood on one side of the hearth ready to feed the newly laid fire, as she faced the man for whom she'd grown quite fond.

His flashing eyes roamed with admiration from the top of her head to her bare feet, her toes curling nervously in the long fur. 'Twas near a quarter mark earlier that he began to unbraid her hair, running his fingers through its luxurious length. Now 'twas loose and free flowing down her back, a thick strand spilling o'er her weather-tanned shoulder attempting to hide one delicious pink nipple from his view. He reached forth and pushed the offending strand back, amazed at how soft was her skin, amid the flickering backdrop produced by the firelight that could not hide her natural beauty. As his hand drifted down to cup her now fully exposed breast, she lifted herself to him with a dazzling smile. 'Twas breathtaking. Rhyah had never experienced such strong emotions, and yet he was certain he appeared much calmer than he felt. Although he'd held her hand upon occasion, even stolen a kiss in the hallway, they'd not taken things this far 'til tonight.

The vicious wounds upon his own shoulder were now healed, leaving him with pink slashes 'cross his otherwise perfect skin, which would fade away slowly but surely to a mere memory of the event. His heart pounding a rhythm of desire, Storrm reached forward to gently touch the scars, tracing them with her long fingers 'cross his bare chest then ever downward to his navel, bringing a stuttered gasp from the Fay. He forced himself to slow things down, for he wanted this time to be truly unforgettable, and taking her face with both hands he drew her slowly toward him, closing the gap 'tween, kissing her hungrily.

Through the past moon 'twas not what the Second in Command said, 'twas what she didn't say during their many marks spent together, that made him realize how afraid she was, how much she wanted to love and be loved. He was confident he could provide her with what she wanted. If she would allow such. So, he'd held back, gained her trust, forgiven her frequent, sudden, and usually confusing changes in mood, and built their relationship. Finally, she was his.

Storrm's heart raced with guilty yearning. She couldn't deny her rising desire, she wanted this man, more than any other man she'd ever wanted afore. But he was not Mystynn. Still, her hands trembled as they reached for Rhyah's chest, the slight shimmering effect of his skin near hypnotic, the contrast of the pink scars against his natural warm glow of Allure, demanding her touch. Her fingers strayed toward his navel, his muscled belly tight and rock solid. Her eyes widened in expectation as her gaze drank in the hardening of his shaft, lifting, inviting her touch there as well, but suddenly his strong hands were pulling her closer and she took hold of his thick wrists to prevent him from letting go. She needed him. Their lips met, his tongue entwining with hers, and time stood still. 'Twas as if they were the only two in the entire Keep.

Rhyah's tongue plunged deeper, one hand cupped the nape of her neck while the other slid under the curtain of her long hair down her back to her hips, and he crushed her against his strong body. He'd felt her emotion. He never wanted to let her go.

Storrm stood on her toes to meet the Fay, her tongue and his dancing together, her hands pulling him closer, one knee rising up his side to his hip as his hand slid to her leg, holding her spread 'cross his pelvis, the pressure not enough for either of them. They wanted more.

His firm shaft caressed her 'tween her legs, rubbing up and down through the gathering moisture, the blood rushing in, preparing her for his invasion. Tingling, warming, tiny spasms began to make her shutter. This was going faster than they'd planned. Breath stuttering, both gasping, Rhyah could take no more, and lifting her off her feet, her legs locked around him and his hands pulled her hips tight as he drove into her with one smooth powerful stroke. Harder he plunged, Storrm's head upon his shoulder, holding onto him for the ride as he pushed in and pulled out, faster and deeper, setting a rhythm that she fiercely met, his strong arms giving them the leverage they both needed, and within moments took them o'er the edge of ecstasy toward which they'd cried.

Rhyah had waited 'til Storrm reached her climax afore he'd allowed himself to spill his seed and didn't want to pull out once his orgasm was attained. Even standing up, holding this beautiful woman against him, cupping her hips in both hands to keep them locked together, he would mind not, maintaining this position 'til the sun dawned. Pushing slightly in and out, his pelvis pressuring hers, he was rewarded with the expression in Storrm's eyes telling him that she could and would go again. What a remarkable woman, he thought, afore pulling out and lying her down on the fur rug. Leaning o'er her on one elbow, his tongue slid in and out of her welcoming mouth, those gorgeous lips open and inviting. As he licked them sensuously, his imagination had him at another place he wanted to lick, and he allowed his hand to explore her muscled body. Slowly his hand drifted downward 'tween her legs, her hips rising to meet his fingers as he slid one deep inside her. Then there were two fingers inside while his thumb rubbed o'er the center of her desire, and within mere moments, she was at the precipice of ecstasy again.

Shaking his head and smiling wickedly, he slowly pulled his fingers out, covered with her warm juices, so he could taste her. Honey sweet, he watched with feverish eyes as Storrm took his hand and drew his fingers to her own mouth. Eye to eye, he could feel himself rising to the challenge, but he had other plans for this one. Kissing her again, he dragged his tongue slowly down the soft skin of her long neck, teasingly down 'tween her breasts afore giving careful attention to each in turn. Flicking the sensitive nubs, nibbling gently, he gave her a taste of what was to come. Her hands eagerly pushed his head downward as the moisture 'tween her legs near spurted forth in anticipation. His warm tongue swirled through the mound of tight red curls and then spreading her with his long fingers, he stared at the beauty afore his eyes. Her hands pushed harder and he slowly obeyed, licking and teasing mercilessly, his tongue mimicking another member of his body. She tasted so good. Firmly his tongue licked up and down, around and around, in and out, and within moments he was rewarded once again. Storrm's head came off the rug hard and fast, her face a mask of intense pleasure and a moan of sheer delight burst forth from her lips as the juices 'tween her legs burst forth into his mouth.

Shifting his position to lie next to her with one knee 'tween her legs, he leaned again on his elbow and held her while the spasms lessened, then gently caressed her flat belly. Meeting her gaze, her face that of extreme fulfillment, he asked, "Are we done?"

Storrm's smile was wicked as she narrowed her eyes and replied with a resounding, "You don't get away that easily!"

Rhyah was impressed. And delighted. He licked his lips and took a deep breath to allow him speech capability as he responded, "The night is young, my love. Put yourself in my hands."

If his emotions were in better control, he'd have noticed the slight change in her expression upon hearing his words. She was excited for more as Rhyah was proving to be an accomplished lover, but unsure of love itself. Still, they did have many marks ahead of them to thoroughly enjoy whatever this was. She tried to ignore her guilt but 'twas only when she imagined another as her lover, that she was able to relax and let Rhyah pleasure her.

~~~~~ MEANWHILE ~~~~~

Having informed his partner that he would be gone o'ernight on an extended hunt, Mystynn sat miserably upon the ledge in the deep forest, knowing exactly what Storrm was doing, and with whom. His cold tears fell like raindrops to the trees below. If the Fates ever gave them another chance, he'd take it in a heartbeat. 'Twas too late he realized that he'd been wrong. He should have tried. She might have been able to love him. Now he'd lost her for all time.

~~~~~ NEAR DAWN ~~~~~

Rhyah laid beside her, once more on one elbow, and smoothed her disheveled hair out of her face. Even in blissful sleep, Storrm was a creature of immense beauty... and mystery. 'Twas several marks of lovemaking afore they'd finally settled down to sleep in each other's arms, but Rhyah found that even in exhaustion, sleep eluded him.

During their night of passion, Rhyah came to the realization that Storrm didn't know her own mind. Although she'd made love to him and with him for marks, her heart was not keeping up at the same level as was her body. Falling asleep but for a few moments, the dream woman came to him again, beckoning him come to the Icelands. The urgency he felt in that dream made his heart ache with indecision. Agonizing about what to do, he recalled Corbyn's words to him. He controlled his emotions. No one else. And as for Storrm? 'Twas clearly revealed through the night, that she did not reciprocate his love, for she loved another. Humans. He shook his head. But gazing down at her lovely face, he had to admit he didn't really understand love, this had probably been mere lust, with respect of course, but he had no regrets. He'd tried. He'd given it his all, and he could do no more. Besides, what if the woman in the Icelands was truly Queen Bryanna and needed him. He and Bryanna had history. 'Twould be interesting.

He'd found Corbyn and delivered his message. Without Storrm's love, he had nothing to hold him here. Determining that his destiny lay in another direction, his finger lightly caressed along Storrm's freckled cheek, then down her neck. He would miss her. He wondered if she would miss him. He sighed. Storrm was in a terrible situation, he could sense the unrequited love she felt for another. Who was the lucky man? What an idiot he was for denying this gorgeous creature his heart!

Storrm's eyes fluttered open and she initially appeared confused, then realizing where and with whom she was, she presented a shy smile. Rhyah leaned o'er and kissed her lightly, then rolled away, standing up, assisting her up as well. Grabbing her leathers off the floor where they'd been discarded last night, he handed them to her and dressed while she did the same. Silently, he watched her for any evidence that he might be wrong, that she might be able to fall in love with him, but her shy nature, avoiding his gaze, confirmed his earlier deduction. He tucked his chin. "'Twas the most remarkable night I've ever spent with any woman, Storrm."

She licked her lips as she finished lacing her pants, then looked at him with those beautiful blue eyes that made his heart skip a beat. Lust? Love? At this particular moment, he knew not. "I'd have to say that 'twas remarkable for me as well. You are most talented. And caring." Her gaze dipped to the floor as she donned her boots, then back to Rhyah. "You're a good man…" she began, but he stopped her.

Stepping closer, he placed one finger 'cross her lips to silence whatever thoughts she may have had as 'twas no doubt now, that she did not love him. "Let me finish, Storrm. I want you. I think I could love you like no other. But we both know that you love another." When she attempted to protest, further confirming his thoughts, he shook his head again. "No, I will never keep a woman against her will or her own heart. You love another and are free to go. I will not fight to dominate your affections. I will have a woman love me without restriction, or I will walk away. Humans are new to me, but they are not unlike my own Kind. Females tend to deny their own feelings if such is unrequited. 'Til you have let go the one you truly love, regrets will always be 'tween us, and I want more. I want all of you, or none."

Storrm was holding back her tears, trying not to let them flow down her cheeks, but one escaped and when she then wiped it away, more began to stream. She looked down and sniffed. He was right. He was not the one she loved, and she'd never be able to love another than Mystynn. She'd rather be alone than with anyone else. Gaining control o'er the tears, she stated, "Thank you."

"For what?"

"I had thoughts of being with you, and I do love you, you know. In my own way. But you're right. You've confirmed my need and true love for another. Such would always hinder our relationship."

Rhyah's emotions were chaotic, but not as painful as he'd expected. 'Twas an oddly triumphant sadness that he felt. He would miss her, indeed. "And you have confirmed my need and growing affection for another. My destiny lies in the Icelands, with the woman in my dreams. 'Tis time I go to her." Storrm nodded, he'd told her about the dreams and they'd speculated as to their meaning. "Furthermore, you have opened my senses and taught me that I am in control of my emotions. No one can ever take that away from me again."

Storrm was grateful the Fay did not hate her for what she felt she'd done to him. But she knew he'd leave this very day and she had to say her goodbyes. "You shall always be my friend, Rhyah.

I will never forget you, nor do I hold any regrets." Comforted, she turned and made her way to the door. Her life would finally return to normal and she'd make every attempt to get closer to Mystynn. Taking her leave, she then stated, "Go with the One, and may the Fates be kind." Unknown to either, 'twould be the last time they saw each other.

~~~~~~~~~

Mystynn sat on the ramparts of the Keep, his cold tears falling once more, but this time, 'twas with great joy. Storrm loved him. She was his.

~~~~~ THE VOID ~~~~~

A look of pure misery upon her face, Storrm asked, "How did I miss your feelings for so long? How did I not know? I thought the 'Bond allowed us to know everything about each other, to Share all our feelings."

"'Twas I. I Blocked much from you," Mystynn replied with equal misery.

She hung her head in shame, as she'd done the same thing to him. But still, she had to know. "Why? What did I do wrong? Did I displease you somehow?"

The painful truth was difficult to admit, but forging ahead, he told her, "You did nothing wrong, and you could not displease me. I was afraid. I'd been with many females in my span of days, and 'twas a healthy span indeed. I was never rejected but I'd never been in love, either. I thought you deserved more than that. You deserved someone far better than I."

Brightening with his admission, she asked, "You truly loved me? All along?"

"Not loved. Love. From the day I first laid eyes upon you."

THE KEEP
A FORTNIGHT LATER
~~~~~ NEAR THE SUMMER SOLSTICE ~~~~~

Storrm found the Borkahn child in the beehive area, tending her bees. Crytcha looked so much better since she'd been Claimed by Natan and Kayarr, living with her best friend, Flyrra. Nonetheless, she did have a real home and real father, whom she'd not seen in a very long time.

Calling to gain her attention, she pasted a smile upon her face so as not to alarm her. "Crytcha? Darque sent me to find you. Your uncle is here. He's waiting in the Battle Commander's office."

"Uncle Tayatch? He's come for me! I can go home!"

Turning and hurrying down the hall in her heavy, stomping stride, Storrm watched the huge youngster rush off to Darque's office, and certain heartache. She was never one to cry easily but something was making her very emotional since Rhyah left. She wiped the tear rolling down her cheek with her knuckles and sighed as she walked back to the Ward where Mystynn waited for her.

Tayatch of the Borkahn had arrived less than three marks earlier and the news he came to impart was not that for which the child had hoped. Her own meeting with Darque was shortened by the unexpected visit and she'd stayed to hear what the big male had to say, but now she just wanted to get back to her own quarters at the Den. Crytcha would be crushed. She blinked hard to stem the tears, sniffed again, and then cleared her throat. There was nothing she could do. Her emotions in check again she mounted, and alerting the Gatekeepers, she and Mystynn took wing. She was starving and exhausted. Strange. She hadn't really done that much.

Kelseacyr watched from the Ward Gate as the Second in Command and her big green Dragon partner flew away. She chewed the inside of her cheek, pondering what she should do. 'Twas clear that the Second didn't know, but being an experienced Skald, she'd sensed the symptoms, and after careful observation, she knew that trouble was imminent. This could be serious. Should she tell her, or should she go directly to the Battle Commander? After but a moment, she knew whom she had to tell first. Hurrying off, she sought Corbyn the Raven afore he took his own leave to follow the Second back to Drekinn.

A FEW MARKS LATER

~~~~~ THE CLINIC OF THE DRAGON'S DEN ~~~~~

</div>

Storrm had visited Shayla as soon as they'd arrived and now the Healer stood and pondered Storrm's symptoms and complaints. "Lethargy like what you describe, usually comes from working too hard for too long, or a loss of blood, or an infection. However, I want you to know something of which I've just been told." She sucked her bottom lip into her mouth as she made her decision to reveal what had been told her in confidence less than a half mark prior. Corbyn reported from Kelseacyr, the Skald's belief that Storrm was pregnant and that 'twas of the Fay. Shayla had won the argument that they needed to get this under control asap, and not wait and see what happened. If Storrm hadn't come to her, she would have called her into the clinic to discuss it.

After telling Storrm that she was pregnant, and by whom, Shayla was relieved by the other's acceptance and happiness with the situation. 'Twould not be easy on her. "I'm glad you have such a good attitude, and I'm sorry the father can't be notified as well. But you are hardly alone in this!"

Mystynn was just as happy as was Storrm, but the Healer was puzzled when she responded, "No Aunt Shayla, I am alone for now. Please don't tell anyone yet. Let me do it in my own way, in my own time."

Running her fingers through her curly locks to force them back o'er her head, the Healer simply nodded her acceptance of such. "The Battle Commander will have to be informed."

"I'll tell her," Storrm promised. "In the meantime, do you have anything to help with the fatigue? I'm still Second in Command, and I must keep up," she laughed. But Storrm's mirth hid an underlying apprehension that Shayla missed, for no one other than her partner was privy to her prophesy. 'Twas beginning.

~~~~~ TWO DAWNS LATER ~~~~~

Fortunately, Darque decided to change the Guard early, taking command of Drekinn herself while sending Storrm and Mystynn back to the Keep and ordering Kydra and Ragnyrr to take command of the Teams currently out on the mission to locate the missing Warriors from afore the big battle. 'Twas supposed to have been her mission, as 'twas discussed near a moon prior. Storrm wondered at the timing as well as the change in orders but said not a word as she took her assignment, moving back to St Swiftyn's.

Shortly after their arrival, Storrm consulted with Kelsey and the Skald altered Shayla's recently created concoction with the assist of Corbyn, as the baby was growing at an astonishing rate, depleting the Second in Command. She was to drink the concoction once daily. Storrm felt better near immediately. 'Twas a good working solution. For a time.

CHAPTER SIXTEEN

The Dragon's Stash

The Sprite sat down on the middle of the long wooden bench at the matching table 'cross from the Warrior she was somewhat surprised to see. Catching his curious glance, Caleichante addressed the man she recognized from Port O'Teliv so long ago. "My heart aches with you and for your loss." Rygyl looked at her with growing awareness in his eyes, followed by a sad smile. He and his woman, Ariel, along with their 'Bonds, Tegrynn and Zaydarr, had been searching for Dragon teeth, scales, fangs, and Eyes, on the black market. Calei had just made contact with them when she'd found the Krakken, and after boarding she knew not what happened to the pair. They were going back to Drekinn and would return within a sennight, but she wasn't there, off to complete her own mission. Now seeing him again, she felt true sorrow for the sadness he still held in his heart.

"Thank you. I'm not as 'over it', as I profess," Rygyl acknowledged, pulling the braids around his wrist. He had to admit 'twas getting to be an easier burden to bear and the recent battles in which he'd taken part helped ease the pain. Calei glanced to his wrist as he lifted his mug and took another swig. He caught the glance and as had become his habit of late, fingered the loops of tightly braided hair, his own, a promise to his beloved given to Ariel late the same evening they'd met the Sprite. He'd taken it off her lifeless wrist in the blood and gore-strewn field after the battle.

Calei had just arrived from the Keep and was taking a break from the tour. Graasyn had stayed behind, working on the new sign language with the others, incorporating their private signals and some extra battle ones, as well as setting up an additional training schedule with the Warriors, the children, and the rest of the Clansmen. Everyone must be on the same page with all the signs. Calei was a quick study and she'd taken the Commander's invitation to spend a few days at the Den afore she, Graasyn, Diadranei, and Bastyen were deployed to King's Gate to reconnoiter. Their ultimate mission was to infiltrate Evanntyr and discover what the Black was doing with High King Shytin.

She nodded to Rygyl and then stated, "I've learned 'tis a Clan tradition for a male to make such a bracelet to give to his beloved as a promise to vows." She smiled as she fingered her own braids.

With an approving eye upon Calei's wrist, Rygyl stated, "Yes, 'tis."

"Ariel wore them proudly. And she died as should a true Warrior. 'Twas a valiant death. She would not want you to mourn forever. If she loved you enough to make promise, she would want you to be happy, to go on with your life."

Rygyl simply nodded his head. But he noticed that his throat wasn't as tight as 'twould be in the past when thinking about Ariel, and his eyes filled not with tears. He looked up at the Sprite. "I'm getting there." With a smirk upon his lips, he added, "And you begin to sound like my Tegrynn."

"I'm just saying that you wear the promise braids now. Mayhap you will find someone else worthy of your devotion and to whom you can give them. Life goes on, my friend. Change is part of life. Plans have a way of making themselves, without our permission."

Once more, Rygyl nodded his head. Then looking up again, he had a thought. "When we met in that port district, you obviously knew who we were. How?"

"Your Dragons recognized that I am Sprite. I knew that Zaydarr was a cousin of Gunnarr the Mighty Blue. And I knew you were in the 'Bond. That meant that you were Warriors of the Dragon Clan." She shrugged her slim shoulders. "Simple logic."

He laughed. Back then, they'd no idea how much she knew about them. Then he furrowed his brows and stated seriously, "Ariel and I were searching for black market items. You told us you knew where such could be found. Did you speak the truth?"

"I repeat, I am Sprite. And I was Captain of the Elite Guard. Of course, 'twas the truth!" Raising her hand palm forward, she stopped further discussion on that topic. "But I am hungry, and I would eat first, give you information later, for 'twill wait."

They both sat and ate and drank their fill, laughing and talking. Amongst other things, she shared stories of how she and Graasyn met and ultimately mated. 'Twas a mixed blood match that was drawing much fascination throughout the Clan. And although 'twas discovered that Graasyn and Bastyen, the father/son Stealth Team, were of Elven/Human descent, that was not why they'd mated. Love was why. She gave up her life on the island, her rank as Captain, her primary allegiance to the Sprite Nation, to join with that Man. Now they partnered in life and as Team members. And along with Bastyen and his mate, the Elf, Diadranei, they had become the most highly skilled Stealth Team in the entire Resistance. She'd never thought such would be her fate, but 'twas most welcome.

When they'd had their fill, they got up to head to the library. Further baffling the Warrior, Caleichante grabbed a full plate of meat and steamed vegetables afore they left but touched it not. Passing by Thorrn and Tiyya sitting at the end of the table on their way out, Calei frowned, for in that pair she could sense the same misunderstandings, yearnings, and sadness that she'd experienced. Fortunately, Graasyn had come to his senses and they'd put those things behind them. Mayhap somehow Tiyya and Thorrn would, too. Returning her attention to her current task, she stated,

"Come, Rygyl. I will tell you a story that you can then relate to the Battle Commander to complete your old mission." Her voice took on a mysterious tone as she teased, "'Tis a tale from the Beginning and the War of Chaos and involves Drekinn Lair."

MEANWHILE
OUTSIDE THE SPELL DOME
<p style="text-align:center">~~~~~ THE GREAT PLAINS OF DREKINN ~~~~~</p>

Rhyah had left the Keep o'er a moon past, and though he lived there not long, the Fay had befriended everyone and was liked by all. Darque had sent forth Teams to keep him safe along his journey but once past the Far Northlands they lost him when his trail abruptly ended. 'Twas determined that he'd crossed o'er into the Icelands in his preferred Shift as the Wolf, and no word had been forthcoming since.

Rumors abounded about how Rhyah and the Second in Command had spent much time together, and now rumors were flying about Storrm and an expected event in the near future stemming from their time together. 'Twas joyous but secretive, as Storrm had yet to reveal such and refused to acknowledge her condition. Nonetheless, 'twas still early.

Just back from the final attempt to discover any new information about the fate of the Fay, Shasynn and Taniyyah rested on the ledges fronting Byndynn Forest and the steppes that bordered the Great Plains of Drekinn. Thinking about Storrm's obvious state of being, Shasynn mused in envy, hoping Corbyn, Kelseacyr, and the new Matriarch could find a cure for their sterility. And after hearing about the troubles 'tween Zaydarr and Tegrynn and their LifeBonds, Shasynn was troubled. Having hunted afore their return, he and Taniyyah sat side by side upon the ledge. They needed to notify a Gatekeeper afore they flew 'cross the Plains to enter Drekinn Lair. But there was no one about, the skies were clear, and the Hoard had not shown themselves for some time. He turned an appreciative eye toward the female. The flashy orange-gold of her scales in the sunshine, were the perfect match to his own yellow-bronze sparkle.

The 6th Prince of the Highlands had 'Bonded in the second ceremony, but while his eldest brother, Gunnarr, had taken his Human partner as his lifemate, he'd merely felt a deep friendship and respect for his partner, Tiyya, while developing a very strong attraction to Taniyyah, also in the 'Bond. The elegant Dragon shared his desires but they'd yet to share a mating flight, for they were perplexed. Being in 'Bond had them Sharing their emotions, their thoughts, their very lives, but what if their partners didn't feel the same about each other? 'Twould be most difficult to experience the full mating lust while Blocking from their 'Bonds. This could get complicated, as well as annoying. How was such handled back then? 'Twas the very reason Zaydarr and Tegrynn kept Ariel and Rygyl apart.

Taniyyah's Thoughts broke through his own, her voice sultry. *"I'm no history buff and have only begun to access my Memories once again, but I believe the First Warrior and Solvyngarr were not only the first LifeBond, 'tis possible they may have been the only successful LifeBond in that time. And since they mated each other, as have Darque and Gunnarr, such a dilemma would not have occurred."*

That she Heard him when he wasn't openly in the Link, made him realize he was being loose with his Thoughts. He needed to step up or Taniyyah might think him immature and unworthy. *"True. So much of the War of Chaos is shrouded in fading Memories."* Deciding to plunge ahead, he broached the subject they'd tried to avoid in the past. *"However, this is the here and now, and I know that I want you more than any other female I've ever met. And I also know that the Warrior with whom I'm in 'Bond is quite intrigued with the Warrior with whom you are. She likes Thorrn. A lot. Yet she shies away from interaction. Even with what little I've inadvertently Shared with her when my feelings for you have been near o'erwhelming."*

Tan liked his direct style. She didn't play games, and he was honest about what he felt. *"I know. Thorrn is making me crazy, too. The Human male is beyond my comprehension. He can hardly contain his reactions when he is near Tiyya, yet even with my gentle nudges he seems to falter."*

Shasynn's voice held an edge of surprise as he Asked, *"Nudges? You've tried to interfere?"*

She shrugged her broad shoulders. *"Of course! They're in love with each other."*

"You are certain?"

"As certain as one can be of their LifeBond partner and that's saying much, I believe."

Shasynn shook his great head, his scales glistening with the action. He was disgusted. *"Humans. How do they fight so well and love so poorly?"*

Taniyyah was becoming stimulated, her scales darkening. They'd yet to Call a Gatekeeper and once inside they'd not have enough height to achieve that which she wanted. Not to mention that they might not get another chance for some time to come. She Responded sassily, *"I think we should give them a stronger nudge. What say you, my handsome Prince?"*

Shasynn knew she wanted to Share a mating flight with their partners, who, through the LifeBond, would be drawn into their experience, feeling and sensing, everything they did. 'Twas somehow voyeuristic and arousing in an unusual way, and although Sharing such was being discouraged, 'twas not forbidden. Mayhap 'twould push their partners o'er that edge of indecision as well. After all, being in the 'Bond meant they really did know what their partners felt and thought. And although they'd Share the sensations and emotions, 'twouldn't force them to anything they didn't want to do. Their physical and psychological responses were theirs to make. And possibly, enjoy. His husky voice rumbled with his rising… excitement. *"Now?"*

"Now."

Yet, Shasynn hesitated, for this time 'twould be more than just a mating flight. For him 'twould end in forever. His long tongue slipped 'tween sharp white fangs as he ogled Taniyyah. *"I must warn you. If we take flight now, I will Claim you as mine. My heart is on the edge. You have fascinated me since we met at the ceremony. But, as I would not force my LifeBond partner, I've never forced a female to anything she did not want. Would you accept me?"*

Taniyyah's heart pounded passionately as she opened herself to her own LifeBond, holding nothing back. Standing, teasing the big male afore her, she stepped backwards, urging him nearer, afore spinning swiftly about and stretching out her great wings to take flight. *"Catch me and I'm yours!"*

~~~~~ *THE MESS HALL OF THE DRAGON'S DEN* ~~~~~

Thorrn and Tiyya smiled and waved them past, as Caleichante left with Rygyl. But when Thorrn looked back down, the unexpected hunger he felt was not for what lay upon his plate. Glancing 'cross the table, Tiyya's beautiful face met his gaze. Riveted to her mouth, he watched her tongue slip forth, moistening her pink lips. All time seemed to stand still as his vision tunneled to that sweet tongue. He swallowed hard. Her unconscious act forced him to his feet, scooting the bench back roughly with his legs. He was suddenly so hard, he thought he'd choke. His broad shoulders elevated, his meaty fists propped upon the table beside his now meaningless plate, he could not tear his eyes away from her as her brows raised in wonder, afore a deep blush began to rise up the silky skin of her neck.

The aerial dance had just begun, but the teasing 'tween their 'Bonds was now Shared by both Dragons. They'd never felt such strong emotions, not even in battle, and already having such an attraction for each other, they were drawn into that of their partners.

Shasynn strained to reach Taniyyah as she pumped her strong wings, taking them both higher and higher in the mating chase.

The panic of a cornered feral cat was in Tiyya's eyes as she realized they were not alone in the mess hall. Thorrn reached 'cross the table and his big hand engulfed Tiyya's much smaller one. "Come with me," he near demanded, his voice husky with need. She stood up eagerly and they left the area with all haste. She cared not where they went, she just wanted privacy. She wanted him. Now.

Taniyyah reached the peak of her first climb and plunged past Shasynn as the powerful Dragon immediately tried to stop her. He tucked his wings and began to dive faster and faster, to catch up.

Thorrn pulled Tiyya along as she finally matched her step to his. As soon as they reached the first alcove, he turned around. Backing her up to the wall and pushing his chest against hers, he kissed her hard. Tiyya threw her arms around his neck and held on tight as their tongues entwined in the heated embrace. His shaking fingers inadvertently ripped open the front laces of her pants, as his calloused hand pushed down her flat belly, fingering the mound of tight reddish blonde curls with his long fingers, afore sliding lower, and deeper.

Shasynn caught up with Taniyyah and stretched forth his claws, just catching the scales on her hip. Straining to secure the grasp, Taniyyah twisted, turned, and beat her wings hard, with Shasynn following, taking them upwards again to an even higher level than afore, where they repeated their plunge.

Tiyya moved her hips, pressing against his fingers, seeking relief from the urgent need, her breath stuttering. Thorrn was well endowed and his leather pants felt like they were going to crush him as he dragged his hand back from his exploration, wet fingers his reward. Breaking the kiss, he licked the sweet juices off his fingers, his forehead on hers as he attempted to gain control. The strength of the reaction her taste evoked, scared him. He didn't want to hurt her. He was too much for her, he needed to slow down, make sure she was ready, but he could feel the powerful wing strokes of his 'Bond, the frenzied excitement rising to near fever pitch, as he struggled to seize his prize. Catching his breath, Tiyya's shaky voice broke through his thoughts. "She rises again, she plunges again, he catches her, again, next time, he won't release her. She wants him. Please, we need to go somewhere, anywhere!"

Thorrn near dragged Tiyya, who was trying her best to keep up with his long strides, holding his hand just as tightly as he held hers, into his private quarters. Their journey took them past many speculative, amused, and knowing glances, as they pushed past even more without bothering to notice. Locking the heavy oak door behind him, he finally released her, but their hands were all o'er each other, stripping down.

Shasynn's strong talons gripped his lover and she turned to him on the third plunge. They'd reached their highest level yet, and locking talons together, their wings tight to their flanks, they stopped flying and dropped into a wildly spinning free fall.

Naked at last, Thorrn gathered his prize in his strong arms and laid her down on the fur rug at the hearth. Shasynn and Taniyyah fell faster and faster, locked together, scale to scale. Chest to chest, Thorrn fell upon her and with savage passion he took her. Tiyya gasped with the initial moment of pain but she was so wet 'twas gone in an instant. She met his every thrust, pounding a rhythm of pure ecstasy, talons gripping and holding tight, his hands slipping off her sweaty hips he tightened his grasp for more leverage to allow him deeper penetration as Shasynn did the same to Taniyyah. She was so tight, she felt so good. Her moans of pleasure spurred him on, and he moved inside her, quickening his thrusts as with their heartbeats, free falling toward the ground, racing faster and faster toward the peak of ecstasy. As Tiyya screamed in pleasure, Thorrn groaned, seed burst forth filling her completely, spilling o'er skin and scale.

Just afore the two Dragons had to break apart or hit the ground, the Sharing abruptly ended. The loss of the additional sensations sent the Warrior rolling onto the soft fur of the rug as if pushed, near exhausted, a look of pure bliss upon his handsome face.

~~~~ *A FEW MOMENTS LATER* ~~~~

As his heart rate slowed, realizing what they'd done, Thorrn was appalled. Lying on his shoulder, he jerked his hand away from Tiyya's silky strawberry blonde hair and looked down at his spent nakedness. Beside her. The woman he really wanted to impress. He covered his face with his hands and peeked out through his fingers when he heard her giggle. Her reaction to the discovery emboldened him and he asked, "What just happened?"

She laughed louder. "Don't tell me I have to teach you that, as well?"

His face turned as crimson as was his vision when in Battle Lust, as he sputtered trying to say something that made sense. But nothing came to mind. All he could think of was how good she'd felt, how much he wanted her again, how much he loved her, and how fearful he was that he'd just thrown it all away.

Tiyya took pity on him and drew his hand back to her cheek where his fingers seemed to caress down her neck of their own accord, amazed at the silky texture under his calloused hands. His touch felt good to her and she didn't want him to stop. "I believe we just experienced our Dragons in mating flight. We Shared what they did and felt, although it appears that we did and felt just what they Shared." As a thought suddenly came to mind, she asked, "You weren't a virgin, were you?"

The question was not meant to be demeaning and he knew 'twas time to lay all his cards on the table. In his mind, even though 'twas a tad rough, they didn't just have sex, they'd just made love, and he hoped 'twas how she felt as well. Mayhap he could still salvage the situation. "I was not. But I've never felt comfortable... doing it... just for fun, and I've never felt a need, such as the other Warriors speak. I've wanted someone special, and it's been a long time. I apologize if I wasn't knowledgeable enough to satisfy you, and especially if I hurt you. But I'm willing to learn. I'll do anything. I just want you. Again."

For a Warrior of his prowess, such sentiments were frankly surprising, as well as the fact that he'd been more than enough for her, amazingly skilled as if he read her mind, touching her and filling her perfectly. Tiyya realized she was blushing yet again. Now 'twas her turn to tell the truth. She hesitated fleetingly and Thorrn held his breath awaiting her response. "All this time, I've hoped and dreamed of being with you. But I thought that you were like all the rest and couldn't possibly want me. I'm no virgin either, but like you, I've waited a long time for someone special. Satisfy me? That's a laugh. My greatest fear was if we ever got together, I'd not satisfy you! I think our Dragons did us a huge favor, because otherwise 'tis likely we'd never have gotten past our shy 'hellos'." She understood his concern. She could see it lingering on his face. "I was not forced to such."

He wanted to kiss every freckle upon her entire body, one by one. Since they were scattered everywhere, 'twould be most enjoyable and take a very long time. He could think of no better way to spend such time. Pushing off his elbow and straddling her, he held himself up on his hands and knees as he stared at the sweat sheen on her skin, the sparkling droplets of moisture trickling 'tween her breasts. Those breasts that fit perfectly into his large hands. She ached for him to cup them again and reached forth, drawing her fingertips down his ribs toward his navel then ever lower toward the junction 'tween his legs. The heat coming off his rock-hard body made her squirm with longing, her eyes drinking in the chiseled muscle from head to toe, while his perceived not only her strength, but her grace and beauty. As both his confidence and his manhood grew, he had to have her. He nodded in confirmation of her statement. "We are not puppets on strings. I want you, Tiyya. I think we should try this again, a bit slower, and see where our own emotions take us." She could not have agreed more, and as he used his knees to spread her willing legs, she smiled. Lowering himself onto her, their bodies melded together flawlessly, the weight of him on her hips, the fullness of him inside her as with a single, slow, deep thrust, he near sent her o'er that precipice of delight. Pulling his face to hers, their lips met, and his tongue sought entrance once more.

A FEW MARKS LATER

~~~~~ THE ARCHIVES OF THE DRAGON'S DEN ~~~~~

</div>

Regynn had been working in the Archives non-stop since they'd returned from the mission. Darque was encouraged by his report, but Regynn had been disappointed he'd not been able to return with the Kreegare. Trying to second guess the mysterious Elven Commander was impossible, so to get his mind off the events of the past winter, he'd plunged headlong into his Clan Historian duties. At the very least he was certain the Kreegare would not align with the Black. That was something of a success.

Bringing an offering of a hearty meal with her, which Regynn wolfed down voraciously, Caleichante began a search through the oldest maps in the Archives with the Warrior's assistance. Finally, she tapped her finger upon the latest scroll exclaiming, "There! 'Tis the Lair of Neeshinkyandor, a mighty warrior of the ancient Highlands. 'Tis the oldest mountain upon all Kadoor, and therein lies much treasure still, me thinks."

Rygyl stood beside the Sprite at the table, peering o'er her shoulder as she pointed to a tall mountain on a large faded map in the middle of an even larger, and very ancient, scroll. Gingerly holding down his end of the scroll he leaned forward to get a better look. Nothing was familiar. "I don't recognize anything. You say this is close to where we are now?"

"I say it can't get any closer," she stated with some sarcasm as she glanced up at the young Warrior. Regynn had been elsewhere during the search after providing Calei with the scrolls, but now walked o'er to them as he listened. "Look here. And here.

And here." Pointing to various places, she asked them both what they might recognize. "Remember that most of the obvious landmarks are gone, most of the major regions altered, some more so than others, but if you use your imagination you will see." She moved her finger to encircle a large region on the map in the northernmost section. "These are the Icelands." Then she moved slightly south and butting up along that same border, outlined an even larger area. "This is the Far Northlands." Then she moved her finger down again and out to the west and stopped on an island in the middle of the ocean. "This was once an island with another name, but 'tis now known as…"

Squinting, Regynn slowly finished her thought. "The Island of Dreams."

Calei smiled and nodded. Rygyl stared at the Elder Warrior who now stood with a triumphant expression, his muscled arms crossed o'er his chest. Regynn knew where Calei was taking them. Irritated, Rygyl then shifted his gaze to the Sprite as the sun began to dawn upon him. Intensely he studied the map o'er her shoulder as Calei's finger moved back northward to the shoreline. Moving eastward and then dropping downward in a squiggly line, tracing through part of the landmass on the map, she said, "This is the current shoreline of the Sea of Dreams."

About midway along that southward section of 'shoreline', lay the Lair she'd named earlier. Rygyl was speechless and finally stammered, "But, that means, THIS is that mountain! Drekinn Lair sits upon the remains of that one." Regynn glanced knowingly at Calei but said not a word as they turned their gazes in unison to Rygyl. His gaze shifted from one to the other with confusion, and then it hit him. "No. It can't be. Are you trying to tell me that we sit not upon it, but IN it?"

Calei laughed. "Yes, in it, indeed. Surely you've wondered about all the many ancient Spells upon the caverns, the corridors, the illusory Spells making the open caves upon the cliffs appear to be short and not winding into the Lair itself? The fact that the light is ever present in some caves and reflects from the gems you see in the Cave of Jewels? I hear that it waxes and wanes with the sun itself." Calei was ever amazed at the ignorance of Humans for their own history. "Where did you think all that came from?"

Calei and Regynn sat down together at the table as Rygyl hurriedly, yet carefully, gathered the scroll and left to make report to the Commander. 'Twould complete his mission with Ariel and mayhap 'twould give him that final closure. At least 'twould help. Regynn thought about the map briefly and then stated, "You knew this when you came. I know you've been wandering through the Lair below the Den, and that you have had a particular interest in the excavation going on in the Cave of Jewels. Just how stable can an ancient treasure stash be? Do you think the Lair could collapse, or present a danger to us in other ways? Mayhap there still be some ancient Protection Spells we've not yet identified?"

She took a deep breath. "I came here to see if my conjecture had merit, and then to discuss my thoughts with Darque. But I met Rygyl upstairs afore I could do that." She shrugged her shoulders. "Everything is dangerous. However, I think 'twould be wise to learn just how stable we are. If I'm correct, and this IS the Lair of Neeshinkyandor..." She trailed off and Regynn merely nodded. 'Twould be both good and bad.

Suddenly Regynn looked up, his expression clearly urgent. "Sydrayyah Calls. She says we're to meet Darque and Gunnarr in the Cave of Jewels with all haste."

Swiftly, Calei stood and followed the Warrior out of the Archives toward the dungeons of the Den, where they'd be walked through the Spell Door via Sydrayyah.

Arriving soon thereafter to the Cave of Jewels, they found several others huddling close to the far side where they'd been carrying out their exploratory excavations along the wall of the cave. After chipping and cleaning a small section of the wall, they'd discovered much more than that for which they'd bargained and had Called Darque to come see for herself. Darque stood and glared. Regynn, Calei, and Rygyl stood in awe at her shoulders. There afore them, a portion of the wall itself, was part of a Dragon's Eye, the hilt of a sword, what could only be a shield, the edges of talons, fangs, and more, all compacted aside multiple exquisite precious gems. 'Twas exactly that which Calei had warned. They were literally standing within a Dragon's stash. The wall was not made of rock, 'twas created by piles of ancient treasure. But if they tried to remove anything 'twas highly likely an ancient Protection Spell might kick in and/or just cause the cave, and mayhap the entire Lair, to collapse. 'Twould be disaster. Accepting her Magic bearing ally's recommendations, Darque ordered nothing removed. 'Twould take much study. But for now, all appeared to be stable. As long as no one got greedy. She bit her lip in frustration at the loss of a veritable mountain of treasure. Scales, teeth, fangs, Eyes, ancient weapons. They were surrounded with the very items that could help them in the war effort but could make use of nothing. Not to mention they'd be unable for the time being, to enlarge or modify any of the caves for living space.

CHAPTER SEVENTEEN

Best Of Three

Regynn and Cathay stood beside Darque, King Gabriel, Rakkah, and the spirit of Abriya on the ramparts of the Keep's great wall, gazing down at the approaching entourage from the Sakyn Forest. Slapping the Battle Commander on the back, Regynn grinned broadly. "See? What did I tell you?" Cathay rolled her eyes but ensured her lifemate did not see her do so. Darque simply smiled as did the King. Rakkah, ever vigilant, did not like the odds of vetting this entire army. Abriya was eager to see her old friend once again. She'd have to get Ardyth to interpret, as she didn't have to use up any of her energy to manifest to the 'Seer of the Dead', and she and Tammra could then have an elongated and much delayed conversation.

The Kreegaren had suddenly appeared within a league of the Keep a mere few marks prior. Tammra had been wise to allow the Resistance forces time to be notified of the Elven Assassins' arrival so there would be no doubt of their intentions. Friendly fire was the worst betrayal.

Her entourage too large to bring directly into the Ward through the portals, they'd been drawn inside the Dome o'er the past mark and deposited upon the long and wide rock bridge that led to the gates of the Keep. Now Tammra Dayo herself walked toward the gates followed by near fifteen hundred Assassins. She was indeed glorious in her cloak and armament, her shoulder length black hair fluttering in the gentle breeze. Tammra was built more like a Clansman than like an Elf, broad shouldered, muscled, and hardened, though 'twas clear by her posture, she was proud of her heritage and confident in her skills. A sword at each hip, bow 'cross her shoulder, shield 'cross her back, blades strapped on both thighs, both forearms, and in both boots, one had to be an idiot to doubt her expertise. The Assassins were fully cloaked in black as was their trademark, and no faces could be seen. Only Tammra and those flanking her, had their hoods pulled back.

Tammra signaled to her troops to stand and they immediately stood stock-still as she closed in on the huge stone gate, looking up at Regynn, then examining the rest of the ones now gazing back at her. Loudly enough for all to hear she stated, "I seek entry. We need to talk."

Gabriel nodded to Darque who spoke. "You and your troops are welcome here. Enter…" She began.

But Tammra stopped her. "No." Indicating Leis, Dyra, Cassiopeia and the eldest Elf she'd ever seen, standing behind and beside her, she stated, "Just we five. My troops will wait here for my decision."

Gabriel poked Darque in the ribs, indicating he understood what she wanted. "Let me handle this," he said quietly.

Darque nodded toward the Gatekeepers, and the huge gate slowly creaked open just wide enough for the five of them to enter, the great chains reversing their pull to shut the gate behind them.

WITHIN MOMENTS

~~~~~ THE WARD OF THE KEEP ~~~~~

</div>

After introducing her group and ensuring that Orayalyn would be welcome to stay regardless of the final decision of the Assassins, Gabriel stood afore the Elf, already knowing she was honest. The test was that he had to get her and her troops to stay with them, to swear fealty to him and his crown and to stand under Darque's Command, for although the Elves had already done this, the warrior afore him now did not ally herself with the Elven Nation and neither did any of her troops. Not only that, she was ancient, highly experienced, skilled, knowledgeable, and not easily swayed, while he was clearly young with little experience. He'd have to play this well and may the luck of the Fates be with them all. As they eyed each other, Gabriel broke the silence. "You must be the Elven warrior of whom I've heard so much lately. Tammra Dayo." He stepped closer to her, and as they met, he reached forth to take her offered arm in grasp, feeling no withdrawal. She smiled as he introduced himself. "I am Gabriel."

"King Gabriel," Tammra replied dryly, noting his slight uneasiness with the title. Then she turned with him and leaving Orayalyn, Leis, Dyra and Cass standing opposite Darque, Rakkah, Regynn and Cathay (Abriya had disappeared), they began to walk side by side, stopping a short distance away. Darque stayed Rakkah and Regynn both, as she chewed her bottom lip, wondering what was transpiring. Still, the pair were within earshot of their enhanced senses.

Gabriel merely smiled and stated, "If you will. As is Darque's position, 'twas a matter of birth order." He did not feel they should waste any time and got down to business. "My philosophy is to keep everyone alive by joining forces against the Evil One. The Resistance could use your help."

Tammra liked his style. Direct. To the point. "I've a philosophy that has kept me alive." She then looked at the King, cocked her head and spoke audaciously, "I bend knee to no one whom I can defeat."

But Gabriel blinked not. He simply stated, unruffled, "Do you make challenge, then?"

Now not quite so sure she had the upper hand on this one, she said slowly, "Yes."

Rakkah and Regynn were beginning to sweat. Darque simply grinned in perceptive anticipation, for she now knew where this was going, and reached out her arm to block them both from moving, shaking her head to keep them silent.

Gabriel's smirk was contagious, as he questioned, "Would you be satisfied with a contest?"

Now Tammra understood what he was up to but had no idea how he thought to gain her fealty by losing a contest. Her expression teasing, she thought to give the King an out, and replied, "'Tis traditional."

But Gabriel kept digging himself in deeper. "Best of three?"

Surely he didn't think... Tammra nodded, a leery expression upon her face.

The young man who appeared no different than any other of the Warriors she could now see beginning to surround them in the Ward, continued politely, "As the one challenged, the first trial is my choice, correct?"

Still leery, Tammra licked her lush lips and stated, "Of course."

"Knife throwing." Upon this declaration, Rakkah near choked then near ran o'er Darque to get to the King, and Regynn and Cathay had to help restrain him.

What? Tammra mused. She was beginning to think this King was too cocky for her to swear fealty to him. But, since 'twas clear they were going through with this charade, she'd fully expected him to choose the sword or spear (after all, he was a Warrior), either of which she felt confident in winning. She could out swing any Warrior living today.

Regynn gripped tightly onto Rakkah and whispered in his ear, after which the big man who looked so much like the King himself, stood rocking in place while gritting his teeth, fire burning in his eyes. At least he didn't need to be restrained any longer.

Darque beckoned to some of the bystanders, and Alric the Weapons Master along with some others, quickly set up a knife throwing range and target. But the King showed more skill than expected with throwing a blade, winning the contest by more than a handbreadth, and gambling that he might be saving sword for last, Tammra chose wrestling as the second trial. She was enjoying this. 'Twould be sad when they had to leave. It had taken her so long to get her brethren to agree to the journey along with the possible outcome. But, after stripping down of heavy wraps, outer clothing and weapons, Tammra was shocked at how hard she had to work to gain the win. Panting with the invigorating workout, she was rivetted. Now they were tied.

Taking a few moments to rest and drink, Gabriel stood beside Darque and the others. Sheepishly he stated, "I thought I could win that." He shook his head. "But no matter. I still have the final draw." His eyes twinkling, even Rakkah understood now, that his half-brother had played the trial well. Working the conversation rapidly to him being the one challenged, and knowing he could not lose at throwing weapons, he didn't care what Tammra chose as her trial. Win or lose, his last selection would tell the tale.

Completely surprising Tammra, he chose the bow. "Bow?" Dumbfounded, she continued, having a difficult time speaking through her snickers. "You would challenge an Elf to a duel of bow? Are you mad? Or do you simply not want my Assassins to join the Resistance?" Gabriel grinned boldly as Tammra shook her head.

Once the setup was completed, Tammra used her own bow to fire her shots, all dead center. Gabriel then stepped up to the line. She smirked.

But unbeknownst to Tammra, Gabriel was not a born and bred Clansman. He'd been raised by the People. No one shot bow better than his adopted tribesmen. Using unorthodox and frequently altering stance, making each shot with an added flair, every one of her arrows were split when he finished. Tammra had never seen such mastery, such skill... such showmanship. As she accepted that she couldn't beat him, her musical laughter rang forth through the hush of the Ward, all spectators having held their collective breaths as they watched their King soundly beat the Elven Commander, but fearful to cheer when he did. Her laughter broke their silence and roars of approval echoed throughout the Keep. After near a quarter mark of celebration, Tammra stepped forth, took a firm grasp on Gabriel's arm, and announced for all to hear, "You are indeed worthy. Tammra

Dayo shall bend knee to King Gabriel and the Resistance!" Going down on one knee for the formality more than the actual need, Gabriel touched the back of her head with the flat of his sword. Rising and crossing her arms o'er her chest, she added, "The Kreegare acquiesce to Darque's Command!" Her declaration was met with even more raucous cheers of approval as the rest of her forces were brought inside the Ward.

<center>~~~~~THE VOID ~~~~~</center>

Storrm had not said a word in a very long time. When she felt Mystynn's arms around her she questioned, "What is it?"

Mystynn had felt the warmth under Storrm's cheek. If anywhere else, her tears would be falling, weeping quietly. "I had the feeling you needed to speak. After all these revelations, I thought a break might be prudent. Are you alright? Do you wish to continue?"

She laughed. He was ever-thoughtful. She had begun to feel a tad o'er whelmed. Gazing upwards, Mystynn's green eyes were not as stunning as the glittering ones upon which she'd become dependent for her well-being since taking his 'Bond. 'Twas then she realized something. He was not comfortable. "Mystynn? Your human form is quite handsome."

Tenderly, he replied, "I wish to please you."

"But I didn't fall in love with a human."

Mystynn's brows furrowed and he searched her eyes, his own reflecting his fear of losing the one woman he loved with all his heart, and whom he was convinced he'd already failed once. He tried to respond but found he could not, and he tried clearing his dry throat. He was not very comfortable in this form, but he'd do anything for Storrm, suffer any humility, be who and what she wanted him to be. He would not fail her again.

Afore he could find words, she stated, "I fell in love, deeply, madly, passionately, in love, with the 2nd Prince of the Highland Dragons." She reached up and kissed his soft lips, and then leaned back, critically shaking her head. "'Tis not this I desire. When will the real you return?"

Mystynn growled deep in his chest but try as he might, he could not contain the joy that spilled o'er as he took her back into his arms, his glistening scales already beginning to cover his morphing body as the Prince rapidly regained his birth form.

Storrm nodded and smiled, then allowed him to wrap her in his lengthening wings. Hugging her tightly to his chest once more, she closed her eyes and Shared his vision. "Break o'er," she murmured, much pleased.

NEAR A SENNIGHT LATER
~~~~~ DARQUE'S QUARTERS AT THE DEN~~~~~

</div>

Storrm glowed in happiness. She'd just finished her report and would soon be returning to the Keep, but she had to tell her. Facing her sister, she could barely contain her joy as she blurted, "I'm pregnant!"

Darque was astonished. Her sister hadn't known that already? It seemed everyone in the Keep knew the Second in Command was expecting, with the exception of the Second in Command. Slightly envious, she chuckled, glad her sister was finally making the joyous announcement, and burst forth laughing, "I'm so happy for you!"

"And yes, I knew I was pregnant, I just wanted to make sure all was well afore I made an official declaration." She winked at her sister and they shared a hug.

Darque frowned. The contact and her expertise told her one thing as her senses added to the story. "You are weakened. Are you well?" She placed her hand upon Storrm's swollen belly. "You're past the first trimester. You did wait a long time! Who is the father?"

Storrm's mood took a definite turn and sadly she responded, "Rhyah."

Darque was confused. "You and the Fay? Why didn't I know this?" She snorted. "Why didn't I SENSE it?" Nonetheless, this could mean trouble for her sister. For all of them. A tri-blood child. There was no prior similar pregnancy to draw from for information on how this would transpire. Apparently the child was developing very quickly, for the Fay had not been with them for long and had only just left less than two moons past. Which would leave Storrm…

Raising her hand palm forward, she stopped her sister's rampant thoughts. "Yes. I know. The baby is developing very quickly. Quickly enough that I already know she is female. I've named her Skyya, to which she is responding. And I'm already using a potion that Kelsey concocted to give her what she needs from me, to keep her from depleting my resources. Don't be angry with them, I swore them to secrecy. Besides, 'tis clear now that I'll not be pregnant for long, and how can that be bad?" She shrugged her shoulders in flippant disregard for the issues. Biting her bottom lip, she sighed and then continued, "I'll be fine, stop worrying."

She knew what Darque was thinking. 'Twas a huge health risk. And Rhyah was not within contact range to be told of his impending fatherhood. At any rate, he might not even survive his undertaking to the Icelands. 'Twas as close to a suicide mission as they came, no one truly expecting to hear from the Wolf again. 'Twould be sad if Skyya never had the chance to meet her father. But, as usual, she'd told Darque not to worry. If only she could stop herself, she thought, as she and Mystynn took wing back to the Keep.

CHAPTER EIGHTEEN

The Package Deal

The Raven soared 'cross the waters and slipped into the porthole alongside the Krakken as he'd done many times afore, through the past many winters. He was fatigued, as he'd searched for the Krakken for some time afore seeing her distinctive black and gold sails billowing on the horizon. Morphing mid-air, Corbyn stood facing Myrrdin 'cross from his desk. Warm greetings were exchanged, for these were good friends. Although no one, not even Lyran, Myrrdin's First Mate, knew of this meeting, everyone knew of the enduring friendship 'tween the Fay and the Elven Prince.

Corbyn glanced at the bottle of Drekinn Whiskey sitting undisturbed in the middle of the table. Seeing 'twas b'Spelled to remain there, he was puzzled. His gaze now resting upon the Ship's Master, his expression asked the question.

"Sit, my friend. I'll open a new one." Myrrdin pulled up a chair and they sat together, sharing the whiskey while he told the tale of the bottle. "'Twill remain there 'til Caleichante returns to share it with me, as per her promise."

Taking a sip of the amber liquid, Corbyn sat back and relaxed. "Her mission was a success. She is now mated to the Warrior Graasyn and living at St Swiftyn's, fighting for the Resistance."

The Ship's Master shrugged his shoulders as he too, sat back and took another sip. "'Twas a promise, and I keep my promises. She, too, will keep hers, and one day we will share this bottle.

'Twill be the next time we see each other, the next time she sets foot on the Krakken."

Acknowledging the Elf's pledge and moving forward to his own, Corbyn stated, "Your honor and loyalty to your friends has always impressed me. 'Tis why I'm here now. I have a contract to offer and I can think of no other to fulfill such. 'Twill be extremely dangerous but with a critical outcome for which I will pay you well." Leaning forward, he set the glass down as he reached toward his pocket.

Myrrdin laughed, sat forward, and stayed Corbyn's hand. "Your coin is not good here!" Noting the confusion upon the Fay's face, he continued, "You saved my life. Allow me to repay that favor as often as I can."

Corbyn was Heir Apparent to a vast fortune but being cursed, coin was difficult to come by and he was grateful. They grasped arms afore leaning back again to discuss the contract. "I cannot give you many details, for I have few to give. The situation is fluid. However, within the next few moons I believe I will be in need of long-term package care, requiring comprehensive secrecy. No one can ever know of our arrangement and you will be the only one to know upon whom you entrust the care."

Myrrdin recognized of what he was speaking, but 'twas bewildering indeed. "How long will the 'package' require upkeep?"

"At the very least, thirteen winters," the Raven stated, his eyes locked onto Myrrdin's.

Children on Kadoor came of age once they'd gathered thirteen winters. His eyes opened wide and he blinked several times with the validation of his thoughts. He'd heard the blossoming rumors of Storrm's pregnancy, hadn't everyone? But thus far, they'd been only rumors. He took another sip as the one person upon whom he could trust for such a task, came to mind. Plans already forming, he asked, "And how will you make the delivery?"

Corbyn leaned forward again, his elbows upon the table. Catching the gaze of his good friend, he responded, "Personally."

Such a confirmation of Corbyn's intended involvement was impressive and Myrddin raised his eyebrows. "How will I know where to meet you?"

"I will find you."

"How will I know when?" he asked, running one finger around the edge of his glass.

"I will provide more information as it becomes available, and as I can. If I cannot without compromising security," he sighed and sat back once more afore finishing his statement. "Simply expect the unexpected."

Not much to go on. Myrrdin smiled. 'Twas intriguing. "'Tis a very interesting proposition."

"You agree, then?" Corbyn asked, with some slight trepidation. If Myrrdin refused, his options to protect Skyya were near zero, and he'd promised to do so.

Slamming his now empty glass upon the table, he sat upright and emphasized, to Corbyn's obvious relief, "Of course! Nothing could stop me, for you have stimulated my curiosity. I look forward to fulfilling this contract, my friend."

MEANWHILE AT THE KEEP

~~~~~ STORRM AND MYSTYNN'S QUARTERS ~~~~~

</center>

Storrm struggled to wake from the recurrent nightmare, but 'twas as if a noose were tightening around her neck, dragging her under the canopy of wakefulness as the cruel voice growled at her with the same despicable warnings she'd heard near nightly o'er the past several dawns. "I See it. I Hear it. 'Tis an abomination and I will kill it. There is nowhere you can run, nowhere you can hide. I will find you and kill you all!"

With a mighty effort she woke, sitting bolt upright in a cold sweat. Mystynn tried to soothe her back to sleep by wrapping her with his wing, but she rolled out from under and stood up. His luminous eyes now fully open, understanding bloomed as the look on her face told the story. "Again?" he questioned.

Still shaking, her hand cupping her growing belly, she nodded. "'Twas horrible. I know 'tis the Black. Somehow he has found a way into my mind, infiltrating my thoughts." She did not finish the idea that suddenly occurred to her. She'd rarely had nightmares in her span of days. These began after she became pregnant and the disembodied voice spoke as if 'twas the babe to which he referred. But this time had her convinced. 'Twas no dream. 'Twas the Black himself. She frowned. 'Twas either that, or she was losing her sanity.

Mystynn could think of no way the Black could fulfill his promise, if 'twas the Black and not just a nightmare caused by Storrm's chaotic hormones. Mayhap 'twas a result of the potion she was now forced to drink several times a day to get any benefit. Once more he tried to comfort his beloved. This pregnancy was harder on her than either of them had imagined. They'd been at the Keep since afore announcing the pregnancy to Darque. Mayhap a change of scenery would help? He would speak to Darque when the sun broke o'er the horizon. Mayhap joining the mission to find the deployed, or even being assigned back to the Den. 'Twas the home of her birth, after all.

Storrm tucked herself back under his wing, but he knew she slept not. Nowhere they could run. Nowhere they could hide. Why not? And just how would he find them? Mystynn pondered the likelihood of the nightmares being real. An abomination? Was Storrm worried about having a tri-blood child? No. 'Twas he who was worried. About everything.

OUTSIDE THE DOME

<center>~~~~~ A FEW DAWNS LATER ~~~~~</center>

Storrm leaned back against the tree trunk and then decided to sit down instead, stepping o'er to a large flat rock. She reached into her pack and pulled out the bag of potion, but 'twas empty. So tired. She sighed as Flyrra walked closer. The silver haired young girl reached forth to touch Storrm's belly and cocked her head as if listening to something. Or someone. "Little one is growing fast."

"What?" Storrm questioned, her brows furrowed.

"The baby is growing fast, and this takes much from you," Flyrra stated flatly, afore withdrawing her hand and looking at the Second.

Storrm was initially amused but then she understood that Flyrra wasn't being playful. She was being literal. Curious, she asked, "You know I'm pregnant?"

"Yes."

When the little girl did not say more, with a smile, and thinking 'twould be a cute response obtained, Storrm encouraged her to continue. "How do you know this?"

"I can Hear her. She is of mixed blood, as am I."

Storrm's smile abruptly dropped. "What do you mean, you can Hear her?"

"She is stretching her Magic. She is broadcasting quite clearly. Sometimes she is so loud that I can Hear her from the other side of the Keep."

"You've Heard her that far way?"

"Yes. And just this morning, I Heard her when you and Mystynn were flying in from the Bog, to pick me up."

Storrm could feel the blood draining from her face. Attempting to clarify, and hoping she was wrong, she asked, "Afore we entered through the portals?"

"Yes."

Storrm squinted and bit her bottom lip. Anxiety growing, she asked, "How long have you Heard her?"

Innocently, the child responded, "Since shortly after Rhyah left." Then sensing Storrm's fear, Flyrra hurriedly added, "She knows not what she is doing. She means no harm."

Now quite alarmed, Storrm stood up and Told Mystynn, *"Come back now! We have a problem."*

~~~~~ LATER ~~~~~

After concluding 1) that 'twas Flyrra alone (that they could ascertain) Hearing Skyya, and 2), neither Flyrra nor Storrm could communicate with the baby to keep her from broadcasting, Kelsey tried to comfort the Second in Command. "Skyya is growing quickly, she will surely join us soon and then we need not be concerned with her Voice."

Storrm was near panic. She'd not divulged to the Skald that Skyya's Voice had been Heard 'cross the protective shield of the Dome. Although she felt Flyrra was innocent of such a transgression, she was convinced that someone had Heard Skyya's rambling broadcasts and had given the information to the Black. And now the Black was using that information against her. He could very well find them using Skyya's Voice, just as he'd promised, not to mention that he'd been able to use Skyya to infiltrate the Second's thoughts and dreams. Not only could the Lairs be compromised, so too, could their personal safety. "How do you know she won't continue to do this after birth? Have you ever known of this to happen with other pregnancies?"

Kelsey knew not why Storrm was so upset, other than hormonal imbalance, and admitted, "Well... no. I have never heard of this afore. Nor have I found anything in the Archives. Although we've acknowledged half-bloods, I know not of any other tri-bloods." Dismally Storrm replied, "I'm sorry. I know you're trying. But we're shooting our arrows in the darkness."

Kelsey knew that Storrm was correct, but with nothing else to say on that subject, she continued, "I know you're having a difficult time, and I have made some alterations to the formula for your potion. It should give you extra energy and help you feel better."

"Thank you, Kelsey, I do appreciate you." Storrm sighed and got up to leave the clinic.

"There are no others than Flyrra who say they've Heard the baby. But I understand the risks," the Skald said apologetically. "The simple solution is for you to stay inside the Dome 'til her birth. Should not be long now. Do you want me to speak with Darque or will you?"

Storrm stiffened. "I'll speak with her," she sputtered quickly, then walked away without looking back.

Kelsey pondered the Second's odd behavior, but there were so many reasons that made perfect sense that there was no reason to search for any others, and shrugging her shoulders as she watched Storrm leave, she turned and went back to her research.

~~~~~ A FEW DAWNS LATER ~~~~~

Mystynn was as concerned as was Storrm and 'tween them, they'd asked for assignment to search for the missing Warriors, thinking that out in the field they'd draw less attention to the Lairs. And 'twas always the possibility that there was a spy reporting to the Black. Mayhap once outside they could distance themselves, ending the threat. But Darque had refused to allow her to go. The pregnancy was taking a heavy toll on her sister and she wanted Storrm to be close to the Skald. Neither Storrm nor Mystynn revealed the full truth of their circumstances, sensing they should keep all to themselves for everyone's protection. So, they'd asked for and received a change in Command to Drekinn Lair. Darque decided if Storrm wouldn't stay with the Skald, she'd send the Skald with Storrm. Which she did. But none other than Storrm, Mystynn, Flyrra and Corbyn know about Skyya's Voice. The silver haired little girl had been sworn to secrecy with the promise that she would be the one to announce their secret to everyone, AFTER Skyya's birth, which delighted Flyrra. Since the fiasco of Rhyah's rescue, she'd never disobey the Second's orders again, therefore, they knew the child would keep her promise 'til her own death. And since no one mentioned even the nightmares to Kelsey and she was much needed at the Keep, she returned in but a few dawns.

Nevertheless, the nightmares continued and Storrm and Mystynn both felt the Black was somehow Hearing Skyya. Her ever-present companion, the Raven, made an attempt to cover Skyya's Voice, but as they'd feared 'twas determined after a thorough examination, that such could not be accomplished without harm. Corbyn did have a slightly different angle in that he didn't believe the Black had the capacity to Hear such, but he concluded that if not the Evil One himself, then 'twas someone either stronger than he, or closer, who was reporting directly to him, thus making Storrm's nightmares legitimate threats as well as confirming the distinct possibility of a spy.

Storrm and Mystynn became more reclusive as the issues stacked up and soon, no one thought much about not actually seeing or speaking directly to either of them. Their Command duties Relayed through the Link, they tried not to say aloud that which they each tried to Block from the other: that Skyya's survival was threatened as well as was the Resistance, and there could be but one way to protect them both. Desperately they sought another, the prophesy now looming in their minds, even as they carefully began to orchestrate their final strategy.

NEAR A MOON LATER

THE ISLAND OF DREAMS

~~~~~ THE PRIVATE CHAMBERS OF BENETYK

OF THE SPRITE ASSEMBLY ~~~~~

</div>

Benetyk was worried. He and Frynbec had faced much closer scrutiny since the return of Prince Kevon along with that meddling little bitch, the Elven Princess Anastasia, and their 'business dealings' with the Sorcerer were getting more and more difficult. They must be careful. Nonetheless, the Sorcerer's impatience was growing, and they had to find a way to fulfill his last demand. Even though expecting the visit, he was startled at the knock on the door and nervously stated, "Enter."

As Frynbec crossed the threshold into the newly renovated chambers, he questioned his longtime friend and associate. "You are certain no one can hear?"

"Not with the new panels I had installed. No Spells, nothing to notice," replied Benetyk.

"And of course, the ones who did the installing are now…?"

"Provisions for my nephew."

Although the boy had originally been useful in helping the pair to cover up their mutual crimes along their rise in the Assembly, he was becoming a burden to their safety. They'd not truly needed his repugnant cravings for some time and yet, to keep him quiet they had to continue to provide for his desires. "It seems that he requires such with increasing frequency," stated Frynbec. "He is becoming as bad as the Pitch. How long will you continue to provide him with victims to squelch the thirst he has developed for Life Force?"

"'Til I can come up with a decent plan to get rid of him without facing backlash," replied Benetyk with disgust. "I've even considered having him kidnapped and taken to the Pitch, but who then would I hire, and who would take care of them? Besides, he is all the family I have left. He was my sister's only son."

"Does he not begin to show his addiction?"

Reluctantly, Benetyk answered, "I believe I've noticed a certain sallowness to his skin of late. I know that I must do something, and soon."

Frynbec squinted and stepped closer, speaking in a low voice even though he knew they could not be heard. "Your nephew has served us well, but he is addicted to Vampyrism and cannot be trusted. We must now think of ourselves. However, we cannot do the deed, 'twould bring too much attention and be very difficult to cover. Mayhap we should take advantage of the Sorcerer's wish to capture the Krakken."

They'd been trying to find a way to do that for many moons. "What do you mean?"

"The boy craves power, control, wealth, as well as the life energy he Draws from others to their deaths. All we have to do is get him to believe that by setting the Spell he'd gain control of the Krakken, and he'd do anything to get on board that ship."

"Myrrdin is too intelligent to be duped."

With an evil leer, Frynbec revealed his plan. "Yes, but he is in need of a new crewman and I've taken the liberty of circulating a rumor that, among other things, his next contract is extremely dangerous, and he expects many to be lost in the effort. Besides, he has his weaknesses and your nephew is a very good actor, having hidden his depravities even longer than you knew."

Benetyk's eyes narrowed with the revelation his 'friend' had been prepared for the presentation of this idea, and apparently believed there'd be little to no discussion required to obtain his consent. Circulating rumors could very well return to haunt them. He was getting the ugly feeling he was being manipulated. Choosing to keep such thoughts to himself for now, he said, "If the boy has any idea 'twill lead to his own death…"

Frynbec was frustrated. In his opinion 'twas the perfect resolution and they had no other choice. "He will note your uncertainty. Besides the fact that he will eventually turn on us, do you not hate him for taking your sister Beyond?"

Benetyk stared in astonishment. "You have found proof of this claim?"

Frynbec hesitated not, even while the memories of taunting the boy into Draining his own mother, came to mind. They'd needed someone disposable to assist them to gain their seats in the upper tier of the Assembly and the boy, with his perversion just rising, was perfect. Still, if and when the boy decided to tell his uncle about their early discussions… "I've tried for many winters, as have you. There can be no proof, but all leads to that conclusion. You know this as well as I," he spit forth angrily.

Benetyk considered. The Sorcerer demanded that the Spell be delivered quickly but they'd not found a disgruntled crewman. And such a search near had them caught more than once. They'd have to find someone soon or face the wrath of the Sorcerer.

Frynbec's plan would be the perfect escape for them and getting rid of his nephew had become necessary. The sooner the better. "I will speak to him tonight. He will be on the Krakken afore Myrrdin sails again, or I will force him Past the Veil myself. And follow him Beyond."

Frynbec licked his lips at that notion. 'Twould leave him alone to gather all the riches. Deviously, he replied, "Be careful, my friend. The boy must not suspect the truth. Play on his cravings. His desire for power."

"I will talk to you later," Benetyk answered, his lip curling at the eagerness Frynbec displayed, near salivating with the prospect of his nephew's demise. 'Twould not be clean. He was beginning to wish he could rid himself of his friend as well. 'Twas clear he could trust no one.

CHAPTER NINETEEN

On The Run

Since they'd been stationed back at the Keep, Mystynn felt much safer because it provided many places for Storrm to hide from public view. But although they'd become quite reclusive there as well, continuing to reinforce their plan, they did have to get out occasionally, their duties taking them back and forth 'tween the Keep and the Bog as Kydra and Ragnyrr continued to pursue their mission to the Outlands.

One of the first things they did was ensure King Gabriel was well ensconced in the Keep, and ever aware of their primary duties, under Rakkah's orders an entire detail of Warriors now surrounded them at all times. Rakkah and the King were well known, and though Storrm and Mystynn made them aware of their suspicions of a spy, they did not make them aware of their reasoning for such a deduction. Still, even though there were more people at the Keep, 'twas felt the King was safer there than he'd been at the smaller Training Facility at the Bog, with more Warriors to provide protection, for the spy could be anywhere. If there was a spy.

~~~~~ STORRM AND MYSTYNN'S PRIVATE QUARTERS ~~~~~

They'd both been edgy since returning from the Bog earlier. Their voices broke the evening's extended silence in unison with, "I'm sorry." 'Twas shock upon their faces as they realized they'd just spoken the same thought aloud. When Mystynn attempted to speak again, Storrm placed her hand o'er his muzzle and shook her head. "No. Let me." Stepping back, she sat on the fur rug on the stone floor in front of the hearth. 'Twas beginning to get cooler at night, and the fire was lit once more, as 'twas not difficult.

'Twas one of the benefits of having your own Dragon. Mystynn stretched out beside her, and facing each other, she stated flatly, "You and I both know that neither of us Called to the Gatekeepers to open the portal this afternoon."

Mystynn's great tongue slipped out 'tween his glossy fangs, and then back inside his mouth nervously. 'Twas exactly what he'd been thinking, too.

Storrm noted his discomfort, and continued, "Skyya's Magic is strong, but she knows not what she's doing and now she's not only Calling to the Hoard, she'd going to let them in! She opened that portal. I don't know how, but I know she's able, and cannot be stopped. And we don't know if she can be stopped even after she is birthed." Storrm tried not to cry, the entire situation was becoming tragic. Even though they'd both faced this possible future scenario, they'd been praying hard that 'twould not happen.

Mystynn did not know what else to say, so he repeated, "I'm sorry."

"For what?"

"For forcing you away and into Rhyah's arms. For causing this to happen. If I hadn't been such an idiot..."

"No! I'm sorry. I'm sorry for not telling you how I felt about you, for Blocking my thoughts and emotions, for..."

"You did nothing wrong, 'twas entirely my fault, I Blocked so much..."

"Stop!" Storrm wiped away more tears and then coughed to clear her throat, sniffed and continued, "We can't blame ourselves, or each other. I Blocked from you, too. We were both at fault, and neither at fault. 'Tis no fault. 'Tis all in the prophesy. The prophesy you knew about afore you took my 'Bond, and that I learned soon thereafter. The prophesy we both hoped would not happen." She swallowed, and her voice calmed a bit. "But 'twill not be thwarted. Everything is unfolding at 'twas Told." She sniffed again, and then with resolve, she lifted her chin and caught his eyes. "I will do anything to protect her. 'Tis the only way out. The only way to keep Skyya safe."

Mystynn hung his great head in sadness, cold Dragon tears dripping down his muzzle, creating an icy puddle on the floor.

Her voice cracked with emotion as she asked, "Mystynn?"

"Yes?"

Still hoping their plan could result in a different ending, yet aware it may not, she answered, "I love her so much. If it all comes down to the worst, you must help me. I cannot do it alone."

"I will be with you, always. You will not be alone. Wherever you go, we go together."

"Promise? You know that Dragons cannot lie to Humans. I know I can be most stubborn."

"I promise. I will find a way."

After they'd both gathered themselves, Storrm curled up under Mystynn's wing and laid there, each finding comfort in the other's closeness, watching the flickering of the fire throughout the long night.

~~~~~ EARLY THE NEXT MORNING ~~~~~

Neither had slept and when dawn finally broke, Storrm crawled out from under Mystynn's wing and dressed quickly. Once she pulled on her boots she asked, "Are you ready?"

"I am. You have but one item to acquire. I will ensure we have the rest by the time you return. Are you up to this?"

"Yes, I am fine. You are certain the Illusion Spell will work as we've discussed?"

"Pfffft. You question my skills?" he asked with the funniest look on his face that Storrm had ever seen, making her laugh out loud. Then, serious but now steady, she nodded in appreciation, turned about, and left on her undertaking.

~~~~~ THE CLINIC OF THE KEEP ~~~~~

As Kelseacyr worked on her order, Storrm stated casually, "I just wanted to make sure I have enough, so I don't have to keep coming back here daily. 'Tis becoming tedious. And we might be called out again, leaving me stranded." With minimal emotion, Storrm played her part well. The lines had been rehearsed multiple times so that the Elven Skald would not suspect deception, and Storrm was rather pleased. She'd never thought of herself as an actress.

Kelsey carefully laid several smaller bags into a larger one, ending up with three full large bags, then handed them to the Second. "I've made up as much of the supplement as I can. I don't have enough of the raw materials to do more now. But this should last you while you're here on rotation."

"Thank you. I'll be very busy, and this will save me time and effort while I'm in charge here at the Keep. I appreciate it very much."

"So, when do you expect to roll back here? I wouldn't want you to be away for too long. I'd need to see you, to make sure everything is going well."

"I'll do my best, but Mystynn can relay my condition if I can't find the time. Don't worry, if anything happens, I'll come by personally, and when we rotate out, I'll make sure I stop by first," Storrm stated brightly as she left the clinic, the heavy bags slung o'er her shoulder.

~~~~~~~~~~

Winded by the time she arrived at their quarters, even enhanced, what would not have given her trouble afore, was giving her definite trouble now. She chewed her bottom lip fretfully as Mystynn added her contribution to their saddlebags. "Darque knows nothing about what we're doing," she stated, guilt written o'er her face.

Mystynn glanced up from his task and caught the worry in her eyes. "Nor does Gunnarr."

She nodded. They'd struggled for moons trying to think of another solution to their predicament. Every scenario came back to this plan. They had but one tiny chance. Get far enough away to birth Skyya without the Hoard's knowledge then bring her back safely into the protection of the Domes, or make the Hoard think she didn't survive. They could not come up with a plan to fake Skyya's death as long as she yet lived in the womb, so the only plan that would work was to birth her alive, and either fake the death at that moment, or get her back to safety. Such meant that they had to run, they had to hide. No one could know where they were, for who knew how she was being Heard? Who knew if 'twas someone providing information without their own knowledge, if 'twas the Black, or if 'twas a spy? If they got far enough away to keep the spy or the Black from Hearing Skyya, they had a slim chance of survival. Still, slim was better than none.

Packing only essential supplies, they left their quarters intact so nothing would appear out of the ordinary. Throughout the day, Storrm mentioned to several people that she would be quite busy for a while going back and forth 'tween the Bog and the Keep, and that she'd continue to relay her orders through Haniyyah. Then, just after midnight and under a Mask of Allure, Mystynn added Storrm's packs upon his already loaded saddle, and taking off from the Ward, they left the Keep, Skyya opening the portal. No one saw them leave. They'd said no goodbyes. Not even a Gatekeeper noted their departure.

They'd left behind an Illusion of themselves that would appear randomly, just often enough and in various places to make everyone believe they were still there. The illusion would stand up to visual inspection but not at close range, and would make them appear to turn a corner, or disappear into a crowd, if anyone tried to get their attention. 'Twas most realistic and since they'd taken great pains in becoming so reclusive, no one would suspect they weren't really anywhere at all, for quite some time.

A FORTNIGHT LATER

~~~~~ IN A SEASIDE TAVERN AT PORT O'DREAMS ~~~~~

Myrrdin was distracted. Upon the first night after making port, he'd lost yet another crewman to a fight in the alley behind this very tavern. The owner was a friend but had no information to provide, although they both suspected 'twas a set-up, for since then he'd had no luck in securing another hire. 'Twas dangerous to make your living upon the high seas, although he'd not had such difficulty in many a winter. In the meantime, his contract with Corbyn was in the future and he pushed it to the back of his mind as he made plans for satisfying a new one. He needed another hand and was at least one short, and if they didn't set sail soon, he'd miss his opportunity.

He frowned when the increasing noise became unbearable, sat upright, and slammed his glass of wine upon the table, the thick cut of heavy cypress reverberating with a loud thunk, gaining everyone's attention while exclaiming, "ENOUGH!" The tavern instantly became silent, his hard stare unnerving to those who'd attempted to drag the man outside, kicking and screaming into the night. His crime? An unpaid tab. He'd pleaded for leniency but the owner, to whom he owed much coin, was unimpressed. From the argument, Myrrdin ascertained the man was broke and had no job, while a pregnant mate with three other little ones, waited at home. He'd admitted to making a mistake by running up a tab he knew he couldn't pay. Although he seemed sincere in his desire to try to work off his debt, the tavern owner refused, saying he'd let it build up too far. Myrrdin was a sucker for a hard tale, especially when it involved children, but he was no fool. Still, he'd obtained most of his men in just this manner, and they'd all become excellent crewmen for the Krakken. They were hard workers who were grateful, honest, loyal, and to whom he owed his life more times than he cared to count in the many winters since he'd taken command as Ship's Master. Besides, this one was young and appeared strong.

With a slight bow and shaking his head, the tavern owner spoke emphatically under his breath, "M'lord Myrrdin, this one's not worth your effort! He'll lie to you, he'll steal from you, like he stole from me!" The tavern owner glared o'er his shoulder at the man, still on the floor, a terrified expression on his boyish face. Tapping his temple with one finger, he stated, "He's not right."

The man's skin was extremely pale, even for a Sprite, but that could be from the bruises beginning to show around his eyes, one near swollen shut from the scuffle. Then again, Myrrdin mused, 'twas dark in the tavern and his friend had given him the same warnings with every new crewman he'd hired in such a manner.

Myrrdin was in need and 'twas as if he'd been blackballed throughout the port. No matter, he'd survived such prejudice afore. Being an Elven Prince living amongst the Sprites, he'd learned to let it go. He picked up his wine and without losing eye contact with the man on the floor, he drained the glass, replaced it on the table a tad more gently this time, and stood up. Everyone moved aside. Now casting his gaze to the tavern owner, he stated quietly, "Put his bill on my tab and have him brought to the Krakken forthwith." He started to walk toward the door but hesitated as he stepped past the man. Noting his now puzzled expression, he smiled slightly and asked, "What's your name, boy?"

"Kyntik."

Myrrdin nodded. The name was familiar, but he could not draw forth the memory. Oft' times Magic bearers passed along their names in similarities through the generations. Although he had a slight sense of foreboding, 'twas likely from the wine. They'd been in port far too long. He wanted to get back into open waters where he felt free and could shuck this stifling sense of confinement. "I'll have someone send a note to your mate to reassure her of your safety, and that you will be unavailable for the next few moons."

LATER
~~~~~ MYRRDIN'S OFFICE ONBOARD ~~~~~

His voice crystal clear and smooth, Myrrdin recited the law of the Krakken as he'd done many times afore. "As long as you work on this ship, you will be compensated. Once your debt is paid in full, you are free to leave at the next port to which we dock, otherwise you work 'til we dock where you want to leave. Credit is not extended on the Krakken. Reasonable meals and water are free as are necessaries, otherwise you will pay for your extras, including replacement weapons and clothing, entertainment, spirits, and gambling. There is no unauthorized fighting amongst the crew. I do not tolerate theft. You will live within your means and will continue to be paid 'til you take your leave. Port privileges are earned, not given. Pay is offered upon the full moon. If you wish, part of your pay, however much you desire, can be held back. This cannot be retrieved once set in place and will not be given to you 'til we return to Port O'Dreams, which can vary from several moons to several winters, depending on our business ventures. None will be kept from you at that time, and careful records are in place to ensure no issues. Being a Ship's Hand can be dangerous as the high seas are frequented by pirates, some of whom may be our clients, therefore, if you do not survive for whatever reason, all coin owed you up to the time of your Passing will be paid to your mate or another of your choosing. If you break these rules your fate is in my hands and I usually choose to Quarter Dance. If you accept these terms you will now be in my employ and under my law. If you do not, you will pay off the debt you owe me now, or you will be handed o'er to the Guard."

His eyes widened as he listened, and when Myrrdin mentioned the punishment he preferred, he had to swallow hard or puke. If one body was pulled in four different directions by others who were Dancing away, that body would be torn apart viciously, explosively and with great agony. Not even a drop of blood would be left on either side of the Dance, and when they returned to the Krakken, the one so punished would be but a memory. 'Twas an ancient form of corporal punishment oft' times used by the mariners as 'twas the least messy, but 'twas also the most horrifying. He was beginning to think he'd made a monumental mistake allowing himself to be brought aboard. Sputtering in disbelief, he replied, "But, I can't leave! What about my mate?"

Myrrdin pushed the paperwork 'cross the desk and simply continued to stare at the young man for a moment, during which time Kyntik said not a word but did not appear the least contrite. This one might be a bit of a challenge. Leaning forward on the desk he laced his fingers together, rested his elbows upon the wooden surface, and stated slowly and clearly, "Mayhap you should have thought of her last night, or any one of the many nights afore that, by report. I am not certain you understand the situation, son. I did not pay your debt for your convenience, I did so for the sake of my friend, the owner of that tavern, and for the sake of your woman and children, who deserve better. I worked hard for that coin and I expect my crew to do the same. I have given you a fair deal, yet 'tis still your choice." Myrrdin felt a twinge of nostalgia and hoped his 'traditional incentive' would work as well as it had in the past, for he'd not used it in a very long time. He took a breath and continued. "But afore you make any decision, mayhap you should take a look out that porthole."

The young Sprite kept his eyes upon the Ship's Master as he stepped haltingly toward the porthole. Once there, he looked out for but a moment, his pale appearance now enhanced by real dread. Without a word, and barely able to breathe, he turned back to Myrrdin. Beginning to tremble, Kyntik stumbled to the desk, took the quill, and penned his signature upon the document, making him a crewman of the Krakken.

Once 'twas official, Myrrdin sent the man with his First Mate, Lyran, to get a meal afore starting his shift. Lyran would help him find a rack later. From now on, he was not Myrrdin's concern. They had work to do and needed to set sail as soon as possible. But afore he gave that order he went topside and standing on the quarterdeck he bowed to the new Captain of the Elite Guard,

Naftaleah, who, along with three of her Guardsmen, stood upon the dock waiting for the man to exit the Krakken so they could take him into custody.

Naftaleah was promoted after Caleichante's successor, Natanamia, was deployed to the Resistance with her troops, and she was already achieving a reputation. Myrrdin also had a reputation throughout the island and no one would dare cross either of them. Smiling, she waved, stood down her Guard, and left for Dream Hold and their other duties. She'd Heard Myrrdin as he Called for assistance through the Links they shared with their Ties just after the man was brought aboard, and knowing Myrrdin's methods, they set the usual 'incentive'. Naftaleah wasn't Caleichante, but she was well pleased to learn that she could still strike fear in the hearts of others. She'd stood with Calei on these missions afore and was honored that Myrrdin let her continue their tradition. Grinning, she thought the whole thing went rather well.

NEAR A MOON LATER

~~~~~ SOMEWHERE IN THE FAR WEST

OF THE RAZOR'S EDGE ~~~~~

</div>

Mystynn returned from his hunt to find Storrm sleeping in the cave where they'd taken refuge just a few dawns past. Starting a small fire, he began to heat up the space for her, and cooked the meat after skinning and cleaning the huge ellka. Storrm stretched and slowly woke to the delicious aromas. She smiled when she realized where they were and what he was doing, and the simple gesture warmed his soul. He'd tried so hard to make her as comfortable as possible, but 'twas difficult. "No worries," she said, their old habits of Blocking each other's thoughts a thing of the past now. Holding her ever expanding belly, she stood up slowly and stretched.

Suddenly Corbyn flew in, his iridescent black feathers a'gleam with moisture from the morning fog. Shifting on the fly, he landed lightly on his feet in front of them just as they started to eat. "No time! Quickly! Leave everything and take wing NOW!"

Storrm glanced to Mystynn, then dropped the meat back in the fire and with his assist, scrambled up to the saddle they never took off anymore. All their bags were packed as well, ever present on his broad back, but the food he'd just made, along with a full bag of her potion, was lost as they took wing into the foggy skies, just moments afore a Hoard squadron arrived at the cave. 'Twas their narrowest escape thus far.

Once they knew they were not being followed, Corbyn, as the Raven, led them to another cavern system, leagues to the north and further west. Settling them, he presented Storrm with the bag of potion she could not have replaced, receiving a hug in return. He felt horrible. And he was worried. They were running out of places to hide, and there was no real way to determine how much longer they need do so. Having been unsuccessful in attempting to get them to return to the Keep, to let Darque know, to let the Resistance help, he had to admit they were right. There were not enough Teams to protect the pair once the Black found them, and if Skyya opened the portals, none of the Lairs would be safe. And just how did they keep finding them so fast? Even with Skyya broadcasting randomly, 'twas not strong enough for just any Magic bearer to perceive from a distance. Every time they were found, he'd noted not one amongst their chase team who could have managed. Yet someone had to be Hearing her, listening for her. That would require much effort, along with some decent Magic. Fay level Magic. Something the Hoard didn't have available to them, to his knowledge. So, who was Hearing Skyya?

He gasped. Wait. Brannyn was now Right to Second to the Black. His brother, the Falcon, had infiltrated the Hoard after Corbyn was sent into exile, and stood shoulder to shoulder with his Second in Command, the Destroyer. His mind drifted back to a recent conversation with Darque, which at the time he'd not believed. Now? They'd sat in her office, sharing glasses of the finest whiskey he'd ever tasted, discussing who might be the spy. "Could it be Brannyn?" he'd asked reluctantly. Darque had replied, just as reluctantly, "I believe 'tis possible that your brother could lose himself to the evil with which he is surrounded. Does anyone have the strength it takes to withstand such an onslaught?" But 'twas her memory of Brannyn's own words, that had made him tremble. Long ago, when the Fay and the Battle Commander first met, he told her, "I have done things for which I should have shame, I should have regrets. I have neither. I do what must be done."

Had he turned? Worse yet, could Brannyn be the Sorcerer?

CHAPTER TWENTY

Deception Discovered

The Destroyer carefully chose his victim, taking the youngest, the smallest, the least likely to suspect his deceit and unable to defend himself. He was also certain the child he'd lured away from the others had no relatives amongst them so that the rest of the group would not recognize the flaws in his Magical transformation. Tossing the broken body of the little boy into the ravine, he completed his Shift and joined the party of refugees. He'd savored killing the child even though he'd had to hurry for he'd likely not get another chance and he'd needed the boost in energy. His Shift was not perfect but as long as everyone was distracted, he could get inside the Keep. He'd have to continue to Shift quickly but in his own mind, his plan was flawless.

The Sorcerer swore the Keep was still there as were all the Lairs of the Resistance despite their unsuccessful efforts to locate any of them and although he hated to admit such, he was correct. The Black's necromancer had attempted to take this glory from him, but he'd have none of that. He was Second in Command and would abduct that little bitch Flyrra, himself. The thought that mayhap the Black would give her to him as reward made him salivate and wiping the drool from the corners of his mouth on the back of a filthy sleeve, he ignored the discomfort this Magic caused him and concentrated on maintaining the Shift, while hiding amongst the adults of this group of refugees.

'Twould be his third attempt to enter the Keep. Thus far he'd been required to wait too long and was unable to do so, in another's form. This time, he was confident of success. He'd learned much from his past attempts and 'twould help him once he got inside. The Warrior Kayarr had yet to return and he knew his form well after interrogating the Pitch who'd let him escape, afore Draining them without mercy. Flyrra would do anything to help the Warrior. He'd never truly believed the rumors of her strength and her ability to differentiate truth from deception. She was a half-breed, making her Magic weaker, not stronger, and the Destroyer would fool her with ease.

WITHIN A MARK
~~~~~ INSIDE THE KEEP ~~~~~

</div>

Laratyn's gaze shifted from the group of refugees he and his brothers were vetting, toward the little boy edging his way surreptitiously toward the exit. Staring at the child, he was surprised when they caught gazes and then the boy tore away from his sight, slipping around the corner. No one else seemed to have noticed the little boy. 'Twas odd. Mayhap the child was simply being a curious child, but that look in his eyes was strangely... ancient and malevolent.

Malyrist noted his brother's inattention. "What say you, my brother? Need a break?"

Orasynth now noted the expression on Laratyn's face and asked, "Fatigue? Something wrong?"

Laratyn was fatigued, and he saw no need to alarm his brothers for a lost child, nor did he want to get that child into trouble so early in his tenure with the Resistance. 'Twas only a feeling, he had no proof. He wanted proof. One way or the other. "I need to check on something. I shall return shortly." Laratyn's response was unusually vague, but with the interviews just beginning, neither brother picked up on any sense of urgency that would require them to delay. They waved to Laratyn as he left the area.

'Twas near a mark later when they began to wonder. Having finished the initial process with the latest refugees, a rather small group this time, Mal and Ora decided to find their wayward brother and get something to eat.

The Destroyer had difficulty with the Shift. A small boy had taken too much energy to maintain. He'd needed an adult, one who would not be questioned as he wandered about the Keep looking for Flyrra. And he could not Shift to Kayarr too soon, there'd be too many eyes upon him. The Elf would do nicely.

Attracting his attention, he'd enticed the Elf to follow him as he wandered further and further into the lower sections of the Keep, but midway, the Elf caught up and turned him roughly, for now his disguise was failing. Taking a firm grip upon the Elf, he made his Shift. The surprise in the other's face was such that the Destroyer was able to take advantage and near Drained Laratyn to the Veil. If not for the possibility of another coming down the corridor he would have completed the act, but he had to leave quickly.

Laratyn tried to hold on. He had to survive long enough to warn his brothers. But would they find him in time? If only he'd understood sooner. He'd been confused and seeking answers. If only he'd noted the discrepancies.

The Destroyer walked as fast as he could without attracting too much attention, back the way they'd come, seeking to avoid all conversation, using all his energy to maintain the Shift. The Keep was a veritable maze. Without realizing such, he'd found himself back where the refugees were being vetted. His gaze caught that of Laratyn's brothers as they were walking out to find him. Ignoring their calls, he disappeared into a crowd of residents. He needed to locate Flyrra. Where was she?

Unable to maintain the Shift any longer, he jerked another hapless victim to a darkened corner, Drained him completely and became a member of the kitchen staff. Surely, they would know where was the child.

He struck pay dirt with this Shift, as it seemed Flyrra was popular and everyone knew her. Learning quickly where she could be found at this time of day, he abandoned the kitchens and headed toward her classroom.

~~~~~ FLYRRA'S QUARTERS ~~~~~

The Shift to the Warrior Kayarr had been very difficult. From the reports of the Pitch he'd had a clear image but knew there'd be something wrong. He'd just have to trust the girl would not reveal his deception. She was intelligent enough to understand that the real Kayarr might be in mortal danger. He'd picked up energy along their way back to her quarters, surreptitiously touching and taking what he could without anyone's knowledge. He preferred killing to this, it took too much finesse and he had no time for such. His next Shift would be even more difficult than had been the Warrior, but 'twas the only way he could get Flyrra out of the Keep. And if all went as planned, he'd not have to maintain that Shift for long.

Flyrra was near the last to leave her classroom, thinking about how long it had been since she'd gone out with the Second on gatherings. She missed that. But she knew Storrm was busy with her duties, and she was no longer a priority to the commanders. Not any more so than anyone else. Especially since she could not tell them the location of the Black's Lair. Everyone played their part and did what they could to help in the war effort. She oft' times wondered what part she would, or could, play.

Suddenly someone touched her shoulder from behind. Flyrra knew instantly 'twas not her father come to collect her from class, but she'd hesitated just long enough for the Destroyer to whisper in her ear, "Your 'father' will meet a most horrible end, if you do not cooperate with me now." His gravelly voice and fetid breath made her cringe, memories clawing at her guts. Still, she could have killed him but how to rescue her father if she did not go along with the pretense? That is, if they really had him, which she doubted. Kayarr was too good to get caught by the likes of the Hoard. However, she could not allow her friends to be harmed because of her. Besides, she'd promised not to use her Magic in the Keep or against anyone of the Resistance ever again. Darque and Storrm and all the others had given her a new life. Thus far, she'd given little in return. And this one had breached the Keep.

With sudden clarity, she understood that no one could truly protect her, she would always be a target, endangering everyone. Mayhap this was how the Fates had chosen to give her the opportunity to avenge her mother's death, and to play her part in the war. If she returned to the Lair, she could do much damage afore they killed her. Mayhap she could take out the Black himself. Then and there, she determined she would sacrifice herself for her new-found family and friends.

Taking the Destroyer's cold hand, she led the way back to her quarters. It sickened her to touch the Elf. His voice made her shiver in revulsion, the glint in his eye was evil, the memories of his past advances had bile rising in her throat. And when he made his Shift to Storrm, her eyes filled with tears.

~~~~~ DEEP IN SOUTHEASTERN WYNDSYR FOREST ~~~~~

'Twas cold and Storrm was a bare shell of her former self. Having run out of potion days past, she couldn't eat enough fast enough to counter what Skyya was taking. Still, she managed. Moving from place to place, they'd not stayed anywhere for more than a few marks, barely able to let Storrm rest and eat afore they were off again, the numbers of their Hoard followers growing. At first just a mere handful, at last count 'twas o'er a hundred.

Mystynn and Corbyn had been talking quietly together for near a quarter mark when they heard her wake. Corbyn had reconnoitered the Hoard contingent giving chase and 'twould seem whoever was Listening, traveled with them. They had to further distance themselves, no stops as they'd done so far, despite the fact that Storrm required sleep and nourishment. They needed to leave the Razor's Edge and go north. Bringing her some food, she waved the roots away. 'Twould be all she could do, to consume the meat. Stuffing the offered feast into her mouth she ate voraciously, embarrassed at her enthusiasm when she noted the amused expressions on the faces of her audience. Wiping her mouth on the sleeve of her leather shirt, for napkins were now luxurious and distant memories, she licked her lips and stated brightly with more energy than she felt, "Where to next?"

Despite her bravado 'twas clear that Storrm could not keep this up, and so Corbyn had chosen to go all the way to Winter's Edge in the Far Northlands. Mystynn broke the news. "I know 'twill be a long and difficult journey for you, but 'tis nowhere suitable any closer and Winter's Edge can provide us good security, for few even know of its existence. Mayhap we will finally be far enough away that Skyya's Voice will no longer be Heard."

Storrm knew they could not Push their way there faster than normal flight, for Skyya had near died with their initial attempt to fly through the timefold, leaving her a most difficult journey, indeed. But 'twould be worth it if they could stay there in hiding long enough to birth Skyya and then get back to the Lair. She nodded, took a deep breath, and finished her meal as she mounted. Quickly Mystynn took wing, just missing the Hoard who had found them yet again. The Raven's beady black eyes glittered in anger, as he followed the big Dragon.

THE KEEP

~~~~~ NEAR A FORTNIGHT LATER ~~~~~

</div>

Darque had returned to the Keep and sent word to Storrm and Mystynn to make report. Although Haniyyah had Responded, Darque repeated her desire to speak with her Seconds face to face afore they rotated back to Drekinn. While waiting for them, she and Tammra had discussed the Assassins' role and Resistance strategies long into the night. Finally, they finished their mead and the Kreegaren Commander stood to take her leave. "Your wish is my command, Darque. 'Twill be child's play for my forces to bodyguard Storrm without her knowledge. We shall present our initial report by dawn."

"I thank you. I know 'tis selfish of me to ask such, but I have been very concerned. Storrm has not made report in person in o'er three moons, and although many have said they've seen her and she makes all her reports on time, no one has been able to tell me they've spoken face to face, and all reports have gone through Haniyyah. And, she's yet to answer my summons. This pregnancy has been very difficult on her. Kelseacyr wants her back in the clinic. I want her there, too. I'm worried."

"Fear not, Darque. We will find her," Tammra said. But as she turned to make her exit, she was near o'erwhelmed by an old sensation of warning. 'Twas something she felt when things were about to take a drastic turn toward the worst-case scenario. She'd not felt her warning sensation this strongly since the ancient ambush, and she hesitated. Darque's attention was back on her paperwork. Surely this sensation was off beam. 'Twas a simple assignment, what could go wrong? Setting aside the feeling, she shook her head, shut the door behind her, gathered Leis, Dyra, and Cass, and walked purposefully down the hallway to begin their assignment.

~~~~~ DAWN ~~~~~

'Twas not long after Darque sent the Kreegaren Commander on her private mission that Tammra and her Assassins returned with strange news. As the Battle Commander processed what she'd just been told, Gunnarr left to hunt. They'd need their strength. Heading to the Mess Hall, she planned on getting a good meal herself, not sure if she were more upset or confused with what her sister had apparently done. It made no sense.

As Darque walked into the dining area, Natanamia rushed toward her, so excited she glowed. "Darque! Where is he?"

Gunnarr was just outside the Dome and Felt the bewildered emotion Darque Pushed as she asked, "Who?"

"Kayarr! I heard he was seen in the Keep. I thought he'd be with you...", Natan's voice trailed off, a questioning look upon her face. As she spoke, she knew something was wrong by the equally questioning look upon the Battle Commander's face.

Darque felt blindsided. The Kreegare had just reported that Storrm was gone. The Illusion Spell was well wrought but with the breakdown they noted, Tammra estimated 'twas likely they'd been gone for near three moons. She and Gunnarr were preparing for an extended search to find and return Storrm and Mystynn to the Keep. And if Kayarr was back, the Gatekeeper would have reported such to her. As she'd heard the Sprite's voice, she'd turned, but afore she could speak, a hush fell o'er the hall as everyone took notice, staring at Orasynth and Malyrist carrying the broken and Drained body of their brother, Laratyn. As the sun began to dawn upon her, she Spoke with Gunnarr, *"Come home now. I need you."*

WITHIN MOMENTS
~~~~~ THE BATTLE COMMANDER'S OFFICE ~~~~~

</div>

Darque led them into the large room and cleared her desk afore standing behind it. Facing the growing crowd, she watched them step aside while the Elven brothers walked through and carefully laid Laratyn's body upon the smooth oaken surface, fury in their eyes. "What happened?" she asked.

Orasynth's emotions barely in check, he made his report. "We were vetting a new group of refugees. He felt something was amiss and excused himself, saying that he would return shortly. We caught sight of him later, but he seemed distant and did not acknowledge us, so we followed. We lost him without a trace. 'Twas the War Dogs Drys and Horace who found him in one of the back corridors."

"Was he already Past the Veil?"

"No. But upon his last breath he seemed to be babbling. He said someone had slipped in. A child who was not a child." His face took on a look of confusion as he continued, "And then he added something about tarnish upon the metal." Orasynth had run out of words. Choking, he attempted to clear his throat and swallowed hard. He simply stood, his face a mask of agony, waiting for the Commander to speak understanding into his brother's seemingly senseless loss while Malyrist stood at his shoulder, jaw set.

Gunnarr's deep Voice penetrated Darque's thoughts. *"Find the imposter posing as Kayarr and you find the intruder, for 'twill surely be the one who forced the Elf 'cross the Veil. I am entering the Keep and will be with you soon."*

Darque listened to her partner and hesitated not a heartbeat. Her gaze sweeping to Natanamia, she spoke to the entire room. "Find Kayarr. Bring him to me now."

Natan glanced around and nodded to the rest of her team, but afore they could leave, Regynn stepped forth, staying the Sprite with his hand upon her shoulder. "I think that search would prove fruitless by now, as 'tis unlikely our intruder is the one who appears as Kayarr. The boy's last words indicated that he knew this, and he provided the only clues he could."

Darque's eyes narrowed. "What do you mean?"

"He said that someone slipped in. 'A child who was not a child.' Kayarr would not have had to slip inside, but he would have attracted much attention. And then there's the other thing he mentioned. To the Clan, to most humans, the phrase 'the tarnish is upon the metal' speaks of broken trust. One might think he was referring to the imposter Kayarr being untrustworthy. But knowing Elves as do I, I think Laratyn was being literal."

Natanamia's quick mind leaping ahead, she questioned, "Someone who was at once a boy and then a Warrior with tarnished weapons? We seek the Fay?"

"Probably not." Regynn shook his head and stated to her and Darque, "Such would be a sloppy Shift for the Fay. Possibly another Race, not as strong in Shifting."

Darque readily grasped the idea. "One who dared to do such would be burning through his Magic and would have to make quick Shifts. The child, Laratyn, Kayarr... but that means, he or she could be anyone, or anything, by now."

While she spoke, Axyl and Ardyth entered the room and were now standing in the back with Haniyyah and Bryynn close behind along with a growing crowd of Warriors as Regynn replied. "Yes, so Laratyn was warning us not to seek out a particular person or Warrior. If we seek only Kayarr, we will miss the intruder."

Orasynth stepped forth, his voice, his posture, his emotions, all action. "Commander, I think we have a bigger problem. Flyrra was seen going back to her quarters with Kayarr." Malyrist, Gylrann and Gylragg, nodded in agreement. 'Twas such a report that had Natan seeking him.

At that moment, two more Gatekeepers entered to report that Kayarr was approaching the Keep with eleven Eagle Warriors, and hearing the end of the last statement, added that Flyrra was not with them.

One of the Gatekeepers newly arrived, stepped forth. "Sir? Flyrra is safe. She went out less than a quarter mark past, on a gathering outing."

Darque began to suspect the worst, as she questioned, "With whom?"

"Commander Storrm," she replied, and suddenly all eyes were upon her as she looked with eyes wide from one person to the next.

The intruder had moved quickly, indeed. If 'twas the Hoard, and it could be no other, then they'd be taking Flyrra back to their Lair. They might never have a better opportunity. If Storrm were in trouble, she'd Call. Bringing her home would have to wait, for Flyrra's rescue, along with the destruction of the Black and his

Lair, took precedence. Storrm's Sword would be missed, but there was no time to chastise her Second. Darque's head turned questioningly to the Kreegaren entourage. Without another word, Tammra Dayo glanced to her brethren, grit her teeth as the Battle Lust began to rise, and nodded their readiness to assist.

<center>~~~~~ THE QUARTERS OF NATANAMIA AND KAYARR ~~~~~</center>

'Twas an eerie sensation they felt when they ran into their quarters, Crytcha right behind. The Call to Arms had sounded throughout the Keep and all children were immediately sent to their parents or to the protection of the barracks to be armed and set in defense mode. Crytcha stood wordlessly in the corner watching her Claim parents as she waited. She was wearing her headband as usual. She never removed it and they had not the heart to ask her to. Even though it no longer glittered as 'twas getting dull with wear, 'twas her most treasured possession.

Natan spoke first. "I do not like this."

Kayarr caught her gaze toward the elder of their two Claim children and then dismissively returned to his task of changing out his leathers and weaponry. "She is her best friend and her sister by Claim. She has a right to go."

"But she is just a child!"

As he finished buckling his thick leather forearm bracers and adding his blades, he replied, "She is a very powerful child, as is Flyrra, each in their own way. And she's a member of the Clan and the Resistance, who has already fought and killed in this war."

"She has fought Humans, not Dragons."

He glanced toward Crytcha, who remained in the corner waiting stoically. "She likes her odds. As do I."

Natan quietly armed up, ensuring Kayarr's bracers and pads were properly adjusted as he reluctantly did the same for her. Crytcha required no such armor, standing silent and ready, holding the huge stone hammer o'er her massive shoulder. 'Twas no mercy in her deep-set narrowed eyes.

Kayarr tried one last time. "You should stay home, Natanamia." His gaze flashed to Crytcha, who barely nodded her head in agreement. "If anything happens to us, Flyrra will need someone here for her."

She shrugged her shoulders and flatly stated, "I have to go."

Suspicious of the expression on his mate's face, he asked, "Any other reason than your command? Darque will allow you to stay to protect the Keep."

"'Twill be the first time we have a true location on the Lair."

Flipping his hand o'er his shoulder, he stated, "We will track them."

But Natan was insistent. "You know we can't follow quickly enough, they will leave no trail to track, and 'twill take too long!"

"We have many Free Dragons to fly us."

"Flyrra is alone with her kidnapper. They travel a'foot, and the Dragons can't see through forest canopy."

"They can scent her."

"No! I must go with you! They take her directly to the Black's Lair, and they will kill her afore you can track her!"

Having just finished lacing his boots he stood upright quickly, and with frustration 'cross his dark face and in his now dark brown eyes, he exclaimed, "Natan! What's going on here? What are you not saying?"

She met his gaze and answered calmly. "I can follow her directly. I can see where she is at any time."

Suspicion replaced anger once more as he asked, "How can you do such?"

She clasped her hands together and sighed. 'Twas still difficult to talk about her little sister, and what she'd done filled her with guilt as 'twas considered a violation of trust for her people. "Sprite parents Tie to the spirits of their children. 'Tis similar to how we Tie to the Water Dragons. But Niamia wasn't allowed this." She hesitated afore she admitted the truth. "So, I did it myself, not long after you brought Flyrra here. Her spirit will lead us directly to them. I just need Seek her, and she will Show herself to me."

~~~~~ WITHIN HALF A MARK ~~~~~

"May we fight well, and may the Fates be with us," Darque told them as she issued her blessing, just after they'd gathered their forces in the forest outside the Dome. Then as one, they began to move.

They traveled fast and light, mostly a'foot, with near two hundred Dragons flying low o'er the treetops. From her intel, the Black had triple that at his disposal. Those in the 'Bond led the others for their own protection and to keep a lid on their enthusiasm, for they did not want to throw the salt early. 'Twas surmised that the kidnapper was the Destroyer himself, and he must not know they were being followed so quickly. 'Twas clear the Hoard's plan was to take Flyrra and lose any rescue effort in the delay of discovering her missing. The Lair of the Black had been sought for winters, and never found. The Destroyer did not believe 'twould be found now, his Magic Masking their trail. 'Twas his thinking that even if they sensed the Mask, 'twould lead them nowhere. But no Mask could suppress the spirit Tie 'tween Natan and Flyrra.

Darque and Gunnarr flew at the head of the aerial assault forces. This was not just a rescue mission. This was their chance to end the war. Darque's intel had advised that his foot soldiers were mostly at Evanntyr with less than a thousand at his Lair as trust 'tween the Hoard Dragons and the Humans was dismally low, mayhap as a result of the efforts of the Sentinel and Brannyn the Falcon, working together from within. The Free Dragon with amber hues to her scales, had been inside the Hoard longer than had Brannyn himself, and had saved the Fay from an ambush just after he'd taken his promotion to Right to Second to the Black. And even though the Black had them outnumbered by Dragons,

Darque had far more ground forces than he could possibly imagine, still thinking they'd annihilated the Clan in the last battle. Natanamia and her Sprite and Elven squad, along with Kayarr and the Eagle Warriors, led those forces along with near three hundred Free Warriors, near five hundred of the People of the Daggogh and the Gordatch including their Night Beasts and Night Wings, and although no one could see them, one thousand Kreegaren troops were roving their perimeter, protecting their flanks. The other five hundred Assassins had been split 'tween the Keep and Drekinn for protection if they were attacked.

Assassins were not frontal assault fighters but had wholeheartedly agreed with this mission once they heard of whom they were after. The chance to kill the Black and rescue a little girl was too tempting for Tammra to pass up, especially when she discovered the girl was Elven. Despite Natanamia trying to clarify Flyrra was half Sprite, Tammra just smiled, turned, and gathered her Assassins. She, like Myrrdin, knew the 'cousin' Races were one, and having any Elven blood, made her Elven. Besides, Leisalarr and Dyraserrah, who flanked her even now, once humbled her into remembering that all life was precious. The past was the past and she was in the fight again. And there was always the possibility of meeting the one they were now chasing, face-to-face once more. She'd lived eons for that meeting.

Fryya, Walkyr, and Brecca reluctantly stayed behind, waiting with the few remaining Warriors and Free Dragons to defend the Keep if such became necessary, and to listen for any news of the battle. The blood-red 7th Prince, Bryynn, whose powerful Enhancement Magic, allowing him to absorb and/or project his or another's Magical powers to those of his choosing, and his partner Ardyth, the Seer of the Dead, who could channel the spirits of those who had Passed, giving them the ability to do as they'd done in life, along with the lovely petite green Haniyyah and her huge, muscled Warrior LifeBond Axyl, joined the rescue mission. That left all communications going through

Rolf and Nalwynn, based at Drekinn, and the surprising 'Bond of Aspynn, the Prince Maakayyel, last surviving sibling of the past Matriarchs and Gunnarr's uncle. Maakayyel's Link was so strong, he could Hear any focused thought to him, clear 'cross Kadoor. Since taking the 'Bond he'd been pushing himself to try to Hear unfocused thoughts, but thus far, he'd had little success, Hearing only occasional random ones. Now Maakayyel was in Command of Communications o'er Haniyyah and Nalwynn.

While Natanamia continued to guide them all, her Tie leading them unerringly along the trail Flyrra and the Destroyer just passed through, she reported to Kayarr, ensuring Maakayyel passed the information to Darque and Gunnarr above. Working their way through the forest, she turned not her head to her life-mate, as she spoke. "I believe that Flyrra knows you are not held captive by the Hoard."

"You've made contact already?"

"Following the Tie isn't like making contact, but I am getting some emotions. Not as clearly as would Diadranei, but enough to deduce why she left, knowing the truth. She thinks to sacrifice herself if need be, to try to take down the Black and as many of the Hoard as possible, afore they take her down."

"She's always been a very courageous, but impulsive, little girl."

Natan didn't answer, as she continued her efforts to keep them on track.

After passing along yet another change in direction, the Dragons adjusted their flight pattern and they traveled through the days and into the nights, staying always just a few leagues behind the Destroyer and his hostage. He would not hear them, as his own Mask would blunt any outside sensations from penetrating. They were safe as long as they stayed out of sight.

MEANWHILE

~~~~~ THE LAIR OF THE BLACK ~~~~~

</div>

The Black growled his delight with the newest report from his necromancer. He'd located Storrm and Mystynn again. They'd traveled out of the Razor's Edge and deep into the Far Northlands, but they would go no further, as the abomination growing in her womb was near ready to be birthed. His madness apparent in his eyes, he vowed to destroy them afore this went any further. Storrm and that bastard of hers must die, and Corbyn must not gain the throne of the Fay.

The situation was reminiscent of the Last Holocaust. A low menacing growl emanated from deep in his chest. They were close. This time he'd leave nothing to chance. This time he'd watch o'er their efforts himself. 'Twas the only way to be certain they did not fail him again.

Leaving the Lair, he cared not that the Destroyer would arrive within a few dawns with Flyrra. His Second in Command could handle the girl 'til he returned. What did he pay him for anyway? Flyrra could wait. The other could not. Telling the Sorcerer to expect him soon, he exited the caverns, laboriously climbed around the cave entrance and up the side of the cliff to the top open ledge and without hesitation, launched himself, flanked by Third Fighter Brannyn and a handful of his Hoard taking wing to Winter's Edge.

CHAPTER TWENTY-ONE

Battle Of Darden Caverns

'Twas near dusk and the Destroyer was livid when they arrived, the girl now hooded as per the Black's standing orders. His glorious leader was nowhere in the Lair, and word was, he'd left days earlier for some place in the far north. He'd pushed hard to get here this fast, and he spit in anger as he attempted to find anyone with any authority, eventually discovering the necromancer and his Right to Second were gone as well. No one to glorify his efforts, no one to whom to brag. His lip curled in disgust.

He threw the scrawny little girl into a cell, her hands still tied and hood intact, and went in search of someone to destroy to dissipate his anger. But shortly after he'd left the area, Flyrra removed both the hood and the ropes around her wrists, using her flexibility and strength alone. She'd done so many times in the past. 'Twas simple enough to force the guards to remain silent and let her out of the cell. Once free she made them rip their own vocal cords out of their throats so she could leave them without the ability to call for help, fleeing the area as they suffocated and bled to death, the gurgling sounds fading into the distance as she made her way into the upper chambers.

It didn't take long for Flyrra to discover neither the Sorcerer or the Black were at the Lair, and no one knew when they'd return. She was disappointed. Evidently her capture was of less importance than was another issue. But she could still kill the Destroyer and set up chaos, decreasing the Hoard's numbers so Darque and her forces, who she knew were following and would arrive at any moment, could manage to destroy the Lair itself, ensuring the Black would have no safe haven to which to return. 'Twould force the Hoard on the run, making them more vulnerable and decreasing the odds against the Resistance. To make her plan effective she just had to avoid getting killed too early in the fighting.

Within moments, Flyrra's acute hearing alerted her that Darque's forces had arrived, swords swinging, Flame streaming, penetrating the Lair, killing everyone in their path. 'Twas not long afore 'twas all hand-to-hand combat within the confines of the caverns, vast as they were, for streaming Flame would have killed even their own in such an environment. Those Dragons who'd made it outside the caverns, were battling the Teams o'er head in a vicious aerial attack.

She hurried through the corridors, seeking the Destroyer. A bully, his spineless ass would be found... there! Triumphantly she faced him as he tried to gather his belongings to make good his escape. Catching him off-guard, her control was still tenuous, and she was surprised at his strength. Avoiding her direct gaze, he too, was surprised at the power the despicable half-breed displayed.

'Twas a standoff at best. Flyrra tried but could not keep him still, let alone kill him, and her strength ebbed with his continuous struggles against her Hold. Needing to find a distraction, he chose with disdain and suddenly the Destroyer Shifted. Flyrra was startled. She was standing afore her mother, Niamia. 'Twas only for a heartbeat, but 'twas all he needed. Losing her control, he reached for her, forcing her withdrawal. Struggling to reset her Magic, she slipped and sat hard on the stone floor of his chambers, a position in which she'd found herself many times afore. He laughed at the horror reflected on her face as he came ever nearer.

Just afore the Destroyer touched her, Gylragg came out of nowhere, stepping 'tween the pair, blocking his advance. Niamia disappeared as the Destroyer Shifted back to himself, sword already in swing. 'Ragg pushed Flyrra back, missing his block, and the Destroyer struck his thigh as he twisted away. Blood spurted forth from the open gash, as 'Ragg turned and near hamstrung the Destroyer with his counter swing. 'Twas enough for the Black's Second in Command, and he ran past the child and her defender into the outer corridors, calling for Hoardsmen to finish them.

Just as they exited the small chambers, 'Ragg and Flyrra were met with a dozen Hoardsmen and were forced back into the lesser corridors. The Elf could find no ready organics in the endless stone of the cave, and if he used Flyrra, her power would diminish. 'Twould leave them both weakened and vulnerable, fighting off all twelve of the enemy. Flyrra used what strength she had left to Hold them at a distance, but they ferociously continued to push against her Magic, the fear of what would happen to them in the torture chambers if they failed, fueling their enthusiasm. Flyrra and Gylragg could do naught but continue to withdraw.

~~~~~~~~~~

As Ardyth entered the Lair, she did not hesitate. She'd felt the many spirits that filled the caverns rushing her, seeking retribution upon the Black for their tortuous deaths, and with Bryynn's Magic to enhance her Gift, she opened herself to them. Shocked by her rapid transformation from petite female to Elf, Sprite, and Human, warriors and peasants alike as spirit after spirit entered her body and fought viciously, the Hoardsmen they encountered stood little chance against their vengeance. Slashing their way deeper into the caverns to the main chamber, her sword swung everywhere at once as Bryynn, Haniyyah and Axyl followed, defending her flanks, butchering their way along in the wake of the powerful Seer of the Dead. The spirits were so pleased to be back in the fight, that each shared the body one by one, vacating quickly with another eagerly replacing, as Ardyth rapid-channeled them, not even trying to control her 'guests', as they turned their rage and impotence into a reckoning upon the Hoard afore finally crossing the Veil for good.

Axyl was a killing machine, protecting his 'Bond, his lifemate, and the 7th Prince. His huge muscled arms swung sword so hard, even the man-made steel cut men in two and made Dragons run away, as he and Ardyth cleared their path further into the vast caverns looking for Flyrra. Still, Axyl was a hardened Warrior. This was too easy, he thought, as they continued to fight. Where were all the Black's troops? But of even more importance, where was the Black?

<center>~~~~~ BACK AT THE CLINIC ~~~~~</center>

Chynnar paused from cleaning up her counter and watched Kelsey, busy at her own tasks. Neither had spoken since Fryya left with Walkyr just half a mark earlier. The boy had yet another Vision of the upcoming battle and Chynnar was perplexed. "I'm confused. I know not what to do."

Kelsey furrowed her brows at the sound of Chynnar's voice as she tried to understand just what the girl was talking about. She'd been distracting herself from potential incoming wounded, by working on her sideline project. She and Corbyn had been studying the infertility issues of the Highlands, seeking the reasons behind the situation as well as to devise a solution, and she believed there was a strong correlation 'tween stress, including feelings of guilt by association (the Black was a Highland, after all), and infrequent mating flights. That was a double issue: their increasing efforts in the war leading up to the Last Holocaust and their increasingly reclusive nature since that time. These issues, along with so many single Highlands whose lifemates had Passed, seemed to have more to do with their infertility than some kind of Spell. She'd also interviewed the Matriarch on several occasions and had discovered some interesting findings from Synahmarr's Memories that might support her theory. And, Prince Maakayyel had shown unduly high interest, giving no reason, as well as having supplied much information without saying from whence it came, which gave her pause.

Just trying to gather together all this information and put it in some kind of logical order, she sighed, shifted her thoughts, met Chynnar's gaze, and stated, "I agree. I've never encountered anything like this. I've been researching in the Archives but have found nothing helpful for his situation. Since his birth, the boy's Visions have been stronger than any other Seer in history and I've found nothing to control them." She knew 'twas not what the other wanted to hear but had to add, "'Tis likely to be to his demise."

Chynnar sighed. "I know all that. There's something else. I wasn't certain, but now I think…" she began, but stopped.

Curiosity and trepidation shone in the Elf's eyes. "What?"

Lifting a stack of papers upon which she'd written many notes, she said, "Well, I've been keeping careful records of the details of the Visions Walkyr has had about this battle, and tonight I've noted some discrepancies."

"You mean, he faltered in the telling?" Kelsey had a hard time believing that, Walkyr was too honest, his memory too long.

"No, not exactly. I'm not even sure 'tis possible, but this Vision has repeated itself and I wonder if he isn't having more than one jammed together. The frequency has increased along with the intensity. I think mayhap 'tis not that the details have been changing, but that he is getting more detail." Setting the papers down on the counter, she leaned one hip against it.

"Well, Cayell did think Walkyr might be Seeing the battle rage both inside and outside the Lair."

Chynnar shook her head. "No, 'tis more than that. The details to which I am referring seem to, well, they seem to create…" she threw up her hands in surrender and blurted, "I think he may be Seeing more than one battle."

Kelseacyr's brows furrowed and she and the youthful Senior Healer simply gaped at each other for a moment. Then Kelsey came o'er and perused her notes, while Chynnar gave her mentor all her ideas, all the many reasons she felt the way she did.

Each specific detail meant little alone, but together they added up. Could another battle be brewing elsewhere? 'Twas just a thought, a feeling, and they had no proof. Darque's orders were for Maakayyel to Listen, not Send, unless 'twas a dire emergency. If they Sent a message now, would it be intercepted, or be a distraction and cause more trouble? Even the boy reviewed his Visions as of one battle. But if Chynnar was correct, the Battle Commander and her forces could be in more danger than they could imagine.

With determination, Kelsey laid down the papers and grabbed Chynnar's hand, pulling her out of the clinic and down the hallway to the Ward where they'd find Maakayyel, watching and Listening on the ramparts.

The mighty Dragon peered down upon the two Healers as they finished their story, then pondered the meaning of the Visions along with them. Briefly in Link, he gazed at them again. "I am not certain my message has been Received. The battle has already begun."

~~~~~ HIGH ABOVE THE LAIR OF THE BLACK ~~~~~

The Hoard Dragons had emerged swiftly from the Lair below to join those attempting to defend, shortly after Darque's ground troops entered. Darque and her Teams fought through the time-fold, Pushing their way here, there and everywhere using the native Highland Magic of enlarging space for their own purpose, speeding them along without regard to outside influence, giving their opponents no forewarning, and attacking ferociously. Suddenly appearing outside the 'fold, their fangs, talons, and Dragon Swords made swift work of the startled enemy forces.

As the battle heated, she thought she Heard Maakayyel, but 'twas not something she could ponder as they continued to fight. And, her intel told her the Black had more troops than this. She had to think the Hoard were at least two hundred shy at this location. Where could they be? Mayhap they'd moved them to

Evanntyr? She'd not yet received a report from the Stealth Team she'd sent there, and she hoped Graasyn, Bastyen, Diadranei and Caleichante were still alive and well. But Diadranei was a powerful Empath and should have been able to Send her something by now.

Frowning, ever aware of the potential for ambush, she returned her attention to the slaughter of her enemies, leaving the rescue of Flyrra to her ground troops in the Lair below.

~~~~~~~~~~

The Kreegaren forces were everywhere at once, their ghostly black images as they traveled in their unique Dance, unseen to everyone in the torch lit shadows of the caverns. Not giving the enemy any chance, they Drained, Danced, and Drained again and again, securing cave after cave in the labyrinthine system as they helped protect their new allies and searched for the child.

They gained much respect for the People, watching them use their special weapons made of the razor-sharp wings of the Rochas, known as Star Wings and Fans. The People were expert archers, but 'twas their throwing weapons with which they displayed much skill in the oft' times narrow spaces, and of which they used swiftly and with lethal resolve, pulling and throwing from holders under their arms, along their ribs, on their forearms, shoulders, hips, and thighs, taking down Hoardsman after Hoardsman within the Lair with blinding speed, retrieving their weapons and throwing again. When in close quarters with not enough space to effectively throw, they used them as blades, showing great skill in hand-to-hand techniques as the enemy dead stacked up.

~~~~~~~~~~

As Gheryh retrieved their weapons, her huge shaggy Night Beast, Ryygg, protected their flank afore they climbed o'er the dead to exit this cavern and catch up with Kyrag and his Night Wing leading the way into the next section. Suddenly Kyrag stopped moving. Gheryh and Ryygg stepped up beside him as they eyed the line of four Hoardsmen blocking their passage in the flickering torchlight. With a slight smile, Gheryh stayed Ryygg from charging ahead, afore she glanced to her mate. Without a word, Kyrag gave Bayl a nudge, the creature launching off his elbow, and watched as his giant fox-faced bat-like hunting partner flew o'er the enemy's heads. They saw him not, as Bayl's hide was near black and he was silent in the hunt, but they felt the gusts of wind and heard the flapping of his thick leathery wings beating o'er head in the shadows. Such startled them and they spun 'round seeking the cause.

Bats no longer lived in these caverns, and the Dragons that did, were outside fighting. But they'd never encountered any-thing like the Night Wing. Half the size of his Handler yet only a fraction of his weight, Bayl had recovered well from hideous wounds inflicted by Hoardsmen winters past and had become adept at killing them. Humans were much easier to kill than their usual fare of the huge antlered ellka and the heavy bodied moun-tain cats, even easier than the mountain deer and goats. But Humans were not taken back to the fire and were shared not with the tribe. Humans were killed to protect them, not to provide for them. Still, their blood was sweeter than any other animal he'd encountered in his span of days and as far as Bayl was concerned, blood was blood and 'twould give him energy to continue fight-ing. He'd fought with Kyrag during the attack on their village in the Talons, and he'd fought with him in the battle to Draw the Domes. The accomplished hunter lived to please Kyrag.

Bayl soared past the Hoardsmen threatening his Handler and his mate, coming to rest against the ceiling a short distance be-yond. Lethal talons grasped his perch and he wrapped his wings snugly about his body as he prepared to take his vengeance once more. Closing his luminous eyes to increase the terror effect, as fear would slow their responses, he listened to their breathing and waited. Hanging thusly upside down, he'd already sized up the hunt, his strategy simple. With his long fangs, wicked claws, blinding speed, and formidable strength, the Humans would be dead afore they could gather their wits, and then he would drink.

Within a few breaths the Hoardsmen located the terrifying creature hanging from the ceiling in the shadows. Soundless, their throats paralyzed with fear, their faces became masks of horror as Bayl's eyes snapped open. 'Twas the last thing they saw on this side of the Veil.

When Bayl had drunk his fill, Kyrag held out his arm and the Wing obediently flew to him, leaving the carnage where it lay. Snugging up against his Human, wrapping his long tail around Kyrag's waist, his hind feet sitting on his self-created perch and wings laid close to his flanks, Bayl rested his head o'er his Handler's shoulder and hugged on for the ride as they continued deeper into the caverns, Gheryh and Ryygg following close behind.

~~~~~~~~~~

Natanamia and Kayarr fought with brutal aggression as they beat back the Hoard, helping to clear out the Lair one swift kill at a time. Natan took a cue from her new friends, the Assassins, and when opportunity allowed, she drained her enemy. If unable to achieve a sufficiently solid grasp to outright kill them, she could weaken them and thus gain her advantage in the fight, saving her energy, for which she felt no guilt.

Kayarr's swinging sword sang in the caverns as if creating a music of its own. His bracers and shoulder pads, made in o'er lapping layers of thick leather cut and tooled to appear as feathers, were covered with blood, but 'twas not his own. Time and again he used his Gift of uncanny awareness of danger to keep them safe as they led the ground troops courageously in the battle, searching for the Black, and their daughter.

~~~~~~~~~~

Crytcha needed no protection other than the Kreegaren keeping the enemy from o'erwhelming her, restricting her movements. Beating them down with her fists, swinging her War Hammer in a massive arc, she crushed the enemy without mercy. Bones splintered, blood, guts, and body parts splattered 'cross the walls and floors. None of the Hoard had ever seen such a being afore. None of them would live to tell the tale. But all Crytcha cared about was finding her sister. Where was Flyrra?

She'd cleared this cavern and began to climb o'er the many bodies to exit, as she did not want to be caught against a wall. Abruptly she looked up into the huge muzzle of a Hoard Dragon. Her eyes widened, but not in fear. She'd never seen one of these Dragons up close afore, and she was fascinated with the fact that she could see so much in their eyes. Hatred, cruelty, greed, arrogance, and more, did she see there. She could practically smell their evil.

But the Dragon was still larger than was she, despite her great size. Nonetheless, such as this one was responsible for harming her sister. Wasting no more time, she set her jaw and swung her Hammer hard. Downward. Hitting the beast's foreleg, surprising him with her tactics, the Dragon was knocked back on his own ass afore she went to work on his enormous muzzle. Hitting him square 'tween his wide set eyes, the Hammer sunk deep, injuring the brain. His Healing thus fettered, she continued to strike 'til the beast's head was near crushed. Surely, he'd not Heal from that, but she was not satisfied. Driving her blocky hand under his foreleg, she ripped through his thick skin and plunged into his chest cavity, tearing out his still beating heart. Now, she was satisfied. Stepping o'er the creature's remains, she knew not that during the struggle she'd lost her treasured headband, lying broken and ruined in the bloody mess she'd left behind. Entering the next passageway, she continued her search for Flyrra.

~~~~~~~~~~

The Hoard was losing the fight. The Destroyer was now convinced they could not defend the Lair, nor did he care. From the number of Resistance ground troops, he was also convinced that no one would remain alive from this battle who could report to the Black, thus ensuring his own safety. All he need do was escape. And that meant he had to fight his way through the still crowded main cavern to reach the exit.

When he arrived there, he couldn't believe his luck. There stood one who could help him get past the others. He'd seen these two together, understood they were twins. Making his Shift, he ran directly toward the young Prince who'd just found himself without an opponent for a few breaths and exclaimed, "Come quickly! I found the girl!"

'Twas unthinkable and Gylrann hesitated. There afore him stood Gylragg, but 'twas not 'Ragg. Even having never seen the man afore, 'twas clearly the Destroyer, for could be no other. And having attempted to lure him away from the others using his twin's guise, 'Rann was startled by the implication that his brother was dead, and the Destroyer hesitated not. He reached for Gylrann, who scarcely sidestepped quickly enough to avoid his vile touch, and the fight was on. Battling against the image of his own brother, hoping against hope that he yet lived, made it difficult to use full force and his strikes were all too easily deflected. Surrounded, the others were in their own skirmishes and they'd not know what was happening at any rate, unable to determine who or how to help. As they continued their battle, 'twas becoming clear that he might actually lose.

His breath coming fast, his heart racing, 'Rann allowed the anger to build, but control to counter, and he struck true upon the other's shoulder, near cutting off his arm. The pain and force of the blow caused the Destroyer to lose his focus and his Shift, and suddenly Gylrann was facing a new threat. His Magic weakened by the drain of sustaining the form of another followed by the Healing of his shoulder, the Destroyer regained his full strength within a heartbeat of making the change to his true Elven form by reaching forth and instantly Draining one of his own who made the unfortunate mistake of coming to his aide.

The Destroyer missed not a beat and 'Rann was barely able to maintain against the ferocity of his renewed attack.

The Destroyer had eons of experience o'er Gylrann but was also driven by greed and 'twas no honor in him. Gylrann recovered his footing once as they exchanged brutal strikes but having to step wide to miss the next swing, he lost his balance. His eyes followed the sword arc of his enemy as it came ever nearer, knowing whatever move he made now would be too late. Still he would not give up and crouching to try to roll out of the way he abruptly heard the loud metal on metal reverberation of a solid block against the Destroyer's incoming swing just afore 'twould have cleaved him in half. His astonished gaze traveled up the thigh-high black leather boots of Tammra Dayo.

Her voice low and menacing, her eyes never leaving the Destroyer as they began warily circling, each seeking an opening, she stated with perfect control, "Go. Your brother is defended by Flyrra down that corridor to your right. She cannot hold off the Hoardsmen all alone for much longer." Licking her lush lips with a look of fiery anticipation upon her face, jaw set, and chiseled muscles tensed, the black-haired Elven beauty balanced her sword lightly o'er her forearm, tip toward her enemy, as Gylrann did what he was told. 'Twas without a doubt, an ancient grudge match forming behind him as he entered the corridor.

~~~~~~~~~~

Gylrann fought his way through the tunnels of the caverns, following his twin sense to locate his brother and Flyrra. When he did find them, the little girl's strength was waning, Holding them but unable to force them to suicide as they struggled against her Magic, pushing her and Gylragg deeper into the darkened tunnels in their retreat. 'Ragg was severely injured, maintaining pressure on his thigh with both hands, pushing himself along with his good leg and one elbow while Flyrra was half dragging him o'er the stone floor. They'd been steered into a dead end and would soon be exhausted. 'Twould be then that the Hoardsmen could finish them off. Still, despite 'Ragg trying to get her to do so, the little girl would abandon him not.

With Flyrra and 'Ragg's Magic dangerously low, 'Rann had to move fast. Using his newly acquired Dance techniques to attack the Hoardsmen from behind, he melted into the darkness, Draining them and moving on, dropping the enemy from the back of the pack through to the prize. All they saw was a gauze-like mist. 'Twas so fast, they knew not what was happening and were all dead within a few heartbeats, leaving 'Rann more energized than ever. Grabbing his twin and tossing him o'er his shoulder, he then instructed Flyrra in what was about to happen as she wrapped her thin arms and legs around his bare torso, gaining the skin on skin contact that was required. And then, afore the dumbfounded eyes of a handful of approaching Hoardsmen, they simply vanished, to appear behind the incoming men. 'Ragg Shared in the energy of his brother and was able to Heal himself enough so that he could join him in Draining the newcomers. Then taking Flyrra by the hand 'tween them, they vanished again.

~~~~~ MEANWHILE ~~~~~

Tammra faced off with her old nemesis. He'd gained his call name from her. Seeing him again dredged up cruel recollections of the far distant past and she had to clench her teeth to keep from flinching with revulsion. He was the destroyer of her family, her childhood, and near destroyed her future. She'd struggled for ages to distance herself from him and the memories, his vile betrayal of his own Kind, and the resultant stain left upon her family and her people. She was too young to prevent his escape after 'twas revealed he was a spy for the Hoard, nonetheless, her success in the Elven forces came from her ever-simmering hatred of her stepfather, what he'd done, how he'd treated her and her mother, and her endless driving need to prove her worth to herself and to King Lucien. But she'd ultimately failed the King and his sons, a vow of revenge her only reason for living. Now at last she had the chance to finish it, to finally leave the past in the past.

As the Destroyer curled his lip, his swing coming so very close to her gut, she countered and twisted, forcing his blade up and o'er her head. Stabbing her sword toward him, he managed to sidestep just in time to avoid being skewered. Tammra did not allow frustration to foul her technique and reined in her temper, meeting and countering every swing of her enemy, a slight smile appearing in her focused expression as she noted that the Destroyer was becoming fatigued. Just as she stepped back to swing 'round, she felt the moisture underfoot and slipping, she found herself on her butt against the wall, her sword still in her hand.

The Destroyer could not miss the opportunity to cause more grief, and as she tried to regain her feet, he charged her, pushing her back to one elbow. Leaning closer, he leered and then he Shifted. Her mother. He wanted her last vision to be that of her own mother making the killing strike, sending her Beyond. Tammra's eyes narrowed but not in defeat. In a fraction of a candle drip she took advantage of his hesitation, driving her sword in a vicious uppercut just preventing his final stab into her chest. Twisting the blade now embedded deeply in his guts, she rolled out from under him as he slowly fell to his side, losing the Shift with a groan and a look of pure shock upon his agonized face.

As the Destroyer slowly bled out, Flyrra and the twin Elven Princes entered the cavern and ran to Tammra's side. Pointing to the little girl, her voice growled through clenched teeth as she spit forth her anger toward her nemesis. "I am no longer a child, for you to terrorize!" Then realizing such as these gave her a new reason to live on, she proudly declared, "I am Tammra Dayo, and you take your last breath with MY face emblazoned upon YOUR memory! May you forever be entrenched in the Hades of the Fade!"

~~~~~~~~~~

As the clang on clang of swords, the groans and grunts of effort, pain, and death diminished, the Resistance forces cleared the last of the caverns, ensuring all the Lair's defenders were either Passed the Veil or on the run. 'Twas then that Darque Heard the deep Voice of Maakayyel as he repeated his earlier message of the Healers' belief that there was yet another battle. Choosing not to give chase to the handful of stragglers to avoid any further casualties, Darque had Regynn use his new Flamite to turn the cavernous system into unusable rubble. They had not the manpower to maintain the Lair nor to defend it and 'twas nearing midnight so its complete destruction was the only option. The Black would find no respite here. But where was this other battle? A horrible feeling made the hair stand up on the back of her neck. Storrm.

Flyrra ran to the Battle Commander, trying to ignore the way some of the Warriors averted their gazes and whispered to each other. Her acute hearing picked up one such conversation 'tween them. He'd seen her as she'd used her Magic. "I could not avoid watching, 'twas as if my eyes were glued to the scene and I could not rip them away, nor close them. I've never been afraid of the fight, but this... she wasn't even touching her enemies, yet she had such control o'er them, forcing them to ravage themselves in the most gruesome ways... they knew what was happening but could do nothing to prevent such. They could not stop 'til they'd Passed the Veil. 'Twas terrifying."

Her large wasp-shaped black eyes dripped tears down her triangular face as Darque reached for her. Pulling her close, the Battle Commander knelt beside her and looked at her questioningly. Her breath coming in stutters, she blurted, "The Black has gone after Storrm! They're somewhere north!" But even the little girl knew 'twas not enough information for them to find the Second in Command fast enough. If 'twas where the rest of the Black's forces had gone, Storrm and Mystynn stood not a chance. Flyrra had used the Compulsion to make her enemies talk afore she'd killed them, and she continued, passing along what she'd learned. "He called her an abomination! He said he has to kill the hybrid, and he can't let the Fay take the crown!" Once again, she winced with the uncertainty of her information. It made no sense. Severely traumatized, she just repeated as best she could. She loved Storrm as much as she loved her family.

Darque squinted. At first what Flyrra said didn't make much sense to her, either. But then she realized the truth. Storrm and Mystynn were alone out there, and they were being tracked. The 'abomination' must be Skyya. And who in Hades knew or cared what that part about the Fay's crown meant. She had enough to deal with.

Directing everyone to the Den at Drekinn flying through the timefold, 'twas not a full two marks later when they all met in the Pits. Crytcha had to be left behind and was making her way to the Lair as fast as she could underground, but they could not wait for her. Gathering Flyrra, Ardyth, Axyl, Bryynn, Haniyyah, Regynn, Kayarr, Natanamia and Tammra Dayo into a huddle, they debated on how to find the wayward Seconds. They could not rescue that which they could not locate, and there was no Tie involved here. Gunnarr had attempted to Call, but Mystynn's Link was still being Blocked. And they did not want to divide their forces for fear of an ambush as they'd likely be facing at least two hundred of the Black's minions.

Once again, 'twas Regynn who stroked his chin and innocently mentioned, "Seems like a prophesy scenario to me," while turning his attention curiously to Darque, who knew every one of them.

Darque's brows furrowed as she tried to recall anything involving her sister. Her mind flashed back to her own prophesy but dismissing that as a possibility she found herself glancing up to discover Walkyr and Fryya arriving upon a Free Dragon.

CHAPTER TWENTY-TWO
The Prophesy Unfolds

Fryya and Walkyr had been trying to pass the long marks waiting by exploring further into the Keep, Horace and Drys following along with them. When the big War Dogs not only stopped but sat down in a deserted hallway deep in the bowels, they assumed their constant companions were simply fatigued, and joined them. Suddenly, Walkyr began to shake and Fryya held onto him tightly, managing to roll up her vest and place it under his head to keep him from injury against the floor. Soon the Vision eased. "That was quick, Walkyr. What did you See?"

Walkyr was surprised to be where he'd been when the Vision began, as lately he found himself in his bed or at the clinic after every Vision. He sat up with a little assistance from his best friend and after thinking about the fact that Horace and Drys had warned them of the impending Vision, saving him from injury, he told her what he'd Seen. "Yes. 'Twas very short." He took a breath but was not as fatigued as usual. With a distant expression he shared with Fryya.

She bit her bottom lip as she tried to understand the details of this one. "A Snowy Owl? Carrying a bloody leather bundle? O'er the forest?" He'd also felt great effort and agony along with the presence of Storrm and Mystynn from afar, as if they'd been there, Calling to him. Even so, although the Vision was as clear as a painting, he'd simply Seen an unknown forest region and the owl, nothing more. Her nose wrinkled. "That's strange, Walkyr. Even for you." But they were both bothered by the idea that he seemed to have heard the Voices of the Seconds in Command.

Walkyr just nodded in agreement. 'Twas not that they Called for assistance, 'twas more like they'd wanted someone to know where they could be found. But then again just what was the huge white owl carrying in that leather bundle? And why did that forest scene look so familiar?

Abruptly he thought he understood. Surely the owl was a spirit, for he was white, and the bundle must have been the spirits of Storrm and Mystynn as he carried them to the Beyond 'cross the far horizon. And for certain 'twas the scene of a battle. With a gasp he knew why the area was so familiar. He remembered where he'd seen it afore. Racing up to the Ward, they enlisted the aid of one of the Free Dragons, leaving the Keep under the guise of going to the Bog. Once outside the Dome, the youngest Warriors directed the poor Dragon to take them to Drekinn Lair, arriving in time to see the others crowded around Darque.

Leaping off the Dragon afore he even had time to make a solid landing, Walkyr ran to Darque, Fryya close behind. Breathlessly he told her, "The Hoard has found them!"

Darque grabbed his slim shoulders. "Where are they? Have you Seen them?"

'Twas no time to give the frustrating details of the Vision, he wanted to try to avoid it happening. That meant they had to find them fast. "The tapestry!" he wheezed, his breath stuttering from the fatigue of the recent Vision followed by the flight and then the run 'cross the soft deep sands. "The one hanging upon her wall. 'Tis there we'll find them!"

With sudden clarity Darque recalled the strange way Storrm had acted that day in the caverns below o'er three winters past as she'd showed her the tapestry upon which she labored. "Storrm, 'tis stunning! Where did you get the inspiration for such?" she'd asked her sister, admiring the workmanship of her weaving. Storrm had shyly replied, "'Twas of a great battle within a cave. Do you really like it?" Then she'd stared at her own work as though 'twas of another's skills. Darque continued, "I know not this battle. 'Twas Legend Song? 'Tis not familiar," as she'd tried to make out all the details within the barely begun work. Storrm had been nervous when she'd responded. "Mayhap you'll recognize it when I get more finished, my sister. 'Tis hardly enough there now, for you to tell 'tis a cave." She'd sounded oddly serious and although she'd smiled and laughed, the mirth reached not her eyes. 'Twas somehow sobering. She'd avoided Darque's question, but she'd not be thwarted. "Tell me more, I wish to know about this great battle. I thought I knew them all." Then she'd stared at Storrm, trying to decipher any hidden meaning behind her words. She'd felt there was something wrong, but then Storrm had turned suddenly toward the cave exit where Mystynn came striding up protectively. Her face lit up upon seeing him, but there was a sadness Darque couldn't explain, in the depths of Storrm's deep blue eyes. "Mystynn thinks I need some fresh air," she'd said. Then taking Darque's hands and catching her gaze, she'd continued, "I've been given much in this life. Daughter to the Battle Commander, sister to the Second, live 'Bond with Mystynn the Green, Second Prince of the Highland Dragons. No matter where our destinies may lead us, together or distant, never doubt my love for you, Darque." And then she'd turned away too quickly for Darque to confirm whether that was a tear in her eye, and walked swiftly out with Mystynn, leaving her quite bewildered. The memory had faded, but not the tapestry.

Now convinced as well, she exclaimed, "She's there! Come with me!" Darque led the way and all followed swiftly down to Storrm and Mystynn's quarters under the Den. Piling up in the entry, everyone studied the beautiful needlework, but no one recognized the area. Just as Darque began to despair, Haniyyah squeezed past the others and shuffled her way into the room followed by Ardyth, to take a closer look. Discussing briefly with each other, they then turned together. Ardyth spoke while Haniyyah nodded. "We believe this is an area in which I lived a short while afore I moved on to Ice Mist Falls. I did not see it from this level, but Han did." Looking up at the Dragon, Ardyth faced the group and her Commander once again, shrugged her shoulders and stated, "Of course there is no certainty, but we think 'tis Winter's Edge."

EARLIER

~~~~~ WINTER'S EDGE ~~~~~

</div>

Storrm panted in her efforts to speak aloud. "Is she capable of surviving on her own yet?" She and Mystynn had been trying to avoid using their Link as 'twas one of the ways they'd surmised the Hoard was locating them, trying to find a reason that did not include the babe, although 'twas probable she was the unwitting culprit. Skyya knew not what she was doing and had no control o'er her actions, but such had them at an impasse in the long, grueling run, and they'd gone as far as Storrm could manage. She could take not one more step. Asking Corbyn again, she reiterated her question. "Will she live outside the womb? Is she ready? Tell me, for I fear I can go no further."

'Twas close to first mark and the Raven had just returned, flying into the cavern past Mystynn who stood guard, awaiting their destiny. Corbyn had been spying upon the Hoard, still trying to discover who was Hearing the babe as well as keeping tabs on their position. The big Green silently waved him deeper into the system to the very end, where sat Storrm upon the dirt floor, her back against a rock formation at the far wall, the light from the flickering torches surrounding her.

Shifting to his Fay form, his hands upon the swollen belly of the one he served, he felt for the answer. Looking up into Storrm's beautiful blue eyes, filled with a quiet determination despite her pain and fatigue, he knew as well as did she, that the cycle of his curse was close to ending once more and 'twould be the Warrior's last battle. "She actively seeks entry to the outside world. She is viable. She is strong. But she is stubborn, and this process will take much longer than you have left afore the Hoard arrives.

They are even now on their way. There is one amongst them who not only Hears her random Calls but can follow the Call of her blood as did I follow the Call of Grifynn and Shayla after the Last Holocaust." He now accepted that one was at least part Fay, the evil necromancer he'd been trying to identify for eons, known only as the Sorcerer, and he shook his head. His long, feathery layers of dark chocolate-to-black hair softly fluttered with the action afore he tucked a thick strand of it behind his pointed wing-like ears. "I estimate they will arrive by first light."

"How long afore Skyya will be naturally birthed?"

Hesitating but a moment, for he didn't want to raise her hopes, he stated frankly, "Mayhap another two dawns." 'Twas his best guesstimate.

Storrm sighed in frustration and disappointment, for she knew they didn't have that long. If not for the Hoard on their trail, the birthing process alone would be hard enough, but she could have managed. After all, she was a Warrior in 'Bond, and women had been having children successfully for ages. "Once birthed, will she continue to Call to the Hoard?"

Mystynn ambled in at that moment, his love for her clear in his dazzling green eyes. Corbyn replied, "I think not. At any rate, I can then provide cover if she does. As we've discussed, I can and will, keep her safe."

Mystynn could tell with a glance that Storrm was done. They'd not been at Winter's Edge for more than a few dawns, and the journey here had taken much from her. With Skyya so close to being birthed, Storrm was unable to maintain her strength and once she Passed, so too, would he. But he'd long since accepted their fate, and he'd not make this more difficult than 'twas already. "I'll stand with you here and defend you to the Veil, or I will take you anywhere. Just tell me what you want to do."

Storrm had long ago given up the hope they could birth the child safely anywhere. She prayed that Corbyn was correct and once birthed Skyya's Call would no longer be heard by the Evil

One, and that her native Magic would be contained 'til she could be taught how to do so herself. Smiling at her partner and the love of her life, she nodded in acceptance, closed her eyes, and made her decision. They had nowhere left to go and had run out of options. 'Twas time to put their final solution into play. Her long red lashes seemingly dusting the ceiling, she looked up and addressed them both, "We make our stand here. I will take Skyya myself. Corbyn, you can then transport her to your place of safety." Her hand in the air, she waved off his response, "No, don't tell me where. I have an idea, but I don't want our hopes to be divulged to the Sorcerer, we know not the power of his Link."

Both males were troubled, but 'twas the only plan they had. The only chance for Skyya to live and fulfill her destiny. Corbyn replied, for Mystynn could not speak o'er the tightening of his massive throat. "If I am to take the babe and clear the cavern afore the Hoard sees me, you have but a few marks to complete the act of which you have chosen."

Storrm licked her lips and with her troubled gaze upon Mystynn, stated, "These past few moons have been a frantic race headlong to the Veil. But the race is soon complete and 'tis the first break we've had. Please, Corbyn, allow Mystynn and I some time to ourselves to say our goodbyes afore we set this plan in motion."

Corbyn still had no idea that Skyya's destiny was to help fulfill the end of his own curse. The Fay was ignorant of the prophesy concerning him, and Storrm and Mystynn had chosen to keep it so. Distraught at his role in this affair, he could think of nothing helpful to say and simply nodded and turned, striding out of the area toward the entrance. Winter's Edge was spectacular to behold. But this time, he could not appreciate the beauty afore him. He stared off into space, 'cross the forest canopy, unable to even attempt to Listen to what the two were discussing. His stress levels were at an all-time high. 'Twas horribly parallel to when he'd left Hellyn and his unborn son, only to return from the wild goose chase upon which someone had sent him, to find them slaughtered in their private chambers. 'Twas the beginning of his curse. A fate he felt he deserved for abandoning them that night. For allowing their deaths to occur. Storrm had been his for less than four winters and as always, he'd not be present when the one he served, the one he'd grown so very fond of, needed his help the most. 'Twas his guilt that kept him from sensing the prophesy bespoke to her just after she took the 'Bond.

Mystynn laid down beside his beloved, scaled chest flat on the cool dirt and stone, his face at eye level with Storrm. His long, warm, wet tongue slipped forth and sensually tipped hers. She swallowed hard as he nuzzled her face with his nose and she stroked his snout with her fingers, hugging him closer, needing his warmth, his affection, his love. Hot tears spilled o'er her cheeks to mix with those of her partner. Her hands were small, and although not as small as Darque's, they were just as strong and calloused for she'd held a sword since she was but a toddler. Unable to find her voice for once, she and Mystynn quietly held onto each other as the moments dripped away. Her heart ached not just for herself and Mystynn, but for her daughter who would never know her mother, and unlike her own, would never return. She mourned for her sister, who even now was mounting a rescue effort that was doomed to fail. She also mourned for the Resistance. She wasn't ready to give up. She'd thought they'd have many winters, fight many battles, mayhap even to see the end of the reign of the Evil One, the end of the war. Her breath stuttered with the strength of her emotions. 'Twas not to be.

Mystynn's huge paw and sharp talons gently caressed her swollen belly, calming the spasms. From him, she felt no doubts, no jealousy, only a sadness that he was not the father and that they'd not be able to share in Skyya's raising. He was also saddened by how much time they'd lost to misunderstandings, and guilt-ridden that he'd pushed her into the arms of another, to a life he'd thought she both desired and deserved. But prophesy could not be evaded and what was to be, would be. The depth of his devotion was astonishing. She touched his wet face, once again amazed that a Dragon's tears were so cold. Finally, their voices broke the quiet in unison, saying, "I love you."

As the bittersweet echoes drifted away into the shadows, Corbyn returned. Dragging their eyes from each other, his deep voice became their path back to the present. "They near. We can wait no longer."

Mystynn stood up, gazed longingly at his beloved once more, and then turned about, striding toward the entrance in full Battle Mode, his extended and sharpened talons scraping along the stone, his great nostrils puffing smoke with each breath as he prepared his Flame. His task was to keep the Hoard at bay for as long as possible, for once they entered the cave 'twould not be long afore they'd be inundated. The plan was simple. Storrm would take the babe and Corbyn would fly her away. No one would know but Corbyn and those with whom he entrusted the babe, that she'd not Passed along with her mother in this battle. If she was thought dead, she was safe, as were those with whom she would be living.

Mystynn could kill far more of the Hoard initially, than could Storrm in her condition. She would remain in the deep recesses of the cave and as he lost ground, he would retreat to her. They would make their last stand together, defending each other, doing as much damage as they could for as long as they could, and then they would Pass together. Nothing could prevent that now.

He took up his stance at the entrance and gnashed his fangs with Storrm's stifled groan. Blocking much of her pain, as soon as the deed was done he Healed the gaping slash 'cross her belly, but she'd lost much of her Life Source, something he could not completely restore, as he had to ration his Healing. In a mere few heartbeats, he felt the Fay sweep past his shoulder. Looking up, he was surprised to see not the Raven, but a huge Snowy Owl clutching a blood-covered leather bundle, flying northwest toward the

Sea of Dreams. Turning his great head to the southeast, his raptor's vision allowed him to see the Hoard approaching in the far distance. Corbyn mentioned something o'er two hundred, as if that mattered now. Their numbers had grown as they'd managed to evade their pursuers. 'Twas bizarrely flattering.

Sharing through the Link he Felt Storrm rise slowly but stubbornly, trembling as she drew her Dragon Sword with both hands, leaning against the rock wall behind her for support. Her leather shirt was missing, and wearing only the width 'cross her breasts, her bracers, boots, and pants, weak, traumatized, already covered in her own blood, she'd fight as long as she could to give Corbyn time to ensure Skyya's safe delivery. Once the task was complete he thought to return and assist in the battle but 'twould be too late, as would the arrival of Darque and her forces. He hated to deceive the Battle Commander but 'twas necessary to protect the child. If not Skyya herself who'd Called to the Hoard, evil eyes could be anywhere, and the fewer who knew her fate, the better. Even General Gunnarr knew not the truth. Grimly he prepared himself as the Hoard closed.

THE SEA OF DREAMS
~~~~~ LESS THAN A MARK LATER ~~~~~

As the Raven, Corbyn could not have handled the weight of the bundle, but even as the Snowy Owl, he was getting fatigued. Still, he flew as fast as he could, carrying his precious cargo ever into the dawning skies. He must find the Krakken and get back quickly enough so that he could save Storrm and Mystynn. Just how he was supposed to do that, however, eluded the Fay, his thinking clouded by the desperation of the unfolding events.

THE DEN
~~~~~ MEANWHILE ~~~~~

Leaving Walkyr and Fryya at the Den to wait for Crytcha, Gunnarr growled for the rest of them to follow, and with

Haniyyah, Bryynn, Axyl, and Ardyth in the lead, they Pushed their way toward Winter's Edge. But the journey would still take at least a few marks even using Bryynn's Enhancement Magic to speed them along. Darque and Gunnarr were not only concerned that they'd not get there in time, but that they'd not be at the right place when they did. They'd have no second chance. Still, with o'er a hundred Dragons and Warriors making this trip, the odds were better than at the last battle. A battle they'd won with few losses. Darque didn't want to think of the potential losses in the battle they would soon enter.

~~~~~ WINTER'S EDGE ~~~~~

Storrm Shared Mystynn's vision and Yelled encouragement as the first Dragons landed, Flaming full stream to counter against the Green's own. Mystynn held firm at the cavern's narrow entrance, Listening to Storrm as she warned him, *"Above you!"* Billowing forth Flame, his fangs and talons flashed. *"Watch your flank!"* Mystynn turned his head just enough to get a lock on the enemy trying to squeeze past him on his right and reached forth with a mighty swipe of his great hind paw, slicing into the Dragon as he cried out in pain, but was slashed 'cross his own chest while distracted. The Healing was fast in them. For every stroke, slice, bite, and burn he inflicted, his Magic was weakening, and although they were forced to fight him a handful at a time at the entrance, he was losing ground, his own Healing stretched to the limit.

All too soon he was forced backwards, deeper into the cavern. Once inside, the enlarged space would no longer provide him backup. *"Mystynn! O'er head!"* Without even a glance the powerful Green reached up with one paw, rearing on his hind legs to inflict as much damage as possible when he Heard, *"Behind you, hit him!"* The searing pain of Magical burn 'cross his back and tail distracted him for but an instant, when he felt the fangs of another Dragon sink deep into his foreleg. Near blinded with fury along with the added pain, the Dragon he now faced attacked, wasting not a moment. Able to effectively fight either the ones in front of him or the ones behind, not both, Mystynn turned to savagely defend his flank, trying to keep them all focused on him and away from Storrm. But there were so many.

As he retreated deeper he felt his Magic failing, his Healing slowing. Slashing viciously with both forelegs, he failed to block another strike, this time 'cross his snout. The gush of blood momentarily blinded him for real this time and he was forced to use more of his weakening Healing to allow him to continue the battle. He'd already accepted that he'd not be able to help Storrm once they found her. Valiantly, he struggled to keep all the Hoard Dragons engaged with him, ferociously battling against the absurd odds.

Roaring forth his curses in Dragon Tongue, he raised their ire, distracting them from thinking about their original mission to seek and destroy the babe. By the time they found Storrm, they'd be too incensed to care about anything other than the massacre. Although they'd tried to prepare for the level of brutality with which they were being met, to his shock and disbelief the odds had steadily increased against them. Corbyn had counted near two hundred. He'd lowered those numbers significantly in the last mark and intended to continue to do so. He threw himself into the fight, recklessly increasing their anger to make them finish the deed quickly, and yet, he had to maintain for as long as possible.

Suddenly he Heard Storrm's battle cry as yet another of the monsters slipped past him. Turning, he retreated to her, the change in tactics causing confusion in his pursuers. She'd managed to do severe damage to the Dragon, but he'd not be injured for long. On her knees, leaning on the hilt of her Sword, she gasped, "I tried, Mystynn! He crawled out of reach of my Sword. I could not give chase."

Mystynn hesitated but a heartbeat, and taking her Sword from her hand, he cut the hapless Dragon to shreds, decapitating him in the process, for daring to hurt Storrm. His mind a chaotic mix of Battle Lust, pain, and guilt, he managed to give the Sword back to her within a few breaths. "You did well. Hang on just a bit longer." He'd sustained multiple lacerations, talon gashes, fang bites, and Flame burns, and had lost several of his scales, but the pain he felt the strongest was the sense of failing Storrm. Her face covered with blood, he could see the Dragon had slashed her thigh and her Life Source was running again. Turning, he faced the rest of the incoming Hoard in the huge cavern. But instead of attacking all at once, they unexpectedly came to a halt, holding back. Parting, they allowed one very large Dragon to step forth through their midst as a hush fell o'er them. 'Twas the Black.

Storrm stayed on her knees behind Mystynn, crouched and holding her still swollen belly in case any took notice of her actions, as she watched the eerily hushed approach of the leader, the most heinous of the Hoard, through Mystynn's massive legs. Mystynn expanded his great chest seemingly growing to twice his size, and locked gazes with the vile creature. With less than a dozen Dragon lengths 'tween them, the Black halted. Storrm could feel the heat she experienced during great stress, but this time she felt as if she were on fire. An aura appeared around her as wisps of smoke began to rise and her skin felt tight and began to ripple as if 'twas thickening. Mystynn didn't have to see her to know her Dragon blood was finally showing its influence. But there wasn't enough time for her to develop the full potential. 'Twas too little, too late.

In response to Storrm's condition, fear filled the Black's eyes, mixed with burning rage and astonishment. He'd seen this afore. Just once. 'Twas her sister upon the battlefield at the beginning of the Battle for the Dragon Clan. 'Twas his past come back to haunt him.

The hybrid status of the Aalanna Grifynn siblings was the direct result of the Black's horrific experiments afore the Last Holocaust, his attempts to eradicate Man along with total enslavement of his own Kind. But such had backfired on him. Here to ensure they finally had her and 'twas no mistake, he trembled at what he'd allowed to be created. He had to kill it. 'Twas not some prophesy he sought to destroy, not even to prevent the crowning of the future Greatest King. First and foremost, he must stop her and her Kind from continuation. Darque had shown similar traits but she could not reproduce with the High Prince for they were life-mates and Dragons mated for life. But this one? His fear of what she might be able to do made him keep his distance, and his loathing prevented him from seeing the reality. Storrm held onto her belly protectively and he smirked. Turning his back upon the two, he walked out 'tween his forces, all slobbering in perverse expecta-tion. As he passed through, his cruel growl could be heard rum-bling through the cavern. "Finish it."

At precisely the moment that several Dragons rushed them, Mystynn Heard a distant voice. Corbyn had completed his task and was on his way back to help.

~~~~~ APPROACHING WINTER'S EDGE ~~~~~

In her mind Darque Heard him. Deep, masculine and un-characteristically apologetic, she Heard Brannyn Speak. *"For what 'tis worth, I am sorry."* Her vision enhanced, Darque watched with fury as the Black took wing outside the cavern, tak-ing with him several other of his Dragons, and the Fay. Darque and Gunnarr could Feel the battle that had raged in the distance as they approached Winter's Edge. How had she missed the hints, the signs, her sister coming so close to telling her outright of her prophesy? Her senses told her 'twas here they'd find Storrm and Mystynn, and she Felt the desperation of the battle that had taken place. Using their sign language, she gave her orders to her forces, hope sinking as she realized that although the Hoard had not yet seen them, they were already vacating, following the Black into the horizon. She swallowed hard. They were not standing to fight. They were leaving.

~~~~~ DEEP IN THE CAVERN ~~~~~

Their level of injury and fatigue slowed their reactions and in the span of a few breaths, Storrm could not suppress the screams of pain as the blood poured forth. Her chest fileted, she rolled o'er to her back, her cleaved heart pumping her Life Source upon the floor of the cavern. She could not breathe, could not even lift her Sword. In her final moments she looked for Mystynn, reaching out for him, his body scorched by Flame, unable to stop the flow of blood from his own heart, his Healing exhausted. The same Dragon who had just struck her, struck again with lightning speed, hitting true on Mystynn who now stood 'tween them, and as he fell backwards, he stretched his foreleg for her hand, just touching fingertip to talon. As their Life Source emptied unchecked from their bodies, Storrm used her last bit of energy to Speak with Mystynn, the communication through the Link taking place in the blink of an eye. *"Mystynn, I can't hold on any longer!"*

Despite the circumstances, he lovingly Replied, *"You may let go."*

But still, she could not. *"Then Skyya is safe?"*

"Corbyn has delivered her. She is safe."

Relieved, yet in unbearable pain and anguish, she Asked, *"Must we go?"*

Gently, the big Green responded, *"We must."*

Knowing she was too weak to do this on her own, she Exclaimed, *"Remember your promise! Don't let me back out, for the pain of leaving her is much worse than any battle wound, and far beyond my expectations."*

Mystynn was aggrieved for his beloved and choked out his promise. *"I will not forget."*

The Black escaped, but they could sense the arrival of Darque and her forces and knew they were fighting their way through those Dragons still in the caverns, to get to them. Soon, Corbyn would arrive. So close. Her blurring vision could almost make out her sister in the distance entering this very cavern. Darque's Dragon Sword was swinging, Gunnarr's defiant roar boomed in her ears. But, 'twas too late.

As Storrm slipped away, Mystynn Blocked her memories of the horrible pain, the devastation, all the events of the past winter, and especially of her child. For leaving a battle and leaving Skyya would be her biggest and most difficult challenges. She was not one to give up, but she must. So, he did just as she'd requested of him moons prior when they began their run. If he was lucky, he could get her through the Void quickly enough to dodge any mishaps. But how? He had to distract her. Human form might work.

Despite all, Storrm could sense a cocoon of sorts, all around her body, her Dragon blood rising to protect her. Oddly, she felt as though she were encased in scale. She smiled at Mystynn who smiled back with longing in his luminescent eyes. Then, in slow motion they watched the incoming stream of Flame that would obliterate all evidence of their deceit. Storrm's hearing and vision dimming fast, she closed her eyes for the last time upon that side of the Veil...

~~~~~~~~~~

As Darque made the final kill strike on the last Hoard Dragon trying to block her way, she found herself surrounded by death. No Storrm. No Mystynn. Trudging forward through the blood and gore, Gunnarr leading the way, they frantically searched the cavern. Her Warriors were close behind as they finished ensuring all the enemy who'd not fled earlier, were indeed lifeless. But Darque was not glowing in victorious Battle Lust. Desperately she tried to locate that which she knew in her heart, she would not. As the rest of the Teams stood guard at the entrance, Tyndall and Fyndarr and Daayn and Kashiyann, who fought courageously at Darque and Gunnarr's sides through both battles, efficiently standing in for their absent Seconds and Thirds, gathered 'round, for each of them knew what their Commanders would find. Anxiously they watched as Gunnarr threw oft' times un-identifiable Dragon parts aside, clearing a path to the back wall of the cavern. And then his forward momentum came to such a sudden halt, Darque ran into him. Knowing the reason, feeling the emotions Shared 'tween them, she could not stop her response, yelling, "NOOOOOOO!" He lifted his huge head as she regained her senses and ran 'round his shoulder, his heart-wrenching roar reverberating through the caverns as she caught sight of what lay upon the stone floor at his feet.

She fell to her knees beside the bloody and charred remains of Storrm and Mystynn, and simply stared. No further words could she speak. Gunnarr's roar echoed through the caverns and then finally disappeared. As the last echo faded away, he stood as a silent sentinel. No one approached their Commanders in their grief, leaving the cavern and returning to the entrance to await their orders. Trembling, in guilty disbelief Darque reached forth to touch what was left of Storrm's beautiful long red hair still piled up with picks intact, her cheek, her arm bracers. From the wounds inflicted, along with the Flame, 'twas clear the babe did not survive, but 'twas also clear Storrm should have been a pile of ash and she was not. The phenomenon was chalked up to their Dragon blood, but the potential eluded the Battle Commander. "Send them home," she stated in a flat voice. Halfheartedly, Gunnarr Relayed the order to the others and they retreated a short distance but refused to completely abandon them at the scene.

Darque walked blindly out of Winter's Edge, speaking softly into the chill air as if addressing someone only she could now see, "I failed her." As she walked slowly, the Raven came soaring in, Shifting to stand upon the cliff ledge, his own failure plain to read in Darque's expression. Holding tightly onto one of Storrm's braids secured by the picks she'd given her as a gift so long ago, she stopped when Fryya and Walkyr dismounted from one of the Free Dragons. Fryya ran to her, leaped into her arms and rocked with her, smoothing her bloody hair away from her filthy, sweaty face. Darque's eyes were empty as she stared 'cross the forest, mumbling o'er and o'er, "They're dead. They're dead. They're dead."

~~~~~ THE VOID ~~~~~

...afore opening them again within the eerie whiteout. If Storrm could still cry, her face would be wet against Mystynn's chest as he held her shuddering body, racked with pain, reliving the entire experience.

Storrm's eyes were full of agony, but not for the physical wounds they'd just suffered. She knew for certain that they must Pass. They'd not been able to avoid the Hoard to have the baby in secrecy and even if they had, her existence was now known, and she'd be hunted without mercy. 'Twas in the prophesy that she now recalled with shocking clarity. 'Twas her destiny. But these facts did nothing to make her feel better. "Is she really safe? Did Corbyn get her out of Winter's Edge?"

Still concerned about how she might change her feelings toward him now that she knew the truth, he stated quietly, "Yes."

"And did they suspect? Did the Hoard know the baby was already gone, that she was still alive?"

"There was much going through the Link during the battle. I monitored all. No. They had no idea. To sacrifice oneself for another is an act of extreme compassion. Such is not in them to understand, and so, no, they did not and do not, suspect."

Relief filled her heart, yet she was still miserable as she beseeched him, "I deceived my own sister! 'Tis an offense from which she will have no healing, no succor. How could I do this to her?"

Mystynn, now back in all his glorious green scaled brilliance, tried to provide what comfort he could. He sat, his leathery wings wrapped around her, one talon under her chin lifting her face to his. Even his deep rumbling voice was back to normal. "When can be revealed that Skyya yet lives, Darque will at least have an understanding."

"But will she have forgiveness?"

"For you, eventually. She loves you dearly."

Pondering what he'd just said, she then asked, "For herself?"

He hesitated, choosing his words carefully. "I have great respect for the Commander. No one can surpass her battle strategy or fighting prowess. Yet, she holds herself to a much higher standard than she does others." He stopped and dipped his chin to peer into her eyes. "Will she ever forgive herself for our Passing?" Shaking his massive head, he finished. "I think not."

Storrm hung her head and began to back away sadly.

He wasn't certain if she were backing away from him or from the situation. Their journey could wait. He would try to offer her some hope, anything to help ease the pain reflected in those blue eyes. "There is more, my love. Do you wish to continue?"

"More? You can show me what's happening outside the Void, past the point of our deaths?"

"Officially, we've not gone there yet, but yes, Highlands can move through the Veil and can alter time for our own perception. 'Tis how we know so much about our futures. Besides, I am a Prince. I have a bit more power than most."

Storrm squinted. "What exactly, does that mean?"

"It means that I can show you what's happening outside the Void, past the point of our deaths." Smiling, he beckoned to her, "Come."

Storrm readily stepped forward, clutching his great chest to her cheek, her eyes closed in anticipation as he enfolded her possessively with his leathery wings.

CHAPTER TWENTY-THREE

The Final Sleep

Corbyn's sudden arrival had prevented Myrrdin from telling Kyntik about his family. The Fay had come and gone without a word, dropping the bloody leather bundle on Myrrdin's table. Then Shifting on wing from the owl to the Raven, he flew away immediately. 'Twas puzzling, but then this entire affair was puzzling. Nonetheless, he put his own plan into action and within a half mark of Skyya's arrival, Myrrdin had transferred her to Islyth in complete secrecy, with orders to deliver the baby to his friend on the Northern Cliffs of the Island of Dreams. He encouraged his Tie to be swift, but they were not far from the island at that time and her task should not take more than a few marks for one so swift as Islyth. He warned the Water Dragon that his friend knew not to expect her, that she was not to allow herself to be seen by anyone else, and to say nothing. 'Twould be understood.

'Twas a mere half day later that Myrrdin had an uneasy sensation crawl up his spine. The Krakken 'felt wrong'. The 'package' arrival and this uneasy feeling were initially thought to be related, but once Myrrdin climbed to the top deck, 'twas evident the Krakken was b'Spelled, heading straight toward the Ocean of Fears at a speed most incredible. His first thought was Kyntik and his gut churned with realization. He sent Lyran to collect the man.

~~~~~~~~~~

Sitting at his desk Myrrdin awaited his latest crewman but when Lyran brought him in, he stood up. Just the look in his eyes, made the boy begin to shiver. Without guilt, Kyntik lied to save his own ass, groveling, "Forgive me, m'Lord Myrrdin! He had my family. He said he'd kill 'em!"

Myrrdin's eyes were hardened, his expression difficult to read as he came out from behind his desk, stepping closer. "I would have gone to the ends of Kadoor, to help you free them."

"He said he had you in his pocket! You're no Sprite, you have no allegiance to us! Said 'twas you who got my family killed! I should've known better than to trust him o'er you, but I was in shock," he pleaded, his lies piling one on top of another.

Myrrdin squinted. How would the boy know his family had been killed? Myrrdin himself, had only just heard about the incident. The Elite Guard had the two Assemblymen, Frynbec and Benetyk, under arrest after linking them to the murders of Benetyk's nephew's family, as well as having all the gathered information on their spying activities. They'd apparently done the deed to eliminate the trail to them. Naftaleah sent word to Myrrdin that the pair had expected the boy to die at sea, but they'd not known they were under suspicion and although the Guard had tried to save the innocents, they'd been too late. He grit his teeth in disgust. Kyntik probably knew not the truth of their demise and would probably care not. Nonetheless, 'twas the proof for which he was looking. He was not fooled by the other's bodacious falsehoods. Impatiently, he demanded, "Tell me how to stop the Krakken. Tell me what is this Magic."

Now Kyntik began to sweat. He'd guessed why he'd been near dragged into the presence of the Ship's Master, but he'd not cared about his family. He'd never cared. All he knew now was that 'twas obvious his lies had fallen on deaf ears and he was losing control of the situation. He needed to impress the Ship's Master with his influence. Sneering, he bragged with upmost confidence, "She can't be stopped. The Spell will take the Krakken to Port O'Kings where the Sorcerer awaits us even now. She will be mine after you are taken," he stated with arms crossed o'er his chest, and a smirk on his face.

Now Myrrdin knew what he was up against. He snorted. "The Sorcerer will have you hanging by your cock and balls in the dungeons of Evanntyr within a mark after you arrive! He gives no gift that will not benefit him. Think, man! This Spell was Cast in blood, and in blood 'twas evoked. Only blood will stop it. Whose death do you suppose that will require?"

The question frightened Kyntik, and the scorn upon his face turned to an expression of horror. After several moments, he hung his head. Even knowing what was to come, he spoke the truth, for he suddenly realized that Myrrdin was correct, and that he would receive far worse from the Sorcerer. The fact that the Spell was binding by blood meant that he would have to Pass by someone's hand, to stop it. He'd been fooling himself all along. The stories of the atrocities committed upon those held in the Pits of Hades by the Sorcerer's torturer, came unbidden to his mind. He squeezed shut his eyes but could not slow his racing heart as the sun abruptly dawned upon him. He'd been betrayed by his own uncle, and there'd be no rescue or chance of ransom forthcoming. His only hope was that the Ship's Master would be merciful, but given their situation, 'twas unlikely. Shaking, he could not look upon Myrrdin's face as he replied, "Mine, and the Krakken's."

"So be it," Myrrdin replied with a sharp edge to his voice that Kyntik had never heard afore. Myrrdin was beyond furious. He should have seen through this one's lies. He'd become lax, and now his ship and his crew were paying the price. He thought about the bottle of Drekinn whiskey still sitting in the middle of the table in his quarters. And then there was the blade he'd obtained from Grifynn as his final passage payment. 'Twas Darque's, one of a matched set of four, and still lay in his safe on the wall. 'Twas his duty to return it to her when the time was right, as he'd promised. He owed much to many, and now he was letting everyone down. Anger burned, and grabbing Kyntik's collar, he thrust the man forward, stumbling along the corridor with First Mate Lyran as another crewman met them.

With concern in his pale eyes, Lyran took report from the other crewman and then stated, "Dragons on the horizon, Sir. ETA within the quarter mark, but we've yet to get the Krakken to answer the helm."

"Activate the Final Sleep," Myrrdin stated resolutely.

Distressed, Lyran replied, "But Sir! We can take them! We'll never abandon you, nor the Krakken!"

Angrily Myrrdin replied, "She cannot answer her helm, we've been betrayed." He gestured to the crewman standing just off his First Mate's shoulder. "Take him to the bilge and find the Spell. I expect it to be in the form of an ax or a blade as 'twill be imbedded in the wood. Lyran, set up our defenses, prepare the Krakken, and meet me below with two others."

The First Mate smiled wickedly. He knew what the Master was planning, and 'twas more than justified for what this one had done. He pulled his short broadsword and turned about, exclaiming o'er his shoulder as he ran up the corridor, "Aye, Sir!"

Kyntik began to whimper, tears in his eyes as the full realization of what they meant to do, began to dawn upon him. Roughly, the crewman pushed him along through the darkened and deepening corridors.

MYRRDIN'S QUARTERS
~~~~~ A FEW MOMENTS LATER ~~~~~

Staring at the bottle upon his table, Myrrdin fought back his emotions. The Krakken was his first ship, his only ship, from the day he'd laid eyes upon her as she'd returned to Port O'Dreams after a vicious encounter with pirates. The former Ship's Master had fled and left her to be ravaged, while the pirates took everything, including her trim, hand carved woodwork, port windows, furnishings, and every scrap of metal within, both functional and decorative. She was barely a husk of her former glory. Once the pride of the Sprite Nation's Mariner Fleet, she hadn't aged well, having been ill-used, poorly managed, mistreated, and taken for granted. After the attack she couldn't even sail home on her own, being dragged in by Dragons who'd found her half full of water.

Myrrdin hadn't lived on the island for long at that time, but he'd acquired enough coin to purchase the wreck from its former owners. Driving a hard bargain, he'd had enough left o'er to re-fit her, and through the following winters made her even more magnificent than afore. She became the pride of the fleet once again, but now she was the biggest, baddest, fastest, and most profitable ship as well. Through the many winters in which he'd commanded her, they'd developed a kindred spirit relationship. Everyone thought the Krakken was not only alive in some manner, but was invincible, and that Myrrdin was the reason. The Elven Prince never disputed such. The Krakken was his soulmate, the one to whom he owed his life, and upon her, he spared no expense.

His glance shifted to sweep 'round the tiny cabin. This had been his home since the time of the Last Holocaust. He paused as the sounds of incoming wings grew louder. He knew his men were topside, as they'd vowed to make the fight look real. 'Twould probably mean causalities, but to protect Myrrdin and the Krakken, no one even flinched. His eyes became moist at their steadfast loyalty, and he blinked hard. Then his ire returned and raising his hands he set the Spell into motion, walking out of the room without taking anything, for he could not; everything that belonged here, had to go down with her. At least 'twould be safe from the Hoard. Shutting the door behind him, the glistening sheen of the Spell still trailed from his fingertips as it filled the hallway, slipped under every door, into every cabin and hold, soaking into the very wood and metal of the ship, covering everything under the top deck, afore disappearing to vision. Meeting up with his First Mate, Lyran had prepared the Krakken for scuttle and brought along two of the crewmen, all with expressions of vengeance upon their faces, for they knew well their coming orders and the reason for such.

Once they descended into the bowels of the ship, the original crewman stood with his prisoner, a look of triumph in his eyes. Kyntik was kneeling o'er a blade stuck in the boards of the hull, his hands tied behind him and his head held down by the crewman. By all appearances, Kyntik had been 'persuaded' to lead him to the Spell. "I found it, Captain," he snarled.

As the fight began to rage above, Myrrdin set sentence. Addressing his First Mate and the chosen executioners, he stated, "timing is essential. The death of the Krakken cannot be seen as by design. She must go down as if sent by the fight, or 'twill cause suspicion and the Hoard will try to raise her. Railings and masts will need be sacrificed." As well as his banner, he thought to himself.

"The Water Dragons are holding the Hoard attackers at bay for now. There are more coming, but our Dragons will continue to fight and will be ready to scuttle on your command, Sir." The man was his long-time friend as well as his First Mate, and he knew what was on his Captain's mind. Quietly, he added, "The Krakken's banner has been lowered, Sir. 'Twill not affect the Final Sleep for she's not just a ship, she's a living being, and her banner belongs to you." He pulled the fabric out of his stuffed breast pocket, handing it o'er to Myrrdin. "It has been my sincere honor to work with you, Sir."

Myrrdin nodded with gratitude. 'Twas not unusual for a ship's banner to be dropped when under attack and 'twould not be seen as so. Taking the banner quickly, he shoved it into his own pocket. The decision to scuttle was not an easy one, but 'twas the only option. 'The death of the Krakken' meant that she had to sink to stop the Spell. Being in the privateering business for as long as he'd been, he was ever prepared for all issues, even final ones. But he liked it not. "Are we secured?"

"Yes Sir, the Krakken is ready for her nap."

Myrrdin realized his plight, though unplanned, would provide even greater security for Skyya. If her delivery was noted, they'd think the babe died with the ship. 'Twas as if 'twas meant to be. Holding his hand o'er his pocket, he nodded again. The Krakken might be ready, but he was surely not. Islyth was on her way, chasing down the ship in her headlong journey, bringing along many of her friends, and traveling with the Ties of the crewmen. Speaking to her, he gave his orders. *"You and your friends need hold off the Hoard just long enough for me to break the Spell. I will not need to Tell you when I have done so, for without the foul winds the Krakken will begin to slow, but 'twill not be o'er, and she must go down quickly thereafter, as if by battle. 'Twill take much acting and good timing. You need allow the Hoard to think they won the battle and then retreat underwater without them knowing there were any survivors. Can you do that, my friend?"*

Her Voice angry but crystal clear, she Responded, *"No fail Myrrdin! Hoard stupid! Not one brain amongst them all to share! Supposed to guide to Sorcerer, not attack. We make them fight! Hoard not raise Krakken. Leviathans keep Evil One away."*

Myrrdin smiled at Islyth's accurate assessment of the situation and then his brows lifted. The Leviathans of which Islyth spoke lived in the deepest part of the deepest ocean and were the scourge of the mariners throughout the Ocean of Fears, known to kill Water Dragons and take down entire ships. If they were close, they were already in the middle of the Fears, and if the Krakken slipped o'er the edge of their crevasse 'twould never be seen again, for even the Water Dragons could not swim that deep, the pressures too great for their Magic. He'd have to depend on them to guide her down. 'Twould take many, and if the Leviathans woke, not only would the Dragons be killed, so too, would he and his crewmen trying to escape, for they were not close enough to shore to avoid the deadly creatures. He knew not how many Water Dragons were fighting with them now, but they needed enough to handle his crew, flying them through the waters to safety after the Krakken was laid to rest. He took a deep breath. He had no choice. He'd always known if he had to do this 'twould be serious, and 'twasn't like he'd ever had any opportunity to practice. But 'twas getting more complicated than he'd ever envisioned.

~~~~~~~~~~

The prisoner gulped hard as Myrrdin held him by the back of his neck, pushing his head down and o'er the blade in the hull. 'Twould be just the beginning. His blood was required to stop the foul winds of the Spell, as well as his death, but the two didn't have to happen at the same time. He felt the Ship's Master reach around his throat and then he felt the slice of the blade cutting the skin of his neck, yet 'twas not enough to end his suffering. The worst was yet to come. He sputtered with the burning pain as he watched his Life Source trickle down and cover the blade, soaking into the wood around the steel, the blade lifting up and falling onto the planks as if 'twas a living thing repulsed by his blood. His vision began to blur. He couldn't help himself as he cried out for pity, pleading for his life, begging for mercy, "Please, m'lord Myrrdin! Please! Don't kill me! I'm sorry! I'm sorry! I'll never do it again! I'm sick, I need help, 'tis not my fault!" His breath came hard, and the slow loss of blood combined with the fear and the pain, began to make him dizzy. But he did not pass out, for which he cursed the Fates.

Myrrdin faltered not. The shuffling of the others' boots came to Kyntik's ears as his arms and legs were snatched away from him, turning him o'er and yanking him so that his body just cleared the wooden planks of the hull. Holding him by his ankles and elbows, for they'd not even bothered to untie his wrists, their expressions were frightening, and he cried and pleaded in misery, snot running down his cheeks. Terrified, he finally understood that he was about to die. These would be his last moments this side of the Veil, and if he weren't lucky, he'd end up stuck in the Hades of the Fade to spend an eternity in similar agony. Kyntik choked on his own saliva. He'd never been lucky.

Myrrdin's eyes narrowed and burning with rage he lifted his head and caught each of the men's eyes. "Dance," he hissed without remorse and they disappeared, wrenching the man in four different directions, his body ripped apart, the explosion of blood, gore, guts, and screams, all disappearing as well, but not afore all witnessed the results of such. Satisfied, as they reappeared Myrrdin's hardened gaze met each of the four crewmen with approval and gratitude. Nothing was left of Kyntik as they shifted their stance to adjust for the abrupt yet subtle loss of their breakneck speed.

The Krakken was slowing. The evil winds were gone, but she still could not answer her helm and would eventually take them to the Spell's intended destination. However, her altered speed would take some time to be noticed by their attackers. They had less than a mark at best. After completing his preparation Spell o'er the bilge, he grabbed the blade and tucked it into his pocket, for it did not belong here and he would not leave such filth on his ship. Then Myrrdin led the others as they climbed up toward the roar of the battle. This had to look good.

~~~~~~~~~~

Myrrdin and his First Mate set foot above to the battle already in full swing. Multiple Hoard Dragons were Flaming in from all sides, the crew of the Krakken dodging as best they could with nowhere to hide but awaiting their Captain afore they did anything else. The mainsail and rigging were burning, the masts splintered upon the deck. Myrrdin Called to Islyth, discovering she was just a few leagues north and would arrive within mere moments. Giving his orders, he and what was left of his crew abandoned ship, leaping o'er the sides to join their Water Dragons for the real fight.

Myrrdin didn't have to tread water for very long as he waited for Islyth. Flying up under him, he swiftly mounted just behind her shoulders as she took him deep down into the murky waters of the Fears. Her long journey fatigued her not, as she'd eaten her fill on the way back in preparation for this, Hearing the events as they'd unfolded. Her heart aching for her Tie, she sought vengeance upon the Hoard.

As did the other Water Dragons, deep down they swam afore Islyth turned, and using her powerful tail and short legs she gained speed rapidly, traveling in a straight line. More speed, they needed more, so her dorsal ridge would not get stuck in the scales of her enemy. Punching upwards, they had little time to target the Hoard Dragon as Islyth could not fly, only soar, and they missed their opportunity to perform the 'spinning saw' attack strategy of the Water Dragons. Islyth didn't waste their efforts, and with her short muzzle and hard head, she hit the Dragon square in his groin, then grabbed hold of his hind leg and near bit it off, causing the Dragon to drop like a rock into the sea in great pain. As he sunk beneath the waters attempting to hide long enough to Heal, he was met by many other Water Dragons, whose fierce group attack, along with their most powerful jaws, made short work of him in his weakened state, unable to use his Healing quickly enough to replace his much-damaged leg and exit the waters.

The sea churned red with blood as hundreds of Water Dragons attacked fiercely, but as many of the Hoard that they killed, so too, did they die. Islyth dove deeper and faster than ever, and Myrrdin dared not use his Magic to reduce the pressure on his ears. Knowing they would soon burst, he squeezed his eyes shut and grit his teeth, funneling his Magic to Islyth to give her more power for the maneuver. The timing had to be perfect as well as the angle and upon this, their third rise from the depths, they were successful. The Hoard Dragon was in range, and Islyth immediately pulled her tail up tightly to her chest with her front paws while extending her dorsal ridge and tucking her head for the spin. Myrrdin held on close, his chest against her broad back, arms and legs wrapped around her. Backwards she rotated with such speed into the neck of the Hoard Dragon, she decapitated him. The headless torso followed what was once attached to it, into the frothy red foam below as Islyth gracefully spread her leathery webbing and wings and dove back into the sea, narrowly missing being struck by a stream of deadly Flame.

The battle raged on as the Water Dragons punched up from the depths, biting, spitting their forced streams of water that could decapitate or dismember, their dorsal ridges fully extended. Multiple Water Dragons latched onto a Hoard Dragon and pulled him into the waters to his death. But 'twas time for the final sleep. The Krakken had taken a beating. Those crewmen still defending her saluted, then ensured the last of the Hoard were engaged and would notice nothing amiss. If they could survive the next few moments, they had a good chance to get away. Islyth and Myrrdin swam under her hull and the Water Dragon spit forth her stream of water, cutting the hole into the Krakken's side. Joined by twenty others, less than half with Ties, they helped guide her down toward the lip of the Leviathan's crevasse, leaving First Mate Lyran above with orders to abandon the fight as soon as the Krakken was laid to rest.

'Twas most difficult even with their combined strength, to avoid the current trying to sweep her o'er the edge. The battle above had not brought the huge creatures' attention, and for this, Myrrdin was grateful, as the Krakken hit the muddy bottom, then tilted precariously, bringing much trepidation afore she became stable. Sending the rest back up, with Islyth he set her anchor to keep her where she lay. Staring at her final resting place he was positive there would be no way the Hoard could ever raise her. At least she was safe from desecration. Now for the rest of those for whom he was responsible.

As they began their long ascent to the surface, Islyth suddenly became alarmed. The Leviathans had seen them and were rising. Most of the Water Dragons were not fast enough to outswim the monstrous creatures, even with a head start, and Myrrdin gave his orders for all to escape and leave the Fears as quickly as they could. Now that the Krakken was gone, the Hoard cared not to continue their efforts, for 'twas for Myrrdin and his ship, they'd come. Finding not either, they abandoned the fight, and noting the shadows of the Leviathans 'twas decided the Krakken had fallen into their crevasse and awakened them. They could safely report to the Sorcerer that she was gone, and the giant creatures of the Fears would take care of all who were still alive in their territory. Satisfied, the remaining Dragons took wing toward Evanntyr.

The Leviathans were drawn not only to the disturbance caused by the Krakken settling upon the edge of their home, but to the smell of blood in the sea. Their long, poisoned tentacles flayed outward to capture the Water Dragons and their Ties, grabbing onto them and dragging their helpless bodies into their great maws to be devoured alive. O'er half of those who'd assisted to guide the Krakken down were lost, but not Islyth, and those still above were able to get to the Sea of Dreams in safety, unseen from the skies, enforcing the impression that all had perished.

CHAPTER TWENTY-FOUR
Return To Winter's Edge

They'd brought their downed brethren home from the battles and had joint funeral pyres just the day afore, for all but the Seconds in Command. Now Storrm and Mystynn lay side by side upon the massive pyre in the middle of the sands. Wearing that which she'd worn in the battle, her Dragon Sword having refused to leave her side, lay upon her breast, her hands cradling it close. Darque knew not what 'twould do once the fire did its work, but the Sword could not be destroyed and so they left it where it chose to lay. If not Darque herself, the Sword would find another Warrior, she was quite sure. There were so many who could use such a powerful weapon.

Licking her dry lips, Darque hesitated for what seemed to those present to be a lifespan afore her voice resounded through the Training Pits of the Dragon's Den for the second time in less than a day. "One Warrior down, one Dragon down, a sister and brother have Passed." 'Twas oddly flat and unemotional as if she was not even there, her eyes glazed o'er. 'Twas not as 'twas the day afore. Gunnarr remained silent and expressionless. Reverently, the witnesses chanted, "They kept their Oath unto the last." Many moments slipped by 'til Darque spoke again. "And how do we honor these, our brethren?" She received in response, "In Legend Song they will live again." 'Twas spoken without the usual enthusiasm, as a shroud lay o'er the Pits like a damp fog, clinging to them, soaking into their skin, making them shiver with o'erwhelming sadness.

'Twas not a dry eye in the Den, with one exception. Darque watched seemingly without emotion as the fire roared to life, burning brightly, taking the spirits of Storrm and Mystynn to the heavens. In her hand, her knuckles turning white with the strength of her grip, was a single long red braid meticulously washed clean of blood, curled and held together with scrimshawed hair picks.

EARLY SPRING

SIX MOONS LATER

~~~~~ OFFICE OF THE BATTLE COMMANDER ~~~~~

</div>

It had been a long, difficult winter, but spring brought healing to most, memories of the horror and the loss, pushed to where they should remain. In the past. No one had blamed Corbyn, but Corbyn himself. The Goddess Morrigan had remained atypically silent after Storrm's Passing and with nowhere else he was needed, he'd moved in temporarily with the Clan at the Keep, though he'd said little to anyone and was rarely seen outside the clinic without Shayla, Chynnar or Kelseacyr. The Raven grieved. Like so many others, Storrm's loss weighed heavy on his heart.

Flyrra was returned to the Keep by Dragon along with Walkyr and Fryya, days afore Crytcha arrived traveling a'foot. She could have gotten there much faster than she did but Darque was not concerned. She had Dragons keeping watch o'er her progress. The child of the Borkahn also blamed herself, though 'twas ridiculous. There was nothing she could have done to prevent what happened, but the long journey was good for her.

When Crytcha returned from the battle without her beloved headband, she found to her stunned delight a multitude of different headbands of all colors and materials covering her rack at home and spilling o'er onto the floor, all handmade by Clansmen who appreciated her and her brave efforts in the rescue. Crytcha felt accepted at last.

Immediately after the battles, Darque had promoted 3rd Stable to 3rd Flight, making official their desire to be called Mace Flight. She mused o'er all those they'd lost in the last two battles, knowing their swords would be missed. Forcing the knowledge of losing her sister and her unborn niece as well as Mystynn the Green, to the back of her mind, she'd recalled Kydra and Ragnyrr somewhat reluctantly took their promotions. Pulled back in from their search mission, 'twas not grief but something else that set a damper on their interest. They'd discharged their Third Fighter duties efficiently, but mayhap they were not destined for higher ranking. Besides, they'd been shaken badly by the battles in which they'd not even participated. 'Twas not cowardly, as they were both good fighters. 'Twas once again self-blame for what they were unable to prevent.

For many moons prior to the battles, the new Seconds had worked with the Elves and Sprites in the vetting process, showing much interest in diplomatic matters of all kinds. Ragnyrr was becoming a skilled negotiator and Kydra matched his kindness with a level head. Yet, if not Kydra and Ragnyrr standing at her side from now on, then who? Darque recognized she had to find new assignments for them but could think not of it now.

In the meantime, if she could find a suitable option for the current Seconds, she was considering promoting Tyndall and Fyndarr to Seconds in Command, and Daayn and Kashiyann to Thirds, as they'd stepped readily and quite effectively into those roles during the battles. And they were rotating through with her 'tween the Bog, the Keep, and Drekinn, while Kydra and Rag were deployed. She'd ordered her Seconds in Command off again on their search mission within a moon after the funerals and received little protest from the still grieving pair. Mystynn's little brother seemed inconsolable, while the rest of his family were quietly adjusting to the loss. Darque didn't want to make any final command decisions 'til she had a sit-down talk with them.

The winter moons had come and gone, the Spring Melts near o'er. Darque finished writing the proclamation of which they'd requested and scrawled her signature upon the bottom. Then she lifted it up and studied it. The Warriors of Second Flight had arrived just a mark prior, making a formal request of which she agreed without reservation. Third Flight had nicknamed themselves 'Mace Flight' from the time they'd taken the 'Bond and she'd already acquiesced to their desire to be so named officially. Why not name them all? No longer would the Flights be numbered. From this day forward, they would name themselves, and Second Flight requested the honor of taking the name of the former Second in Command, in her memory. Second Flight would forever be known as Storrm Flight. She'd ask First Flight for their suggestions, later.

When she'd returned from the battle she'd had to break the news to Aalanna, and she in turn had told Grifynn, and they'd not spoken about Storrm since. Afore the pyre had grown cold that day so long ago, Darque had pushed her sister's braid and picks to the back of the drawer and to the back of her mind. There was much work to do. The mission to recover the missing Warriors was continuing and now the Hoard was on the run. Many were caught and killed in successful routing missions, but they dared not attack Evanntyr directly and her Stealth Team was still out of touch. They were not dead, for she'd know, but whatever they were doing, she hoped 'twould bear fruit soon. Nevertheless, Diadranei was a very powerful Empath and surely they knew of what had happened, and of…

Deliberately she lowered the parchment and sat quietly staring at Storrm's Dragon Sword lying 'cross the top shelf on the far side of her office since it had found its way there after the funeral. Although with her blessing some had tried to Call, it remained there, unmoving. Darque refused to Call. She could not.

Afore these morose thoughts consumed her, she gathered her emotions and her riding gear. Gunnarr was waiting. There was something she needed to do, that she'd been avoiding for some time.

~~~~~ WINTER'S EDGE ~~~~~

Flame had cleansed everything into the furthest, deepest, darkest corners. What burn marks remained were now hidden under a layer of dirt, leaving the cavern pristine. The surrounding forest had healed itself and there was little evidence that a battle had ever been fought here. A reverent hush washed o'er the land. Only the soft rustling of the newly budding leaves in the gentle breezes, could be heard.

Her booted feet dangling o'er the edge of the cliff, Darque sat in front of the cave and looked out o'er Winter's Edge. 'Twas surreal. She could almost feel her sister, as if she was standing behind her once again, ready to back her up, take her commands, follow where she would lead them. Even to leap off the wall of the spectator's decks into the Training Pits below. She'd always taken for granted that Storrm would be there. 'Til the LifeBond they'd been inseparable and as her Second in Command, she was only a Thought away. Now, her voice was just a memory, her never-ending babble that had always aggravated Darque, would be welcomed and was much missed.

Gunnarr had not looked forward to this visit but he'd known 'twas inevitable. As a Human, even with Dragon blood, and as a female, she would need to see it again. Stand here. Look. Remember. He sighed. No. 'Twas not because she was Human, or female. 'Twas because she was compassionate. Responsible. And this was where her sister and his brother were forced Past the Veil. Storrm and Mystynn now walked with the brave. As a Highland, knowing Dragons could and did travel through the Veil, he understood that Mystynn could very well be at his side at this very moment. But he still wished he could see him, hear one more joke in their endless banter about who was the strongest or the best looking... he shook his great head, 'twas no telling if or when such might occur, for those Beyond frequently were never heard from again. He glanced at his lifemate. "There is no shame in tears."

Flatly, she replied, "They won't help her now."

"They would help you," he emphasized.

Darque didn't move, didn't respond. She tried to push aside the emotion and dissect the strategies, the similarities in the battles. She would not allow such to happen again. Not that the two were similar, but the pairings were. Near four winters past, she and Storrm had followed their father to Evanntyr, fighting their way through the castle in his footsteps only to lose him and be thrust right into the Battle for the Dragon Clan, where they were victorious. This time, in the Battle of Darden Caverns they were the victors only to plunge into the Battle of Winter's Edge where they lost her sister, her unborn niece, and Mystynn the Green.

She would never forgive herself. In the deepest recesses of her mind she fought to cage the terrible revelation that Storrm and Mystynn had betrayed her, lied to her, purposely misled her, to their own destruction. Yet even with such knowledge, knowing the reasons why such was done, she could find forgiveness for them. Eventually. But not for herself. Surely she could have done more, worked faster, been there for her. Had she found them earlier, they'd not be dead now. Regardless of the fact she had no idea they were in need, she could not help but think that had they gone to Storrm and Mystynn's rescue first, they would have survived, and mayhap the Evil One would have met his demise. 'Twas her fault. She'd failed them. "I should have known where they were, how much trouble they were in. How could I not have known?"

"Because Skyya was Calling to the Hoard and Storrm took great pains to hide from you and everyone else, in their efforts to survive and to do her job: protect the Resistance."

"But how did she do such?"

"She learned from the best. You." He sat down beside her and shrugged his great shoulders. "With the information you had, you chose correctly. 'Twas a successful mission. You rescued Flyrra, destroyed the Black's main Lair, and he and his Hoard have been thrown into chaos. They are still on the run and have gone into hiding." Softening his tone, he added, "Darque, you cannot know everything. You cannot be everywhere."

She shivered as her own sentiments echoed back to her. She'd told another this very thing, had used those very words.

Gunnarr's voice faded into the rustling of the forest leaves in the breeze, her hearing muted by the intensity of her despair as she sat staring blankly 'cross the region. And still, her emotions would not flow. She'd yet to cry. The dam would not break.

As she listened to the leaves rustling, the playful Voice was a bare whisper into her soul. "I've got your back," she Heard, and yet, 'twasn't the same as the Link. 'Twas more like how Diadranei and Anastasia Pushed their emotions to others. She glanced at Gunnarr sitting beside her, his long tail wrapped o'er his feet, wings tucked to his flanks. There was no one else around for leagues. Her inattention had made her mistake what she'd Heard. "Thank you," she told him.

'Twas as if he'd not been listening as he turned his great head toward her. Curiously, he asked, "For what?"

"For," she began, but the odd look on his face made her hesitate. She must have imagined it. Shaking her head, she cast her gaze back 'cross Winter's Edge. "Nothing. 'Twas nothing." She bit her bottom lip.

~~~~~ THE VOID ~~~~~

Storrm was not happy. "She Heard me, I know she did! Why did she not believe?"

Mystynn tried to explain. "When one heart Speaks, another may Hear, but when that heart is closed, so, too, the ears."

Storrm huffed. Darque was still angry, hurt. "Mayhap I can return as does Abriya? Speak with her face-to-face?"

"That is yet to be determined my love, and we'd have to be on the other side of the Veil to even attempt such, not here in the Void."

Storrm considered. "Will we be able to continue this tour through Memory on the other side?"

"I know not for certain. I'm sorry."

She frowned.

"Are you ready to continue?" he asked, hopefully.

In answer, she stepped up and hugged him, closing her eyes once more.

CHAPTER TWENTY-FIVE
Leahnyah

Although now retired, Leahnyah was not only a highly respected Skald of the Sprites, she'd come from a long line of Skalds and warriors from afore the Separation. Myrrdin could think of no other more capable for the task he'd set.

'Twould be the first time he'd seen the baby since handing her to Islyth mid-ocean just o'er nine moons past. Once he'd returned home after the battle, he'd helped the Elite to convict both Assemblymen, and with his testimony added to the evidence they'd gathered o'er the past several moons, the spies were sentenced. Given the choice to take the Quarter Dance or be exiled and allow the Sorcerer to find and punish them, they'd surprisingly accepted the former and sentence was carried out forthwith. He felt Skyya was safer now, but not safe enough to be raised openly. He'd heard nothing from Corbyn, although such was not unexpected, and chose to keep his plan in place.

Things had been extremely hectic but were finally slowing down and taking a rare break from work on his new investment, a small ship compared to the Krakken, he'd ridden the few marks 'cross the island to the northwestern cliffs to finally have that face-to-face meeting with his good friend. Leahnyah had always lived a secluded lifestyle with few visitors, even fewer o'er the past several winters, but 'twas as she preferred. She had a small but tidy home, her own gardens, and grew or hunted for all that she needed to survive.

The tall, elderly, but still agile Sprite, stepped forth from the small cottage holding the babe in her arms. Without formal greeting, she stated, "I've been calling her Leah, after my mother."

Redheaded and blue eyed, the child looked remarkably like Storrm, and he noted the slight uplift to her ears appearing to be the only outward sign of her mixed blood heritage. Taking in her features and wondering if she'd shown any Magical talents yet, he nodded without a word. Although alone, Leahnyah was always busy, and feeling his visit was an intrusion, he stated apologetically, "I'll not stay long. Nor can I return or hear of her progress 'til she is of age, without sacrificing her safety. And yours. I will arrange payment for her upbringing and the added burden to your life."

Standing on the path leading to her front door, she held the babe up for him to take, but raising his hand, he took a small step back and shook his head. She smirked. The famous, or mayhap infamous Ship's Master afraid to hold a baby? Rejecting his offer, she stated, "'Twould not be wise. Such payment would be traceable."

He'd known she'd be against accepting anything from him and came prepared. "Then you must take this," he said while handing o'er a large bag of precious gems. "No, do not even think to refuse. 'Twill cover your combined needs for many winters, and most think 'tis not uncommon for one of your skills to be paid in such a manner."

She snorted. Yes, many did think that a Skald would be paid well for her services although such was not the standard and was why she kept up her fighting skills. Even though she had little of value, she could be a target for brigands. Not surprised that he'd not returned to take the babe, she asked, "And just who is this beautiful child, who is evidently now mine?"

Myrrdin's smile faded as he replied somewhat reluctantly, "Skyya Storrm Rhyah."

Leahnyah recognized the surnames, as well as the potential the babe was the answer to a prophesy. Although she'd suspected such, she'd not had proof 'til now. Skyya was a 'tri-blood' child, and her eyes widened. "Mayhap I should not have been so curious."

He furrowed his brows and acknowledged her concerns. "You must know her real name in the event that something happens to me. And if 'tis suspected that she yet lives, she will be hunted. Even without the spies in the Assembly, your life will also be in danger. You must be mindful. And I must apologize."

Although she'd had a passing thought the child might be Myrrdin's when Islyth first brought her, 'twas only because she'd known the Prince since he'd come to the island, he'd never taken a mate, and she'd had that sliver of hope that he'd found some bit of happiness. 'Twas a solitary life he lived. He was a good friend and she wanted the best for him. Surely his true love was out there somewhere. May the Fates help bring them together. She lifted her chin and without any sense of fear, replied teasingly, "'Tis a burden I shall bear... only for you, m'lord."

Myrrdin had to laugh but returned quickly to his serious tact. Staring at the child with admiration, he caught a lightning-like flash in her eyes as she looked to him. 'Twas the tell of the Fay. But if Skyya had done anything noteworthy, Leahnyah would have mentioned it by now. Breaking his gaze, he looked to the Skald again and warned, "Keep her ignorant 'til she comes of age. Then she can make her own decisions."

Leahnyah considered what those decisions might entail. Surely a trip to meet her famous and most powerful aunt Darque? Mayhap the Sprites would be fully engaged in the war and with the Resistance by then. This little one would be welcomed by the Dragon Clan as a Warrior. That is, if they could forgive her for being alive. Skeptically, she asked, "Mayhap the reason for all this secrecy, will be less by that time?"

He sighed, as he acknowledged his friend's earlier thought about the prophesy. "Not likely, I'm afraid."

She nodded. 'Twas now all too clear why Myrrdin chose her. 'Twas not just for their friendship. "Then she must learn to handle her Magic when such begins, as well as the art of war; how to shoot bow and swing sword." It had been long since she'd trained anyone, even longer since she'd fought in battle. She was more than honored by his trust.

Understanding her to mean that Skyya had not shown any Magic thus far, and she may not even have any, for 'twas not a given simply due to her bloodline, he moved on. "Indeed. And I can think of no better Trainer for the child."

"You flatter this Elder Sprite, m'lord Myrrdin."

He'd never believed the Sprites and Elves were a separate Race. In his mind, they were all one and the same. "I speak the truth, Leahnyah. There were no better swordsmen or bowmen for our people during the war, than you and yours." He sighed, looked at the chubby cheeked baby again, and with some hesitance, stepped closer and touched her face lightly. Skyya immediately grabbed his finger and locked on with a left-handed grip he found amazing. Then the baby yawned and closed her eyes and without losing her grasp, she laid her head upon Leahnyah's shoulder and fell asleep. Her peaceful face was the vision Myrrdin held onto as he gently broke her grasp and took his leave without a word, both the Ship's Master and the Skald knowing 'twould be many winters afore he returned. Yet Leahnyah sensed the life paths of the Elven Prince and the tri-blood would cross again. Puzzled by this feeling, she watched Myrrdin as he mounted his chestnut horse and rode o'er the hills toward the sea, never looking back.

~~~~~ THE VOID ~~~~~

Storrm's emotions were mixed. "She's so beautiful."

"As are you," Mystynn replied with a loving smile.

Storrm blushed with his affections. "Will she grow up happy? Will she return to the Clan? Will she become a Warrior?"

"We do not know the future, my dear one."

"Why?" she asked, her face a mask of confusion.

"It hasn't happened yet," he responded, his own face in a similar state of expression.

"But you've shown me events that happen after we Pass, and yet we've not Passed. 'Tis so puzzling. I begin to understand why the spirits behave so strangely. Ardyth once told me they would come and go seemingly at their own leisure, never considerate with their timing and not giving her necessary information, mayhap thinking she already knew. Waiting for them to return was oft' times fruitless and frustrating. Yet, although they appeared unreliable, I now believe 'twas difficulty with time perception since there is no time movement here. If we walk for a league and then come back, there might have been but a heartbeat change, and yet if we walk away just three steps and return, many winters might have passed. Am I accurate in this?"

"Quite. As I've indicated afore, once interrupted 'tis very hard to find my place in the streamline of Time and Memory and trying to pinpoint something that happened after our Passing, takes even more effort."

"But it can be done, correct?"

"Oh yes, it can be done."

Storrm pouted. "I suppose 'twould be easier from the other side of the Veil?"

"Well, now that you mention it, yes. 'Twould."

She looked about them. They were in a holding pattern; the whiteness of the Void was never ending. 'Twas then she had a thought. Excitedly she exclaimed, "Arrrrgh! How slow can I be?"

His expression pained, he asked, "Is that a real question?"

She squinted. "This conversation begins to sound familiar." She pondered momentarily and then shook her head. "Never mind. I know how we can help Darque and the Resistance!"

Frustrated the big Green stated, "We can't go back. 'Tis far too late, and I thought we were done with that notion."

"No, that's not what I meant. I know how we can help from Beyond." Smiling broadly, for she was truly delighted, she kissed his long neck. "I'm ready to go now." Holding onto his thick-scaled elbow, they turned and walked together into the whiteness, Storrm explaining her idea in a never-ending stream of chatter, while Mystynn simply reveled in her touch and the sound of her voice.

CHAPTER TWENTY-SIX

The Dam Breaks

The Dragon Matriarch sat at the head of the huge half-round table, surrounded by her Ancients, her luminescent eyes shining with something... secretive. Darque was not certain what Synahmarr was thinking and it baffled her.

It also baffled her that Synahmarr had summoned them to Fire Heart instead of Speaking through Gunnarr's Link, and even Gunnarr knew not why, as he stood behind her in the massive conference room of the castle where he'd been hatched and raised. Syn's voice was regal, her speech reminiscent of her aunt Maahayyel. And yet Syn was her own Dragon: intelligent, strong, decisive, and not easily swayed. Nonetheless, Darque had convinced Syn to alter the ancient LifeBond Magic. She didn't want to lose another Warrior. And since so many of the Highlands had been forced Beyond, with each ceremony the risk of more Blood Calls going to them was rising dramatically.

She'd listened for some time while the Matriarch explained the alteration of the Spell and how 'twould work, but 'twas Synahmarr's revelation that the Dragons who were on the other side of the Veil needed persuasion to leave and re-join them in the war effort, as well as the fact that they'd not know how, that made things a bit more of a challenge. Of course, those who'd Passed as LifeBond partners could not return, but those Dragons who'd not yet 'Bonded would now be free to answer their Blood Call. However, they would require an anchor to keep them here, and that would have to be their Human partner. Darque thought about her mother, considered the anchor for her father's spirit. They could speak to each other and Aalanna could see him, but Grifynn could not fight. She wondered how this would work 'til she was reminded that Magic was boosted by skin to skin contact and 'twas explained that the Dragon would attach him or herself upon the skin of the Human, in living color and detail, although not in true size. 'Twould appear as an intricate tattoo.

Darque was skeptical. "A tattoo? You mean like, ink?"

Synahmarr wrinkled her leathery muzzle into a toothy grin and patiently answered. "Yes. 'Twill be very much like ink."

A multitude of questions arose in her mind and she asked, "But how will that work? Will the Warrior then be able to fly? How will they fight?"

Syn's great paw lifted to stop Darque's flight of ideas. "They will still Share their thoughts and emotions freely, but the ink will be seen as an ordinary tattoo while the Dragon 'sleeps', 'til he or she is awakened as when Called forth to battle or when they sense danger to their partners. Then the ink will detach and transform, growing into a full-sized Dragon who will be as in life, able to do what they could afore they Passed." With this information a slight smile of hope crossed Darque's face, and Synahmarr reluctantly continued, "Since this will be the first time the Magic is Brewed with this alteration, I know not everything, however, they will have limitations of which I do know. Their time upon this side of the Veil in such a capacity will not be infinite, and they must re-attach to their partner within a few marks to regain their strength. There is no way to know precisely how much time they have, but 'tween them they each will feel the need to come back together. 'Twill be dependent upon many factors, including how long it had been since their last 'awakening', and how much energy they expend while 'awake'. But understand, if they are separated for too long, both will be dragged to the other side. Nothing I can do will prevent such. And of course, if the Human is killed, the Dragon will return Beyond, taking their Human partner with them Past the Veil as do you now."

'Twasn't a perfect solution but Darque knew how much effort Synahmarr had put into altering the greatest Greater Magic Spell of all time. "This could work. But you mentioned they needed some encouragement?"

"Yes. Those Beyond do not perceive time or need as do we, and these misunderstandings could keep them from answering the Call appropriately. But do not fear. None who offer their Blood Call will be dragged 'cross the Veil again, they simply would miss the binding. That, and the fact that the Dragons will need to be taught just what to expect once they 'cross, may create some mishaps."

"'Mishaps'? Oh yeah. So, all we need do is get someone who is already Beyond to try to convince them to make the leap, as well as teach them to attach?" Darque's infamous temper began to flare. Sarcastically, she continued, "That shouldn't be too difficult."

Warrior Mynx had become her best friend and having the Human around, Synahmarr recognized Darque's mood and ignored the slight. "Mayhap not so difficult. I have heard from Beyond that a pair of LifeBond partners have already begun to do what is required."

Darque thought about the Matriarch's aunt Kaahayyel and the Warrior Tannyr, one of the first Teams to cross in the big battle. "Which Team?" she asked.

"They do not describe well, nor do they name them, but they do mention she has red hair, and her Dragon is green." Synahmarr sounded apologetic, as she understood of how little use this was, but Darque felt 'twas a'purpose as a dig for her moodiness. All this told her for certain, was the human half was female. Her thoughts shifted to Loryyn and her partner, Krynnarr, as well as Ariel and her partner, Zaydarr, both Dragons brothers of Synahmarr. Darque hesitated, reining in her retort. Exchanging barbs would get them nowhere. "That could be near any of those who have Passed. Have they nothing else?"

Now for the clincher, for Syn was certain there was something to this, that only the Battle Commander would see, and 'twould be of great importance. 'Twas why she'd insisted upon this face-to-face meeting. "Yes. It seems those Dragons in the Beyond thought there was nothing more they could do 'til this one Passed. They say she is relentless in her efforts and will not shut up. They are considering her plan simply to get her to do so. And, she sent a message for the Battle Commander."

Darque swallowed hard and tilted her head slightly as her eyes began to widen in disbelief. Sucking in her bottom lip, she nodded to the Matriarch to continue, for she didn't want to assume anything. She didn't want to raise her hopes.

"'Twas a message I thought might have meaning to you." She paused. Squinting, she continued, "The Warrior wants you to know that she will always have your back."

Her hand o'er her mouth, Darque began to tremble, and taking an unsteady step backwards, the emotional dam finally broke. Her breath coming in gasps and hot tears flowing, Gunnarr reached forth with both his forepaws to provide support and prevent her from falling on her butt in front of a very surprised Matriarch, his own tears flowing down his muzzle and splashing onto the stone floor.

<center>~~~~~ PAST THE VEIL ~~~~~</center>

"She heard me!" Storrm exclaimed.

"'Twasn't you she heard, 'twas just the message you sent," Mystynn teased her.

"Oh, shut up!"

Storrm had tried very hard to get the message through and hadn't been able to use more than a few words or they'd be forgotten in the translation. Mystynn knew she'd counted on her sister understanding with just the message, and the incessant chatter information was simply an unexpected bonus which guaranteed her identification. "I believe that 'can't shut up', is a well-known characteristic of yours, and 'twas the mention of such that gave Darque her first real clue."

Storrm bit her bottom lip and looked a tad upset afore she replied defensively, "Well, 'tis also a characteristic that will increase the success of the coming LifeBond ceremonies!"

Mystynn hated to see her troubled in any way. "You are remarkable, and I am very lucky to have you."

Her mood elevated instantly and with a wide smile, she stated, "I love you, Mystynn."

He chuckled at her quick changes of temperament, of which he'd never grow tired. Life, or rather death, with his irrepressible woman, would never be boring. "And I love you, my dear."

Throwing her hands in the air, she turned and spoke o'er her shoulder as she briskly walked away. "Break o'er! Come, we have work to do!"

Mystynn rolled his huge, glittering green eyes afore lumbering after her red braids swinging past those luscious hips. He'd do whatever she wanted, follow her throughout Beyond, seeking all those Dragons who'd Passed, spreading the word that they could now answer the Blood Call. In the end, time would be their ally.

THE NURSERY PITS
~~~~~ FLIGHT OF FIRE KEEP ~~~~~

'Twas the largest egg in the batch of thirteen. O'er a moon past, it rolled ever so slowly 'til it came to rest completely isolated against the edge of the sand pit, and there it lay. 'Til tonight. Just afore Synahmarr turned to leave, the egg suddenly trembled, then rocked violently. She heard a slight cracking sound afore it stopped moving once again.

Making a thorough examination, she could find no crack in the surface and so Synahmarr watched intently for near another mark. This one was eager to enter the world. She'd only laid them this past winter after much encouragement from Mynx, her most trusted confidant. Her brows furrowed. She prayed to her

Ancestors that Corbyn was correct, and that soon-to-be-hatched Dragonette was no offspring of the Black.

'Twould be so wonderful, not to mention helpful, if the unknown male who'd supposedly Claimed her, came for her now. She'd know. She paused, wrinkling her elegant snout. Would she know? She'd asked Corbyn to release her altered memories but 'twas such a sloppy effort of the one who'd performed the original Magic that he'd been concerned about making things worse. In fact, the alteration was so bad, Corbyn had been appalled. She shook her head. She could not afford to lose what memories she still had, and after the Raven made a few adjustments they'd decided enough was enough and she'd just have to live with it as 'twas. At least he'd been able to convince her, for the most part, of the possibility of another's Claim. Enough so, that she'd agreed to lay.

Such a large batch was certainly a surprise, but a most special one. They'd tried to keep the eggs a secret, but they'd not stayed so for long, as not only was this the first batch of Highland eggs laid since afore the Last Holocaust, 'twas o'er double the average number. Rumors were inevitable. 'Twas known throughout Dragondom that the Matriarch had been kept prisoner by the Black and without a lifemate coming forth, there was speculation. But even without, one had to wonder how she'd been Claimed when her flight had been limited, and how had she had so many eggs with such limitations? That is, if she was Claimed after she was captured, as the rumors suggested. 'Twas fact that the size of the batch came from the height of flight and number of loops flown. Or was it a fact? So many theories. So many talking behind her back.

The egg moved not again and Synahmarr sighed, finally turning away and vacating the warmth of the lava heated nursery sands.

CHAPTER TWENTY-SEVEN

To Claim A Princess

His mood foul, Radryagg sat upon the cliff ledge fronting his cavern in the snow-covered mountains of the region separating the main landmass of the Rol Dan from the Sakyn Forest. His chin hung to his chest, his eyes scanned 'cross the continually frozen landscape. He'd not stayed to participate in the first LifeBond, nor had he been present for the more recent third, and he'd not return for the next, even though he was fully aware of his obligation if he did receive the Blood Call. He hoped he would not.

During the first ceremony he'd returned home to the Rol Dan to recruit more of his fellow Dragons, bringing them back for the second. But once Synahmarr was found alive, he'd withdrawn and returned home for good, where he'd lived in seclusion since just after the Last Holocaust, when he'd failed her, when he thought he'd left her to die alone by the claws and Magic of the Black and the Sorcerer. How had he not known she yet lived? How could he ever face her again? Although she knew not who he was, he knew her.

He'd Claimed her upon orders. He'd been on an important mission, working with the brother of the Last Dragon Matriarch, infiltrating the Hoard. 'Twas a fluke, a sideline mission, one he'd taken for the good of their Kind. Yes, she'd sent him away, but saving the one he'd Claimed should have taken precedence o'er their original mission. And making matters worse, she was the Princess of his Kind. 'Twas a cowardly retreat and a transgression for which he could never forgive himself. How could she?

His mind filled with ancient Memories. Shortly after the Last Holocaust, Maakayyel, the brother and youngest sibling of the recently elevated Matriarch, Maahayyel, was sent on a covert three-fold mission: to discover what was causing the Highlands to be sterile, uncover the truth of what had happened to his uncle, Kaahayyel's lifemate, and try to find Synahmarr, his missing niece. Kaahayyel was the eldest in his line and the previous Matriarch, who'd abdicated to her middle sibling after her lifemate died in his own efforts to find their wayward daughter.

Recruiting his good friends and fellow patriots, Hadryagg and her brother, Radryagg, both highly trusted, it wasn't long afore they discovered rumors of a cave in the highest peaks of the southernmost region of the Razor's Edge. Supposedly, 'twas where the Black had holed up since his near fatal injury at the end of the War of Chaos. To their horror, the Black had not only survived, he was slowly and insidiously gathering his Hoard once again.

The three Dragons were young, and although the name of the Prince was well known, not so how any of them appeared. Nonetheless, taking no unnecessary chances they disguised themselves and after much effort located his Lair, managing to infiltrate the territory of the Black. 'Twas here they'd expected to find that for which they sought, on all accounts. If 'twas a Spell that the Black had put upon his own Race, limiting all but the Matriarch herself to laying their precious eggs, they must learn how it could be reversed. And if Kaahayyel's lifemate had been killed by the newly reestablished Hoard, such confirmation might lead them to find Synahmarr.

And find her, they did. Her mind controlled by dehydration and starvation, torture and propaganda, Synahmarr did not know whom she could trust, believing only what the Black told her using his foulest brainwashing techniques. She was being kept in a large enclosure but was not strong enough to fly high or for long. Still, she was being prepared for a Claiming ritual by the Black himself, who planned on using the Princess, hoping her powerful Magic and familial ties could help him to infiltrate the Matriarchy itself.

Upon Maakayyel's orders, Radryagg managed to get to the Princess, and after much effort, finally convinced Syn that she was being used and the Black was responsible for her father's death. Headstrong but not stupid, she saw the truth, but she was still too weak to escape. Radryagg wanted to help her, but ashamed of her own role in the happenings, admitted to him that the Black was preparing to Claim her in the morning and there were too many guards to prevent her escape. Rad had snuck past those guards, he knew she spoke the truth. There was no other option. He had to Claim her himself. Sacrificing his own ability to ever take another, he was able to stimulate her enough to fly one loop which would not be seen as odd to her guards, and then taking her upon the ground, he Claimed her as his own. Would there be eggs from such a mating? He doubted it at the time. But, 'twas interesting. Unable to take another, he'd fantasized about the unusual mating for many winters.

Synahmarr was more satisfied than she'd ever been. She loved this male. Her eyes sparkled with desire, but 'twas no time, and she'd ruined any further chance of a life with him. At least she'd had this. "You must leave me here. I can't go, but you have a chance to escape."

Miserably, Radryagg exclaimed, "When he finds you have been Claimed, he will likely kill you!"

She nodded her affirmation. "I understand. 'Tis all I deserve. But he may not, one never knows. I am too weak and would never make it. Now go! You must get out now, for 'tis certain he will kill YOU."

"I will not leave you. I love you, I can get you out of here, get you past the guards, I know I can! You must try, Syn!"

She hesitated. The young Dragon standing afore her was the same she'd wanted since she was birthed, but he was not noble, not of royal parentage, and her father had forbidden them from even being friends. Now everything was o'er. Her life, their chance. Gone. Firmly she declared, "Go. I order it as your Princess."

Rad's expression dropped, his scowl evident. He could not disobey such an order. She did not love him. She was just doing her duty to avert the Black's Claim by allowing another's. Leaving reluctantly, he took one look back o'er his massive shoulder, but her eyes closed, unable to watch his retreat.

Barely managing to make his escape, he'd reported to Maakayyel, whose scowl matched his own, but there was nothing to be done. The following dawn, when the Black discovered Syn had been Claimed already, he'd sent out troops to find the culprit and bring him in to be executed. In the meantime, the Sorcerer altered her Memories of the event, leaving Syn with the belief 'twas the Black who'd taken her Claim.

For many winters, Maakayyel and his cohorts were convinced the Black killed Synahmarr in a fit of rage, her usefulness gone. Maakayyel thought 'twas the only way out for his niece, while Rad could not defend his own actions. His dismay slowed his reflexives and made him reckless. He was captured. But afore he could be killed, a mighty battle raged, leading to the Last Holocaust. His sister managed to free him in the midst of the fighting as she'd remained inside the Hoard as their contact but was severely wounded in the effort. Unable to find her, Rad had once more retreated to Flight of Fire with the Prince. 'Twas soon learned, however, and much to his relief, that Had, although mortally injured, was Healed by a strange woman with the Call of altered DNA in her blood, with something she'd referred to as 'blood elixir' mixed with 'life crystal', of her own creation. Left upon the battlefield in the pitch dark, Hadryagg Healed, returning as a rogue in the Hoard, known as the Sentinel.

Rad continued to stare 'cross the barren landscape. What to do? He knew not. If he presented himself to the Matriarch, she might not even know him, and his audacity could be a death sentence. However, he'd recently learned that Maakayyel had been Called and was now in the 'Bond, living at the Keep of St Swiftyn's. His eyes narrowed as he pondered his options.

The Fangs Of Solvyngarr

Bullaga was sightseeing. The big apricot fawn male had been all o'er St Swiftyn's looking for a place to bring Drys, who would be having her pups at any time. He was rather proud. 'Twasn't every day another litter of War Dog pups was born. In fact, the last litter was afore the Battle for the Dragon Clan and they'd been sired by his late friend, Bensyn. Drys and Horace, belonging to Fryya and Walkyr, were of that litter. Although they were not the only Dogs at the Keep now, as many Free Warriors were paired, Bullaga was the only Dog given free roam.

Bull was still moving a bit slowly in his recovery from the wounds he'd received in the Battle of the Domes, and he sat down to rest. 'Twas then he heard the faint scraping sounds. His huge head turned this way and that, seeking the origin of the noise. Sniffing and listening, he stood up and ambled further down the hallway into the shadows, and then back a bit, and then closer to one wall where he stood quietly, his flop ear pressed against the stone.

War Dogs were very intelligent, bred for protection and fighting. He knew whatever was making that sound was worth locating, as it could be a weapon. The sound was distinct. 'Twas metal on rock in a scratching/banging rhythm as if hitting the wall. Since no Warrior or Clansman was near to create such a sound, 'twas something wrong. He determined to find his master, the Elven Skald, Kelseacyr. She'd know what to do.

As he slowly began his long walk back toward the upper levels of the Keep, a leather ball rolled past his great paws and stopped against the wall where he'd heard the tapping sounds. Racing down to capture the lost ball, was the little blonde girl known as

Kryn. He liked that child, she always had a ready hand for an ear scratch. He sat down and waited for her.

Kryn ran o'er to pick up the ball and as she stood up, her eyes scanned from the floor to the ceiling with awe. Bullaga happened to be looking in the same place at the same time and even his Dog intelligence knew they'd located something of great importance. Kryn trembled, her eyes widening as she took a grip of Bullaga's loose skin at his shoulder, and together they hurried to the clinic to make report to the adults. 'Twas that for which they'd all been searching.

~~~~~ THE LIBRARY OF THE DRAGON'S DEN ~~~~~

Regynn lifted his mug of Vydna once more, toasting his friends who'd gathered this evening to relive their first adventure, o'er fifty winters past. Sitting in the bar section of the library of the Clan, Regynn could not remember such good times in many a winter. "Much water under that bridge, my friends!" He laughed, and after guzzling down the last of his drink, reached forth with the jug to refill all 'round. Halfheartedly, Ardryyn, Kryllyn, and Caleichante held forth their mugs for more of the strongest drink in which any of them had ever imbibed. They'd all sworn to each other earlier that the Human would not win this contest, nonetheless, they'd never tasted this fiery drink afore and now were not certain they'd be able to keep that promise. Still, 'twas a riotous good evening, and they'd spent the last four marks telling and retelling how the entire event on the ship had occurred, each adding details and embellishments as the tale grew larger and Regynn's role became the stuff of Legend Song.

Ardryyn drained his mug once again, and as his vision blurred and his tongue began to stick to his teeth making it more and more difficult to think clearly, he pushed the empty mug 'cross the table toward the Warrior, shaking his head as he conceded his challenge. "You could outdrink Myrrdin!" he exclaimed in near disbelief.

Kryllyn hesitated then followed his brother in the action, indicating no more for him, either. He'd had enough for several lifetimes. Still, the camaraderie they'd shared this evening was something he'd never forget and of which they might never repeat. The war made everything uncertain. One had to share good times when one had the chance. Regardless of how he might feel in the morning, he'd never regret this time together with their old friend.

Caleichante was still holding onto her mug with both hands, sipping away at the latest refill. As lithe as she was, one might think she'd have conceded marks past, but she'd kept up admirably and now might outdrink the brothers. But outdrink the Warrior? In her musical voice, she stated, "No, I think not. Regynn, you win! This Vydna of yours is remarkable. You say you drank this as a child?"

Regynn's clear voice was still steady as a rock, as were his hands and his thinking. No trace of how much he'd consumed was evident. 'Twas astounding. "Yes. I grew up with this. Everyone drinks Vydna in the Rol Dan. 'Tis more readily available than water!"

Calei replied, "Speaking of the Rol Dan, if you'd not been from there, you would never have recognized the poison in those barrels and all this might never have happened. Our history would have changed dramatically. We can, and could never, thank you enough."

Regynn shook his head. "No need for thanks. I'm just grateful I was there, and all worked out well. You did the hardest part, after all. You neutralized all those barrels of poison."

Ardryyn and Kryllyn spoke o'er each other saying, "With your help! We just had enough energy Drawn from you, to take care of all twenty-seven. We'd have been hard pressed to do more, without forcing you Past the Veil!"

Everyone laughed, but then Regynn became quiet, and stared off into space. His mind elsewhere, Caleichante's brows furrowed.

Her gaze shot from the Warrior to the brothers, who now realized there was something very wrong. Was it something they'd said?

Regynn's face took on a dark and urgent expression as he caught the eyes of the others at the table. Leaning forward, he questioned firmly, "Twenty-seven barrels?"

Calei put her hand up to silence the brothers. All business now, the effects of the Vydna fading with the adrenaline pumping into her body, she responded with apprehension, "Yes. Twenty-seven. What say you, Warrior?"

The vision of the cargo hold that had remained in the back of his mind unsettled for all these past winters now clear and stark, he answered with confidence, "There were thirty barrels."

"Thirty?" all three exclaimed at once. Calei shook her head to clear her senses and again silenced the brothers, their faces the epitome of confusion. "You are certain?"

Regynn rolled his eyes, and Calei sat back in her chair. If he'd said there were thirty barrels, then there were thirty barrels. The brothers tried to recall the room, counting the barrels again and again in their minds, but they kept coming to the same number. Twenty-seven. Nevertheless, there was no doubt in Regynn's mind, he knew what he'd seen, and what he'd seen were those three extra and seemingly lost, barrels. Now he related the story of entering the cargo hold for the first time and how he felt a warm tingling sensation, thinking 'twas the air a'foul from having been closed up so many moons. "Calei, could that sensation have been Allure? Could a Spell have been broken by my entrance and could such have caused those three barrels to 'hide' from your vision?"

The Sprite chewed on the inside of her cheek afore nodding her head. "I believe so. If the room was b'Spelled, 'tis possible that Spell did exactly what you suggest."

The brothers could remain silent no longer and Kryllyn questioned, "Then those three barrels are still out there?" Shaking their heads, Ardryyn continued, "No, 'twould have been catastrophic to the Island and the Grotto. We sunk that ship where she was, and if those barrels were exposed to the water, that poison would have activated. Not as bad as all thirty, but those three would have caused irreparable damage and there's been no such event." Casting their gazes to the Human, they searched for confirmation of their thoughts.

Regynn was angry. They'd never seen such fire in his eyes. He'd not caught the meaning of his feeling of uncertainty earlier and had let the vision in his mind sink into oblivion. Why hadn't he figured it out sooner? But afore he could speak, Calei did. "Do not blame yourself Regynn. We obtained more intel after you left on the Norryn, and armed with such knowledge, we should have been more suspicious. We know 'twas the Sorcerer who sent that ship. He'd filled it with the poison after purchasing it in the Rol Dan, had the ship sailed around the Dragon's Breath, through the Ocean of Fears, and into the Sea of Dreams, then all the way north to Port O'Dinburra where you were taken, afore he found a suitable 'Captain'. 'Twas not his goal to capture you, 'twas his goal to destroy the Sprite Nation and the Water Dragons. You were an accidental addition and you managed to thwart his scheme, however, he must have set the Spell when he loaded the barrels in case his original plan went awry."

Now Regynn was not only angry, he was frustrated. They'd known all this and never told him. Ah well, the life of a Warrior. Now another thought occurred to him. "You know what type of Spell he could have used, do you not?"

Calei dipped her chin slightly and sighed. "Yes. The only one he could have used to hide some of the barrels from our vision would also keep them sealed from the waters. But this would not last forever, as he would have used it to try to complete his mission should he be discovered."

"So, how long would such a Spell last afore it released the poison to the waters?"

Cracking her knuckles, she stated ominously, "Theoretically speaking, mayhap fifty or sixty winters at best."

~~~~~ THE OFFICE OF THE BATTLE COMMANDER ~~~~~

Kryn and Bullaga had found the door to Shahanalaa. After following them back to the place where 'twas seen, it had taken several sweeps to determine that only they could see it, and that 'twas, according to Corbyn, due to the combination of 'an innocent child' and 'one who has touched the Veil'. "I am not surprised, merely disappointed that I didn't think of this earlier. The Rashei were given the Keep to safeguard, including Shahanalaa, for all eternity. They must have taken my ancestor's suggestion as to how to do that effectively. Even though the Rashei could not have b'Spelled the entry, they could have recruited the Fay to do so." Standing still and quiet, his eyes glazed o'er as did the Dragons when in Link. Finally returning his attention to those in the room, he'd continued, "I've been dredging my own memories for some time on this. I found a single memory of a conversation from my childhood with Abriya, to the reasons why 'tis closed."

"You learned something of Shahanalaa and told me not? Just whose side are you on, Fay?" Darque chastised him.

Ignoring the rebuke, he continued, "There was no information on location, merely the mention that if the Keep were compromised the door would close, and in reverse, once the Keep were no longer compromised 'twould open again."

Darque chewed on her bottom lip. 'Twas truth. The reference was basically useless but 'twas good to know the how and why. Squinting, another notion came to mind. "Could the fact that the door was never closed when she lived here, be why Aalanna could not locate it?"

Corbyn merely nodded. He'd untethered her memories to return to her as she saw things from her past. Without the visual prompt, she would have no memory.

Still, it had been located. But the Keep was still compromised. However, if there was a way to open it, Darque would make that happen. Neither the Dog nor the child could see the door alone, which confirmed Corbyn's theory, but Bullaga patiently sat and stared while Kryn spent many marks drawing detailed pictures. 'Twas fortunate she was a decent artist at her young age. With help from her pictures and from her view of the door itself while Darque adjusted and added, Darque was able to draw even more detailed images, and soon they had an impressively detailed picture of the massive entrance. 'Twas a double doorway, floor to ceiling and twice as wide, without lever, knob, or visible hinges, made of solid rock carved and inlaid with gems, precious metals, and rare natural woods in an intricate mosaic that told a story. Interestingly enough, the ages of the stories differed from top to bottom. There seemed to be some that was obviously ancient, as ancient as the door itself, and then there was a newer level clearly added at some later date.

Back in her office Darque poured o'er the pictures, trying to decipher how to open the door now, for surely the instructions were there to read, when suddenly Abriya appeared sitting upon the armrest of her chair, peering o'er her shoulder. Darque Abriya D'Rienne had not visited for some time. As usual, she bothered not with trivial pleasantries. Her voice distant but so much like her own (the only difference being the slight accent from the woman who'd lived and died speaking Ancient Tongue), Darque listened to the voice of her ancestor as she 'read' the story.

In conclusion, Abriya stated, "You will need the Fangs of Solvyngarr to unlock the doorway to Shahanalaa. They closed when the Keep was compromised by Koryl's curse and will not open again 'til the curse is lifted." She noted the confusion on Darque's face and continued, "I've been doing more research in the Archives. Koryl is no Magic bearer and could not have placed a Spell, but she is a full-blood Rashei. From what I have discovered, with the help of someone more powerful than she, say mayhap the Sorcerer, along with the power of the Book of the Conqueror, a curse could have been placed o'er the Keep affecting all the Rashei within. Consequently, the Book will be required to break the curse and allow the door to open once more.

However,…" She hesitated and dropping her gaze to her lap, her hands clasped together, she continued, "since the Rashei used the Fangs to enforce the lock on the Book, they must be found and used, to open the Book." Now she faced her namesake once more. "And the Fay is correct. The entry was b'Spelled by the Ancients that once 'twas closed, 'twould require both the sight of an innocent child and one who has touched the Veil to see. Kryn and Bullaga qualified for that on both counts."

"Why by the Fates did you never mention all this afore?"

"What?", the First Warrior questioned innocently.

Frustrated Darque exclaimed, "We've been searching for moons, winters! Why didn't you tell us where and how to look?"

Bewildered, the spirit raised her eyebrows. Darque instantly remembered the many

limitations 'tween their two worlds of existence. The spirit Warrior would not have truly known how much time they'd been apart while doing her 'research'. Still, Abriya acknowledged, "Our time is limited when I visit, and I had to allow you to learn much with simple guidance." She shrugged her shoulders. "I knew you'd find the door," she stated confidently as she began to fade again.

Darque mentally summarized their exchange of information, realizing they had no idea where to search for either the Fangs or the Book, but according to Abriya, the Fangs came first. "Wait! How do we find the Fangs? Just what do they look like?" she questioned the fading spirit.

Abriya stopped mid-fade. Floating o'er to sit opposite the Battle Commander upon the edge of her desk, she looked enquiringly at her namesake. As if in deep thought, Abriya gazed around the room. Many times, when she was with Darque she'd felt the sense that her LifeBond partner was near. At this very moment, she could almost feel Solvyngarr touching her, the sensation stronger than ever afore. Still, she could sense only one. They'd been separated. All four Fangs were required to reunite her with her LifeBond partner. Her emotions rising, she would have taken a deep breath if she yet breathed. The Fangs were very powerful indeed, but she'd failed to bring back Sol with them. She'd been too weakened after what had happened, and then lost the opportunity. Lifting her chin, she asked, "What do you mean?"

"I have no idea what they look like or where they are! We've found nothing in the Archives about the Fangs, with the exception of them having been kept in the Lost Room with the Book and your Dragon Sword! None of which have we located."

Abriya's hand brushed Darque's forearm in support afore she placed it back beside her hip on the table. Her emotional status soaked through the room, and Darque's ankle suddenly felt like she'd been hit with a stream of Flame. The First Warrior squinted as Darque reached toward her boot blade, the only one left of a matched set of four that her father had given her upon taking the LifeBond. Quickly, she pulled the blade and laid it atop the desk as it suddenly heated, near burning her ankle. The blade had oft' times felt strangely warm, but never afore had it been this reactive. Watching in wonder, the blade slid 'cross the desk, stopping beside the hand of the spirit.

Staring in disbelief, Abriya's emotions were chaotic. 'Twas one of the Fangs. But where were the other three?

LATER

<div align="center">~~~~~ THE BEYOND ~~~~~</div>

Storrm was worried while eavesdropping on her sister and Gunnarr. "She will not Pass when such happens?"

"No," Mystynn replied with some caution.

Storrm was not convinced by his tone, nonetheless, she asked, "Will she be the same? Mentally? Emotionally?"

"Darque is strong. She will succeed."

"You are certain? There are no others like us. This has never happened afore."

Mystynn hesitated long enough to bring a frown to Storrm's lovely face. He straightened his massive shoulders and stated firmly, "I have the utmost confidence in her ability." Sitting back on his haunches, he admitted, "Other than that, no one can be certain."

Storrm nodded solemnly. 'Twould take the heat of Battle Lust to draw forth the changes, as they began with her afore they Passed. "When is their next battle?"

Dropping his gaze with the ugly truth of the situation, he stated, "Soon."

Storrm listened to Darque and Gunnarr's exchange, trying to let her know she was there for her, knowing the only way in which they could truly help, was to continue their mission Beyond. 'Twas in Darque's plan to have another LifeBond in the very near future. The Dragons on this side of the Veil needed her instructions. Shrugging her shoulders, she turned, and thumping Mystynn playfully on his nose, she pulled his wing gently to ensure he was following afore walking away.

MEANWHILE

~~~~~ THE QUARTERS OF DARQUE AND GUNNARR ~~~~~

</div>

Gunnarr broke the uneasy silence. "My enchantment. What has you in such a lather? What's really going through that complex mind of yours?"

'Twas true. Darque had much on her mind. Finding and retrieving the three lost Fangs and the Book, opening Shahanalaa, managing the newcomers and incorporating everyone efficiently, ensuring the safety of all at Drekinn Lair. It seemed a new concern of major proportions filled every spare moment of her young life. And then there was what had been happening to her, personally. If she had not the support of her lifemate, she felt she could not be an effective Commander, let alone simply survive as had Abriya. Needing confirmation of their relationship, she stated, "I am not Human. I am not Dragon. I am a half breed. You fell in love with a Human. Can you love a half breed?"

Gunnarr flipped his great paw in dismissal. "Don't be ridiculous. Remember that I knew who and what you were afore we mated. Besides, to be precise you're not a half breed. You are a hybrid. And I love YOU. Not what you look like or feel like, or smell like, or um… taste like," Gunnarr had to lick his fangs and swallow twice to handle the drool that such thoughts always produced, then cleared his throat afore he continued. "Although all of that is delightful, 'tis not why I love you."

Darque half smiled but was still troubled. 'Twas time to lay her cards on the table. "I'm changing. When in the heat of battle, I feel something happening to me. Since the beginning of our 'Bond I've felt an intense heat, more so than can be accredited to the Lust. And at Winter's Edge I seemed to grow beyond myself, along with a prickling sensation about my shoulders and down my arms and thighs. 'Twas as if my skin was hardening, thickening as with scale." She shook her head. 'Twas highly implausible, yet in her heart… "I know not how else to describe such. But when the Lust is gone, so too, the changes." She paused as she remembered another battle. "Ama once mentioned she saw an image of a huge Dragon surrounding me, like a mist of my own creation, with swirls of heat coming off my body. But such dissipated quickly and she decided 'twas just her imagination. Yet she described my father's death as an instantaneous funeral pyre, in which he disappeared to char on the stone floor in a mere heartbeat. Although the heat I feel is not uncomfortable, I have wondered if such could happen to me, given my perception of increasing temperatures. Have you noticed anything?"

Calmly, he responded, "You are changing."

A look of pure astonishment o'er her face, she asked, "You've seen it?"

"I can't say that I've seen it, but I know it to be true."

"But, how? Why?"

The Mighty Blue snorted. "You ask for confirmation, not for knowledge. You know how. You know why."

Darque pondered for a moment. She and her siblings were not fully Human, but they'd never thought of the consequences and had only noticed some innate Magic and Dragon-like senses thus far. "What if the changes don't stop? What if I change completely into a Dragon? The morphing of Aba's body finally killed him."

With much wisdom, Gunnarr responded to her concerns. "He was the beginning. You are the result. His fiery Passing was a part of his personal journey and came not only from using the Elixir but as a result of Brannyn's Spell. Nevertheless, his morphing was not like yours and although we know not how far 'twill go, I do not believe 'twill force you Past the Veil, nor turn you into a full-fledged Dragon. I'm more inclined to believe whatever changes you manifest will be uniquely yours, and without a doubt, beneficial."

"So, what do we do now?"

"We wait. We watch. We deal with what happens as it happens. We anticipate with great joy and expect the wondrous. This might have some side effects that could be... quite interesting as well as beneficial," he stated with a wink and a lecherous grin.

Darque was still not convinced but was beginning to see the potential. "If I did form scale, 'twould be as true Dragon scale?"

"I cannot say for certain, but if you are successful, you would be armored against both the kiss of steel and Flame itself."

"So 'twould seem that you think I should let it happen and not fight to contain the changes next time they begin to occur?"

"Most assuredly," Gunnarr replied, perplexed by the question.

The look on his face was so humorous she near laughed out loud, but she was not ready and reminded him, "If I cannot manifest the changes quickly enough, I could Pass as did Aba, or at the very least, such distraction could get us forced Past the Veil by our enemy and either way, forget you not that if I go, so do you."

Gunnarr's confidence faltered not. "I have no fear of such happening. You will not waver, and I can protect you during the process should such need arise." With feigned arrogance he finished, "Besides, failure is not in the prophesy."

Darque was silent for some moments as she considered everything. An unbidden thought came to mind and she slowly asked, "Why did the Morrigan show not these changes?"

She'd used Storrm's Battle Name again and he knew 'twas still difficult for Darque to mention her sister's given name aloud. Gently, Gunnarr said, "We know not that she did not. But you are a full winter elder and her development was always a step behind yours."

'Twas sound reasoning. Suddenly a new thought occurred to her. Eyes widening, she murmured, "Which leaves Fryya."

"True." Gunnarr could sense Darque's need. "You are the forerunner, my jewel. Your experience will guide Fryya's path."

With that knowledge, hesitance became determination. "Then the sooner the better, though more fighting is not my wish."

"This war will not end soon. Battle will come whether we wish it or not, therefore Battle Lust is not only foreseeable in our future," heaving a huge sigh he summarized, "as per intel and personal history, 'twill be not long in the making."

Like a warm hand upon her shoulder, Darque felt the 'presence' again, along with a voice telling her that she was not alone. Her sister still had her back. 'Twas not heard by her ears, instead, 'twas felt in her heart. A wicked smile upon her lips, she locked her gaze to Gunnarr's and fiercely challenged the Fates, "Then let the Hoard rise against us, for I am Darque Aalanna Grifynn! I. Will. Not. Fail!"

THUS ENDS BATTLE OF WINTER'S EDGE

Wait for it! Book 5 in the Darque Legends
series is in the making! Look for :

THE FANGS OF SOLVYNGARR

Coming soon!

Long Live Darque and the Dragon Clan!

Lifebond Rosters

THE FIRST LIFEBOND/FIRST FLIGHT

1. Darque (female-sister to Storrm) and Gunnarr (male, High Prince)

2. Storrm (female-sister to Darque) and Mystynn (male, Second Prince)

3. Kydra (female) and Ragnyrr (male, Third Prince)

4. Axyl (male-brother to Daxx) and Haniyyah (female-sister to Linayyah)

5. Daxx (male-brother to Axyl) and Linayyah (female-sister to Haniyyah)

6. Yanais (male) and Shykiyyah (female)

7. Rolf (male) and Nalwynn (female)

8. Rygyl (male) and Tegrynn (female)

9. Tyndall (female) and Fyndarr (male-brother to Zaydarr, cousin to Gunnarr)

10. Apryya (female) and Dannyrkyn (male)

11. Zoe (female) and Kyrlayyn (male)

12. Ethynn (male-brother to Daylyn) and Makayyd (female-sister to Makyyan)

13. Ariel (female) and Zayddarr (male-brother to the children of Kaahayyel: Fyndarr, Shraadarr, Krynnarr, Synahmarr, and cousins to Gunnarr)

THE SECOND LIFEBOND/STORRM FLIGHT

1. Regynn (male-an Elder Warrior and Clan Historian) and Sydrayyah (female)

2. Astraa (female-sister to Aspynn) and Kaygynn (male, Quad Prince)

3. Tannah (female-sister to Tiyya) and Synddarr (male, Fifth Prince)

4. Daylyn (female-sister to Ethynn) and Makyyan (male-brother to Makayyd)

5. Tiyya (female-sister to Tannah) and Shasynn (male, Sixth Prince)
6. Thorrn (male) and Taniyyah (female)
7. Barynn (male) and Shraadarr (female)
8. Hannah (female) and Izayyah (male)
9. Mikkal/Gabriel (male) and Daynahmyn (female)
10. Rakkah (male) and Petrayyah (female sister to Pelayyah and Sydrayyah)
11. Loryyn (female) and Krynnarr (male)
12. Daayn (male-elder brother of Tonn) and Kashiyann (female-sister to Krydann who has been missing since the time of the Last Holocaust)
13. Tannyr (male-eldest brother of Tonn and Daayn) and Kaahayyel (female-sister to Maahayyel; mother of Fynddarr, Zayddarr, Synahmarr, Shraadarr and Krynnarr)

THE THIRD LIFEBOND/MACE FLIGHT

1. Aspynn (Astraa's sister) and Maakayyel (male-brother of Maahayyel and Kaahayyel; uncle to Gunnarr and his siblings, and of Fyndarr and Synahmarr)
2. Soryn (male) and Pelayyah (female-sister of Petrayyah and Sydrayyah)
3. Drysalyn (female) and Danniagg (male-brother of Korriagg; cousin of siblings Radryagg and Hadryagg)
4. Prysym (female) and Rasparyn (male)
5. Valkyn (male) and Zymaalynn (female)
6. Alyyse (female) and Kyralayah (female)
7. Paydynn (female) and Korriagg (male- brother of Danniagg; cousin of siblings Radryagg and Hadryagg)
8. Kytahna (female) and Dylordynn (male)
9. Hadyn (male) and Delfyyan (female)
10. Maddyx (male) and Varrdayyn (male)
11. Mace (male twin to Mynx) and Maddokyn (female)
12. Darrtan (male) and Illsyyah (female)
13. Baylis (female) and Maklarynn (male- brother of Lyrriynn)

Author's Bio

Born in Connecticut and raised in the Midwest, Derrien Relyea grew up fascinated with mythology, Viking lore, and Dragons. Her vivid imagination was kindled by her highly creative family, encouraging a love of writing and fantasy. She worked her way through Oklahoma City Community College with degrees in Occupational Therapy and Therapeutic Recreation, and later graduated from the University of Oklahoma Health Sciences Center with a degree in Physical Therapy.

Taking her cue from an exciting genealogical history and such authors as Anne McCaffrey, Edgar Rice Burroughs, Jules Verne, and Sir Arthur Conan Doyle, she has embarked upon a new adventure in her life. Please join her at:

http://thedragonwarrior.com

Kudos and credit to my friend and
accomplished artist, Lisa Dixon:

http://lisadixonart.com